Praise for *New Yor*[illegible]

"Greed, vengeance a[illegible] atmospheric thriller dark and disturbing."—*Romantic Times* on *See How She Dies*

"A terrific tale of romantic suspense with plenty of thrills." —*I Love a Mystery* on *The Morning After*

"This book is guaranteed to keep you guessing."—*The Pilot* (Southern Pine, North Carolina) on *The Morning After*

Praise for *New York Times* best-selling author Lori Foster

"This is quintessential Foster; lots of action, lots of laughter, and lots of sex—heartwarming, hilarious, and hot! hot! hot!" —*Booklist* on *Say No to Joe?*

"Foster delivers another sexy and sizzling tale rich in plot and excitement. *The Secret Life of Bryan* is original, poignant, laced with humor and just plain delicious."—*Romantic Times* on *The Secret Life of Bryan*

"A Lori Foster book is like a glass of good champagne—sexy and sparkling!"—Jayne Ann Krentz

Praise for *New York Times* best-selling author Debbie Macomber

"Debbie Macomber's gift for understanding the souls of women—their relationships, their values, their lives—is at its peak here."—*Bookpage* on *Between Friends*

"Excellent characterization will keep readers anticipating the next visit to Cedar Cove."—*Booklist* on *311 Pelican Court*

"A multifaceted tale of romance and deceit, the final installment of Macomber's Dakota trilogy oozes with country charm and a strong sense of community."—*Publishers Weekly* on *Always Dakota*

Praise for *USA Today* best-selling author Suzanne Forster

"A spellbinding tale of murder and intrigue that guarantees a long night of reading suspense."—*Publishers Weekly* on *Every Breath She Takes*

"Dangerous, thrilling and sensual."—*Romantic Times* on *Innocence*

"Absolutely delicious."—*The Philadelphia Inquirer* on *Blush*

Books by Lisa Jackson

See How She Dies

Intimacies

Wishes

Whispers

Twice Kissed

Unspoken

If She Only Knew

Hot Blooded

Cold Blooded

The Night Before

The Morning After

Books by Lori Foster

Never Too Much

Too Much Temptation

Unexpected

The Secret Life of Bryan

Just a Hint—Clint

Say No to Joe?

When Bruce Met Cyn

Published by Zebra Books

Kiss Me Again

Lisa Jackson

Debbie Macomber

Lori Foster

Suzanne Forster

ZEBRA BOOKS
Kensington Publishing Corp.
http://www.kensingtonbooks.com

ZEBRA BOOKS are published by

Kensington Publishing Corp.
850 Third Avenue
New York, NY 10022

First Printing: January 2005
10 9 8 7 6 5 4 3 2 1

Printed in the United States of America

CONTENTS

Stranger in Her Bed

Suzanne Forster

Prologue

"Admit it, Kerry. You'd *love* to have your toes sucked."

"Admit I'd love wha—? I don't remember saying I'd love that—them—sucked. My toes, I mean."

"Just for the sake of discussion, let's say you would. How do you think it would feel?"

Kerry Houston took a quick, furtive sip of her wine. They'd been building toward a moment like this all evening, and it had been all she could do to fight the seductive pull of his voice, especially when it dropped to those sexy lower registers and got all fuzzy and intimate. He'd been given unfair advantage, she decided. He'd been blessed with an instrument that could give a woman the shivering fits and send her running in search of her vibrator.

Only Kerry didn't have a vibrator.

She shifted in the chair, tugging at her silk kimono. Her town house was drafty and normally she went to bed in three sets of flannel. But before they started this little adventure of his, he'd casually suggested a dark candlelit room, loose comfortable clothing and a glass of wine to relax her. Now she knew why.

How would it feel? Wet, warm, slippery, strange . . .

"Squishy?" she ventured.

"Squishy . . . works." He didn't sound too sure. "Would your toes prefer a man or a woman?"

"They'd prefer a podiatrist."

Kerry got no reaction to her diversionary tactics. No

reaction at all. This guy was hard to fluster, and even harder to sidetrack. He seemed as bent on finding her soft spots—literally—as a grand master chess player was on winning a tournament, but a grand master didn't have this guy's focus.

"And would you like this fantasy man to remove your shoes and stockings?" he asked. "Perhaps massage your feet and individually stimulate each toe? Using a decadent chocolate ganache syrup, of course."

"Did we ever establish that I *wanted* my toes sucked?"

"Shhhhh . . . can you hear that, Kerry? Can you hear how hard your heart is beating?"

All she could hear was a faint beeping noise that sounded like her cordless phone when it was low on batteries.

"Did you answer my question?" she persisted.

"If not your toes, then something else? Fingers, earlobes, elbows, kneecaps, pipkin?"

"Pipkin? Isn't that an apple?"

"Kerry," he admonished gently, "the more open and receptive you are, the better this will be. Breathe and let yourself go; imagine that you're floating on a warm water bed and that your every whim and caprice is being indulged. Anything you wish is yours. Whatever you secretly desire in life has already imprinted itself on you. All you have to do is recognize its existence."

He hesitated, letting her float, letting her float . . .

"It's true, Kerry. Pleasure beyond anything you can imagine awaits you. Beyond *anything*, if you're willing. . . ."

Kerry's eyelids were starting to flutter, among other things. The effect he had on her was strangely hypnotic. It was like listening to the music of a dark melodic river. Soothing, and yet there was a single grain of sand in it that gently abraded her senses. It kept her mesmerized. And more importantly, he was right. She ought to at least try to answer his questions. That *was* the point of this exercise.

"I've never thought of my toes as erogenous zones," she said, absently aware of the soft beeping. It seemed to keep pace with her heart, her breathing.

"Well, then, we'll have to find some that are."

"Zones? Erogenous? I don't think I have any."

"Sure you do. The body is one big zone, a veritable playground. There's the back of the knees, the insides of the wrists, the breasts, and of course, the lips, both sets. Are your lips very sensitive?"

Both sets? Kerry's eyes sprang open to a dark, candlelit room. Her stomach was falling through a hole in the earth to New Zealand. "Maybe we should stick to the toes? I think I can feel something tingling." And for sure it wasn't her toes.

"Tingling?" He laughed, and the sound was low-down, steamy sex personified.

"Tingling is good," he said. "Just imagine how it would feel to have the soles of your feet massaged with warm, scented lotion and some nice sharp knuckles, gently working out the knots along the ball. Would you like that?"

She was weakening. *Of course she would.* Was he crazy?

"Feel the deep pressure on your arch and the firm palms of my hand, working both sides of your foot, kneading, pleating with my thumbs. How do you like to be touched? In your fantasies, how does it happen—lightly, firmly?"

"I don't think I have fantasies."

"Of course, you do. Everyone has erogenous zones *and* fantasies. Let your mind run free, Kerry. . . . Visualize a man who becomes aroused at the mere sight of you, magnificently aroused. And say this man is naked so he can't hide his burgeoning desire. Maybe he's a servant and you're a princess."

Kerry rather liked the aroused-at-the-mere-sight-of-her part, but she wasn't sure what one did with a naked serving man when he wasn't serving.

"Hmm, not much reaction there," he said. "Is your finger properly positioned, Kerry?"

She blushed and nodded, hoping he couldn't see her.

"Was that a yes?" he prompted.

"Oh, sorry, yes. It was a yes. My finger is . . . you know."

"I do know. Relax now, Kerry, breathe . . . see yourself flying across a field in a sheer white nightgown . . . you're being chased down by a highwayman on a horse, who drops to the ground when he reaches you, rips open his breeches and passionately takes you against a huge tree."

Oh . . . my . . . oh . . . a ravishment fantasy.

"Anything?" he asked.

"Nope," was all she could manage. If she'd said more, something would have leaped out of her mouth, probably her heart.

"Then how about this one; how about a man who's tall, dark and sexier than sin, and he's right behind you, whispering naughty things in your ear while you're waiting in line at the bank."

Kerry was about to protest when it became apparent that the beeping sounds were not her cordless telephone. They rang out like chimes, and they were keeping time with her heart. Her wild heart.

Did she want someone to whisper naughty things in her ear?

"Well, of course, that depends on the man," she said, feigning aplomb. But naturally, it didn't work. Nothing worked. The chimes had become a chorus and were in danger of being drowned out by buzzing and pinging noises. What in the world was going on?

"I think we've touched a nerve," he said softly.

His irony seemed to generate more sound and fury. Whoops and flashes of light made it look like there was a pinball machine in the room.

"What does this noise mean?" she asked.

"It means you do have fantasies, Kerry. Hot ones. That finger glove you're wearing is registering your vital signs and giving you feedback."

The translucent sheath on her index finger was wired into her computer, much like her mouse and audio speakers were, but Kerry had forgotten all about it until he asked. Apparently it was measuring more than her heart rate. Good thing it couldn't read her mind. The machine would go up in smoke.

"Fortunately, I can take care of that," he said.

"What?" She sat straight up in the chair. "What are you going to take care of?"

"I'm going to take care of you, Kerry. I'm going to devise the perfect fantasy for you. The one you've been waiting for, the one you don't want anyone to know about. Your deepest secret, your deepest need, your deepest desire. I'm going to give them all to you."

The game began to wail like a police siren.

Kerry made an instant executive decision. "Go to sleep," she said, pulling off the finger glove and tossing it onto her desk.

"Kerry, you understand what happens when you voice that command. The game will be over."

"Yes, I have to . . . please, that's it for tonight."

"Are you sure?"

"Go to sleep." Kerry repeated the command firmly, knowing he wouldn't obey otherwise. As a backup she positioned the mouse and aimed the arrow at an icon in the upper corner of her computer screen. It had the image of a man snoozing, a vapor trail of Zzzzzzzs above him and one word below him, SLEEP.

She clicked the mouse and fell back against the chair, watching the computer screen go dark. "Whew," she whistled softly. "Now that was *some* video game! Maybe I shouldn't have set the Sensuality Level so high."

She'd been a game tester for Genesis Software for a few months now, but this was by far the best idea they'd ever sent her for their new adult line. It was an interactive voice recognition game, and it felt like the game guide, otherwise known as Mr. Quick-Where's-My-Vibrator, was right there in the room with her.

She grabbed her legal pad and began jotting notes.

> *I love this game! It's like foreplay only more convenient. You can stop whenever you want to and throw in a load of wash.*

Her next tip was crucial.

> *There's just one thing missing. Your game guide needs a face to go with that voice. Maybe a body, too. Oh, my, yes! Let's give our customers the full experience.*

When Kerry was done making notes, she fell back in the chair and actually giggled. She hadn't done that in a long time. There had been nothing resembling whimsy in her life for some time now. But, crazy as it seemed, she couldn't shake the feeling that there was a new man on the horizon, and that something was about to happen. It felt like the heavens had opened and dropped him into her lap. Of course, that was ridiculous, she told herself. What the heavens had dropped was a compact disk.

She picked up the silky finger glove and felt a sharp little quiver of anticipation at the mere thought of slipping it on. Or was it foreboding? Whatever it was, she dropped the sheath like a hot potato.

"For heaven's sake, girl, get a grip. It's a game. It's *only* a game."

One

Kerry stared at the front door of her house as if it had the power to reach out and grab her. She was bundled up like a linebacker, both for the winter weather and for defensive purposes. She had a mission to accomplish out there in the cold, cold world, but she hadn't gotten any further than this impasse with her door. No surprise there. She hadn't been out of her house in days, maybe weeks.

"The only thing to fear is fear itself," she intoned, wishing she knew who'd come up with *that* line. Obviously not someone who lived in her neighborhood.

She yanked her fur trapper hat down tight, snapped the earflaps under her chin and checked her parka pockets. The pepper spray and police whistle were there, but she wasn't sure what good they would do her. You needed an armed tank for this neighborhood. Just the thought of venturing out made her so nervous she'd seen a psychologist recently, and the woman had told her it was no surprise she was a little paranoid. She had reason.

Kerry lived in an area that had once been the pride of south Philly, but lately the neighborhood had been under siege. A pack of young thugs had moved into the "hood" and claimed it as theirs. Kerry herself had been mugged twice, and the attacks had left her feeling terribly vulnerable.

She should have moved months ago, when the area

started going downhill, but her quaint redbrick town house had been left to her by her grandparents, whom she'd adored. They'd taken her in and raised her when it became clear that her single mom—their only daughter, Paula—wasn't financially or emotionally able to take care of a child. Freed of that burden, Paula had gone off in search of herself, and Kerry had rarely seen her mother after that. Her grandparents were the only real family she knew.

A loud rap on the door startled her out of her reflections. "Kerry, it's Malcolm! Are you in there?"

Kerry struggled to calm her drumming heart. Malcolm lived in the studio above the garage in the back. He was her new tenant, and a sweet guy for the most part, but his mind was a Nintendo game. He actually thought that cell phones and Palm Pilots were part of a government plot to spy on the citizenry. The way he scrutinized Kerry's computer equipment, she assumed that was suspect, too. She had him pegged for a conspiracy theorist and maybe a technophobe. Of course, she hadn't figured that out until *after* she'd rented him the room.

"Hold on, Malcolm," she called out. "It may take me a minute."

The floor seemed to roll beneath Kerry's feet as she started for the door. Her face was flushed, and the way her pulse was skittering, she wasn't at all certain she was going to get there. A little paranoid? She couldn't seem to walk. *Or* talk. It felt like something was caught in her throat—probably her heart. And by the time she did get to the door, her palms were so slippery she couldn't get traction on the knob.

She lived on a side street, but traffic noise roared in her ears as she opened the door a crack.

"Are you okay, Kerry?"

Malcolm's brow was furrowed with concern. He was wearing his navy peacoat and knit cap, as always, and his luxurious beard reminded her of the fisherman's in the

Gorton's ad. He had the guy's great baritone voice, too, except that Malcolm appeared to be at least twenty years younger. His eyes were a surreal delft blue, and there wasn't a line on his face, despite hair as snowy as the deep drifts outside.

"I'm fine," she said, but her shaky voice didn't seem to fool him. It probably wouldn't have fooled anyone.

"Here, I brought this for you."

Her tenant made a quick, awkward presentation of a can of soup. Chicken noodle, Kerry realized by the label. She could remember her grandmother fixing that for lunch on rainy days, along with grilled cheese sandwiches.

"Soup, Malcolm?" Kerry didn't know quite what to say.

"Sometimes I wonder if you get enough to eat," he confessed.

Touched, she opened the door enough for him to step inside. "Thank you," she said as she took the can.

Malcolm had brought little offerings on other occasions, and Kerry hadn't had the heart to tell him not to. She sensed that he wanted to help, and Lord knew, she could use some. Today, however, his other arm was tucked behind his back, making her wonder if he had another surprise in store.

She didn't ask. He seemed preoccupied.

"Santa just mugged someone," he said.

"Oh, Malcolm"—Kerry shook her head—"stop that now."

"No, it's true, one of the nuns from Our Lady of Perpetual Weeping. He knocked her down and took her fanny pack."

Kerry might have laughed if Malcolm hadn't seemed so perfectly serious. She didn't know what Santa he was talking about, unless it was one of the Salvation Army volunteers on the corner down the block. None of them had ever gone haywire that she knew of, but anything was possible.

"Might as well live in Bosnia," Malcolm muttered.

"No kidding," Kerry agreed. If anyone knew how bad it was, she did. The second time she'd been mugged a crowd had collected to watch as if it were a sporting match, and no one had lifted a finger to help her. She'd implored them to call the police, but they'd done nothing except scurry away. That's when the fear had set in. She'd recognized one of them as her own next-door neighbor!

"Kerry, why do you stay?" Malcolm asked.

Kerry didn't have a ready answer, except that she loved the place. The town house had a storybook charm about it that had always made her feel safe and secure, at least while she was inside. The breakfast nook walls were hung with sayings done in her grandmother's hand-stitched embroidery, as was the upholstery in the living room and the cushions on the window seat.

Nothing had been safe from Gramma Laura's needle except Grandpa Dan's buttery-soft, old leather rocker. No one was allowed to touch that chair, even to drape a doily over the headrest, which her grandmother had tried on a few occasions. It was where he'd rocked Kerry endlessly, telling her stories about how wishes always came true if you wished hard enough. And Kerry had probably believed him once, impressionable child that she was.

This was how she kept her grandparents' memories alive, she realized, by staying. But she couldn't tell Malcolm that.

"I'll have noodle soup for lunch today," she assured him. It was the kindest way she could think of to get him to leave. And she did need him to leave. He meant well, but he could get spookier than she was, if that was possible.

"Oh, sure, good," he said, seeming to get her drift.

He turned toward the door, and Kerry saw the bouquet of tulips he'd been hiding behind his back. They were bright spring colors, pink and deep rose reds, sunny yellows and oranges. It wasn't a bouquet, it was a rainbow.

"Tulips, Malcolm? Where did you find tulips in the middle of winter?"

Apparently her tenant had forgotten all about the flowers because his shoulders lifted in surprise. "The tulip store?"

Kerry did laugh at that, and when Malcolm turned around, his blue eyes were twinkling like stars. She accepted the flowers and thanked him warmly, but for the first time since Kerry had rented him the room, she wondered about her new tenant. For a fleeting moment, she wondered if it was possible that Malcolm was hiding something other than a bouquet of tulips.

She didn't ask.

Kerry's cordless phone had become the enemy. It sat on the enormous tower of mail-order catalogs that she'd been collecting since she started working out of her house, and it had begun to ring shortly after Malcolm left. She could have broken a Guinness record with the tower, she imagined. Kerry Houston, Catalog Queen. But that was beside the point.

Her ringing phone was the point. She knew exactly who was calling, which was why she hadn't answered. She'd finally had the sense to turn down the volume, but that hadn't turned off the emotion churning inside her.

One look at the Caller ID number had told her it was starting all over again. The Genesis Software people would not give up! Genesis was the company she'd left three months ago, under the most embarrassing of circumstances, but their Human Resources person kept calling and insisting that she come back. He'd offered her everything under the sun, including more money, big money. She'd actually bundled up today with the thought of going over there to negotiate a new employment contract, that's how much damn money it was.

The man had tempted her, and she'd almost succumbed. But in point of fact, there wasn't a salary big enough to pay for the humiliation she'd been through at Genesis. Even if she could get out her front door, she would never go back there.

She peeled off her hat and the parka, along with several layers of clothing, and piled it all in the leather rocker that sat next to the catalog tower. The weather wasn't the only reason she'd bundled up. The bulk was meant to make a very average, five-feet four-inch woman look less vulnerable. If the local toughs thought she was an undersized hockey player, all the better.

She picked up the phone and dialed the software company's number with purpose and resolve. She didn't know the man who'd been calling as anything other than Phil in Human Resources, but she was ready for him when he came on the line. She didn't even bother to introduce herself. He had to know her voice by now.

"I want you to stop calling me, Phil. I'm not coming back and I never will."

"I've never called you Phil . . . and did you intend that to rhyme?"

Kerry smiled despite herself. Lucky for him that she had smiled or he might have gotten another verbal one-two. It also worked in his favor that he had a great voice. He was no Mr. Quick-Where's-My-Vibrator, but his conversational tones were low and masculine and sort of steamy, like a pot on simmer. That might even be the reason she'd allowed him to call as often as he had. Yes, she rather liked Phil's voice. It shivered up a person's neck like warm air currents. Nevertheless, she had to be firm with him now.

"I'm quite serious," she told him. "I have no desire to work in design anymore. I'm perfectly happy as a game tester, and if you call me again, I'll be forced to report it as harassment."

"Hey, hey, no one's harassing anyone here. If you don't want me to call again, I won't. But could you answer one question? Why are you so adamant? Do you feel as if you were treated unfairly here? Was anyone unprofessional or improper?"

She was treated like yesterday's news, trashed by the boss himself, but it was a highly personal situation and she wasn't going to discuss it with a veritable stranger.

"There's improper and there's improper, Phil. One's about wearing hoop earrings and a leather micro-mini to church. The other's about acting boorishly without a thought to the pain you cause others. I'll let you figure out which is which."

With that, and an icy-bright best wishes for the holidays, she pressed the OFF button and considered herself well rid of the pest and his simmering pot of a voice.

Joe Gamble's telephone headset was calibrated to pick up noises as faint as normal respiration. People breathed and he could hear them. Unfortunately. Because right now he had a dial tone trying to buzz-saw a hole through his head. Kerry Houston had just cut him off at the kneecaps, and he was probably lucky it wasn't higher. She hadn't let him get in one more word, much less the last one.

Damn, it annoyed him when that happened.

It annoyed Phil, too. Technically Philip was his middle name, but since she refused to talk to Joe Gamble, and most everyone else at Genesis, he'd had to resort to the subterfuge. He snapped off the headset and draped it over his halogen arc lamp. Apparently there were still a few people who could not be bought, and she was one of them. He admired her for that, but how was he going to get her back if not with filthy lucre?

The game he'd been uploading suddenly flashed onto his computer screen, distracting him. An array of multiple-choice questions appeared against a background of pink cupids, pouty red lip imprints and silhouetted females of the supermodel variety. It was pretty garish, plus the music playing through the speakers sounded suspiciously like the "Love Boat" theme.

"Preferred breast size?" Joe read aloud.

It wasn't the first question that came up, but it was the first one to catch his eye. A set of multiple-choice answers followed: (a) plums, (b) peaches, (c) Texas grapefruit, or (d) honeydew.

"What?" Joe remarked dryly, "no seedless watermelon?"

He clicked on the FEEDBACK icon, and then RECORD. "The fruit references aren't going to fly," he said, leaving a message for the game's architects. "I don't want to ruin the fun, but is it possible for you pervs in design to think in terms of small, average, full . . . something like that?"

Joe was evaluating a Genesis product in the design stages with a working title of "Build Her and She Will Come." The idea of the game was to let men visualize and create their ideal mate from head to toe, including her physical characteristics, but globular fruit was certain to offend a key demographic who might buy it for their brothers or male friends, namely women. And the title was certain to offend everyone.

He clicked on "Peaches," just for evaluation purposes, of course. Honeydew was excessive, plums were vaguely prepubescent and grapefruit had never been a big favorite. Made his teeth hurt.

An animated cupid thanked him for his answer, and then pointed his little pink arrow to the next question: "Preferred leg length?"

This one had a flower theme. The design team was having way too much fun, Joe thought, as he read the choices under his breath. "(a) Long-stemmed American Beauties, (b) daffodils, (c) daisies, or (d) Christmas cacti."

Joe figured the last one must either be a nod to the season or a woman who didn't shave her legs. He clicked the first one. Okay, so he liked long stems. That didn't make him a pervert, too, did it?

On the right side of the screen was a computer matrix outline of a woman, who was materializing as he made his choices. The woman didn't concern him as much as the cupid, flying around her in a presentational way, pointing to each body part that appeared.

"Fellas? Lose the fruit, the flowers *and* cupid."

Joe scrolled back to the questions he'd skipped over and settled in to finish the game. By now he was curious what this arrangement of X-rated body parts was going to look like when it was finished. Maybe that was a plus. Once you got the woman started, you *had* to finish her.

Oops, he thought with a faint smile. *Better not go there, either.* The game was booby-trapped with double entendres.

Joe's office was also his own personal think tank and where he did most of his creative work when he wasn't traveling on business. The walls were lined with traditional cherry bookcases that groaned with the weight of his varied interests and his research, and he worked at a desk, like everyone else. But most everything in his office was computerized, digitalized and automated. He could open the skylight and look up at the starry sky by speaking to it—the skylight, not the sky. He didn't have a lock on Mother Nature yet, but technology, that he took to its limits . . . because he could.

By the time he'd finished the questions, he was glued to the screen, but not because the game was that good. It was the challenge of making it better that absorbed him. Probably more than it should, considering the state of his personal affairs. What affairs? to be exact. His office overlooked a green belt, planted with Japanese cedars, and there was the equivalent of a winter wonderland right outside his window, but he rarely took the time to look at it, much less experience it. There didn't seem to be any way to unglue himself from whatever the current project was.

A wall panel opened behind him, revealing an office-sized refrigerator and microwave. Joe glanced at his watch, only mildly interested in the lunch reminder. He'd programmed the panel to open at twelve-thirty because he had a bad habit of forgetting to eat.

It was curiosity more than hunger that made him open the refrigerator today. The pizza caught his eye, but he picked up the container of East Indian tandoori instead and popped it in the microwave. It was spicy as hell, which almost let him overlook the fact that it was low-fat and "good for him," according to his assistant.

Moments later he walked to the window with his steaming food, still in its microwaveable container. But it was the wonderland outside that had finally caught his attention. For some reason he was reminded of the Godzilla-like snowmen he'd made when he was a kid growing up on the family farm. He'd even gone on great treks into the woods to find a tree on Christmas Eve because his parents were too poor to afford one. What had happened to that kid?

To say that Joe Gamble worked too much was an understatement. He could have taken an Olympic gold in working. He just wasn't sure why. His married friends had suggested that he was avoiding something, which was a nice way of saying he was a commitment phobe, but how could he be when there'd been no relationships to be phobic about? He'd been married once, almost on a dare, while he was in college. It was a crazy, impulsive thing that happened mostly because her wealthy parents were determined to split them up, and it only lasted a year before his bride decided her doting father was right. Joe didn't have enough money to make her happy. That experience had left him gun-shy, especially now that he did have money, pots of it.

He'd dated over the years, but none of the relationships would have been considered long term. No smart woman wanted to play second fiddle to a man's creative obsessions, and, sadly, the women he'd met had never challenged or absorbed him the way a new idea did. Work had always been enough, but that was changing now. Something was missing. He was restless and unfulfilled, and stranger yet, the only thing that seemed to intrigue him at the moment *was* a woman. Kerry Houston had sparked his interest like nothing else had in a long time, and he had a hunch it was because she was as good at this idea stuff as he was. Maybe better.

A heaping forkful of tandoori got him some rice, raisins and a savory chunk of chicken and sauce. He ate slowly, reflecting.

He'd debated the wisdom of telling Kerry who he really was, but he'd learned over the years that his presence had an inhibiting effect on even the best and the brightest. It was one of the reasons he'd stopped sitting in on the various creative teams' brainstorming sessions and started videotaping them instead, with the members' knowledge, of course. That was how he'd first discovered Kerry Houston, watching her interact on tape as a new designer on one of the teams. He'd immediately given a bonus to the Human Resources person who hired her, a guy whose name wasn't Phil.

Kerry was inspired, and watching her had inspired him. He loved the way she brainstormed. She was quietly intent at first, offering feedback only when she had something cogent to say. But it soon became apparent that she absorbed the collective energy like a sponge, because when she pitched an idea, she was as quick and kinetic as lightning.

Those eyes were like bolts from the sky. And, God, that

attracted him. He would never have described her as a hot number. You couldn't even call her sexy in the way men normally thought of those things. But that *fire.*

At some point an idea would drive her right out of her conference chair, and every head would swing her way, riveted. They might be a little envious of her passion, but they couldn't take their eyes off her. Her color was high and her voice took on heat as she raced to get the flow of thoughts out as swiftly as they came to her. Even her body showed signs of arousal when she got that excited . . . and so had Joe showed some signs, although that had nothing to do with why he was trying to get her back. She was his best person. She kicked butt.

Joe finished off the tandoori and left the container on his desk as he went back to his chair. He'd actually had hopes that Kerry would revitalize his entire design division, and then one day she was gone. She excused herself from a strategy session to take a potty break and never came back. She'd never explained her exit, either, although he'd learned later what happened, and he'd blamed himself. He'd had his people track her down, offering career amnesty, and making increasingly generous offers to get her back, but she'd said no to everything, including him.

He rarely attended company functions, and he'd only met her in person one time. It was a few months after she'd started, and there'd been a meeting in which he'd congratulated her on something. He couldn't even remember what it was now, he'd been so intrigued with the idea of meeting her face to face. He'd expected to see sparks fly when they shook hands. Instead it was an internal reaction, and the sparks were icy hot. His gut would probably never be the same. Most guys would have known that this was the beginning of something incredible. Joe knew it was the end. He had no idea if Kerry felt the same way, but he made a strategic decision to back off the very next day. She was much too valuable to mess with, in any sense of the word.

Joe came out of his preoccupation with Kerry Houston to the frustrating awareness that he'd re-created her on the screen in front of him. The gaze wasn't fiery enough, but it was none other behind the impish smile. Apparently she was determined to annoy him in every possible way. She wasn't even that cute, with her mousy brown hair and the mole near her lip that matched her intensely dark eyes. He'd been going for Cindy Crawford, anyway.

Still, he continued to stare at the image until his body reminded him of the power a woman could have over a man, even when all the poor sucker had was a cartoon characterization of her. There was a tug of anticipation deep in his groin, and various muscles were yanking at the bit. He couldn't tell if he was angry or aroused, but one was as good as the other for his purposes.

Something had to be done about this Houston woman.

Two

"Stuck in your house with no one but a computer-generated hunk in a voice-recognition game for company? *Great,*" Kerry murmured as she hovered at her front window, looking out at the snow-covered bowers of Lover's Park across the street.

She couldn't actually see the four stone paths that radiated like spokes from the park's circular courtyard, but she knew they were there, dozing under the soft white blanket. Also heaped in graceful drifts was the statue the park was named for, a marble replica of a man and woman in a longing embrace. Her grandfather had told her the story of the couple who inspired the statue, and Kerry had been touched by its poignancy. But she couldn't concentrate on anything except her own misery this morning.

"Kerry, come back and play. It's lonely in here without you."

Startled, Kerry turned and saw that her computer monitor was on. It glowed brightly from the maple secretary that was tucked in the far corner of the room.

"Hey, I thought I turned you off!" she exclaimed.

The image of a man's face smiled from the screen, and his sonorous voice reached out as if to touch her. "Are you sure it's me you want to turn off?"

He was dead right about that. Moments ago she'd abandoned him—and the game she was *supposed* to be testing for Genesis. It was possible she hadn't turned off the computer in her rush, but who could blame her. She was being seduced by the dark side! His voice was bad enough. Now she had his face to contend with, too.

George, the game's creator at Genesis, had responded immediately to her feedback about a male face to go with the voice. Maybe he'd already been working on the problem because in record time he'd come up with a breathtaking simulation of Jean Valjean, the lead character in *Les Miserables.* How had George known she loved *Les Mis?*

The new and improved version of "Discover the Secret, Sensual You!" was waiting in her e-mail queue this morning when she woke up. And so was Valjean's wounded, penetrating gaze, his strong features and sensual mouth. The main difference was his shoulder-length waves. This man's hair was shorter, olive-black and cut adorably close to his head, a lush, curly crew.

Of course, she would *never* have called it adorable to his face. Valjean was just such a guy's guy, male through and through.

Kerry's mistake had been to download the game immediately, and nothing had been quite the same since. Whoever had coined the phrase "love at first sight" couldn't have been thinking about a video game. Was it possible to be infatuated with a nonperson, with dots on a screen?

And could she *be* more desperate?

Kerry reached down and yanked up her wool slipper socks. The elastic was going and they kept slipping down. So very attractive it was, too.

"Did I say something to offend you?" the screen image asked.

She insisted on thinking of his face as an image to remind herself that he wasn't a man. He was hundreds of pixels. Too bad she hadn't been smarter about his name.

"No, you didn't, Jean. I'm fine." He'd introduced himself as a guide and given her a set of verbal directions, which included assigning him a name. He'd encouraged her to pick one with personal meaning, and she'd impulsively said Jean, and then she couldn't figure out how to delete it. How she wished she'd said Biff or Game Guy.

"Because if I did," he said, "just repeat the offensive parts, and then say 'Down, boy.'" His smile hinted at irony. "I'm self-editing."

I wish I were!, Kerry thought. If only she could edit some of the lurid fantasies dancing through her brain. He had her thinking about handsome strangers whispering erotic things in her ear at the bank, about plundering highwaymen and huge trees! She could only imagine what her heart rate must be now, after a night of moist dreams about aroused slave boys. But then that was the point of the game, she supposed, to encourage fantasies. She could give it an A+ on that score.

"Are you coming back, Kerry?" he asked. "We can't continue if you won't sit down and play. There's nothing to be afraid of, unless there's something you don't want to know . . . about yourself."

"And what would that be?" she challenged. "Since you seem to know so much about me."

"It's difficult to say, since you refuse to wear the finger glove. But I'm sure we'll find something."

"Are you laughing?" Kerry walked over and peered at the screen. She thought she'd heard suspiciously muffled sounds, but she didn't detect anything in his expression. *"Jean?"*

"Mais, non," he assured her. "How could I possibly take pleasure in your difficulties? That's not what I'm here for."

"And what *are* you here for, pray tell?"

"To free you from prudish notions and blocks to your sensuality."

Now it was all she could do not to laugh. "And you

think quizzing me about my erogenous zones and suggesting smutty talk in financial institutions will do that?"

"It's a start."

There wasn't a hint of sarcasm in his voice, which was more than she could say for hers. "I can hardly wait to see where we go from here."

"Excellent, let's be on our way," he said.

But, of course, he'd taken her literally.

Suddenly the computer screen was awash in color, and music swelled through the speakers. There were clouds, blue sky and a rainbow arch with dazzling colors that changed continuously. A silver bird soared from the bottom of the screen toward the top, dipped and soared again. Kerry recognized the music as "Somewhere Over the Rainbow," and it struck her that all the fanfare was incredibly corny, and yet, she was quite captured by it.

Instead of a brick road, a sparkling staircase materialized, and a woman ascended it. Near the top she became a bird and ribboned through the clouds before soaring off to somewhere unseen.

"What's happening? Jean? Where are we going?"

"On a tour."

"Of what?"

"Of you, a grand tour of Kerry. I'll be your guide, but you're the landscape *and* the traveler, so you choose the itinerary. Where would you like to start?"

"How about my brain? I must be crazy for agreeing to this."

"How about your skin?" he asked, ignoring her comment. "Did you know that there are over a hundred receptors in the fingertips alone? The skin is our most sensitive organ. Of course, you have membranes that are richer in nerve endings, but we'll get to those later. Why don't we start at your toes and work our way up."

"Oh, please, not my toes."

The irony in his expression told her that he was coming to understand some things. Maybe he was programmed to know when he was dealing with a sexually repressed woman who was afraid of her own front door, and *that* was on a good day.

"Let's take a deep breath and start over, Kerry. Are you comfortable? Wearing loose clothing? Do you have a soothing cup of tea or a glass of wine?"

Do I take antipsychotic medication?

"Can't get much looser than this charming sweatshirt dress." She lifted her cup of Quiet Woman herbal tea and saluted him. She decided not to mention the L-tyrosine, an amino acid she'd found in a nutritional supplements catalog that was supposed to be an anxiety-buster. Couldn't have proved it by her, anyway.

"It's okay," she told him, "I'm ready. Lead on, fearless guide. Take me where you will, but be gentle. I bruise easily."

She actually wasn't kidding, and maybe he could hear the sigh of resignation in her voice. She had ducked and dodged and avoided this adventure as long as she could, primarily because it had become personal. It wasn't about testing the game anymore, although she certainly needed the job, and the money. It was about self-discovery and why that seemed to frighten her so. *Was* there something about Kerry Houston that she didn't want to know?

"Kerry, if I'm to be your guide, there are two conditions. First, you will have to entrust yourself to me for this journey," he told her. "And while we're on the subject, how do you feel about that?"

"Entrusting myself to you?"

"Yes, does that make you feel warm or cold?"

Warm or cold? What an odd question. Still, all those receptors he was talking about on the surface of her skin were registering a chill in the air, but the blood flowing through her veins felt hot.

"A little of both. I think I want to shiver."

"Exactly. That's how it's supposed to feel when fear and excitement go head to head. Don't fight those feelings; they're completely natural and the perfect alchemy in which to create . . . something combustible."

Oh, good, she was going to explode. At least she'd be warm.

"I think you're ready for the tour," he said, "but let's try a little experiment first, if you're willing. I sense some romantic pain in your past, and I think that might be getting in your way."

He had to be kidding. *Some* romantic pain? She was riddled with it. She didn't know where to start. All her life she had seemed to invite men who were users and takers. They took advantage, took her for granted, took her for a ride, took her for everything she was worth, emotionally speaking. She was Velcro for the jerks of the world. It was so bad, she'd sworn off the opposite sex three years ago, at just twenty-five. The only exception had been a certain CEO of Genesis Software, and he'd been the biggest jerk of all.

"Is it anything you could talk about?"

"I could talk forever. Got a minute?"

"Let's go for the most painful or the most recent, whichever is shorter."

Maybe he *was* sarcastic? That was probably not a bad thing. She wasn't sure she could relate to a man who wasn't at least minimally sarcastic, not given her affinity for meanies.

"That's easy, they're one and the same," she said. "Picture this, a brand-new software designer for a major company—that would be me—being blown off by the guy who runs the place—that would be him. He flirted with me, at least I think he was flirting, and then he subjected me to the worst kind of public ridicule and humiliation. It was awful."

She shuddered.

"Tell me about the public ridicule part."

So she did. She told him how Joe Gamble had surprised everyone at Genesis by showing up at a company picnic. But it was Kerry who got the biggest surprise because she had no idea who he was when he joined her at a bathtub filled with iced beer and congratulated her on Women-Wealth, her idea for encouraging women to storm Wall Street with a game that simulated trading real stocks. Gamble was notoriously reclusive, and all Kerry, and most of the other employees at Genesis, had ever seen of him was a ten-year-old snapshot in the company newsletter.

He arrived at the picnic fresh from a climbing expedition in the Italian Alps and he was still heavily bearded. Plus, he was wearing sunglasses. How was she supposed to know that the guy who flirted with her and gave her a card with only his e-mail address on it—gamesman@genesis.com—was the president?

She'd sent him an e-mail that night, and maybe it was a little suggestive. She'd said, "Let the games begin, but beware, I've been known to play dirty. Naked at dawn, weapons drawn? Let's see how big *your* gun is."

Okay, it was a lot suggestive. She'd probably had a beer too many at the picnic, but did he have to make such a big deal of it? By the time Kerry found out about her mistake, everybody in the design division was whispering, and Gamble's assistant, a snippy little thing with Altoids breath and bright blue eyes, courtesy of her tinted contacts, had confronted Kerry about her "tacky and inappropriate" behavior.

She'd actually used the words "appallingly lewd" and warned that a sexual harassment suit was in the offing, and before it was over Kerry had been told to fold her tent and leave Genesis. The assistant's parting remark was that Gamble had sent her to deal with Kerry rather than do it himself to avoid "embarrassing" either of them further.

Chicken, coward, yellow running dog.

"I walked out that afternoon," Kerry said, still smarting from the fiery sting of rejection, "and I haven't been back since."

She hadn't told the whole story, but it was as much as

she was willing to say. She'd left that afternoon, but she didn't officially quit until the next day, and it wasn't totally because of Joe Gamble's cadlike behavior. The next morning as she was leaving for work, she collapsed on her doorstep, gasping for air, and that was as far as she got. She'd been dealing with anxiety symptoms because of the muggings, but nothing to compare with these. She'd barely left her house since.

She couldn't blame that on Joe. It was her neighborhood.

Kerry finished her story with a shrug of indifference, but she was sad inside, and even though her "fearless guide" couldn't see it, he could probably hear it. Maybe it was in how she phrased things, her syntax, but he seemed to be able to detect her moods. He was good, and so was the game.

"That was your most recent?" he asked.

"Romantic fiasco? Yes, and my quickest. So now you know why I'm wary of men."

"I know why you're wary of that man. He's not worthy of your pain. He's not worthy of anything. Kerry, save your tears for someone who knows what they cost, someone who will treasure them—and you—because he knows how deep your feelings cut. Don't waste another drop on him."

"Jean?" Kerry sat up to look at him.

He'd spoken with so much conviction—or was it passion—that he'd brought her up out of the chair. She studied his features, surprised at the furrows in his brow, the tension in his mouth. He could have been scowling, but he wasn't angry. She could almost believe that he cared.

"Do you actually feel things, Jean?" she said. "I mean human feelings?"

"I'm not sure. Can a man feel things without a body?"

"I don't know," she said, "but a woman can *not* feel

things with a body. I haven't felt much of anything but fear in quite some time now."

"Which is why I'm here, to help you throw open the doors and windows and feel whatever you want to feel, the entire rainbow."

She smiled and so did he. Was that coincidence or could he see her?

"How do you feel about riddles?" he asked her.

"Pretty much the same way I feel about men . . . but go ahead, if you must."

"I must," he said with a tone of wry forbearance. "Remember the fantasy I promised you, the one that could anticipate your every need, wish and desire? I'm going to need a little more information."

Kerry bent over and hitched up her socks, which made it that much more convenient to get up from the desk and walk over to the window. A fluttery chill passed over her, like curtains caught in an updraft. Maybe she should put on another sweatshirt.

Who said she wanted all those things anticipated?

Several moments passed, and the chilliness felt less and less like a draft. It was her skin. She was a porcupine inside out. The quills pricked her. So far, she wasn't too crazy about this rainbow of his.

Abruptly, she said, "What's the riddle?"

"Are you sure?"

"It's just a riddle isn't it?"

"Kerry . . . is something wrong?"

The way he said her name brought her gaze to the screen, to him. Something inside her lifted and spilled over as softly as sand in an hourglass. It turned on its head, and took her with it. Not that it was a bad feeling. Oh, no, no, no, she would have traveled the world over for that feeling. It was wonderful, as light as a handspring. But that was the good part. His voice did everything else sand could do, too—sift, drift, swirl—and suck you down into its depths.

They should offer medical coverage with this game, Kerry thought. It was dangerous.

"Riddles can be pretty annoying," she said.

"You'll like this one," he assured her. "All you have to do is describe two things you would do with a strawberry that have nothing to do with eating it."

"A strawberry?" Not the kind of puzzle she expected. "Well, they don't make good doorstops. I dropped an entire box of them once. Didn't find the one hiding behind the door until it was too late. Strawberry puree."

The small room was silent except for the soft music coming from the speakers. But outside, the neighborhood hooligans were at it again. There were shouts, cars backfiring. Kerry blocked the sounds from her mind.

"What would anyone do with a strawberry besides eat it? I suppose you could drop it in a flute of champagne."

He lifted an eyebrow. "I was hoping for something a little more imaginative."

"Sorry, I can't think of a thing."

"I can tell you what *I'd* do with it."

"Down, boy," Kerry murmured. His voice had a sexy edge that warned her not to go there, but the remark hung in midair like a helium-filled balloon, daring her to let go of the string.

"Okay, what would you do? Make puree and massage my toes?"

"No, but that's not bad. Actually, if I had a *very* ripe strawberry, I think perhaps I would crush it in my hand, let the juice run down my fingers and pool in my palm. When it was warm, I'd drizzle it over a very tender part of the body and delicately *lick* it off."

"Lick it off," she echoed faintly. "But that would be eating . . . wouldn't it?"

"You're right. Shall we go for number two?"

"No!" She was too far away to turn the machine off. Computers ought to come with remotes, dammit.

"Too bold?" he asked.

"No, no, it was fine. I always gasp as if I'd just finished a marathon."

"Kerry . . . maybe you should come back here and sit down?"

She almost gasped again. "How did you know I got up?"

"The volume of your voice went down. You're either talking very softly or you've moved away. Come on back. I won't bite . . . I won't even lick."

"Gee, darn," she said under her breath.

He laughed, and finally, she did too. She gave herself another moment and then went back, but only as far as the old leather rocker.

"We could go on with the tour," he said, "if you're ready."

"Ready as I'll ever be." What a beautiful thing cynicism was. Those sharp-edged scissors kept everyone away except him. But that was only because he wasn't real, right?

She went back to her desk and sat down, although she would love to have stretched out in the rocker. A little distance would have felt safer, she was sure.

"I'd like you to relax and think about something for a minute," he said. "Think about your sense of touch. What does it mean to you?"

She closed her eyes and dropped back in the chair. "Everything. I love to touch. I love the feel of things. It's very sensual, touch."

"And being touched? How do you prefer that?"

"It depends on who's touching me."

"Who would you like to touch you?"

"Your voice." She barely had the words out of her mouth before her own voice dropped to a whisper. "I'd like it all over me like a big warm blanket."

The husky catch in her throat surprised her. And him, as well. When she opened her eyes, he was staring at her, and he seemed as perplexed as he was intrigued.

"I don't seem to be programmed to respond to that," he said.

Had she actually shocked him? Good, she didn't want to be the only one.

Brightly she asked, "Too bold?"

"I don't seem to be programmed to answer that, either."

Kerry tilted an eyebrow. "Well, you must know that your voice is amazingly sexy. I probably shouldn't be saying this, but I have another name for you, besides Jean, I mean."

"And what is that?"

"It's Mr. Quick-Where's-My-Vibrator."

Was he blushing? Oh, this was fun. His handsome face was now frozen in a perplexed expression, and it appeared that she'd jammed the program. Little Kerry Houston, who'd run from her workplace rather than confront her big bad boss when he had her fired, and who hid from the outside world like a hermit, had just beaten the system! At least she could fluster someone, even if it was only a virtual hunk.

"Let's take a deep breath and start over, Kerry. Are you comfortable?"

Now he was repeating himself!

"I'm just dandy," she said. "How are you?"

He didn't seem to hear her. "Remember the fantasy I promised you, Kerry, the one that could anticipate your every need, wish and desire? I'm going to need a little more information."

Poor Jean. She'd blown his fuses. "I'm not a woman without fantasies, you know. Listen, I have fantasies. I have a few fantasies that might shock you."

He appeared to blink and wake up at that point. "Could you name one?" he asked.

"And I love to touch things, too," she announced. "Do you know what I really love to touch? Buns, behinds, tushies, cheeks. Not that I go around doing that, but they look so firm and springy."

"Kerry—"

"And my favorite article of men's clothing? I know you didn't ask, but in case you're curious, it's a belt. Belts are long and leathery and they buckle in the sexiest way. They're well-placed on a man's body, *if* you know what I mean."

"Kerry—"

"Do you know what I mean, Jean? The place I'm thinking of that belts are close to? Do you have a pet name for yours? I like package, myself."

"Kerry!"

"Yes?"

"I told you that there are two conditions to this journey."

"Yes, I remember, that I entrust myself to you, and . . . hmm—"

"I didn't tell you the second one."

"Oh . . . right."

"The second condition is that you don't bluff. You can't win this game that way. You can't win this game without being willing to lose it, to give everything away. Do you understand me, Kerry? You have to be willing to give everything away."

On some level, Kerry understood exactly what he meant, and now he *was* talking fantasy. She had worked too hard to make herself safe behind these walls. She couldn't give an inch, and he wanted *everything*? Dear God.

Three

"Mmmmmmmm . . ."

"Now there's an interesting sound. You okay, Kerry?"

"Mmm . . . mmm . . . mmm . . . *mmmmmmmmm* . . ."

"I guess that was a yes?"

Kerry sighed deeply and felt a ripple of pleasure spiraling toward her toes. She was draped in her chair with her feet up on the desk, and the desire to stretch was so irresistible she made no attempt to fight it. She didn't even worry how it might look as she arched her back and slowly swiveled her hips, moving her shoulders in a languid counter-rhythm. Another moan slipped out, another contented sigh, another kitten purr of pleasure.

This guy was some tour guide.

He'd suggested a relaxation exercise before they began, and boy, had it worked. She was as flushed and rosy as if she'd just come out of a steam bath, and there wasn't a part of her that wasn't humming.

She'd been uneasy about the exercise, especially when he told her that it involved hypnosis and that he would be putting her in a light trance. But finally she'd agreed to do it. This *was* just a game. What could he do to her, after all, besides talk? But, oh, baby, could he talk. The way other men plied you with fine chocolates and kissed your fingertips, that was how he could talk. Astaire danced like he could talk. Sinatra sang. Jean's voice was steamy stolen kisses in the backseat of an old Chevy. It was fantasy phone sex.

"Kerry . . . are you still with me?"

"I wish," she murmured. It hardly mattered what the man said—it was all sweet seduction.

"You wish?"

"This must be what puff clouds feel like," she said, releasing another languid sigh. "A little breeze, and I would be on my way, floating, floating . . . just floating."

"What do you wish for, Kerry?"

"I could just float all day . . . did I mention I felt like a puff cloud?"

"Kerry, stay with me, girl."

With you? I am so with you, Jean.

"You said something about a wish."

What did she wish for? So many things . . .

No, just one. One little thing.

"Care to share?" he asked.

"Well, I wish I could move." She lifted her arm and it flopped back down. "I'm as limp as linguine. That hypnosis was amazing."

"It only works with a willing subject."

She smiled through drooping lids. "I didn't know I was that willing. This is a little bit of heaven, this weightless sensation. And I'm *so* warm. I've never been so warm."

"You released some tension, and now you're glowing. Technically, it's just blood, rushing to the surface."

"Glowing, yes, that's exactly what it feels like."

When he'd suggested hypnosis, she'd immediately thought of some guy on a stage, making people bark. But the sounds of a babbling brook and chirping birds had overridden her concerns, and the screen was transformed with kaleidoscopic images of slowly swirling pink clouds, sifting sands and dark green oceans.

She found it impossible not to watch.

It was like a peek at infinity.

Her lids were already heavy when Jean's voice entered the mix and he suggested she rest her head. She was gone before her eyes closed, but it had seemed as if he were right there, whispering strange, yet deliciously soothing things in her ear and putting her in a trance with his warm breath. His voice ebbed and flowed like a drug in her bloodstream, and even though she couldn't recall exactly what he'd said or what she'd done, she was quite certain she'd followed his suggestions without question. That was what you did when you were hypnotized.

When she came to she was slumped in her chair like a rag doll and sighing out sounds of satisfaction. She was so mellow her sweater socks were down around her ankles and she didn't even care. But what really fascinated her were the contradictions. Her body felt heavy and light at the same time, relaxed, yet deliciously aroused. Nerve endings twinkled like strings of Christmas lights, but her muscles were as fluid as the music coming from the speakers.

She'd heard about things like full-body orgasms, but she didn't think they were possible, especially if you had yet to have one of the garden variety type. The one smart thing she'd done with the string of losers in her life was to *not* sleep with them. She may have been used, but not in that way. Some protective instinct had kept her from surrendering body and soul to these men, despite their bad boy charm—or maybe because of it.

Her first boyfriend in college was the closest thing she'd ever had to a grand passion. She'd loved him and wanted to give herself to him, perhaps too soon and for the wrong reason. She'd hoped it would bring them closer, but her own desperation should have warned her what would happen. Brad Styles repaid her trust by having sex with one of Kerry's girlfriends the night after he'd taken Kerry's virginity. It was devastating. Most nineteen-year-old coeds would have been able to put it behind them, but for her it was a life sentence because it validated her belief that no man would ever really love her.

Her father hadn't. He'd deserted his family when

Kerry was a toddler, and her mother's bitterness had prepared Kerry to expect the worst from men. Even after Paula was gone, Kerry could hear her mother's warnings, but she didn't want to believe them. She'd had hope and her whole life ahead of her. Without realizing it, Kerry had desperately wanted Brad to prove her mother wrong—and to prove to Kerry that she was worth loving.

After that it was users and losers, men who confirmed what her mother had told her. She might not have consciously known it, but Kerry was afraid to take another risk on a good guy and have her heart broken again. It was easier to lock herself off, and when she did become involved, it was with men who acted exactly the way she expected—and believed she deserved.

With a romantic past like hers, Kerry hadn't spent a lot of time thinking about orgasmic experiences of any kind. But something had happened here today, something incredible. It felt like someone had switched bodies on her. She tried to bring back a detail or two of the experience, but the only thing she could remember were the feelings. Such wildness.

"*Zhhaa—?*" She was trying to say his name, but her voice cracked, and she couldn't clear away the raspiness. Where was her tea? One eye blinked open, and she spotted the cup of Quiet Woman on her desk. Nope. Too far.

"Yes, Kerry?"

"Did anything unusual happen while I was under?"

"Other than the noises?"

Ah, yes, the noises. Kerry could feel one building in her throat now. She tried to stop it, but her eyelids fluttered, and she flushed even warmer, if that was possible.

"Mmmmmmmmmmmmmm . . . oh, my . . . oh . . ."

"Kerry?" The noise *he* made was husky with disbelief. "Does that feel as good as it sounds?"

"Better," she whispered, "oh, much better. It feels like

I want to take my clothes off. I swear it does. Isn't that amazing?"

She laughed and flopped her arms wide. "I'm the original abominable snow woman."

"Original, maybe. Abominable, never."

"Ohhhhhhhhhh, Jean, that is sooo sweet. You're just an old sweetie pie, that's what you are. And I'm just so warm and breathless. You wouldn't mind, would you?"

"Wouldn't mind?"

"If I took something off?" He'd told her not to bluff, but she wasn't bluffing now. She was glowing, alive, and not the tiniest bit afraid.

"I don't think—"

"Oh, right, I'll bet you're not programmed to answer that, are you?" She sighed. "Oh, well, it'll be okay. You can't see me anyway . . . can you?"

He took too long to answer so she hiked up her heavy fleece dress and purposely flashed some leg as she peeled off one sweater sock. It was the blind man test. If she did something startling right in front of him and got no response, he probably couldn't see her. *Or* he was a very smart man.

"Jean?"

Nothing. Maybe one sock wasn't startling enough. She pulled off the other one and dangled the pair in front of the screen, wondering how he'd managed to turn her drafty old town house into a sauna—and her into an exhibitionist.

Not a twitch from the man. She had to bend forward to get a closer look at the screen, but she couldn't detect any signs of life at all, even simulated ones. At the very least his eyes should be dilating. Maybe the computer *was* frozen.

"That didn't bother you, did it?" she asked. "By any chance?"

"Bother me? What was it that should have bothered me?"

"Uh . . . nothing." At least she knew he was there, but

she still had no idea whether he could see her or not. He might have been probing for information. This was becoming a challenge.

"Excuse me, then," she said, "while I finish with this activity that *isn't* bothering you."

His sexy mouth hinted at a smile. "Don't mind me."

A definite challenge. Her mind was generating enough watts of suspicion to light up the neighborhood, but she could not crack this guy's code. Unfortunately, she was *really* glowing now. Some might have called it perspiring.

Off with the dress, Alice.

Years of use had made the crew neck of her dress loose enough to slip off her shoulder. From there she got her arm out—and realized she was dealing with a straitjacket, not a dress. Graceful it wasn't, but she knew better than to stand up and pull the bulky thing over her head. It was ankle length, and she would be too wobbly. Not to mention *exposed.* She could just imagine getting stuck, her arms and head inside, the rest of her outside.

She liberated the other arm and inched the dress down to her behind. It took a near backflip to get it to her ankles. Kicking her feet free was another high point, but it brought more blood rushing to the surface. Her color had to be approaching magenta by now. As she wiped the dampness from her brow, she realized the thermal underwear had to go too, but, then, oops, she would have nothing left but a pair of high-cut bikinis and a tank top.

"Pretty damn sexy," she murmured, when she was finally down to the essentials. She'd never thought of herself in those terms before, but then she'd never undressed for a man in quite this way before. Actually, she'd never undressed for a man in any way, but her guide didn't need to know that.

She straightened her tank top and felt a *zing zing* of electricity run through her. There were a couple parts of her that were still humming—and quite urgently aroused. Her breasts were taut and budded. They didn't seem to care whether the rest of her was glowing or not. They'd just come in from the cold.

"Would you look at that," she whispered in disbelief.

"Look at what?"

"The twins. I look like Cindy Crawford without a bra."

He made a throat-clearing sound, and she glanced up, startled. "Oh, sorry. It's just that I'm so warm and they're so . . . perky."

He seemed to be staring at her, and there was a pensive quality to his expression.

"Jean? You're awfully quiet. Is everything okay?"

"Yes, everything is fine."

"You sound a little tense. Is it me? Am I doing things you're not programmed to respond to?"

"I wouldn't put it exactly that way, but there are times when someone like me . . . when someone like me . . . wishes . . ."

Oh, don't stop now.

She was so caught up with the words she couldn't breathe. But his sea-deep eyes were beautiful. They seemed to be imbued with the ocean's hypnotic power.

Wishes what?

It sounded as if he'd cleared his throat again, and that possibility astounded her. Why would a computer simulation be hoarse?

"Jean? You were saying?"

"There are times when someone like me wishes he were real, Kerry. This is one of those times."

"Oh, me too, Jean. I wish you were real. I really do."

Her voice betrayed her, too. It was so raspy she could hardly get the words out. She grabbed for the tea to clear her throat, but she didn't have a firm grip on the handle, and some of it slopped on the keyboard.

"Oh, God," she whispered, staring at the poof of smoke.

There was a hot, sizzling sound, a shower of sparks, and the computer screen went dark.

Kerry jumped up from the chair and flipped the keyboard upside down to drain the spilled tea. She had a sinking feeling it was too late, the damage had been done, and she had no idea how to fix it. She'd never been into the nuts and bolts hardware. She was an idea person. Or she used to be.

"Jean? Are you there? Are you there? Oh, no, please tell me I didn't short out the keyboard!"

Not only wasn't he there, but the computer didn't seem to be there, either. Kerry did everything she could think of to get it restarted, but it was like trying to resurrect the dead, and she wasn't likely to get any help. It was late afternoon and one look outside told her she wouldn't get a repairman today. It had been snowing again, heavily, and the road was heaped with white.

Distraught, she picked up the game box and was gripped with the crazy need to apologize to it. It almost felt as if she'd killed someone. Of course, that wasn't true. It was a game, and he was the guide. He would be in every single copy that Genesis put out, wouldn't he? All she had to do was get her computer fixed and ask them to e-mail her a new copy of "Discover the Secret, Sensual You!"

It would be Jean in there, wouldn't it?

Somehow she didn't think so.

Four

"Kerry, come back and play. It's lonely in here without you."

Kerry heard the distant plea through a smothering veil of sleep. She was in deep slumber and might not have awakened at all if the hauntingly familiar voice hadn't coaxed her repeatedly.

"Kerry, come back and play—"

"Play?" she breathed into her pillow.

"Kerry—it's me."

She rolled over heavily and laid there in the darkness, vaguely aware that someone was about, and that she was too groggy even to open her eyes. The pale glow permeating her eyelids made her wonder if she'd left the television on in the living room. But she never used the television. She was always on her computer.

"Kerry, it's lonely—"

Her computer? She forced open her eyes to an aura of flickering blue light. It *was* her computer. The monitor was on. How could that be?

"Kerry—"

"Who's there?" Suddenly the voice was perilously close, a male voice.

"It's me," he said. "I'm here with you."

"With me?" Kerry could see nothing except the pulsing light, but her heart exploded with adrenaline. She dug her heels into the mattress and reared up, shoving herself back against the headboard.

"Who is it? Who's there?" She clutched the comforter to her body like a shield, unable to do more than whisper. What was going on? Who was there? Her eyes strained to make sense of things, but all she could see was a dark form silhouetted in the doorway.

The voice wasn't coming from the living room.

It wasn't coming from her computer.

There was a man standing right there in her bedroom—a tall, silent man, haloed by spikes of blue light. If this was a bad dream, it was a very, very bad one.

"Who are you? What are you doing in my house?"

"I'm sorry if I frightened you," he said.

His voice. She knew that voice.

"Tell me who you are."

"You know who I am."

"Tell me who you are!"

"I'm your guide, Kerry. It's Jean."

She couldn't see him well enough to distinguish his features, but she did know that voice. She'd been mesmerized by it. Hypnotized.

"Jean from the video game?"

"I've come, Kerry. I'm here. You can see me, can't you?"

She didn't know whether to be incredulous or horrified. The chill she felt cut to her bones. Either someone was playing a very cruel joke, or she had lost her mind.

"You *can't* be here. You're not real. You're pixels, hundreds of them."

"Not anymore. And it's all because of you."

Kerry didn't know what to do. Terror gripped her as she tried to reason things through. This had happened to her before when she tried to escape her problems with sleep. She dropped fast, deep, and dreamed profusely. Wild flights of hope and freedom. Often she dreamed that she was free of the fears and could walk out her front door. This was one of those. It was wish fulfillment, Freudian wish fulfillment. Either that or she'd taken too much L-tyrosine.

"You're not really here," she told him. "You're some figment of my loneliness and frustration, and I'd like you to go."

"I'm not a figment, Kerry, feel me, pinch me. I'm real."

"No! Stay there!" She threw up her hands, but he was in the room, at the foot of her bed, before she could stop him.

"No further," she told him. *"Please,* I believe you."

Her grandmother's antique lamp sat next to her bed. She stretched over and tried to turn it on, but the key was loose and the lamp wouldn't light. Frantically she twisted it again. Maybe she'd shorted out the whole house. But, then, how could the computer be working?

She kept one eye on the man at the foot of her bed as she felt for a weapon. Her vision had adjusted to the dark, but he was still too brightly haloed with light.

Damn. No electricity meant her curling iron was useless too. She kept it on her nightstand, plugged and ready. Guns frightened her, and the iron got hot enough to sizzle water in less than thirty seconds. She had the scars to prove it. There was a brick stashed under the bed and a baseball bat behind the door, in case of break-ins, but that had never been a problem before this. Her doors and windows were triple locked, and she had an alarm system.

"How did you get in here?" she asked.

"I have no idea. I'm here, that's all I know. Touch me, see for yourself."

Kerry's heart leaped as he held out a hand to her. How could he be here in her bedroom when just this afternoon he'd been the sexy heartthrob on her computer screen, watching her undress? Oh, God!

"You can't be real," she protested. "Because if you're real, then I should be screaming, right? Or calling the police—"

There was a phone on her night table too. She lunged for it, but he was there before she could punch a single number.

The receiver fell to the floor as he caught her wrist. His grip was powerful enough to push her back on the bed and hold her there. Not painful, but firm.

"Don't do that, Kerry. *Hear me out, please.* I am real, but not in the way that you think. I'm only here because you wished that I would be."

"I didn't wish anything of the kind!"

"Yes, you did, just before you spilled your tea."

She shook her head in confusion. She had no idea what he was talking about, and the sheer strength of his hold was terrifying. She might have been able to see him if it weren't for that damn blue light. He was close enough. Lord, was he close.

"Try to remember," he urged. "It's important. You said something like, 'Me too, Jean. I wish you were real.' Do you remember that?"

Someone was crazy, and it wasn't her. Whoever this guy was, he must have been watching her through the window today. He was a Peeping Tom who spotted her undressing and overheard her conversation with the video game.

"There's five hundred dollars in my bunny slippers in the closet," she told him. "Take it and go. I won't call the police. I won't scream. I won't do anything. Please, just take the money."

He released her arm and fell silent, as though he didn't know what she was talking about. *As though he wasn't programmed to respond.* She wanted to throw up her hands. What kind of crazy nightmare was this?

"I don't want your money," he said.

She chanced another look at him and thought she could make out the enigmatic features that had graced her computer screen—the same sea-deep eyes and sexy black hair, shorn close but curly. The same strong, handsome, haunted face. Fine details were lost in shadows, but this had to be him. She couldn't be having a dream this elaborate, could she?

Was it him, Jean, living, breathing, above her?

The comforter had slipped away, exposing her tank top. She took advantage of his retreat and yanked the blanket back, tucking it around her. She'd worn her underwear to bed? That was something she never did. It was much too cold, among other things.

Calming her voice was an effort. "Well then," she said, "if you don't want money, what *do* you want?"

"Actually, it's not that easy to explain."

"Please! *Try.*"

"All right, but I don't want you to take this wrong, okay?"

He retreated farther, walking to the other side of the room, possibly to think about what he was going to say. She waited to see if he was coming back, but he hesitated near a white pine shutter console that had been part of her grandmother's trousseau. The shadows couldn't hide his expression. It was somber and filled with portent.

"There's a curse on me, Kerry, and only you can break it."

She just stared at him. Stared and wished she'd bought a gun for her nightstand. Guns didn't need electricity.

"Kerry . . . you're looking at me like I'm crazy."

"Duh," she said softly.

"I'm *not* crazy, believe me."

"Oh, you're not crazy, but you're cursed? Do you know how crazy that sounds?"

"Yes, I guess it does, doesn't it."

He smiled and she released a helpless sound. "Oh, God, please let this be a dream. It has to be a dream because otherwise I *really* do need antipsychotic medication."

"What kind of curse?" She ducked her head. "No, stop, don't tell me. Don't say anything! I can't go there."

Whatever this was, it was totally outside her experience and she had no idea what to do. She just wanted him out of her bedroom and out of her head. She could hear his voice, reverberating in the lower registers, even when he wasn't talking. It always made her think of water—of rivers and deep canyons. That was a sure sign of insanity, wasn't it? When you started hearing phantom music or instructions from above?

Maybe if she shut her eyes he would vanish in a puff of smoke. All she wanted was to wake from this terrible dream that had taken over her life. She didn't understand what was happening to her. Suddenly, everything was out of control. Her entire world was a flipping TV test pattern. Fear was her constant companion, her only companion, and she was trapped in her own home.

Why was she trapped? What was she afraid of, really?

When she looked up, he was still there, still observing her in that somber, stoic way that Jean Valjean did.

"Oh, all right," she snapped. "What kind of curse?"

He shrugged. "The kind that gets you imprisoned in a video game?"

He didn't sound any better at this hocus pocus than she was. "Yes, but who put the curse on you? And why, what did you do?"

"Good questions, but I'm short on the salient details. Given my track record, I'm guessing it has something to do with pride and power, with lack of humility. There are experiences I've never had and emotions I can't feel, and I won't be free until I've felt them."

"What experiences?" She gave him a wary look as he returned to the foot of her bed. "You're not here to deliver my fantasy, are you? Because I don't really want you all over me like a blanket. I have a perfectly good blanket right here. And there are no strawberries in the fridge. It's the wrong time of year, and as far as belts go, I don't really find them that fascinating."

What else had she said? Quick, what else?

Was he smiling? Always a bad sign.

"I was just kidding about all that stuff, okay? Even if it sounded like I meant it, I *didn't*. It was probably stress or the amino acid I've been taking. Brain chemicals, you know. They can make you do and say things—"

His nod was understanding. "You certainly did that. You said things *and* did things."

"What did I say? What did I do? What?"

"It's okay. You were fine."

"No, really, what did I do? It couldn't have been *that* bad. I remember everything, except . . . oh, dear . . . when I was under hypnosis?"

"Except then," he said.

She didn't like the dark glint in his eyes. "What? Did I do something terrible?" What could be worse than undressing in front of the computer screen?

So many things.

"Did it involve one of the five senses?" she asked. "Touch, taste?"

"I'm not saying anything. You were fine, Kerry. Now, do you think we could finish our conversation about the curse?"

"Not until you tell me what I did."

"Not until we finish with the curse."

Obviously they'd reached an impasse. He said he was short on time. Maybe she could wait him out.

Unexpectedly he laughed, and it was a rich, rugged sound. "You have a gift, Kerry. I've never heard noises like that before."

She frowned.

He nodded.

"All right, all right." A sigh. "Tell me about this curse."

He sat on the end of the bed, positioning himself in the way that guys sometimes did, with one leg pulled up. Doctors were famous for that pose, news anchors, even cowboys, men of some authority, men with a problem to fix.

"Bottom line?" he said. "There's an emotion I've never experienced."

"Which one?"

"The one that makes you shudder."

"Fear? Is that the one you mean?" No wonder he'd been sent to her. Kerry Houston was an expert on shuddering.

"Not necessarily, although fear could be part of it. It's an emotion that can never be mastered by the human will. I can't explain it beyond that, but I'll know it when I feel it."

Now she was curious. Maybe this was one of those lucid dreams, the kind that were so vivid and real you couldn't tell them from everyday life. Was that even remotely possible? And if it was, then maybe the dream had something to tell her. It might be her own subconscious, trying to communicate.

"But you do know who put the curse on you, right? Someone had to—a practicing witch, the computer gods, your ex-wife?"

Irony tempered his smile. "I've come to believe that you can curse yourself. In fact, maybe that's the way it always happens with curses. They're self-imposed and self-fulfilling. But even if that's the case, I'm ready to change. I want to be free."

So did she. Oh, yes, so did she.

"Kerry, there was a moment when I thought I saw you peering back at me through the screen, and it was like waking from a deep sleep. There's a reason that happened to me. There's a reason it was you and there's a reason I'm here. I don't have much time."

"But why was it me?"

"Because you woke me up, because you wished for me to be here? Maybe you even needed me to be here."

Because she needed him to be here. How strange that her grandfather had always said that life had a way of bringing you whatever you needed, but you had to ask, and most people never did.

"Kerry . . . I may be trapped for all time."

Okay, she thought, *so maybe this is a dream and maybe it does have something to tell me.* She could certainly use the feedback. Her life wasn't exactly a picnic in Lover's Park lately. And it probably wouldn't hurt to go along with it—with him—for a while.

"I could be stating the obvious," she said, "but you are here. You are free. Why don't you just walk out that door and go merrily on your way?"

"It doesn't work like that. There are things a man has to learn, things that maybe only a woman can teach."

Her stomach was doing that handspring thing again, and Kerry could hardly contain a sigh. He had her at *things a man has to learn.*

"You know, Jean, I'm not exactly a poster girl for mental health."

"You're perfect."

His voice resonated softly through the dark, tapping at the stubborn barriers that protected her heart. She drew the comforter around her, warding off a shiver.

"What do I have to do?" she asked him.

"Teach me how to shudder, the crash course?"

She laughed at that. "We could put it on video, the companion piece to 'Discover the Secret, Sensual You!'"

"You'll do it then?"

"Honestly, Jean, I don't think that can be taught."

There was pride in the lift of his head, pride and sadness. "Then show me the way back to my soul. Isn't that where shuddering comes from?"

She tugged on the comforter, trying to cover herself, but there was nothing she could do. He was sitting on the other end.

"The crash course sounds easier," she admitted.

"What makes you shudder, Kerry? How does it happen?"

You, she thought. *Don't you know? Can't you see?*

"It's cold in here," she told him. "I should probably get some clothes on."

"Can I help with that?"

Again, Kerry found herself staring at him. *I gave him the wrong name,* she thought. *He isn't Jean Valjean from* Les Mis. *He's* Starman *from the movie.* She had her own personal Starman. He thought it was just fine offering to help a crazy naked lady get dressed. He was from another planet.

"I'll stick with the comforter," she said, "but it would be nice if we had some light in here."

She half-expected him to point a finger at her table lamp and zap it on. Instead, he walked over and began to tinker with it while she gathered up the comforter and created her own igloo. She watched him expectantly, waiting for the moment when light flooded him and she could finally see the details of his face. She was dying to know what he looked like in the flesh, how he dressed and carried himself.

The shadows gave him a graceful, fluid presence, but she was very aware of his height. He was a good-sized man, and as darkly gorgeous as the winter night. She had an instinctive feel for the dimensions of her bedroom, and she could just make out the substantial contours of his hand as it worked the switch of her antique table lamp. She could also remember how it felt on her arm, how much area it took up, how commanding it was.

A slave bracelet encircling pink satin skin . . . a slave bracelet, his hand.

Warmth rushed up Kerry's throat. She loosened the comforter, and had a momentary flash of him reaching for her, lifting her out of her igloo and into his arms. He could do it easily, she realized. He was tall enough that her feet would never touch the floor. Tall enough to curl your bare legs around and ride like a wave to its crest. *Tall enough to bounce your head in the clouds with every rip and swell.*

Wooooooo . . . where was she going with that one?

She lifted her head and felt the dizzy weight of her own eyelids. The warmth had flooded her face and gone straight to her brain.

"I think you've blown a fuse," he said.

She didn't dare laugh. "I have candles somewhere." They wouldn't need light the way she was glowing. She was steamy enough to throw off the comforter and start fanning herself. It was an odd thing having a strange man this close to her in a darkened bedroom. She wondered if he knew how intimate it was, or the effect he was having on her.

If she could find a way to have that effect on him, she could free him from any old curse in a matter of minutes.

The candles were in her closet. She rose from the bed to get them and wondered what he would do. The answer might have frightened her if she hadn't sensed from the first that his purpose was not to do her harm. When she turned, he was there, standing behind her, close enough to feel his heat and breathe in his male scent. It startled her, but he seemed to anticipate her concern.

"Shhhhh," he whispered as he took an armful of votive candles from her. "It's okay."

He began to arrange them in small circles around the room and light them.

For some reason it pleased her to watch him do that, but she wondered about the matches in his pocket. Where did a cursed man who lived in a computer get those? You're having a dream, Kerry, she reminded herself. A revelatory dream. That's why you're going along with it, and that's the *only* reason. Your unconscious is trying to tell you something, and you're going to listen, even if it makes you want to squeal and hide under the bed.

Her questions vanished as she realized he was gone. She looked around the room, bewildered, and saw him returning from the living room, absent the blue aura. He'd turned the TV off, but he was carrying the one remaining candle, and she was finally able to see him. The sinuous flame played its tricks, but she was certain this was the same man she'd seen on her screen.

She wondered if the sexy dark curls on his head had been cropped short to tame them. His lashes were equally dark and feathery. His mouth was even moodier and more sensual than she remembered, given its width, the curvature of his upper lip, the tilted corners. He was better looking than on the screen.

"You bring a word to mind," he said.

"I do?"

"Beauty. You have so much of it."

"I was thinking that about you," she said.

"How difficult is it?"

"Shuddering? It's not hard at all. There are so many ways. Your voice," she said. "Your voice makes me shudder."

He took in her flushed features, obviously pleased. God, how he made her heart beat and the blood hum through her veins. It felt like her body was making music, trying to sing.

A circle of candles flickered from the mirrored dresser, setting fire to the glass.

"Can you tell me how it works?" he asked.

"Your voice touches nerves. I can't explain it, but if I could touch you in the same way, you'd shudder too."

He was wearing a black sweater shirt that buttoned up the front. She slipped a hand through an opening in the comforter and touched the material. What was she doing? The room was so quiet you could hear her fingernails click against the bone buttons as she began to undo them. Her heart was beating unnaturally hard, but it seemed the right thing to do, the only thing. Moments later, the silky material fell away from his torso, letting the firelight reveal him. His abdomen was hard and smooth. Above it, sienna-colored nipples peeked through glossy dark hair.

He caught a breath as she touched his midriff.

Rippling muscles tightened torturously.

"There," she said. "See? See how easy it is? You're a free man."

He laughed and threw back his head. "God," he whispered.

"It worked, right?"

"Oh, no, Kerry," he said, nearly as breathless as she was, "no, I'm still cursed. I'm more cursed than ever."

Kerry was crushed. "That wasn't a shudder? It was a quiver maybe?"

"I don't know what it was, but it was unbelievable."

"Then what's wrong?"

He pressed a hand to the fluttering muscles. "It's an amazing feeling, but I don't think it's the one I'm missing."

"Really, are you sure? I guess we should try something else, then. How do you like to be touched? Lightly? Firmly?"

His lips melted into a smile. "Are you my guide now?"

It was impossible not to smile back. "I could be. Would you like to go on a tour of Jean?"

"Lead on," he said.

"This is just a dream, isn't it?"

"It feels pretty real to me."

Well, of course, she thought, what else would she expect a dream character to say? He wasn't the one under stress and popping amino acids. This was her learning experience. Who cared what he thought?

She solved the problem of her comforter by tucking it in like a bath towel and wearing it like a cape. After that she eased open his shirt to allow more access. The silky material slid off one shoulder and dropped down his arm. It was an incredibly sexy accident. She didn't want to think about how sexy.

A river of muscle, sinew and bone, that's what she was dealing with. His belly button was the only reasonably soft thing she could see. She could start there, but like the apex of a wheel, it would only lead to things that were hard, no matter which way she went. She drew a little circle, keenly aware of the taut heat beneath her fingers, of the sensitive puckers and tucks, and the bull's-eye at its center.

"How's this?" she asked.

He shook his head as if to say "Nice, yes, but still not the right one."

But she had seen the way his muscles sucked in and his shoulders lifted.

She tried those same shoulders and his neck next. There were some irresistibly tawny cords and tendons that actually quivered when she touched them. Now *that* could make a woman want to die, it was so thrilling. What must be going on inside him, she wondered. The same exquisite sensations that were stirring in her? He had such a marvelously responsive body.

"I don't think so," he said.

An idea came to her, but was it too reckless?

"This is only in the interests of helping your cause," she told him. "It's nothing personal."

She tilted up and pressed a breathless kiss to his mouth.

Air jetted from his nostrils, but his expression barely registered the impact.

"Anything?" she asked.

He shook his head.

"No? Really? Are you sure?"

She brushed her mouth over his again, only this time she let her fingers glide down his body, over his hardened abs and across his crotch. Just so very lightly, she brushed him and felt him turn into a girder beneath her fingers. He was certainly built like a human.

A groan shot through him and his whole body quaked.

She stepped back with a secret rush of pleasure. "Congratulations," she said.

"Whoa," he breathed, "I'm still vibrating. What did you do to me?"

She wasn't sure herself. "It was just a touch, and barely one at that. Maybe it was what I *didn't* do."

It seemed as if he needed to sit down to get his bearings. He stepped back and ended up on her bed, but when he looked up at her, he was shaking his head.

"You're not going to believe this," he said with the huskiest of voices, "but I don't think that was it. No, I don't think so."

"What? How could it not be? Your stomach muscles were practically in spasm." She really was at a loss—and then lightning struck again. God, the creative process. She loved it.

"Do you think it could be that you need to touch *me*?" she asked.

She was still bundled inside her igloo, and he looked her over as if to say that he couldn't see how much touching was going to get accomplished with only her face showing.

"Here," she said, "I'll just move the comforter off my shoulder. See, like this." She touched her fingertips to bare skin and quivered. "Oh! Try that."

His fingers brushed her flesh and her igloo fell away. It dropped to the floor, revealing her tank top and bikini panties. She stood there, staring at him, wanting to gasp, gasping deep in her soul where shudders start. That was the moment she knew that something momentous was going to happen to her tonight. He was going to touch her in ways she'd never been touched before, redefine the very word, touch. And not only that, she wanted him to. Let the journey begin. It was only a dream, after all.

And she hadn't shuddered this way in such a very long time.

Five

Whatever you secretly desire in life has already imprinted itself on you. All you have to do is recognize its existence . . .

Kerry heard his voice as if he'd just whispered the words, but he couldn't have. He was doing something much more thrilling and terrifying with his mouth than whispering. He was showing her what she secretly desired. It was the only part of him that touched her body, his hot, whispering mouth.

"Oh!" she cried as he rolled her nipple between his teeth. She felt the sharp edges against her aching flesh, and nearly swooned with pleasure. It was sweet relief. She was stretched so taut that even a nip would have felt good. Anything that released the pressure. How she wanted his hands on her! How she wanted to be touched and squeezed and fondled until she did swoon. She would fall into unconsciousness, aroused only by each nip, by each sharp, unbearably sweet thing he did to her.

It's a dream . . . it has to be . . . I couldn't do this if it weren't.

She had fleeting thoughts of turning away from him, of trying to cover herself, but that was impossible . . . and this was perfect. In some way, it was perfect.

She was naked and wantonly displayed for her dream lover. . . . The comforter had fallen away at his touch, as had her tank top, and she couldn't remember how it had happened. She didn't know when her breasts had come to be bared. How her whole body had come to this wild flash point of desire.

She had to turn away.

This was her last chance.

That thought took hold of her, but when she tried, he spun her back into his arms. Her head dropped back with a gasp and weakness flooded her. Shock burned her face and her jaw fell slack. *What was happening? The more powerful he became, the weaker she got, and that made her utterly breathless.*

"You can't win this game by bluffing, Kerry. You have to show your hand."

"I'm naked," she whispered. "Look at me. What more can I show you?"

"Yourself, show me that."

Show him that.

"The entire rainbow, Kerry . . . it's all yours to feel."

"It's too much feeling."

"Breathe . . . let go of everything else . . . breathe and float . . ."

Her eyelids fluttered, and she became aware of her breathing. It was deep and regular. She was succumbing again, falling more deeply under his spell, and soon there would be no hope for her. Maybe there never had been. A sensation lived in the pit of her stomach. It was as crystal clear as a violin's song. Her body was making music again. She could hear the clarion tones that rang from within, and they were even more compelling than his voice.

A moan slipped out. "Mmmmmmmm . . ."

He gripped her arms, and she was glad. If she made him crazy with her sounds, then yes, she was glad. She wanted power over him, any little bit of power she could get.

They were standing by the console, his legs braced wide and hers between them. He had brought her here to make love to her, female intuition told her that. He had laced his hands through her hair and searched for the secrets in her gaze and said her name. *Said it with hunger.* Passion burned off him like radiant energy—

rough and tender passion—and it was all she could do to stay on her feet.

"A highwayman," he whispered near the lobe of her ear, "who sees a woman running through the fields in a transparent gown . . ."

Who rides her down on his horse and takes her against a tree.

Kerry's toes curled into the carpet beneath her feet. The edge of the console dug into her back, but she was grateful it was there to steady her. She couldn't move against him, but he could move against her. And he did.

"A male slave so aroused by a woman he can't hide it . . ."

His erection burned her belly, and she melted against it like candy in the heat. It was beautiful the way he wrapped her in his arms, protecting her nakedness, and at the same time whispering forbidden things in her ear. *Terrible, terrible things and she wanted every one of them to happen to her.*

"The handsome stranger behind you in line, who murmurs that he has been fantasizing about you in a dress with no panties underneath . . ."

A sound vibrated in his throat. It ran all through Kerry.

He startled her by holding her at arm's length and looking down at her body, admiring her in the way that hungry males do succulent females. She had never thought of herself as edible, but his expression forced her to. His eyes were hot and his mouth was just slack enough to make her imagination run wild. Those moody lips and white, glistening teeth.

What those teeth could do. *Had done.* She felt another bolt of electricity at the thought. Such excruciating pleasure.

"Come with me," he said. "Come with me on a tour of *us*."

He lifted her onto the console and moved between her legs. The inside of her thighs ached with anticipation, and the ache deepened as he moved closer, spreading her legs wider. Pressure built within her, and it was wildly irresistible, one of the more glorious feelings she'd ever experienced.

She hadn't paid any attention to the fact that he was still dressed. She barely knew what she had on. But when he trailed his knuckles up her thigh and toyed with the leg of her bikini panties, it released a shower of thrills. She was down to one skimpy article of clothing, which wasn't doing her much good at all.

His fingers had become her sun, the center of everything. She could think about nothing else. Every move they made riveted her, especially as they delved inside the elastic of her panties and touched the nest of curls there. She was hit by bolt after bolt, and moisture gushed.

He continued his exploration, delving farther.

Kerry's head snapped up, and her breath caught fire.

Lord, how she wanted him to touch her there, deeply, taste her there. But to her surprise, he didn't do either of those things. He shocked her breathless by asking her to pleasure herself.

"What?"

"Touch yourself the way you want to be touched. Show me, Kerry. Show your hand."

She was self-conscious, but with his encouragement, she caressed the curve of her own throat, including the sensitive little pocket just beneath her chin—and decided it must be the softest part of her body. Of course, that was before she got to the insides of her elbows and wrists. Hundreds of receptors? She had thousands. Her thighs were like water and her fingertips, sunlight. They left diamonds everywhere they traced.

God, how she ached, how wonderfully she ached for him.

There wasn't anywhere she *didn't* want to be touched.

He guided her hand to where his had been, and she

had barely brushed the silky curls before the voltage started. A shaking breath slipped from her throat. Her whole body throbbed. For a moment she was swept by the intensity, and all she could do was rock forward. When she opened her eyes, he was picking her up in his arms.

He laid her on the bed, and then he began to undress. Candlelight flickered over him as he pulled off his shirt, and Kerry was dazed by how powerful he looked. His shoulders were wide and muscular, his arms dark with hair. He unbuttoned his pants, but left them on as he moved over her.

His weight pressed her deeply into the mattress, and she gave out a little cry. They really were going to make love, and she was stunned by that possibility. She had to stop him.

"Can you feel that, Jean? Are you shuddering like I am?"

"God, yes, I can feel it." He pulled her into his arms. "It's beautiful, even my breath is shaking."

"Then you're free? You must be free."

Something compelled her to search his face, even though her body ached for his attention. She was quivering for completion, for the journey she'd never taken. But she had to know if he felt the way she did.

"Is this it? Is this the shuddering you were talking about?"

He touched her face, her mouth, but he didn't answer her right away. He looked a little shell-shocked too.

"Kerry, I'm not sure," he said. "It has to come from the soul. This is incredible. I've never felt anything like it, but I just don't know."

Kerry was hurt and bewildered. She couldn't hide it. "How can you not know? You said that you *would* know. I remember."

He studied her searchingly. "This isn't about me. It's about you, your feelings. It's about the rainbow. Let me give you that—"

Her shuddering did come from the soul. He didn't feel that way?

"No," she insisted, "this has never been about me. It's about freeing you from the curse. Why else are we doing this?"

"Because we want to. I can't imagine any greater pleasure than making you happy, than making *you* shudder."

He didn't feel the tremors she felt, this ecstasy? She had failed utterly in her attempts to reach him? That destroyed her. It simply did.

"I can't do this," she said. "I can't go on with it."

"Kerry, don't—"

"I'm sorry, I can't."

She covered herself with her arms and refused to look at him.

"Kerry, for God's sake, don't," he whispered. "There is no curse on me except you. If I can't have you, I don't want anything else. To live like a normal man would be hell."

His rough voice sent a thrill through her. It didn't sound like Jean at all. He sounded desperate, and Kerry was torn. She didn't know what to do. She couldn't let him do these things to her. The feelings were too intimate. They had to be mutual. She couldn't be the only one falling in love.

She looked up to tell him that . . . but he was gone.

This time Kerry got traction on the doorknob the first time she tried. It was even more amazing that she'd been able to walk to her front door, turn the knob, and open it without an internal earthquake. The floor didn't ripple and warp, the lights didn't dance, but her pulse was kicking painfully. And now that she had the door open, she couldn't seem to move.

He was gone, and she had to find out if he'd ever existed. Could she have dreamed him? Was she crazy? Someone had aroused her to the point of delirium last night, but this morning she awoke to burned down candles and her own discarded clothing. He was gone. Parts of her body were still throbbing, and her heart was an aching knot. What had happened? Was she so desperate that she had to dream a man into existence to make love to her?

It didn't seem possible to feel things so intensely in a dream. But if he really did exist, the implications were staggering. It meant that a virtual stranger had come into her bedroom last night and rendered her naked and utterly helpless with desire. Despite all the stories her grandfather had told her, Kerry no longer believed in curses and fairy tales. The man was real, and therefore he must have broken into her house.

He wasn't a stranger, either. He looked exactly like Jean, and he knew about the game. He talked about it. Malcolm's paranoia seemed less scary to her in comparison to this. Maybe her tenant was right. Someone was spying on them through their computers and Palm Pilots. Everyone was under surveillance and it was a government plot.

But why did the government care whether or not she had an orgasm?

She was going crazy. She was.

Icy air gusted through the open doorway. She hadn't thought to put on her parka or flap hat. Talk about shuddering. Her legs began to shake, but her hands were clammy, despite the frigid weather.

She should have called the police immediately. Why hadn't she done that?

She rubbed her arms for warmth. No, it was too soon to bring the police in on something like this. And it was too strange a story. She had to find out for herself what was going on before someone had her carted off to an asylum.

Go outside and check the door, Kerry.

It was early, and the world was still hushed under a

fresh layer of white, but someone had shoveled her walk, she saw. The concrete steps were wet with a film of melted snow. It was probably her neighbor, the retired grocery store manager who'd pretended not to see while she was being mugged. The gangs had made everyone afraid of reprisals, but Kerry would never understand why someone who'd lived next door long enough to know her grandparents hadn't tried to help. She would have taken on the thugs herself if he'd been attacked.

She checked the knob on the outside of the door, but there weren't any visible scratches or marks. That didn't mean there wasn't a break-in, however. A real professional wouldn't have left any evidence. Kerry had no idea what she was dealing with, but this was beginning to feel more bizarre every moment, if that was possible.

"Kerry? What's wrong?"

The whispered question came from behind her.

Kerry nearly slipped on a patch of ice, trying to get turned around. It was Malcolm, standing alongside the house. He'd scared her half to death, but she didn't have time to be upset with him.

"Malcolm, did you see anything odd going on around here last night? Anyone strange lurking around?"

He crept toward the porch, peeking out at her from under a baseball hat. He was bundled up in the pea jacket and a heavy turtleneck that was mostly hidden by his beard. His breath was as steamy as a horse's.

"Why?" he asked, flipping up the collar of his coat. "Has someone been lurking around?"

"I just asked *you* that question, Malcolm."

A smile glimmered. "Oh, yeah, you did. No, I haven't seen anybody. Are you missing something?"

"Not really." *Just my sanity, my dignity, and possibly my faith in mankind.* "I thought I heard noises, but you know how that is. Maybe it was a dream. Thanks anyway."

She gave him a halfhearted wave and started inside. The plan was to beat a hasty retreat, but something stopped her midstride. Her other hand was frozen on the railing, and she couldn't move. It felt as if she were being zapped with electric current. She could not move. Could not. Move.

Dear God, she thought. She was outside, and she couldn't get back. This was her worst fear realized. She was as paralyzed as the statue across the street. She hadn't been out of the house in weeks. What had made her think that she could do this?

At some point she realized Malcolm was on the porch with her. He was trying to help her, but she was so rigid with fear, he couldn't get her unfrozen, either. With some prying he got her fingers unlocked. And then, to her horror, he picked her up in his arms, carried her into the house and dropped her on the sofa.

"Are you all right?" he asked, kneeling next to her. His blue eyes were dark with concern. "Are you sick or something?"

"No—Yes, maybe. I didn't get much sleep last night."

"Should I call the doctor? I could take you to a clinic."

She pulled a woolen throw over her and huddled inside it. "Just c-c-cold," she said. "I'll be fine in a minute."

"How about something to drink? Wine? Whiskey? Something stronger?"

"*Is* there anything stronger?" She managed a little smile. Malcolm obviously thought she needed sedation, and he was right. "Some hot tea would probably help, but I can get it myself."

He crammed his hands in his jacket pockets and shuffled his feet. "Well, if there's nothing I can do, maybe I should be going. *Is* there anything I can do?"

Kerry didn't want him to go. It hit her all at once that she didn't want her odd duck of a tenant to leave. Boy, that was scary. But even scarier was the prospect of being alone with her bizarre fantasies and suspicions. At least Malcolm was someone to talk to, another human being, not an assortment of pixels like Jean. Okay, a gorgeous assortment, but pixels nonetheless.

"Heard any good conspiracy theories?" she asked him.

He gave her a look that said she was scaring *him*.

She tucked the blanket under her chin, brought herself to a sitting position and began to mutter. "Think maybe you could get up, Kerry?" she said. "Think maybe you could make you and your guest a cup of tea? Something herbal? Something calming? And no more L-tyrosine?"

"Kerry, who are you talking to? Are you all right?"

Poor Malcolm. Now he had one more thing to worry about. Her.

"No, I'm not all right," she said impulsively. "I'm lonely, Malcolm. I'm lonely, and I think maybe what I need is a roommate. Would you like to live with me?"

Malcolm was already up on his feet and inching toward the door. "I really have to be going," he said. "I hope you feel better soon."

Kerry shrugged. "Me, too, Malcolm. Me, too."

"Kerry?" Something seemed to have halted Malcolm's progress. He acted as if he wanted to tell her something, but he was rocking back and forth like a self-conscious teenager. "You will overcome your fear," he said, "when there's something more important to you than your fear."

Kerry sat up. "Malcolm? What does that mean?"

"I—uh—" He shook his head, seeming as bewildered as she was.

As the front door closed on her tenant's fleeing form, Kerry gave out a resigned sigh, followed by a bittersweet sigh, which seemed to bring on a huge, wistful sigh. Now she knew how to get rid of Malcolm. That should have made her happy. But it was true, she was lonely. Lonely, confused and afraid.

It was her grandfather who'd always told her if you wanted something badly enough, you should wish for it. "With an open heart," he'd said, "because only open hearts can receive." There were times when she could feel her grandparents' presence so strongly it felt as if they were still about, keeping an eye on her. They knew she hadn't had good luck with men, and it had occurred to her that if some wonderful guy ever did come her way, they might have had something to do with it.

Silly child, she thought.

Her computer sat forlornly on the secretary, silenced by a poof of smoke. Kerry tried to ignore it. She made her tea, drank it and tidied the kitchen, but finally she couldn't postpone the day any longer. She had work to do. There were other games to test and she had to make a living. No more wandering around in a daze. She'd done that all night. She told herself sternly that she could get the computer working again without being tempted to revisit the scene of the crime. She was never going near Jean Valjean or his criminally seductive video game again.

She wasn't.

Well, she wasn't, damnit.

"Jean, are you in there?"

Kerry peered into the depths of her computer screen with a feeling of despair. She could feel the sequence of sighs starting again, but she'd been sighing all day, and she wasn't going there again. She'd been wrestling with what to do all day too. It had taken her entire supply of tea bags, but finally she'd realized that no mattered how frightened—or crazy—she was, she couldn't pretend that nothing had happened.

"Knock knock? Anyone there? Jean?"

"I don't seem to be programmed to answer that," the game guide said.

How like a man, she thought. They weren't programmed to answer the really important stuff. And how like her life. She tried to have a relationship with a computer simulation, and even he turned out to be a jerk.

"Perhaps you would like to start by giving me a name?" the guide suggested.

"You have a name. It's Jean. My name is Kerry and I've played this game before. You must have a record of me somewhere in your memory. Dammit, Jean! look again!"

"You're not in my memory banks, Kerry. I'm sorry."

"Not as sorry as I am."

Kerry sprang from her chair and walked away from the computer. It had become the source of all her frustration and pain, and she couldn't sit there any longer. She had to escape it, or she would go crazy, but how was she to do that? It was also the source of her income. She was trapped in her house and had no other way to make money.

She had to let go of this obsession with Jean and get on with things. Her survival depended on it. Even if there was a slight possibility that he'd ever existed, he didn't now. She lost him the first time when the keyboard shorted out, and she lost him the second time last night when she wasn't able to free him. Whatever the missing emotion was, she had not touched it. She hadn't been able to give him what he lacked, and that had made her feel like a failure. That was why she'd told him to go. She was afraid of the feelings he touched in her and devastated that she couldn't touch him the same way.

Out her window Kerry could see Lover's Park and the defiantly graceful statue. Neighborhood folklore had it that the two young lovers were caught together against the wishes of their families. They were betrothed to others, and their punishment for falling in love was imprisonment. They were kept in separate towers, chained and naked, until they came to their senses and did as their families wished. It was believed that to venture out into the icy winter without clothing would freeze them solid and they would die the moment they touched.

Kerry had wholly accepted the story as a child, probably because the existence of the statue seemed to prove it. Her favorite part was the ending, which her grandfather swore was true. He told her the young lovers missed each other so grievously they felt as if they were dying anyway, and one night, with the help of servants, they both escaped their prisons. A terrible blizzard had blown in, but the passion flowing in their veins kept them warm until they found each other. The moment they touched, they froze, forever inseparable and locked in a lover's embrace.

Decades passed but the exquisite ice sculpture did not melt as much as one drop, even in the hottest summers. The lovers had preferred death to separation, and the statue Kerry saw out her window was said to represent the way they were found by their families, entwined in naked splendor.

The statue was called *Winter Lovers,* and Kerry had often wondered if a love like that was possible. She wanted to believe it was true. She wanted to *believe.* But there was little in her romantic past that would allow her to. She'd had so few good experiences with men . . . until now, she realized.

"Kerry, are you there? Do you want to play the game? If you don't, just say 'Go to sleep' and I'll turn myself off."

Kerry whirled. It was the game guide. "No, wait! Don't go to sleep, don't!"

She dashed back to her chair and sat down. The *Winter Lovers* had given her an idea. *Please let this work,* she thought. *Please please, please.*

The man staring back at her from the screen had Jean's features—the same dark eyes and hair and mouth—but he wasn't anyone she knew. Certainly he wasn't the man who'd materialized in her house last night. He had the blank stare of a computer simulation. He didn't look like he ever had been or could be human.

She began to speak to the monitor, but she wasn't talking to him.

"Jean, I know what it is now! I know how to make you shudder. You have to come back. Please, Jean, come back. I can free you this time, I'm sure of it."

Six

Kerry lay in bed, frowning at the fire ring of burning candles and wondering what kind of stupid you had to be to believe in fairy tales. She'd even arranged the candles in threes as he had. But he wasn't coming back. She had to stop waiting, wishing, hurting so badly she could die with every second that passed, every second he didn't show up. She had to stop.

She rolled over and buried her face in the pillow. *Jean, please. If you exist, don't let it end like this. Find a way to come back. Find a way.*

"Stop this, Kerry," she told herself, "just stop."

She didn't understand why she couldn't let go of this fantasy and put it out of her mind. She wasn't in love with him. You couldn't be in love with someone who existed only in video games and dreams, no matter how lonely you were. But she knew what it was like to be held prisoner against your will, and maybe that was why it had seemed imperative to help him. There had to be some reason she and Jean had been brought together, something for her to learn from the way he'd come into her life . . . even if it was all a dream.

If she could free him, then perhaps she could find a way to free herself.

She closed her eyes and envisioned the cloudlike images that had hypnotized her, hoping they might help put her to sleep. Still, it seemed like hours before she finally did drift off . . . and only moments before a vaguely familiar noise woke her. The beeping was soft and intermittent, but she'd heard it before. She lay there, dozing, her mind searching for connections, and suddenly she was awake, aware. It was the video game. She'd heard the same sound the first time she played the game. There was a feedback loop keyed into the player's responses. If your heart rate went up, it beeped.

Her heart rate had just gone up.

She sat up and scanned the dark room, wondering what was going on. Her eyes were slow to adjust, but as far as she could tell the whole house was dark. The computer couldn't be on, but she could still hear the noise.

She slipped out of bed and put on her heavy chenille robe. She wasn't wearing her usual layers of flannel. She'd hoped the panties and tank top she wore last might somehow magically encourage him to come back. What kind of stupid? *That* kind of stupid. Sadly, there wasn't anything she hadn't tried, including bargaining with the angels for their help.

Her phone! If it wasn't the computer, then it had to be her cordless phone, she realized. It made a beeping sound when it ran out of batteries. She'd probably left it off its cradle.

The moonlight was so bright she didn't need her flashlight to get around. Silvery rays lit her way into the living room, where she began to search for the phone. She usually left it on the catalogs by the rocking chair, but the beep didn't sound as if it were coming from that direction. Where the heck—

"Is this what you're looking for?"

Kerry let out a scream that could have brought her grandparents out of their graves. There was a man standing in the shadows of the front hallway, and she had no weapon, nothing to protect herself. For a second, she thought it was Malcolm, but the intruder was so well-concealed she couldn't tell.

Her voice quaked. "Who are you, and what are you doing in my house?"

"I was under the impression that you wanted me to be here. Was I wrong?"

No one talked that way, except— *"Jean?"*

"Kerry, I came back."

The floor tilted and the lights danced, even though they weren't on. Kerry took that as a sign that she was going to faint, and when she sat down, it was in the old rocking chair. The creaks and groans drowned out her soft exclamation as he walked into the room, and she saw his face.

"My God, Jean, why didn't you say something? You scared me to death."

"I did. Didn't you just hear me? I said, 'I came back.'"

And she wanted him back, but did it always have to be unannounced?

"Oh, never mind." She was dealing with Starman. She had to remember that. "What is it you're holding?" It looked like a gun in his hand.

"Your phone. It's making funny noises."

I would be, too, if you were holding onto me like that.

Forlorn little beeps echoed through the darkness. It was a sound that had always made Kerry acutely aware of her own loneliness, and she rose from the chair to put the phone out of its misery.

"I'll do it," he said. "I know where it goes."

He knew where it went.

He seemed to know where everything went, including her. This was the man who picked her up and set her on the console last night, the man who sent wild delight tumbling through her. Was that magic or madness?

There was no time to stop and ask him if any of this was really happening. No time for that or any of the other nonsensical questions that were piling up in her mind, like what he'd done before he was cursed and why he'd ended up in a video game, of all places. That must have been symbolic. There were other things that had to be taken care of first, before he disappeared again.

"Do you remember when you hypnotized me?" she asked him.

"You're an excellent subject."

"Well, let's hope you are, too, because I think that's the way to free you."

He looked skeptical. "You're going to hypnotize me?"

"Yes, with the help of a Web site that specializes in trances and hypnotic suggestion. Of course, the key suggestions will come from me."

"And what will those key suggestions be?"

"Jean, when you hypnotized me you asked me to entrust myself to you. Now I'm going to ask the same of you. If I told you what I'm going to do, I might create conscious resistance, but I can promise that you will enjoy your journey as much as I did mine."

"You're serious about this, aren't you?"

"Absolutely," she said, hoping she appeared more confident than she must look in her pink chenille robe. "Do you have a better offer?"

"Okay, now that you put it that way." He gave the room a questioning once-over. "Where do you want me?"

A short time later she had him stretched out in the rocker. She was grateful it could handle a man his size, although the chair was tilted so far back it could have been a recliner. She also arranged the computer monitor on the catalog tower so he could easily see the screen. The patterns oscillating on the screen were much like the ones that had mesmerized her.

"All I want you to do is breathe and relax," she said softly. "Listen to my voice and relax. Feel yourself breathing, feel how deep it goes with every breath, and go with it, deeper . . . deeper . . ."

"One condition," he said, his eyelids beginning to droop. "You can put me under but you have to wake me with a kiss."

She tried not to smile. "You drive a hard bargain."

Within moments his eyes were closed and his facial muscles had surrendered their tension. He appeared to be deeply relaxed and, hopefully, deeply suggestible, because her next step was to coach him on being open and receptive to everything she said. When she'd done that she would attempt the feat that she hoped would free him.

She studied his face in repose, admiring the sharp contrasts. Eyelashes as black as soot threw lyrical shadows over features set at dramatic right angles. She was especially drawn to the mouth she was going to kiss awake. He looked almost vulnerable, and she wasn't too comfortable with the idea of taking advantage of him in this way, but it was for a good cause. How else was she going to save him? There was no other option, and if her plan worked, she would explain it to him when this was over—and he was grateful, she hoped.

"As you listen to my voice," she said, "your mind is opening and expanding, and you are experiencing an emotion you've never felt before—a longing that is both deep and beautiful. Relax and let yourself feel it, Jean. Feel it awakening within you, this longing, rising like a flame. Something vital is missing, and you ache for it in every part of your being. It's the hunger in your heart and the fiery urgency in your loins. It runs like a flood through your soul, this need. Feel it, Jean. Let yourself feel it. You ache for the most essential element of life—a mate, a lover, someone to complete you, to fulfill you in every way possible . . . someone to thrill you . . ."

Kerry's mind flicked back to the way he'd aroused her the night before. Pleasure rippled through her, awakening a sensation in the deep reaches of her own belly. Her thighs tightened with that strange humming sensation. Her voice grew breathless.

"Someone who can make your heart leap painfully and send the blood searching through your veins," she whispered. "A woman who can bring you to your knees with a sigh and bring you awake with a kiss. To love her is the sweetest kind of madness, and yet you have no choice. You need this woman, this siren of your soul, and you need her now."

Kerry stopped herself, wondering what she was doing. The way her heart was pounding, she could have been spinning out her own fantasies. Was she programming him to want what she wanted? She cautioned herself not to say anything else, but the suggestions just kept tumbling out of her mouth . . . about how inflamed he was with longing, and how nothing would satisfy him except to make her his own.

"You must possess her, Jean, possess her or die of the longing . . ."

The rocker groaned, or was it him?

Kerry searched his features, aware of their sudden sensuality. His lips were parted and the heat rushing through them was steamy. Even his skin looked a little flushed.

What she had already done was nothing compared to what she had to do next. *Had to.* How could she suggest that he was falling in love and that love could save him, and not follow through with the rest of it? And anyway, she had a backup plan. If the hypnosis worked, and she freed him, she could put him back under later and erase the suggestions.

She traced her fingers over his lips, another irresistible impulse, and felt them quiver. Lord, what that did to her. She was humming everywhere.

"When you wake up, Jean," she said, "you will see the woman you've always loved, the woman you were born to be with . . . and the only one who can save you."

The hand that had touched him was shaking. This was the moment when she had to bring him back, but she was frightened.

Her heart ran riot as she bent to kiss him.

She brushed her lips over his, and a sound she couldn't control slipped out.

His lids flickered and came open. Maybe it was the lashes, but Kerry didn't have a chance. She was instantly immersed in the dark pools that gazed up at her. He was supposed to be the one in a trance.

"Kerry?" He said her name as if he'd just discovered how softly it could be mouthed.

She didn't dare answer. Her voice would give her away.

"You're beautiful," he said, visually searching out every aspect. "I know I've said that before, but this is different, this I can't define."

"It's all right." She tried to stop him, but he caught a handful of her hair and drew her down for another kiss. His mouth touched hers with a force that was magically soft, yet frenzied. It was breathtaking. She was as dizzy as a child on a merry-go-round, and before she knew it, he'd pulled her right into the chair with him.

"Wait, Jean."

"Wait for what? My God, Kerry," he whispered, "can you feel what's happening? Can you feel what you do to me?"

She could feel plenty. She'd landed on top of him, and her chenille robe had come open. He was generously endowed in more places than just his mouth . . . and getting more generous all the time.

"Jean, I don't think—"

"That's right, Kerry, *don't think.* Don't think, just feel. Feel what's happening to me, feel what's happening to you."

She was vibrating. That's what was happening to her. It was no longer a pleasant humming sensation in the pit of her stomach. It was a powerful current, and she could feel it all the way to her fingertips. She was sprawled on top of him and half naked under the chenille robe, which had fallen open and was no protection at all. Neither were the skimpy tank top and French-cut panties.

What had she done? Created a monster, that's what she'd done.

He gazed at her through beautifully drugged lids, and his hands closed around her waist to position her atop him. The way he moved her, willfully nestling her soft curves against his hard ones, sent a sharp thrill through her nether parts.

"Jean, do you think maybe we could talk first? Just for a minute?"

"No, Kerry, I must have you. It's not an option."

His features were dangerously dark. "I need to possess you in every way a man can possess a woman. Every way and everywhere."

"*Every*where?" Her thoughts went spinning to the hardness she'd landed on. His entire body was rock-solid, but the bulge between his legs could only be described as formidable. If what was happening there was any indication, then she was probably too small to be possessed *any*where, much less everywhere.

"Here," he said, caressing her mouth with his fingertips. He tickled her pensive expression into a sensitive smile. "These beautiful lips must be conquered and made soft and slack."

Next he traced a vibrant line down the length of her body to her hip bone, where he curved his thumb deeply into the hollow of her pelvis. "And *here.* This must be made wet and wanting."

There was no question what part he was referring to now. He meant the tender throb between her legs, but he didn't stop there. Kerry was stunned as he smiled and reached around to trace the delicate cleft.

No, not there! She would have tumbled off him if he hadn't caught her and held her firmly with his hands. His dark river of a voice nearly drowned her.

"Yes, Kerry, there and everywhere. This drive is too powerful to fight. Can't you feel it? Tell me that your tender body isn't aching to be penetrated in all the places I touched you. Tell me you don't ache."

She did. God, she did.

She closed her eyes and felt herself swaying with the chair. He brought her back with those persuasive, possessive hands. *What was happening?* If this was the perfect fantasy he promised, then was he the perpetually erect male slave or the plundering highwayman? *Maybe a little of both.*

The rocking chair crooned softly with each movement.

"Come to me," he said.

She'd given him no choice when she hypnotized him. Now it felt as if *she* had none. Her needs were too raw. This ache was too great.

He clasped her by the thighs and guided her to a kneeling position. As her knees came forward and her body came up, she found herself straddling him at the juncture of his thighs. Now she was even more intimately pressed against the molten steel in his pants. Her legs were spread wide, her sex parts shyly kissing his.

The gentle sway of the chair created a steady, glorious friction. It hit her all at once that he was going to make love to her that way, rocking her deeply into orgasm after orgasm. She would straddle him, fully penetrated by his hardness, and rock until she dropped.

Even more shocking, she wanted it that way. She wanted it as urgently as he did. But when she tried to take off her robe, he wouldn't let her, and it became clear that he had something else in mind.

"Wrap your legs around my waist," he told her.

He lifted her into his lap, and once she was settled there, he rose from the chair and took her with him, robe and all. His hands were cupping her bottom, and Kerry thought she would die, it was so erotic. The steam heat of his palms, the placement of his fingers near her most intimate parts. If he moved a hair's breadth, he would be molesting her.

Her thighs clenched tightly against him as she wondered where this reckless act of possession would take place. On the coffee table? Against the wall?

Where would he take her?

But he turned, and she found herself back in the rocking chair, arranged in the most exotic way imaginable. Her robe was hanging open, her arm was flung above her head and long, pale legs were draped over the arms of the chair. The fact that she was wearing panties made little difference now. She was completely exposed to his view, to his whim. He set the chair rocking, then sank to his knees and savored her from that angle, as if he were imagining every forbidden delight known to man.

Her poor mind was riveted on a single thought. *Just look what she'd done with her hypnotic suggestions . . . just look!*

As the chair rocked up, he blew a kiss to the soft pink crotch of her panties. A strange little sound caught in her throat. She tightened with anticipation. He let the chair swing freely for a moment, then caught it and held her there, held her in thrall as he bent over her and aroused her through her panties with feathery touches of his lips and tongue.

If she had a secret garden, then this was a dragonfly, touching down. She could barely feel him and it was the most erotic sensation imaginable. If he stopped, she would die. If he didn't, she would die.

"It's too light," she whispered, "too light, I can't bear it."

But she couldn't be heard over the moaning of the chair, and apparently Jean wasn't inclined to stop anyway. Certainly not in the way that she meant. He actually caught the crotch of her panties between his teeth and pulled the material out, letting air rush into the heat between her legs.

Kerry arched in surprise. Her legs were suspended in the air for a second, and it felt as if the dragonfly were inside her now, gossamer wings beating.

"I don't know what will happen if you don't stop . . ."

"I do."

The chair groaned as he released it, letting it rock gently back and forth.

Kerry groaned, too, as his tongue slid up and down the most sensitive part of her anatomy. The way it languidly swirled, she could have been an ice-cream cone or a cloud of cotton candy. What an exquisite thrill that was, like the point of a baton lightly riding the sole of the foot. His mouth was an instrument of sweet torture. Deep muscles fluttered tightly, and she could feel dampness seeping through her panties.

"Can't bear—" was all she got out. The rest of it died in her throat as he gathered her up in his arms. He kissed her lips lightly, and when she made a sound of distress, he kissed her deeply. Kissed her to her very soul.

"Now I want you on *your* knees," he told her under his breath.

She assumed they would exchange places, and that he would be the cotton candy, but if she was learning anything in this adventure with him, it was not to assume. There was a lovely old Aubusson carpet on the living room floor by the window, and they ended up there, with Jean lying on his back and Kerry on her knees at his head. Her panties and robe were gone now, draped over the rocker, but she was still wearing her tank top, and her breasts were hotly excited. It was sheer nervous anticipation. He hadn't even touched her there, and yet her nipples were flushed and taut. Every shiver rustled the silky tank top against her skin. Every shiver set her more on edge.

He spread her open above him with his fingers, and then he inched her legs wider and wider, bringing her down to his mouth. The tension was fierce and wonderful. Her thighs shook as he tongued her softly and with the eloquence of a maestro. She raised her arms above her and cried out softly, barely aware of how she must look, like a penitent, begging for mercy.

The first orgasm that shook her brought her to her hands and knees. By the second, she couldn't control the tremors anymore. She crumpled to her elbows and then fell onto her side, next to him. He gathered her close with his arm, and she drifted off, into some kind of ecstasy, floating . . . floating. Some time later she felt him easing from beneath her. She drifted again, and when she awoke next, she was aware that he had rolled her onto her stomach, and that he was above her, possibly even astride her, whispering into her hair.

"Stay just as you are," he said, "I'm going to take you this way."

Somewhere inside Kerry was a barely discernible bleat of alarm. It was a frantic little sound that brought Jean close, whispering and touching her soothingly. Apparently he thought he'd frightened her. And he had. But she was also stirred to the depths of her being.

Kerry wondered if she was still breathing.

He moved over her, and his weight awakened something primitive within her, a mating response. His hands were in the hair at her nape, lifting, sifting. It was glorious. She felt his hardness pressing into her thigh and she responded helplessly, lifting her hips in enticement. It was an involuntary response. She wanted him in the most ancient, urgent way a female can want a male. She wanted him there, now, deeply and fast.

She heard the soft whine of a zipper being opened, and her whole body contracted. The familiar feel of denim against her bare legs told her that he hadn't removed his clothes—and that he wasn't going to. This was more than an act of possession, it was ravishment, and he was neither a highwayman nor a slave. He was a phantom lover who would steal his way into her heart, as well as her body. He would hold her in thrall until he'd stolen everything . . . even her naked, quaking soul. Especially that.

"Stay just as you are," he whispered again. "Utterly still."

She tried, but it was nearly impossible not to quiver as he brushed his lips over her uptilted derriere. A hand slipped through the seam of her thighs and lightly caressed her where she was hot and tingling. Wetness gushed at his touch, and nothing more was needed. She was wild to be entered.

"Rock back as if you were still in the chair," he told her.

He guided her with his hands, and she did exactly as he said. She swung her hips and tasted ecstasy. Tasted him.

He took her there, now, deeply . . . and slow.

It was the sweetest pressure in life, a sensation of being possessed and released all at once. Kerry surrendered herself with barely a whimper, shuddering helplessly at the lush thrill of penetration. He thrust into her reaches as smoothly as a hand into a snug velvet glove, and she tightened immediately. Tightened and quivered at the same time. *Possessed and released at the same time.* From the moment he entered her, she was floating in a sea of sensation, a shimmering world of light and sound.

It was delirious. She made pleading noises, unable to help herself. He was weight and darkness and the source of all pleasure. He was everything at that moment. She would be nothing without him. He couldn't leave her. This couldn't end. Even as the floodtide hit her and she knew that she was in the last throes, that this pleasure could not go on forever, she also knew that she had changed. Her body had changed, simply from this one act of possession. Her mind, her spirit, everything had been changed in some way, and she could never go back.

"Our journey isn't over, Kerry."

It will never be, she thought. And when he turned her on her back, she reached for him. They rushed to reconnect in the most intimate way possible, clinging mouths and yearning limbs, all pining for unity and oneness, and she told herself then that he would never leave her. If he felt anything like she did, he never could.

***

The first time she woke up, she realized they were still on the floor, and he was holding her. "We can't stay this way," he said. "Let me take you to bed."

"No, not the bed, the rocker."

"You want to be in the chair?"

"Yes, with you. We can cover ourselves with blankets and rock until we fall asleep. Please."

He gathered her up and gently settled her in the soft leather cradle, then got a comforter from the bedroom and joined her. When they were all bundled up and she was blissfully pressed next to him, her leg draped over his thighs, she wondered if this was what it was supposed to be like between men and women. She'd never had anything like this. She felt whole for the first time in her life.

He'd said he was missing something. It had to be this.

She couldn't ask the question that meant everything—Are you free, Jean? Did it work? But fortunately, there was another one.

Her mouth was so dry it was hard to speak. "You said there were things that men could only learn from women. What things, Jean?"

He shivered as she lightly raked her fingers through his chest hair.

"How to touch like this?" she asked. "How to be tender?"

He rested his chin against her forehead, and she could hear him breathing. She could almost hear him thinking.

"It's not about giving as much as it is about receiving," he said. "Women teach men how to *receive* tenderness—and other things, like love."

His mouth must be dry too. His voice was grainy and thrilling.

"You taught me something important tonight, Kerry."

"I did?" She looked up at him, aware that she couldn't

swallow. It was virtually impossible to swallow. Could you die from that? she wondered.

"It's not about success or personal power or even courage," he said. "Those things keep a man enslaved. It's about love. That's what sets his soul free."

It's about love.

Now she didn't need to ask the other question. It must have worked. He must be free of the curse, and she had been a part of it. She'd given him the key to unlock the cage. Now, for the first time in her life, she could sleep through the night in a man's sheltering embrace, dream in his arms, and believe that he would be there.

The journey was over. Her life had only begun.

Seven

Several moments passed before Kerry knew where she was. The gentle rocking motion conjured thoughts of a boat, anchored in a harbor . . . and then she opened her eyes. Her living room was cast in a bluish haze, but it was light coming from the window, not a TV or computer screen.

Dawn, she realized. The sun was coming up, not going down.

And she was alone.

She pushed off the comforter, wondering if Jean had gone to the kitchen for something to eat. The unsteadiness she felt as her feet hit the floor brought a vivid reminder of the surreal experiences of the night before. She was still shaking; it was that intense. She could hardly believe it had happened. Certainly nothing like that had ever happened to her before.

Her pink robe was in a heap on the floor, but she didn't bother with it. She was too anxious about where he was. Too anxious even to call his name. *Please don't let him be gone again,* she thought. *Don't do that to me. It would be too cruel, like tormenting an animal at the zoo.*

Her kitchen was hazed with blue, too, and a pinprick of fear touched her when she realized he wasn't there, either. The breakfast nook looked out on her snow-covered backyard, as well as the garage apartment, where Malcolm lived. There was no sign of her tenant or anyone else, although she wouldn't have expected to see

Malcolm. He worked at an assembly plant during the day, and whether he was at home or not, his blinds were always tightly closed.

Kerry's mouth had gone dry with excitement the night before. Now it was coppery, bitter. She already knew what she was going to find when she went to the bedroom, but she had to go anyway. A desperate feeling came over her as she scurried through the living room, knowing it was hopeless. *He was gone.*

The entire house looked alien to her. The place that had given her comfort and refuge now gave her nothing but torment because he wasn't there.

"Oh, God," she whispered, "this can't be happening. It is *too* cruel."

Her bedroom was the proof she dreaded. It was exactly as she'd left it, the sheets thrown back the way they were when she'd crept out of bed to investigate the noise. Her bathroom looked untouched, too. There was no trace of him anywhere. Other than her robe on the floor, she couldn't find evidence that he'd ever been there.

Under her breath, she said, "No one has dreams like that."

She stared at the Aubusson carpet with a growing sense of horror. Was she delusional now? She couldn't tell this story to anyone. It would have sounded like the ramblings of a madwoman. But Jean was as real to her as her own heartbeat. Either she hadn't freed him with her ridiculous plan, or she had, and he had better things to do than hang around with a housebound crazy.

She turned in the room, searching for answers that were becoming more incredible than the questions. Maybe his curse required that he pass more than one test, and this was only the first. Now that he'd conquered the maiden, he had to go out and fight a dragon or something. And maybe Kerry Houston really *was* in need of antipsychotic medication.

"Our journey isn't over, Kerry."

She spun around, thinking it was Jean behind her. Someone had spoken, hadn't they? But there was no one there. The sensation that ran up her spine was like an icy breath of air. She clutched her arms and held herself, fighting the pain that flared every time she tried to breathe. What was it he couldn't feel? He had shuddered in her arms and told her that love could free him. What deeper emotion was there than that? She didn't believe the feeling he spoke of existed. It couldn't.

Her body quailed with another chill.

"Damn, drafty old house." She was freezing, but that wasn't causing her to quake from head to toe. It was despair. Despair and a burning sadness. She had to sell this place. She couldn't live here any longer. The neighborhood had gone to pot and taken her along with it. Even her grandparents wouldn't want her to be here now, not like this. How she would get through the ordeal of packing up and moving out when she couldn't even get through her door was beyond her. But if she didn't do something, they would soon be coming for her with a net.

Gooseflesh needled her bare arms and legs.

That was when she realized she was standing in her living room half naked He'd left her in nothing but a tank top, and she was *still* in nothing but a tank top. The awareness nearly made her ill. It was symbolic of her downfall, of the whole mess. It shouted at her that she wasn't just an emotional wreck, she was guilty of frighteningly bad judgment and worse. She'd given in to dangerous urges with a man she didn't even know, possibly at the risk of her life, certainly at the risk of her sanity. Who knew what he might have done to her? Or who he might have been? On a sliding scale of moral character, you couldn't slide much lower than that.

Real or not, he's gone, Kerry, and you're a fool for believing . . . in anything. She rushed back into the bedroom, vowing to put on her three layers of clothing and never take them off. That was when the tears started.

Kerry was sorting through her kitchen cabinets and tossing out old pots and pans when she heard the commotion out front. It sounded like shouting. Probably another fight breaking out, she decided, and went right on sorting. Did she take her grandmother's old cast-iron skillet or not? It was heavier than lead weights, but the sentimental value was great. She put the skillet in the pile to be packed, wondering when she'd become one of those people who turned a deaf ear to the chaos on the streets.

The shouting got louder, and something about the voices caught her attention. One of them was familiar.

Empty packing boxes tumbled over as she dodged through them and headed for the living room's bay window. Outside, the neighborhood thugs had circled an elderly man like a pack of dogs and they were harassing him. Kerry rushed to call 911, even though she was afraid it wouldn't do any good. By the time the police got there, the victim would be mugged and beaten or possibly dead. It had happened to her, and no one had come to her aid.

She hit the TALK button, but couldn't get a dial tone. Either the lines were out or her batteries were dead again. The phone had never worked right, and there was no time to investigate the problem. The harassing had turned into a full-fledged attack and the old man had been overpowered.

"Malcolm?" Kerry saw him fall to the ground and realized who he was. It was her tenant being bludgeoned. "Malcolm!"

She ran back to the kitchen and grandma's skillet. The baseball bat would probably do more damage, but there was no time. There were four or five of them. If she could back a couple of them off, Malcolm might be able to get to his feet.

She shrieked "Fire!" as she ran out the door, and kept shrieking it. When the thugs turned to look, Malcolm struggled to get up, and Kerry began to swing for all she was worth. She didn't hit anyone, but she cut a swath through them, and she was coming back around when she heard Malcolm shouting at his attackers.

"Back off!" he bellowed.

Kerry turned just as he pulled a deadly looking revolver from his coat.

Two of the thugs lunged at the exact moment that the gun's hammer clicked. It was an explosive sound, and they did back off. Immediately. Within moments the entire pack had begun to retreat.

Kerry waited until they were out of earshot before she turned to her tenant. "Malcolm? You have a gun?"

"It's a cap pistol," he said, "but keep it to yourself."

Kerry's grin died on her lips when she saw the real reason the thugs were leaving the scene. It wasn't because of Malcolm's cap pistol. A second gang was approaching, and these were the hoodlums who'd assaulted her. Fear slammed into her like a fist as she remembered the way they'd terrorized her. She even recognized the ringleader, a vicious punk called Axe.

Axe confronted Malcolm with an insolent smirk. "You could hurt yourself with a gun that big, bozo."

"Or I could hurt you," Malcolm declared quietly.

Kerry was surprised at her tenant's soft menace.

Axe's laughter incited the gang to catcalls, but Malcolm seemed unfazed. He was outnumbered and out-armed, but if he was frightened, he didn't let on. This wasn't the Malcolm who assailed her daily with dire news of the world outside her door.

Suddenly the thug nearest Kerry pulled a knife.

"Drop the gun or she's dead!" he shouted.

He dragged Kerry into a choke hold that nearly cut off

her breathing. She could feel the knife blade at her stomach, and she went deathly still. She had the skillet, but apparently her assailant didn't consider it—or her—a threat. She was a convenient means to his end, whatever that might be.

A siren began to wail, and the thugs looked around for a police car. That was all the advantage Malcolm needed. He grabbed the skillet from Kerry's hand and waylaid two of them before they knew what hit them. The arm clamped to Kerry's neck released, and she was free. Her attacker ducked as the skillet whistled passed his shaved skull.

Malcolm was a demon possessed. Within moments he had cleared out every gang member but Axe. The ringleader reached into his boot for a knife, and Malcolm clipped him with an uppercut. On the way down, Axe grabbed Malcolm's ankle and they both dropped.

Kerry picked up the skillet, but they were rolling and thrashing to get the knife, and she couldn't tell where to strike. Fists flew and they grappled like wrestlers. She winced as Malcolm's head hit the pavement, but finally it was Axe who slumped to the ground, out cold.

"You're hurt!" Kerry knelt next to Malcolm's sprawled form. He seemed to be conscious, but blood gushed from a deep cut above his brow.

"A scalp wound," he got out. "It's superficial."

Kerry hoped it was as she tugged on the sleeve of her sweater and used it to blot his face. She wanted to tell him how incredible he was, and how grateful she was for what he'd done. He'd saved her life. But she knew it would embarrass him. He was such an unpredictable man. She would never have expected this of him, not an act of outright heroism.

She was still cleaning him up when Axe began to regain consciousness. Instantly another siren went off. It whooped and wailed so loudly that Axe labored to his feet and fled.

Malcolm pulled a tiny battery-operated case from his coat pocket. He pressed a button and the siren stopped.

"You were the police car?" The noise vaguely reminded Kerry of the sirens that had gone off when she was wearing the finger glove.

A light snow had started to fall and Kerry had no coat. Malcolm heaved himself up and struggled out of his. He draped it over her shoulders. Again, Kerry was surprised and touched. There was something fundamentally different about her neighbor, but she couldn't figure out what it was.

"Are you okay?" she asked.

"Kerry, there's something I have to tell you."

"What's wrong?"

"Wait—" He was trying to pull off his knit cap, but his hands were shaking. Kerry wanted to help him, but he wouldn't let her. He seemed bound and determined to handle it himself, and when he had the cap off, he began to yank at his beard.

He ripped off the bushy patch right in front of her eyes. His moustache went next.

They weren't real, she realized. The beard and moustache were fakes.

Kerry stared at him, totally stunned. Without the props, Malcolm looked a little like—No, that was impossible.

"Jean?" she whispered. "Is that you? What are you doing dressed up like Malcolm?"

"Kerry, listen to me," he said. "Before you say anything or do anything, give me a chance to explain. Promise you'll do that much."

Kerry didn't know whether to nod or shake her head. It took him a minute to get to his feet, but that wasn't nearly enough time to collect her thoughts.

"My name is Joe Gamble," he said.

"What?" She staggered backward and lost her balance. A slippery patch sent her feet out from under her and she landed on the bottom step of her stoop, which, fortunately, was cushioned by a thin layer of snow. Now she *couldn't* say or do anything, but it had nothing to do with the fall she'd taken.

The man she was staring at wasn't Malcolm, her tenant. He wasn't Jean Valjean, her fantasy. He wasn't even Starman. He was the CEO of Genesis Software, and her former boss. He was the straw who'd broken Kerry Houston's back!

"Jean, Joe—whatever your name is—how could you do this? How could you take advantage of another human being like this?"

Kerry was up and pacing. She turned in the street and faced him. The snow was still falling, and her breath was a lacy white mist. But she wasn't cold. For the first time in ages, she wasn't cold.

"You deceived me," she told him. "You've done nothing *but* deceive me."

Joe Gamble was holding a handful of snow to the cut on his forehead. He looked like someone had been using him for a punching bag, which they had. Still, he was roguishly handsome in a brainy sort of way. A thinking woman's roughneck, she decided. She could see a faint resemblance to the bearded adventurer she'd met at the picnic, but she wouldn't have been able to pick him out in a lineup.

"I wanted to help," he said.

"You wanted to help? Who? *Me?* Dear God, what if you'd been trying to harm me?"

He winced, but Kerry couldn't tell if it was his head or his conscience that hurt him.

"I messed up," he said. "I admit it, I messed up badly. But don't I get a little credit for trying?"

"What was it you were trying to do? Traumatize me for life?"

He looked up carefully, one eye squeezed shut. "I was trying to set you free, Kerry. Not unlike the way you, well—deceived me, trying to set me free."

There were several things she wanted to contradict in that statement. She went for the last and most obvious.

"I didn't deceive you," she declared. "No way."

His slitty, one-eyed stare said otherwise.

"You're saying I did? When?" She was shaking her head when it hit her. "You mean when I hypnotized you and suggested that you were in love with me? You mean like that?"

"I mean like that. You said that loving you was the *only* way to save me, and among other things, you whispered in my ear that my loins were aflame and my heart was hungry. 'Possess her or die of the longing.' Remember that one, Kerry? You had a field day with my poor, unsuspecting, unconscious mind."

"Yes, but I was only . . . trying to help."

"My point exactly. So was I."

He took the snow away and she could see his eyes—beautiful eyes, Jean's eyes, fire stirring in them like embers in dark ashes. The fluttering sensation was back, only it was her stomach this time, and it felt more like little white moths than dragonflies. There were millions of them. Moths in a frenzy. Moths in search of a naked porch light. Silly, silly moths.

"As it turns out, you were right," he said. "There *was* no other way to save me."

The moths went nuts at that one. It seemed they'd found their naked bulb. Him. Could she possibly have heard him right? Was he saying that he loved her? Love, the L word? No, she couldn't have heard him right. She was always hearing voices and this was another one—confusing her, tormenting her, saying everything she'd ever wanted to hear.

Kerry refused to let herself react in any obvious way.

She'd exposed far too much to this man who'd said he was cursed. How could he have done that?

"How could you do that?" she whispered.

He started to answer, but she shook her head. He didn't even sound like Jean anymore. He sounded like Phil, the Human Resources guy from Genesis, and that was because he *was* Phil. And Malcolm. And George, the video game's creator. And probably Starman. He'd admitted taking on all those personas to try and get through to her. He was desperate to "break through The Great Wall of Kerry" was how he'd put it. He'd even admitted to altering his voice via some high-tech device so that she wouldn't recognize him as the different men.

But why? Why would anybody want to get to Kerry Houston that badly?

The thought that this might be some kind of prank, and that she could be fodder for the office gossips again, was devastating. Too devastating to bear.

"I won't be the butt of another one of your jokes," she blurted, turning away from him.

"Kerry, this isn't a joke. Whatever made you think that?"

"That humiliating e-mail I sent you before I left Genesis. You didn't even have the courage to come and tell me yourself what you thought of me. You sent your assistant to do your dirty work."

"I never got the e-mail," he said. "Apparently my assistant intercepted it and took it upon herself to deal with you. 'For the good of the company' was the way she put it. When I found out what she'd done, I fired her on the spot."

"You fired her?" Kerry's voice was faint. "And you didn't tell me?"

"How could I tell you when you wouldn't talk to me? The first time I called, you hung up on me. The second time you said if I wanted to sue you I should call your attorney, and then you hung up on me. After that, you wouldn't take my calls at all, so I became Phil."

"Phil, with the simmering pot of a voice," she murmured.

"Excuse me?"

"Nothing."

"You made it clear that you didn't want anything to do with me or Genesis, except as a game tester. Maybe I should have let it go at that, but I couldn't. I'd seen you on the videotapes, and I was smitten."

"Smitten by what? My beauty, my wit or my social graces?" Okay, so she didn't *quite* believe him.

The closer he got, the more Kerry backed up.

"Listen," he said heatedly, "you were dynamite in those sessions, and I wanted you back. I thought it was for the company, but after Jean came to life the first time, I knew it was for me."

Pain stabbed her. Jean. He was Jean, and she had cared about him.

"Congratulations, man of many voices," she said. "You really suckered me good. You actually had me convinced that Jean was cursed and needed me to set him free. How stupid, huh?"

"It wasn't Jean who needed you, it was me. I'd lost my passion for anything but work, and believe me, that's its own kind of curse."

"You were never cursed," she protested hotly. "Your life is blessed. You have everything."

"When there's no feeling attached to what you have, it's meaningless. Everything is *nothing*.

"What I did was wrong," he admitted. "I concocted this whole elaborate fairy tale to get close to you, and obviously I got carried away with the poetry of my plan. I've been known to do that."

The breath he took sounded like a sigh, a weary one. "The truth is, I was worried about you. This neighborhood isn't safe, and you were all by yourself in the house.

I wanted to be around in case you got into trouble, so I invented Malcolm. That's when I realized what was really going on, that you were trapped."

Recognition dawned. "So you pretended to be trapped yourself, as Jean?"

He nodded. "I thought if it became your goal to free Jean, you might be able to get past your own fears. But I didn't realize what it was going to take until Malcolm spoke up in your living room that day. He surprised me as much as he did you."

Kerry remembered it word for word. "'You'll let go of your fear when something is more important to you than your fear.'"

"That's when I knew something was going to happen to Malcolm, something bad. It had to be more important to you than your fear, and I figured if you thought Malcolm was in trouble, you'd stop at nothing."

She stared at him, confused. "But he *was* in trouble."

"Well . . . no, not at first. Those were some kids I bribed to make it look like they were roughing me up. What I didn't count on was the second gang. They were the real thing, and when I saw that punk grab you and pull a knife. . . . God—"

The words balled up in his throat. Muscles locked powerfully, struggling with some unexpected emotion, some savage emotion. "The thought that I'd endangered you when all I wanted to do was protect you—"

Kerry didn't know what to say, but she couldn't let him go on.

He looked away and roughly cleared his throat. "Last night I told you that you'd taught me something important, but I didn't really know what that meant until now. I had to almost lose someone I loved to understand."

"Joe, don't—"

"I felt it to my soul, Kerry. When I thought I'd lost you I . . ."

He didn't finish, but Kerry knew what he was going to

say. And she knew what he was feeling for the first time. There was an emotion welling inside her, too, a new emotion. It was piercingly sweet.

A snowflake landed on her lashes and melted away like a tear.

"I told you I was cursed," he said. "I don't expect you to forgive me for invading your life like this." He looked up, apparently resigned to his fate, whatever that might be. "I'm not asking that, but whatever happens, it's almost worth it to see you this way. Outside like this."

"Oh, my God," Kerry whispered, realizing where she was for the first time. "I'm outside."

Her heart began to race, and she reached out involuntarily. His hand caught hers, and she squeezed it hard enough to cut off his circulation. Any minute now she would fall to her knees because she couldn't walk. She could almost see herself crawling to the stoop. She would never make it back into the house. *What was she doing out here?*

"Let me help you," he said.

He tried to lead her to the steps, but she held him off. She had to do this herself, and she wasn't running back inside. She had fought off thugs in the street without giving it a thought, and she would fight her way out of this.

"Breathe."

He said the very word that she was thinking, and his voice was as hushed as the falling snow. It cut through her rising panic and spoke to the urgency inside her. Instead of struggling with the sensations, Kerry stopped and drew in a breath, and even that first draught of air had a calming effect. The second restored her thought processes, the third her voice.

He was good. Maybe he was even good for her. The way she figured it she was probably going to have to take a chance on that.

"Did you mean it about me being dynamite in those sessions?" she asked him accusingly.

He nodded. "I meant it, Kerry. You are a force of nature."

"And did you mean it about not wanting to live like a normal man if you couldn't have me?"

"I did."

She still wasn't at all sure she ought to forgive him. He had gone to elaborate lengths to deceive her, and yet when she tried to imagine life without Joe Gamble, it made her want to shudder . . . to her soul.

Make your wish with an open heart, because only open hearts can receive.

Kerry's lips curved into a smile as bittersweet as Joe's. *Grandpa,* she thought, *if you had anything to do with this, it worked.*

She reached for Joe, and he pulled her into his arms. They kissed under a veil of new snow, and the last thing Kerry saw before she closed her eyes was the couple in Lover's Park. She had always wondered how it would feel to be that much in love, and now she would have her chance to find out. This was the beginning of a new journey, and Kerry Houston, perhaps the most unlikely of winter lovers, would not be making it alone.

The Marring Kind

Debbie Macomber

One

Could it actually be Katie Kern? Katie, here in a San Francisco bar of all places? It didn't seem possible. Not after all these years.

Her hips swayed with understated grace and elegance as the sleek, sophisticated woman casually walked toward Jason Ingram's table. They'd been high school sweethearts in Spokane, Washington, ten years earlier. More than a lifetime ago.

Sweet, gentle Katie. That was what Jason had assumed until that fateful night so long ago. He'd say one thing for her, she'd certainly had him fooled. Then, without warning, without so much as a clue as to who and what she really was, Katie had brutally ripped his heart out and then trampled all over it.

He caught a whiff of her perfume and closed his eyes, trying to identify the scent. Jasmine. Warm and sensual. Seductive. Captivating, like the woman herself. Like Katie.

But it couldn't be Katie. It just wasn't possible. Jason sincerely hoped life wouldn't play such a cruel joke on him. Not now when he was three days away from marrying Elaine Hopkins. Not when it had taken him the better half of these last ten years to forget Katie. It would take much longer to forgive her.

Her back was to him now as she walked past him, making it impossible to identify her for certain.

Jason downed another swallow of beer. His fiancee's two

older brothers sat with him, joking, teasing, doing their best to entertain him and welcome him to the family.

"Don't feel obligated to attend this potluck Mom's throwing tonight," Rich Hopkins said, breaking into Jason's thoughts.

It demanded every ounce of strength Jason possessed to stop staring at the woman. He wasn't the only one interested. Every man in the St. Regis cocktail lounge was staring at her, including Rich and Bob. She was stunning, beautiful without knowing it, the same way Katie had once been. She always had been able to take his breath away. But this wasn't Katie. It couldn't be. Not now. Please, not now.

"I'd get out of the dinner if I could," Bob added, reaching for his beer. He was Elaine's youngest brother and closest to her in age.

Jason watched as the woman approached a table on the other side of the room. The old geezer who occupied it promptly stood and kissed her cheek. Jason frowned.

"It's entirely up to you," Rich added. "You'll meet everyone later at the wedding anyway."

Wedding. The word cut through his mind like a laser light, slicing into his conscience. He was marrying Elaine, he reminded himself. He loved Elaine. Enough to ask her to spend the rest of his life with him.

Funny, he'd never told his fiancee about Katie. In retrospect he wondered why. Certainly Elaine had a right to know he'd been married once before. Even if it was the briefest marriage on record. By his best estimate, he'd been a married man all of one hour. If it wasn't so tragic he might have been amused. The wedding ceremony had lasted longer than his marriage.

"You must be exhausted."

Jason's attention returned to the two men who'd soon be his brothers-in-law. "The flight wasn't bad."

"How long does it take to fly in from the East Coast these days?"

"Five, six hours." Jason answered absently. He tried not to be obvious about his interest in the woman sitting with the old fart. It wasn't until she sat down that Jason got a decent look at her.

Dear, sweet heaven, it was Katie.

His heart pounded so hard it felt as if he were in danger of cracking his ribs.

In a matter of seconds, ten long years were wiped away and he was a callow youth all over again. The love he felt for her bubbled up inside him like a Yellowstone geyser. Just as quickly, he was consumed with an anger that threatened to consume him.

There had been a time when he'd loved Katie Kern more than life itself. He'd sacrificed everything for her. He assumed, incorrectly, that she loved him, too. Time had proved otherwise. The minute she faced opposition from her family, she'd turned her back and walked away without a qualm, leaving him to deal with the heartache of not knowing what had happened to her. To them.

"I believe I'll skip out on the dinner plans," Jason said, tightening his hand around the frosty beer mug. He deliberately pulled his gaze away from Katie and concentrated on Elaine's brothers.

"I can't say that I blame you."

"Make an early night of it," Bob suggested, finishing off the last of his beer. "It's already ten o'clock, your time."

"Right." The last thing Jason felt was fatigued. True, he'd spent almost the entire day en route, but he traveled routinely, and time changes generally didn't bother him.

Rich glanced at his watch and stood. "Bob and I'll connect with you sometime tomorrow, then."

"That sounds great," Jason answered. "My brother's set to arrive early afternoon." He could barely wait to tell

Steve that he'd seen Katie. His brother was sure to appreciate the irony of the situation. Three days before Jason was to marry, he ran into Katie. God certainly had a sense of humor.

Rich slapped him across the back affectionately. "We'll see you tomorrow, then."

"You've got less than thirty-six hours to celebrate being a bachelor. Don't waste any time." Bob chuckled and glanced toward Katie suggestively. He stood and reached for his wallet.

Jason stopped him. "The beer's on me."

Both brothers thanked him. "I'll see you at the rehearsal."

"Tomorrow," he echoed, grateful when the two left.

If the woman was indeed Katie, and the possibility looked strong, he had to figure out what he intended to do about it. Nothing, he suspected.

Their marriage, if one could call it that, had been a long time ago. He wasn't sure she'd even want to see him again. For that matter, he wasn't sure he wanted to see Katie, either. She was a reminder of a painful time that he'd prefer to forget.

The cocktail waitress delivered Katie and her date's order. While still in high school, Katie had refused to drink alcoholic beverages. Her aversion apparently hadn't followed her into adulthood.

"Can I get you anything else?" the cocktail waitress asked as she approached his table.

"Nothing, thanks."

She handed him the tab and he signed his name and room number, leaving her a generous tip.

He toyed briefly with the idea of casually walking over and renewing his acquaintance with Katie. That would be the civilized thing to do. But Jason doubted that he could have pulled it off. He was angry, damn it, and he had every right to be. She'd been his wife and she'd deserted him, abandoned him and all their dreams.

Her family had openly disapproved of him when they'd first started dating at the end of their junior year. He'd never completely understood why. He suspected it wasn't him personally that they objected to, but any involvement Katie might have with someone of the opposite sex. Someone not handpicked by them.

The man she was currently with was exactly the type her parents preferred. Older, rich as sin, and pompous as hell. Quite possibly they were married. It wouldn't surprise him in the least.

Ten years ago Jason hadn't been nearly good enough for the Kerns' only child. Her family had had no qualms about voicing their disapproval and so Katie and Jason had been forced to meet on the sly. Dear, sweet heaven, how he'd loved her.

As their senior year progressed, it became increasingly apparent that her parents intended to send her away to school. Then Katie had learned she was headed for a private girls' college on the East Coast and they knew they had to do something.

The thought of being apart was more than either one could bear. They'd been determined to find a solution and eventually had. Marriage.

The night they graduated from high school, instead of attending the senior party the way everyone expected, Jason and Katie eloped across the Idaho border.

It had been romantic and fun. They'd been giddy on love, and each other, certain they'd outsmarted their families and friends.

During the wedding ceremony, when Katie read the vows they'd written themselves, her eyes had filled with tears as she'd gazed up at him with heartfelt devotion. He never would have guessed that her love would be so untrustworthy.

Jason's stomach clenched as he recalled their wedding night. He nearly snickered aloud. There'd been no such animal. If they hadn't taken time for a wedding dinner, they might have had a real honeymoon. Jason had no one to blame but himself for that. He'd been the one who insisted on treating Katie to a fancy dinner. She'd been cheated out of the big wedding she deserved and he wanted to make everything as perfect for her as possible.

He'd been nervous about making love and he knew Katie was, too. She'd been a virgin and his experience had been limited to one brief encounter with his best friend's older cousin when he was sixteen.

After he'd paid for the hotel room, they'd sat on the edge of the bed, holding each other, kissing the way they always did. In all the years since, he hadn't met a woman who gave sweeter kisses than Katie. Not even Elaine.

Just when their love for each other overtook their nervousness, the door had burst open and they were confronted by Katie's irate parents and the local police. The horrible scene that followed was forever burned in his memory.

Katie's mother wept hysterically while her father shouted accusations at them both. The police officer had slammed Jason against the wall and he'd been accused of everything from kidnapping to rape. The next thing he knew, Katie was gone, and he was alone.

He'd never seen her again. Never heard from her, either.

Correction. She'd signed the annulment papers in short order. No letter. No phone call. Nothing. Not even a good-bye.

Until tonight. Thirty-odd hours before he was scheduled to marry another woman. Then, lo and behold, who should he see but Katie Kern. If it was still Kern, which he doubted. Her parents had probably married her off to Daddy Warbucks a long time ago.

In the beginning he'd waited and hoped, certain she'd find a way of contacting him. He'd believed in her. Believed in their love. Believed until there was nothing left. Eventually he'd been forced to accept the truth.

She'd sold him and their love out. She wanted nothing more to do with him.

Briefly he wondered if she remembered him at all. He'd wager she'd obediently followed her father's blueprint for her life.

That was the way it was meant to be.

Jason stood and strolled out of the lounge as if he hadn't a care in the world. He didn't so much as glance over his shoulder. It gave him only minor satisfaction to turn his back on Katie and walk away from her. He'd go up to his room, take a long, hot shower, and watch a little television before turning out the lights. The next couple of days were sure to be busy. He didn't need the memory of another woman clouding his mind before he married Elaine.

He got as far as the lobby. If he could have named what stopped him, he would have cursed it aloud.

Katie, after all these years. In San Francisco.

He looked back just in time to see her leaving the lounge. Alone.

What the hell, he decided. He'd say hello, just for old times' sake. Ask about her life, perhaps bury some of his bitterness. Even wish her well. It would do them both a world of good to clear the air.

He waited by the pay phones.

Although the lighting was dim, it didn't take him but a moment to realize he'd been right. It really was Katie. More beautiful than he remembered, mature and sophisticated, suave in ways that had been foreign to them both ten years earlier. The business suit looked as if it had been designed with her in mind. The pin-striped skirt reached midcalf and hugged her hips. The lines of the fitted jacket highlighted everything that was feminine about her. Her reddish-brown hair was shorter these days, straight and thick with the ends curving under naturally, brushing against the top of her shoulder.

Jason pretended to be using the phone. He waited

until she'd strolled past him before he replaced the receiver. He spoke her name in a manner that suggested he'd recognized her just that moment.

"Katie? Katie Kern?" he said, sounding a bit breathless, surprised.

She turned and her eyes met his. Her lips parted softly and her eyes rounded as if she couldn't believe what she saw.

"Jase? Jase Ingram?"

Two

"Jase? Is it really you?" Katie raised her hand as if to touch his face, but stopped several inches short of his cheek. "How are you? What are you doing here in San Francisco?"

Jason buried his hands in his pants pockets and struck a nonchalant, relaxed pose, wanting her to assume he happened upon her just that moment and had spoken before censuring his actions.

"You look wonderful," she said, sounding oddly breathless.

"You, too." Which had to be the understatement of the century. He almost wished she'd gone to seed. She was more beautiful than ever.

"What are you doing here?" she asked again, not giving him time to answer one question before she asked another.

"I'm in town for a wedding. My own."

"Congratulations." She didn't so much as bat an eyelash.

His gaze fell on her left hand, which remained bare.

"I've never . . . I'm still single."

He wasn't sure congratulations would be in order. He was tempted to blurt out something spiteful about making sure she knew what she wanted the next time around, but restrained himself.

"It'd be fun to get together and talk about old times,"

he said. But before he could claim that, unfortunately, he simply didn't have the time, she nodded enthusiastically.

"Jase, let's do. It'd be great to sit down and talk." She reached out and wrapped her fingers around his forearm. Regret slipped into her eyes and she bit down into her lower lip and glanced toward the cocktail lounge. "I . . . I don't know that I can just now—I'm with someone."

"I saw," he murmured darkly. So much for playing it cool. She was sure to realize he'd spied her earlier now.

"You saw Roger?"

"Yeah." No use trying to hide it. "I was in the lounge earlier and thought that might have been you."

"How about dinner?" she suggested eagerly, her excitement bubbling over. He hadn't counted on her enthusiasm. "I haven't eaten and . . ."

"Some other time," he interrupted stiffly. He certainly didn't intend to join her and Daddy Warbucks for the night. He had never enjoyed being odd man out, and it wasn't a role he intended to play with Katie.

"But . . ."

"I just wanted to say hello and tell you you're looking good."

Her eager excitement died as she stiffened and moved one step back as though anticipating something painful. "There's so much I have to tell you, so much I want to know . . ."

Yeah, well, he had plenty of his own questions.

"Please, Jase. I'll make some excuse, tell Roger I've got a headache and meet you back here in an hour. I deserve that much, don't I?"

"All right." He may have sounded reluctant, but he wasn't. He had plenty he wanted to say to Katie himself, plenty of questions that demanded answers. Perhaps he should feel guilty—after all, he was marrying another woman in a couple of days—but God help him, he didn't. Maybe, just maybe, he could put this entire matter to rest once and for all.

"I'll meet you in the dining room," he said.

"I'll be there. Thanks, Jase," she murmured before turning and hurrying back to the cocktail lounge.

Jason headed up to his room and phoned for dinner reservations. It wasn't until he stood under the pulsating spray of the shower that his hands knotted into tight fists with a rare surge of anger. Katie had betrayed him, abandoned him, rejected his love. He'd waited ten long years to vent his frustration, and he wouldn't be denied the opportunity now. Once again he experienced a mild twinge of conscience, dining with another woman without Elaine knowing. His excuse, if he needed one, was that getting rid of all this excess emotional baggage was sure to make him a better husband.

At least that was what Jason told himself as he prepared to face the demons of his past.

Katie couldn't quell the fluttery feeling in the pit of her stomach. The last time she'd felt this anxious about seeing Jase had been the night they'd eloped. Her cheeks flushed with hot color at the memory of what happened, or, more appropriately, didn't happen. Her heart ached for them both, and for all the might-have-beens that never were.

With her heart pounding and her head held high, she walked into the hotel lobby, half expecting Jase to be waiting for her there. He wasn't, and so she headed directly for the restaurant.

Although he'd approached her, he hadn't seemed any too happy to see her. She understood his dilemma. By his own admission, he was hours away from marrying another woman. Katie should be pleased for him, glad he'd found a woman with whom to share his life. What an ironic twist of fate for them to run into each other now.

He was almost married and she was practically engaged. Roger had been after her to marry him for months and his pleas were just beginning to hit their mark. The last time he'd asked, she'd been tempted to give in. He was kind and gentle. Affectionate. But what she felt for Roger didn't compare with the hot urgency she'd experienced with Jase all those years ago. That had been hormones, she told herself. Good grief, she'd been little more than an eighteen-year-old kid.

Jase was already seated when she joined him. The hostess escorted her to his table. He'd changed clothes, and damn it all, looked terrific. Just seeing him again stirred awake a lot of emotions she'd thought were long dead, long buried. But then, she'd always loved Jase.

"So we meet again," he greeted with a telltale hint of sarcasm. One would think he'd already experienced second thoughts.

Perhaps it hadn't been such a good idea to meet after all, Katie mused, but damn it all, he owed her an explanation, and for that matter a hell of a lot more. She'd pined for weeks for Jase, waited, believed in him and their love. She'd literally been ripped from his arms and never heard from him again.

Katie made a pretense of reading over the menu, something Jase appeared to find fascinating. She made her selection quickly and set it aside.

"Tell me, what've you been doing these last ten years?" she asked, wanting to ease into the conversation. There'd been a time when they could discuss anything, share everything, but those days were long past. Jase was little more than a stranger now. A stranger she would always love.

Slowly, he raised his head until his gaze was level with hers. She'd forgotten how blue and intense his eyes could be. What surprised her was how unfriendly they seemed, almost angry. She'd always been able to read his moods, and he hers. At one time they were so close it felt as if they shared each other's thoughts. Just when it seemed he was about to speak, the waiter approached with a bottle of Chardonnay.

Katie rarely indulged in alcohol, but if there was ever a time she needed something to bolster her nerve, it was now. The first sip, on an empty stomach, seemed to go straight to her head.

"Let's see," he said after their server left, sounding almost friendly. Almost, but not completely. "After I signed the annulment papers you sent me, I joined the Marine Corps."

He mentioned the annulment documents as if they meant nothing to him, as if it were nothing but a legal formality, one they'd discussed and agreed upon before the wedding. Surely he realized what it had cost her to pen her name to those papers. How she'd agonized over it, how she'd wept and pleaded and tried so hard to find a way for them to be together. It would have been easier to cut out her heart than nullify her marriage. Her fingers closed around the crystal goblet as the memories stirred her mind to an age and innocence that had long since died.

"When my enlistment ended with the Marines, I went back to school and graduated. I work for one of the major shipping companies now."

"West Coast?"

"East. I'm only in San Francisco for the wedding."

She noticed that he didn't tell her anything about the woman he was about to marry, not even her name.

"What about you?" he asked.

"Let me see," she said, drawing in a deep breath. "I attended school, majored in business, graduated cum laude, and accepted a position with one of the financial institutions here in San Francisco." She downplayed her role with the bank, although she was said to be one of the rising young executives.

"Just the way Daddy wanted," he muttered.

Katie bristled. "If you recall, my parents wanted me to go into law."

"Law," Jase returned, "that's right, I'd forgotten."

That wasn't likely, but she let the comment slide. They'd both carried around their hurts for a long time.

The waiter came for their order and replenished their wine. Perhaps it was the Chardonnay that caused her to risk so much. Before she could stop herself, she blurted out, "Didn't you even try to find me?"

"Try?" he repeated loudly, attracting the attention of other diners. "I nearly went mad looking for you. Where the hell did they take you?"

"London . . . to live with my aunt."

"London. They don't have phones in England? Do you realize how long I waited to hear from you?"

Katie bowed her head, remembering how miserably unhappy she'd been. How she'd prayed night and day that he'd come for her. "She wouldn't let me," she whispered.

"And that stopped you?"

She swallowed against the tightness gathering in her throat, combating it with her anger. "You might have tried to find me."

"Of course I tried, but it was impossible. I was just a kid. How was I supposed to know where they'd sent you?"

"I told you about my father's sister before, don't you remember? We'd talked about her and how my parents wanted me to spend the summer with her before I went away to college. She's a law professor and . . ." She hesitated when the waiter returned with their salads.

Inhaling a calming breath, she reached for her fork. The lettuce was tasteless and she washed it down with another sip of wine. That, at least, calmed her nerves.

"Your aunt—sure, I remembered her, but I didn't have a name or an address. Someplace on the East Coast, I thought. A lot of good that did me." He tossed his hands into the air. "I don't possess magical powers,

Katie. Just exactly how was I supposed to figure out where you were?"

"You should have known."

His mouth thinned and he stabbed his fork into the lettuce. "Perhaps it'd be best if we left sleeping dogs lie."

"No," she cried emphatically.

He arched his brows at her raised voice. She wasn't the timid young woman she'd once been, shy and easily intimidated.

"I want to know what happened. Every detail. I deserve that much," she insisted.

The waiter, sensing trouble, removed their salad plates and brought out the main course. Katie doubted that she had the stomach for a single bite. She lifted her fork, but knew any pretense of eating would be impossible.

Jase ignored his steak. "I did everything I knew how to do to locate you. I pleaded with your father, asked him to give me the chance to prove myself. When I couldn't break him, I tried talking to your mother. The next thing I knew they slapped a restraining order on me. It wasn't easy for me, you know. Everyone in town knew we'd eloped, then all at once I was home and you were gone."

"I'd never been more miserable in my life," she whispered. He seemed to think being shipped off to a heartless, uncaring aunt was a picnic. "I loved you so much . . ."

"The hell you did. How long did it take you to sign the annulment papers? Two weeks? Three?"

"Five," she cried, nearly shouting.

"The hell it did," he returned, just as loud.

The entire restaurant stopped and stared. Jase glanced around, then slammed his napkin on top of his untouched dinner.

"We can't talk this out reasonably, at least not here," she muttered, ditching her own napkin.

"Fine, we'll finish this once and for all in my room."

Jase signed for their dinners and led the way across

the lobby to the elevator. They stood next to each other, tense and angry on the long ride up to the twentieth floor. She paused, wondering at the wisdom of this, as he unlocked the room. She relaxed once she realized he had a mini-suite. They wouldn't be discussing their almost-marriage with a bed in the middle of the room, reminding them they'd been cheated out of the wedding night.

"All right," she said, bracing her hands against her hips. "You want to know about the annulment papers."

"Which you signed in short order."

She gasped and clenched her fists. "I signed those papers while in the hospital, Jason Ingram. I ended up so sick I could barely think, in so much pain and mental agony I was half out of my mind."

The color washed out of his face. "What happened?"

"I . . . went on a hunger strike. My aunt constantly stuck those papers under my nose, demanding that I sign them, telling me how grateful everyone was that they found me before I'd ruined my life."

Jase turned and stood with his back to her, looking out over the picturesque San Francisco skyline.

"Day after day, I refused to sign them. I insisted my name was Katie Ingram. I wouldn't eat . . ."

"You could have phoned me."

"You make it sound so easy. I wasn't allowed any contact with the outside world. I was little more than a prisoner. What was I supposed to do? Tell me!"

Her question was met with stark silence.

"I tried, Jase, I honestly tried."

"You ended up in the hospital?"

The years rolled away and it felt as though she were a naive eighteen-year-old all over again. The tears welled in her throat, making it difficult to speak "In the beginning I thought the stomach pains were from hunger. I'd lost fifteen pounds the first two weeks and . . ."

"Fifteen pounds?" he whirled around, his eyes wide with horror.

"It was my appendix. It burst and . . . I nearly died."

"Dear God." He closed his eyes.

"My mother was there when I came out of surgery. She looked terrible, pale and shaken. She pleaded with me to sign the annulment papers and be done with all this nonsense. She claimed it was what you wanted . . . I was too weak to fight them any longer. You're right, I should have been stronger, should have held out longer, but I was alone and afraid and so terribly sick. I remember wishing that I could have died—it would have been easier than living without you."

Jase rubbed his hand along the back side of his neck. "I thought . . . assumed you wanted out of the marriage."

"No. I tried to hold out, really I did. More than anything I wanted to prove that our love wasn't going to fade, that what we felt for one another was meant to last a lifetime."

"Then I signed the papers," he whispered, "and joined the Marines."

"When I came back, you were gone."

The distance between them evaporated and he brought her into the warm circle of his arms. "I'm sorry, Katie, for doubting you."

"I'm sorry for failing you."

"We failed each other."

"I loved you so much," she whispered and her voice cracked with the depth of emotion.

"Not a day passed for five years that I didn't think about you."

His kiss was soft and sweet, reminiscent of those they'd once shared. An absolution, forgiveness for being young. For not trusting, for allowing doubts to separate them as effectively as her parents had once done. For giving in to their fears.

"If only I'd known," he whispered. His lips grazed her cheek, seeking her mouth a second time, and Katie tried not to think about this other woman Jase was about to marry. But when he kissed her again, any guilt she might have experienced died. She turned her head in an effort to meet his lips, expecting him to kiss her with the hunger she felt, the hunger he'd fired to life with the first kiss. Instead, his mouth simply slid over hers in moist forays, back and forth, teasing, coaxing, enticing.

Excitement began to build, fires licking awake the tenderness of what they'd once so freely shared.

After what seemed like an eternity, his mouth settled completely over hers and he kissed her in earnest. Jase groaned and wrapped his arms around her, lifting her from the floor, grabbing hold of the fabric of her suit, kissing her with a hunger that was so hot she felt the heat emanating from him like the warmth coming from a roaring fire.

"All these years, I believed . . ."

"So did I." She wept and laughed at the same moment.

"I loved you so damn much."

"I've always loved you . . . always."

He kissed her in a frenzy of hunger and breathless passion. When his tongue broached her lips, she was ready, her lips parted, welcoming the invasion, greeting him with her own.

He groaned again.

His hands unfastened her suit jacket, slipped it from her shoulders and let it fall to the floor.

She twined her arms around his neck, panting, breathless with wonder and shock. "Jase, oh, Jase, what are we doing?"

Three

"We're finishing what we started ten years ago." Jason repeated Katie's question without really hearing the words. He slanted his mouth over hers and devoured her lips with a hunger and need that had been buried deep inside him all these years. He sank his hands deep into her hair, loving the feel, the taste, the sense of her.

"Jase, oh, Jase."

She was the only person in the world who'd ever called him Jase, and the sound of it on her lips was more than he could stand. He took possession of her mouth before he could question the right or wrong of what was happening.

Her hands struggled with the buttons of his shirt while he fumbled with the openings to her blouse. They were a frenzy of arms, tangling, bumping against each other in their eagerness to undress. The raw, physical desire for her all but seared his skin. He sighed when he was finally able to peel the silky material from her shoulders and capture her breasts with both hands, fondling them while kissing her lips.

Their kisses became desperate as their hands caressed each other. Jason was never sure how they made it into the bedroom. He didn't stop to turn on the light or shove back the covers. He'd waited ten years for this moment and he wasn't about to be cheated a second time.

Their clothes were gone, disappeared, evaporated like the early morning fog over the bay. All that existed in that moment was their overwhelming love and need for one another.

He gently placed Katie on the mattress, then joined her, kneeling above her. She wrapped her bare, sleek legs around his thighs and raised her hips in unspoken invitation.

Through the haze of his passion, he saw her stretch her arms toward him, silently pleading with him to make love to her. In the dim light of the full moon, he watched as the tears rolled from the corners of her eyes and onto the bedspread. Her tears were an absolution for them both, for the hurts committed against them, for the long, lonely years that had separated them.

"Love me," she whispered.

"I do. God help me, I do."

His entire body throbbed with need as Jason eased forward, penetrating her body with one, swift, upward thrust. Katie buckled beneath him, sobbing with an intense pleasure as she buried her nails in his back. Her heels dug into his thighs as she rocked against him, meeting each pulsating stroke, riding him, pumping him.

He cried out hoarsely at the explosion of his climax, rearing his head back, blinded by the pure, unadulterated pleasure, breathless with the wonder and the shock.

He loved Katie. He'd never stopped. If anything the years had enhanced the emotion. He didn't speak as he gathered her in his arms. He was grateful when she didn't feel the need to discuss what they'd shared. If they stopped to analyze what had happened, they might find room for regrets and Jason experienced none of those now.

He eased next to Katie, keeping her wrapped protectively in his embrace. Her head was on his shoulder, her legs entwined with his. He stroked the silky smooth skin of her back, needing the feel of her to admit this was real. She was in his arms the way she should have been all those years ago. He dared not think beyond this moment, or look into the future for fear of what he'd see. Eventually he felt his mind drifting toward the mindless escape of sleep.

Katie woke when Jase stirred at her side. She rolled her head and read the illuminated dial of the alarm clock on the nightstand. It was three minutes after two.

"Are you cold?" he whispered, kissing her neck.

"A little." She assumed he meant for them to pull back the covers and started to climb off the bed.

His hand stopped her. "No."

"No?"

"I'll warm you."

He'd already done an excellent job of that, and seemed intent on doing so again, this time without the urgency or haste of the first.

"Jase," she whispered, unsure if they should continue. Her head, her judgment had been clouded earlier, but she was awake now, prepared to put aside whatever emotion had driven them earlier. "We should talk first . . . we need . . ."

"Later. We'll discuss everything later." He captured her nipple between his nimble lips and sucked gently.

Katie sighed and curled her fingers into his hair as the sensation sizzled through her. It didn't seem possible that he could evoke such an intensity of feeling from her so soon after the first lovemaking.

He loved her with a slow hand and an easy touch, whispering erotic promises as his lips explored the sensitive area behind her knees, then moved up the small of her back, eventually making his way to the nape of her neck. Shy and a little embarrassed, Katie couldn't keep from sighing. Again and again he coaxed a response from her, insisting she participate fully in their loveplay. She hesitated, reluctant, fearing recriminations in the morning on both their parts, but she held back nothing, including her head and her heart. She was his and had been from the time she was seventeen. His in the past, the present, always.

"I've dreamed of us like this," he whispered between deep, bone-melting kisses. "Some nights I'd wake and feel an emptiness in the pit of my stomach and realize I'd been dreaming about you."

Katie ran her fingers through his hair. "I can't believe you're here."

"Believe it, Katie, believe it with all your heart."

He entered her then and the sweetness, the rightness of their love was almost more than she could bear. Locking her arms around his neck, she clung to him on the most pleasurable ride of her life.

Eventually they did fall asleep, but it was from sheer exhaustion. Jase shoved back the sheets and they lay, a tangle of arms and legs unwilling to separate for even a moment. She'd never known happiness like this. She should have realized, should have expected it to be fragile. She just didn't know how breakable it truly was until the phone jarred her awake.

The piercing shrill sliced rudely through their lazy contentment.

Apparently jolted out of a deep sleep, Jase jerked upright and looked around as if a fire alarm had sounded.

"It's the phone," she murmured, only slightly more awake than he.

Blindly, he reached for the telephone, nearly throwing it off the nightstand. It rang a third time, the loudness causing Jase to wince.

Katie looked at the clock and groaned aloud. It was nearly nine and she was due to meet with the vice president of Grand National Bank, Roger, and two other bank executives at ten. She couldn't be late.

"Elaine." Jase shouted the other woman's name and glanced guiltily toward Katie. "Sweetheart. What time is it?"

Sweetheart? He spent the night making love with her and he had the gall to refer to Elaine as *Sweetheart?*

"It's nine, already? Meet your Aunt Betty and Uncle Jerome for lunch? Sure. Sure. Of course . . . all right, all right, I'll say it. I love you, too." He rubbed a hand down his face and ignored Katie.

Katie didn't know if she could listen to much more of this without getting sick to her stomach. Tossing aside the sheet, she climbed out of bed and headed for the bathroom.

Slapping cold water on her face, she stared at herself in the mirror and didn't like what she saw. Her reflection revealed a woman who'd been well loved. Well used. She wasn't the woman in Jase's life any longer. Elaine was. Jase was engaged to marry the other woman.

A sick sensation assaulted her. She'd always been a fool for Jase, and the years hadn't changed that. But she wasn't about to become embroiled in an affair with a married man, or a near-married man.

"Katie."

Feeling naked and shy, she looked around for something to cover herself and grabbed a towel. Securing it around her torso, she walked back into the bedroom with her chin tilted at a regal angle.

"Mornin'," he murmured, yawning loudly. He sat on the edge of the mattress, a sheet wrapped around his waist, studying her. The appreciative look in his eyes said he wouldn't be opposed to starting the morning over on a completely different note.

How dare he act as if nothing had happened. "That was your fiancee?"

His face sobered and he nodded. At least he had the good grace to lower his gaze. "I'm sorry about that . . ."

"Not to worry—it's well past time I left." Doing her best to conceal her nakedness, she reached for her blouse, jamming her arms into it without bothering to put on her bra.

"What are you doing?" he demanded, as if it wasn't evident.

"Dressing." She glanced at her wristwatch and groaned. "I have to be in a meeting by ten. If I hurry I can get home, change clothes, and make it into the office before then."

He looked stunned. "Don't you think we should talk first?"

"I don't have time." She found her skirt and stepped into it, hastily tugging it over her hips and sucking in her stomach to fasten the button.

"Like hell. Make time."

"I can't. Not this morning." Then, realizing he probably had a point and that they did need to talk, she sighed expressively and suggested, "Meet me this afternoon."

"I can't."

"Why not?"

"My brother and his wife are arriving. Later I've got the wedding rehearsal and a dinner."

An unexpected pain momentarily tightened her throat. "That says it all, doesn't it?"

"Don't do this to me, Katie. We made love. You can't just walk out of here. Not now, especially not now."

"You're marrying Elaine." She made it a statement, unsure of what she wanted. They were different people now, not teenagers. He had his own life, and she hers. By clouding their heads with the physical they'd stepped into a hornet's nest.

"Elaine," he repeated and plowed all ten fingers through his hair, holding his hands against the crown of his head as if that would help him sort matters through. "Hell, I don't know what to do."

"Let me make the decision easy for you. *Elaine. Sweetheart. Of course I love you.*"

His face tightened. "I'm in San Francisco for my wedding. I told you that."

"I know." She sounded like a jealous shrew, but she

couldn't help herself. Although it was painful to say the words, one of them needed to. It hurt, but it was necessary. "It's too late for us, Jase," she whispered, unable to disguise her misery. "Far too late."

"I suppose you're going to marry Roger," he accused, tossing aside the sheet and reaching for his pants. He jerked them on, stood, and yanked up the zipper. "He's perfect for you. Did your father handpick him?"

It was so close to the truth that Katie gasped. "Roger is generous and kind and caring and . . ."

"A pompous ass."

"I've never met Elaine but I know exactly the type of woman you'd marry," she cried. "She must be a simpering, mindless soul without a thought of her own."

Jase's eyes narrowed into thin slits.

"Let's just end this here and now," she shouted, throwing the words out at him like steel blades. Stuffing her bra, pantyhose, and shoes into her arms, she headed for the door.

"You're not walking out on me. Not again."

"Again?" she challenged. "That's the most ludicrous thing you've ever said to me." Turning her back on him, she took a great deal of pleasure in hurrying out of the suite and slamming the door.

"Katie! Don't you dare leave. Not like this."

As far as she could see, she didn't have a choice. Jase was marrying Elaine. He loved the other woman—she'd heard him say so only moments earlier. It was too late for them. Spending the night with him was quite possibly the worst mistake of her life. What a deplorable mess they'd created. She hadn't meant what she'd said about Elaine. She didn't even know the woman, but his fiancee certainly didn't deserve this. Katie was so furious with Jase and herself that she wanted to weep.

Despite the fact that her underwear was crunched up in her arms, she hurried down the hallway toward the elevator.

"Katie. For the love of heaven, stop."

Katie groaned aloud when she realized Jase had followed her. Barefooted, and with no shirt, he caught up with her at the same time the elevator arrived.

"Jase, please, just leave it."

The doors glided open and a middle-aged man wearing a pin-striped suit and carrying a garment bag stared openly at them. A blue-haired lady in a pillbox hat, who held a small dog under her arm, inhaled sharply.

Her dignity lay in a pool at her feet. Nevertheless, Katie stepped into the elevator and silently pleaded with Jase to let her go. He returned her glare and joined her.

"We've got to talk," he whispered heatedly, standing next to her as if nothing were amiss.

"It's too late for that."

"Like hell."

The two other occupants of the elevator moved as far away from them as possible. Fully aware of her state of undress, Katie wanted to crawl into the nearest hole and die.

"Jase, it's over."

"Not by a long shot. We'll discuss what happened now or later, the choice is yours."

"You're getting married later, remember?"

The elderly woman huffed disapprovingly.

Jase turned and glared at her. "Do you have a problem?"

The dog barked.

Never had it taken an elevator longer to descend to the ground floor. Katie was convinced she'd die of mortification before the doors opened to the opulent hotel lobby. The two other occupants left as if escaping a time bomb.

"We need to sort this out," Jase insisted in low tones.

She offered him a sad smile, and with as much dignity as she could muster, which at this point was shockingly little, she stepped out of the elevator.

"You're walking out on me again," Jase shouted, calling attention to them both. "That's what you've always done, isn't it, Katie?"

"Me?" She whirled around and confronted him, her voice tight and raised. "You're the one who abandoned me. You're the one who left me to deal with everything." Then, swallowing a sob, she turned and ran out of the hotel.

Four

Jason resisted the urge to slam his fist against the polished marble column when Katie literally ran out of the lobby. It was obvious nothing he said was going to convince her to stay and sort through their predicament.

Defeated and depressed, he walked back into the elevator and punched the button for the twentieth floor. Luckily he had his room key in his pants pocket or he'd be locked out of the suite, which at this point would have been poetic justice.

Once inside his room, he slumped onto the sofa and leaned forward, placing his elbows against his knees. It felt as if the weight of the world rested squarely on his shoulders. The last thing he expected Katie to do was run out on him. To prove how completely unreasonable she was, her parting shot was that *he* was abandoning *her.* That made no sense whatsoever. He didn't know how she could even think such a thing.

Fine, he decided, if that was the way she wanted it. Good riddance. He was better off without her. But he didn't feel that way. He felt the same empty sensation he had the night they'd eloped and her parents had literally ripped her out of his arms.

Although he comforted himself with reassurances, Jason didn't believe them. He'd loved Katie as an eighteen-year-old kid and God help them both, he loved her now. Nothing had changed. Except for one small, minute detail.

He was scheduled to marry Elaine on Saturday.

Elaine. Dear God, how would he ever explain how he'd spent the night with another woman? He didn't even want to think about it. Until now, Jason had always thought of himself as an honorable, decent man. He'd have to tell Elaine—there was no way around it.

Dread settled over him like a concrete weight. He expelled his breath in a long, slow exercise while he sorted through his options which, at the moment, seemed shockingly few.

He couldn't possibly marry Elaine now, not when he still loved Katie. Love! What the hell did he know of love anyway? Sixteen or so hours ago when he first arrived in San Francisco, he'd assumed he was in love with Elaine. He must love her, Jason reasoned, otherwise he'd never have asked her to be his wife. A man didn't make that kind of offer unless he was ready, willing, and able to commit the rest of his life to a woman.

Whether he loved or didn't love Elaine wasn't the most pressing point, however. He needed to decide what to do about the wedding. Really, there was only one choice. He couldn't go through with it now. But canceling it at the last minute like this was unthinkable. Humiliating Elaine in front of her family and friends would be unforgivable.

Elaine didn't deserve this. She was a wonderful woman, and he genuinely cared for her. The wedding had been no small expense, either. Her father had a good twenty grand wrapped up in the dinner and reception. Jason had invested another five thousand of his own savings.

He leaned against the sofa and tilted his head back to stare at the ceiling. It would be the height of stupidity to allow a few thousand dollars to direct the course of his life.

By all that was right he should put an end to the wedding plans now and face the music with Elaine and her family before it was too late, no matter how unpleasant the task. Again, the thought of confronting his fiancee and her family, plus the dozens of relatives who'd traveled from all across the country, boggled his mind.

Something was fundamentally wrong with him, Jason decided. He was actually considering going ahead and marrying Elaine because he felt guilty about embarrassing her and inconveniencing their families. First he needed a priest, then a psychiatrist, and that was only the tip of the iceberg.

No clear course of action presented itself and so Jason took the easy way out. As painful and difficult as it was, he'd confess to her what had happened with Katie and then together, Elaine and he could decide what they should do.

He showered, dressed, and still felt like he should be arrested. Actually, jail sounded preferable to facing his fiancee and her family. He'd deal with Elaine first and then find Katie. If his high school sweetheart, his teenage wife, thought she'd escaped him, she was wrong. As far as he was concerned it wasn't even close to being over between them.

With an hour to kill before meeting Elaine and her aunt and uncle, he drove the rental car around the streets of San Francisco, allowing his eyes to take in the beauty of the sights while his mind wrestled with the problems confronting him.

He arrived outside Elaine's family home at noon.

Elaine stood on the porch and smiled when he parked the car. She was petite, slender, attractive, and as unlike Katie as any woman he'd ever met. His heart ached at the thought of hurting her.

Jason remembered the day they'd met a year earlier. Elaine worked as a secretary in the office across the hall from him, efficient, hardworking, ambitious. She'd asked him out for their first date, a novelty as far as Jason was concerned, but then he appreciated a woman who knew what she wanted. It didn't take her long to convince him they were good together.

As time passed, he discovered that they shared the same goals. Her career was important to her and she'd advanced from being the secretary to the vice president to lower level management and was quickly making a name for herself. She'd surprised him when, two months before their June wedding, she'd decided to change jobs and had accepted a position with a rival shipping company. It seemed a lateral move to him, but her career was her business and Jason was content to let her make her own decisions.

"Did you sleep well?" she asked, wrapping her arms around his neck and bouncing her lips over his.

It was all Jason could do to keep from blurting everything out right then and there. He might have done exactly that if Elaine's mother hadn't stepped onto the porch just then. Helen Hopkins was an older version of Elaine, cultured and reserved.

"It looks like the weather is going to be lovely for the wedding," Helen announced, sounding pleased and excited. "It's always a risk this time of year, and I want everything to be perfect."

Guilt squeezed its ugly fingers tightly around his throat. Elaine was the only daughter and her parents had pulled out the stops when it came to her wedding. He wondered if it were possible for the Hopkins to get a refund at this late date, and was fairly confident that would be impossible. It was too late for just about anything but biting the bullet.

Elaine's Aunt Betty and Uncle Jerome were both in their early eighties and spry, energetic souls. They greeted Jason like family . . . which he was about to become, or would have if he hadn't run into Katie.

"I'm pleased to make your acquaintance," Jason said formally. He glanced toward Elaine, hoping to attract her attention. The sooner he explained matters to her, the better he'd feel. Or the worse, he wasn't sure yet. It might just be easier to leap off a bridge and be done with it.

"I thought we'd have lunch out on the patio," Helen said, gesturing toward the French doors off the formal dining room.

"What a lovely idea, Helen," Betty said, leading the way outside. Her husband shuffled along behind her. A soft breeze rustled in the trees as Jason followed along. He could hear birds chirping joyously in the distance, but instead of finding their chatter amusing or entertaining, he wanted to shout at them to shut up. As soon as the thought flashed through his mind, he realized his nerves were about shot. He had to talk to Elaine, and soon, for both their sakes.

"I need to talk to you," he whispered urgently in Elaine's ear. "Alone."

"Darling, whatever it is can wait, can't it? At least until after lunch."

"No." If she had any idea how difficult this was, she'd run screaming into the night. He was two steps away from doing so himself. The need to confess burned inside him.

"In a minute, all right?" She flew past him and into the kitchen, leaving Jason to exchange chitchat with her vivacious aunt and uncle until she returned with a pitcher of iced tea.

"What time did you say your brother was arriving?" Helen directed the question to Jason as she sat down at the round glass and wrought iron table. A large multicolored umbrella shaded the area, although the sky had turned gray and overcast. Jason's mood matched the gathering clouds. He felt as if he were standing under a huge cumulus, waiting for lightning to strike.

"Steve and Lisa should be here sometime around two," he answered when he realized everyone was waiting for his response.

"He had to be here to organize the bachelor party," Elaine explained.

"Naturally, Rich and Bob will help out. You met them last night, didn't you?" Helen passed the hard rolls to Jason and he nodded. He wasn't likely to forget Elaine's brothers. He'd been with Rich and Bob when he'd first seen Katie.

"They got him so drunk, Jason decided to make an early night of it, remember?" The salad bowl went from mother to daughter.

Jason was about to explain that the lone beer wasn't responsible for his 'early night,' then thought better of it.

"Don't pick on your fiance," Betty advised Elaine, winking at Jason.

"At least not before the ceremony," Jerome added, chuckling.

Helen spread the linen napkin across her lap. "You can't imagine what our morning's been like, Jason. Elaine and I were up at the crack of dawn, running from one end of town to another. It's been a madhouse around here."

"I can't believe you slept half the morning away. That's not like you." Elaine dug into her shrimp-filled Caesar salad with a hearty appetite.

"I . . . I had trouble falling asleep," he muttered, certain her entire family knew exactly what he'd been doing.

Elaine gifted him with a soft, trusting smile. Not once since they'd decided to marry had she expressed doubts or voiced second thoughts. If she was experiencing any such notion now, it didn't show.

"Just think," Betty said, glancing fondly at her niece. "At three o'clock this time tomorrow, you'll be a married woman."

Married. Jason broke out in a cold sweat.

Elaine reached across the table and squeezed his

hand. "I'm the luckiest woman in the world to be marrying Jason."

He actually thought he was going to be sick.

"Isn't love grand?" Betty murmured, and dabbed at the corner of her eye with her napkin.

By the sheer force of his will, Jason managed to make it through the rest of the meal without anyone noticing something was amiss, although he considered it nothing short of a miracle. He never had been much good at subterfuge.

He managed to answer Jerome's questions about the shipping business and make polite small talk with the women. Elaine glanced at him curiously a couple of times, but said nothing that led him to believe she'd guessed his true feelings.

"I want to steal Elaine away for a few minutes," he insisted when they'd finished with their salads. He stood and held his hand out to her.

"I keep telling him he'll have me for a lifetime after tomorrow, but he refuses to listen," Elaine joked.

Helen glanced at her watch and Jason knew what she was thinking. Steve and Lisa's flight was due to land in little more than an hour and he was a good forty minutes away from the airport.

"Ten minutes is all I'll need," he assured Elaine's mother.

"Take him out into the garden," Helen suggested indulgently.

Jason wanted to kiss his future mother-in-law. The more private the area the better. Elaine was known to have a hot temper at times and he was sure she'd explode. Not that he blamed her. Heaven almighty, what a mess he'd made of this.

The garden was little more than two rows of flowering rosebushes in the back side of the property. A huge weeping willow dominated the backyard. Elaine swung her arms like a carefree child as they strolled toward the cover of the sprawling limbs of the willow.

"I know you, Jason Ingram. You want me alone so you can have your way with me." Before he could stop her, she wound her arms around his neck and planted a wide, open-mouthed kiss across his lips.

"Elaine, please," he said, having trouble freeing himself from her embrace. She was making this impossible. The woman was like an octopus, wrapping her tentacles around him, refusing to let him go.

"Loosen up, sweetheart."

"There's something I need to tell you."

"Then for the love of heaven, say it," she replied impatiently. She leaned against the tree trunk and waited.

Jason's heart ached. He found it difficult to meet her gaze so he stared at the ground, praying for wisdom. "Before we go ahead with the wedding, there's something you should know about me."

"This sounds serious."

She hadn't a clue how serious.

This wasn't easy, and he suspected the best place to start was in the beginning. "You know that I was born and raised in Spokane."

"Of course."

"At the end of my junior year of high school . . ."

"Are you about to tell me you had a skirmish with the law and I'm marrying a convicted felon?"

"No," he snapped, thinking that might be preferable to what he actually was about to tell her. "Just listen, Elaine, please."

"Sorry." She placed her finger across her lips, promising silence.

"I started dating a girl named Katie, and we were deeply in love."

"You got that sweet young girl pregnant, didn't you? Jason Ingram, you're nothing but a little devil."

"Elaine," he snapped, growing impatient. "Katie and I never. We didn't . . . No."

"Sorry." She squared her shoulders and gave him her full attention.

"As I said, Katie and I were deeply in love." He could tell that Elaine was tempted to say something more, but he silenced her with a look. "For whatever reasons, her family didn't approve of me. Nor did they think we were old enough to be so serious." He glanced her way and found he had her full attention. "Her parents had plans for Katie and they didn't include a husband."

"I should hope not," Elaine said stiffly.

"But Katie and I vowed that we wouldn't let anything or anyone keep us apart." He experienced the same intensity of emotion now as he had all those years ago. "When we learned that her family intended to separate us, we did the only thing we could think of that would keep us together." He sucked in a deep breath and watched Elaine's eyes as he said the words. "We married."

"Married." She spit out the word as if it were a hair in her food. "That's a fine thing to tell me at this late date."

"I know . . . I know." Jason couldn't blame her for being angry.

"Jason Ingram, if you tell me that you've got a wife you never bothered to divorce, I swear I'll shoot you." Her eyes flashed fire, singeing him.

"We didn't need to bother with a divorce," he told her quietly, sadly. "The marriage was annulled."

"Oh, thank heaven," Elaine murmured, planting her hand over her heart, her relief evident.

This was where it got difficult. Really difficult. Now was the time to mention how, through no one's fault, he'd run into Katie right here in San Francisco. Now was the time to explain how, when they saw each other again for the first time in ten years, they realized how much they still loved each other. Now was the time to explain how one thing led to another and before either of them was fully aware of what they were doing they ended up in bed together.

Now was the time to shut up before he ruined his entire life.

"Is there a reason you never mentioned this other woman before?" Elaine asked, sounding suspiciously calm. "You asked me to marry you, Jason, and conveniently forgot to mention you'd been married before."

"It was a long time ago." Canceling the wedding was as painful as anything in his life, including his own father's death.

"You should have told me."

He agreed completely. "I know."

"Well," she said, doing that sighing thing once more, as if to suggest she'd been burdened but not overly. She could deal with this. "We all make mistakes. It's understandable . . . I appreciate you letting me know now, but I must tell you I'm hurt that you kept this from me, Jason. I'm about to become your wife, but then," she whispered, "we all have our secrets, don't we?"

It was now or never. Jason held his breath tight inside his chest. "I loved her. Really, truly loved her."

"Of course you did, but that was then and this is now." She frowned, but seemed willing to forgive him.

Now. He opened his mouth to tell her everything, but the words refused to come. His heart felt like it was about to burst straight through his chest.

"Elaine." Her mother called, and Elaine looked toward the house, seemingly eager to escape.

"I'm not finished," Jason said hurriedly, before she left and it was too late.

"I'll be right back." She kissed his cheek and hurried toward her mother's voice.

Jason clenched both fists and squeezed his eyes closed as he sought a greater source for the courage to continue. Swearing under his breath, he started pacing, testing the words on his tongue. Elaine had a right to know what had happened. It was his duty to tell her.

She returned breathless and agitated a couple of moments later. "Darling, it's a problem with the caterer. We specifically ordered pickled asparagus tips for the canapés, and now they're telling us the order came in without them."

"You're worried about asparagus spears?" Jason couldn't believe what he was hearing.

"It's important, darling. Mother's on the phone with them now. Is there anything else, because this is important. I really need to deal with this. Mother thinks we may have to run down and confront these people right here and now."

"Anything else?" Jason knew he was beginning to sound suspiciously like an echo. "No," he said hurriedly, hating himself for the coward that he was.

"Good." She smiled broadly and then raced back to the house.

Jason stayed outside several minutes, condemning himself. Thanks to the years he served as a Marine, his swearing vocabulary was extensive. He called himself every dirty name he could think of, then slumped down onto a bench.

"Jason," Helen shouted from the back door. "Don't forget your brother."

"Right." He made his way back to the house. "Where's Elaine?"

"She's dealing with the problem with the caterer. It's nothing for you to worry about." She escorted him to the door. "We'll see you at five, right?"

"Five."

"The rehearsal at the church."

"Oh, right, the rehearsal." Jason didn't know how he would get through that, but he hadn't given himself any option. As far as Elaine and her family were concerned, the wedding was still on.

Five

A headache pounded at Katie's temple like a giant sledgehammer. Keeping her mind on track during this all-important meeting was almost impossible. She wanted to blame the wine, but she knew her discomfort had very little to do with the small amount of alcohol she'd consumed. Jase Ingram was the one responsible for her pain, in more ways than one.

Katie lowered her head to read over the proposal on the table, but her thoughts were muddled and confused, refusing to focus on the matter at hand. Her mind and her heart were across town with Jase.

"Katherine?"

She heard her name twice before she realized she was being addressed.

"I'm sorry," she murmured, "what was the question?"

"We were thinking of tabling the proposal until next week," Roger supplied, frowning slightly.

Katie didn't blame him for being irritated. She'd been useless as a negotiator this morning. Her thoughts were a million miles away with the girl she'd once been. At eighteen life had seemed so uncomplicated. She loved Jase and he loved her and their being together was all that was important.

"Tabling the proposal sounds like an excellent idea. Forgive me if I've been inattentive," she said in her most businesslike voice, "but I seem to be troubled with a headache this morning."

"No problem, Katherine," Lloyd Johnson, the first vice president of Grand National, said kindly. "Your headache may well have given us a few more days' time, which is something we could all use just now."

Katie smiled her appreciation. "Thanks, Lloyd."

The men shifted papers back inside their briefcases. Soon the meeting room was empty save for Roger and Katie.

She knew she owed him an explanation, but she could barely find the courage to face him after her lie from the night before. She'd said she wasn't feeling well then and had him drive her home so she could sneak back to the hotel and rendezvous with Jase. It was an ugly, despicable thing to do to a man who genuinely cared for her.

"You're still not feeling well, are you?" Roger asked gently.

"I'm doing slightly better this morning." Another lie. She was worse, much worse.

"Tonight's our dinner engagement with the Andersons," he reminded Katie, eyeing her hopefully.

Katie groaned inwardly. She'd forgotten all about the dinner date which had been set weeks earlier. Had she arrived at her usual time this morning, she would have seen it on her appointment calendar. Instead she'd rushed into the office, barely in time to make the meeting.

The Andersons were longtime friends of Roger's. The couple was in town to celebrate their wedding anniversary and had invited Roger and Katie along for what promised to be a fun-filled evening on the town. They were going back to the Italian restaurant where they'd met fifteen years earlier. Fresh from graduate school, Roger had been with Larry that night as well.

Katie suspected Roger wanted to show her that he wasn't as much of a stuffed shirt as it seemed. With his friends he could let down his hair, as if that was what it took to convince her to marry him.

"You'll feel better later, won't you?" His eyes were almost boyish in his eagerness.

She couldn't refuse him, not after the callous way she'd dumped him the night before. The irony of the situation didn't escape her. She hadn't been eager to join him for drinks at the St. Regis. Roger knew she didn't indulge often, but he'd insisted they had reason to celebrate. They'd worked hard on this deal with Grand National Bank and would be meeting with the first vice president. It was a small coup and so Katie had given in.

She'd never thought of herself as a weak person. After her marriage was annulled she'd promised herself that she wouldn't allow anyone to control her life ever again. Yet here she was, trapped in a relationship with a man her father considered perfect for her. A man who constantly pestered her to marry him.

Marry.

By this time tomorrow Jase would be married. In her mind's eye she pictured him standing in a crowded church exchanging vows with a beautiful, sophisticated woman.

"You seem a million miles away." Roger waved his hand in front of her face, dragging her back into the present, which, unfortunately, was as painful as her dreams.

"I'm sorry."

"About tonight?"

She owed Roger this even if she did feel like staying at home, burying her face in a bowl of chocolate ice cream. But she couldn't do that to Roger, and it would do her no good to sit home and cry in her soup. Or in her case, ice cream. What was done was done. Jase would marry his "sweetheart" and they'd both get on with their lives.

With time and effort they'd put the one small slip in their integrity behind them. Pretend it didn't happen. That was the solution, she realized. Denial. For the first time since she raced out of the St. Regis, Katie felt comforted. Everything was going to work out. She'd forget about him and he'd forget about her.

They'd gotten along perfectly well without one another this long. The rest of their lives wouldn't matter.

Now if she could only make herself believe that.

Standing outside the jetway at San Francisco International, Jason waited for his older brother and his wife, Lisa, to step from the plane and into the terminal. If ever there was a time Jason needed his brother's counsel it was now.

The minute he spied Steve and Lisa, his heart lightened. He stepped forward, hugged his sister-in-law, and impulsively did the same with his brother, squeezing tightly.

"That's quite a welcome," Steve said, slapping him across the back. "You ready for the big day, little brother?"

"Nope."

Steve laughed, not understanding this was no laughing matter. Jason felt about as far from being ready as a man could.

"I need to talk to you as soon as you're settled in at the hotel." His eyes held his brother's, hoping to convey the extent of his distress.

"Sure."

Jason led the way toward the baggage claim area.

Lisa eyed him skeptically. "Is everything all right?"

He longed to blurt out the whole story right then and there, but he couldn't.

"Jason?" Steve pressed. "What's wrong?"

He exhaled sharply. "I'll fill you in later. Come up to my room as soon as you're settled, all right?"

Steve nodded. "Something tells me you've gotten yourself into another fine mess."

Jason couldn't wait to see his brother's expression when Steve learned this "fine mess" involved Katie Kern. Three years his elder, Steve had played a significant role in advising Jason when he'd lost Katie the first time. The two had talked long and hard in the days and weeks following his and Katie's elopement. Frankly, Jason didn't know what would have happened if it hadn't been for his brother.

It seemed to take an eternity for Steve and Lisa to get checked in at the hotel. Jason returned to his own suite, but he couldn't sit still. He paced and snacked on a jar of peanuts out of the goodie bar that cost more than anybody had a right to charge. And waited, impatiently, for his brother.

By the time Steve arrived, Jason had worn a pattern into the plush carpet.

"All right, tell me what's got you so worked up," Steve said and helped himself to a handful of peanuts.

"Where's Lisa?" Jason half-expected his sister-in-law to show. A woman's perspective on this might help.

"Shopping. It's only three hours until the rehearsal and she didn't know if she'd have time to hunt down those all-important souvenirs after the wedding. Mom's visiting Uncle Philip and he's driving her to the wedding tomorrow," he added unnecessarily.

Jason sat down across from his brother and rammed his hand though his hair. "I saw Katie Kern."

"Who? . . . Katie?" Jason recognized the instant his brother made the connection. Steve's face tightened. "When? Where?"

"Last night. Here. The crazy part was she was sitting in the cocktail lounge downstairs having a drink with some old fart."

Steve watched him closely. "Did you talk to her?"

"You might say that," he muttered, rubbing the back side of his neck. "The fact is we did a whole lot more than talk."

"How much more?" Steve asked cautiously.

"We . . . ah, spent the night together."

Steve vaulted to his feet. "Oh, God."

"My sentiments exactly," Jason muttered. "I couldn't help it, Steve. Damn it all, I love her. I always have."

"But you're marrying Elaine."

"Maybe not." This wasn't exactly news to Jason. He'd wrestled with his conscience all day. The guilt was eating giant holes straight through his middle. He regretted cheating on Elaine, but not loving Katie.

"All right," Steve said, sounding calm and rational, "let's reason this out."

"Good luck," Jason said under his breath. He'd been trying to do exactly that all day and was more confused than ever.

"Where's Katie now?"

"I don't know. She ran out of here first thing this morning." He didn't confuse the issue by explaining Elaine's untimely phone call and how it had set everything off between them. "Get this. Katie ran out of here, claiming I was doing the same thing I'd done before by abandoning her."

"You? She betrayed you."

"She didn't," Jason returned heatedly. "Her parents shipped her off to her aunt's place in England. She had no way of contacting me." He didn't mention the hunger strike or that she'd nearly died when her appendix ruptured.

"You believe her?"

He nodded. Perhaps because he so desperately wanted it to be the truth.

"You were little more than kids."

"I loved her then and God help me, I love her now."

Steve sat back down. "What about Elaine?"

If Jason knew the answer to that he wouldn't be in such a state of turmoil. "I decided this morning that the only fair thing to do was tell her . . ."

Steve stopped him by raising his hand. "That would be a big mistake."

"I slept with another woman, Steve. I can't just stuff that under the carpet."

His brother jerked his hands back and forth in a stopping motion. "You might think confession is good for the soul, but in this case I don't think so."

"I tried to tell her."

"What does she know about Katie?"

Steve assumed that he'd confessed his teenage marriage early on in their relationship, but he hadn't. "Only what I was able to relay this afternoon. I intended to tell her everything, but chickened out at the last minute."

"Thank God. The worst thing you could have done is tell her about what happened last night. Even the advice columnists think it's a bad idea. You read 'Dear Abby,' don't you?"

Jason stood and jammed his hands into his pants pockets. "Okay, so I don't say a word to Elaine about Katie. Don't mention a thing about last night. That doesn't change the way I feel."

"What do you mean?"

Jason took in a deep breath. "I . . . don't know that I want to go through with the wedding."

"What? You're joking. Tell me you're joking!" Steve was back on his feet. His brother had turned into a human pogo stick. He fastened his hand against his forehead and slowly shook his head.

"How can I marry Elaine now?"

Steve glared at him. For a minute, he seemed to be at a complete loss for words. "You're right, you're right," he said finally. "This is one of the most important decisions of your life and marriage isn't something to be taken lightly."

Jason felt part of the burden lifted from his shoulders. Steve understood. If no one else, his brother would stand at his side, support his decision, help him through this mess. Together they'd muddle through the same way they had as boys.

"But, Jason, have you considered the ramifications of canceling a wedding at the last minute like this?"

He'd thought of little else all day.

"Elaine's family has invested a lot of money in this." Why his brother felt it was necessary to remind him of that Jason didn't know. It was something he preferred not to consider at the moment.

"I know."

"Lisa mentioned that the wedding gown came from The Young Lovers. She said there wasn't a gown in the entire store under five grand."

Jason knew that, too.

"You're sure you want to cancel the wedding?"

"They're having pickled asparagus tips," Jason muttered, knowing it was a completely illogical statement.

"Pickled asparagus tips?" Steve repeated.

Jason shook his head to clear his thoughts. "Never mind." It seemed a damn shame to marry a woman he wasn't sure he loved because she planned to top the canapés with asparagus. He didn't even like asparagus. He'd never liked asparagus, and generally he enjoyed vegetables.

"I have to tell her, Steve," he murmured. "Even if it means ignoring Dear Abby's advice. Then Elaine and I can make an intelligent decision together." Surely his fiancee would realize that if he fell into bed with another woman only two days away from their wedding, something wasn't right. True, there were mitigating circumstances, but that didn't excuse or absolve him.

"I hate to see you let Katie do this to you a second time," Steve said, sitting back down and reaching for the peanuts. "There are people in this world who are just bad for us."

Jason had never thought of Katie in those terms but he didn't want to get into a verbal debate with his only brother.

"What's she like these days?" Steve inquired.

"The same." The outward trappings were more sophisticated, but it was the same wonderful, generous Katie.

"Daddy's puppet?"

Jason knew what Steve was doing and he didn't like it. "Leave her alone."

"Alone. I don't intend to contact her if that's what's worrying you. She ran out on you, remember? It isn't the first time, either, is it?"

"I said stop it," he shouted.

"All right, all right." Steve raised both hands. "I apologize—it's just that I don't want you to make the biggest mistake of your life."

"Trust me, Steve, I don't want to, either."

Six

The church was filled with people Jason didn't know. The priest directed traffic while the organist practiced the traditional wedding march. The musical score echoed through the sanctuary, bouncing off the ceiling and walls, swelling and filling the large church.

Everyone talked at once and soon Jason could barely hear himself think. Rich and Bob and their wives and children sat impatiently in the front pew. Bob's wife bounced a squirming toddler on her knee. A handful of kids raced up and down the aisles, refusing to listen to Elaine's mother, who chased after them.

Jason's stomach was so tight he didn't know how he'd make it through this rehearsal without being sick. He had to talk to Elaine, explain what happened with Katie, despite his brother's advice. He felt he owed her the truth.

Once he confessed the error of his ways, they could reason everything out like two mature adults and decide what they should do. The only clear answer, as far as he could see, was to cancel the wedding.

Steve elbowed him in the side. "Father Ecker says you're supposed to step toward the altar as soon as Elaine starts down the aisle with her father."

At the mention of his fiancee's name, Jason turned toward the back of the church, hoping to find her. He hadn't seen her since lunch. Quite possibly she was still involved with the asparagus tip disaster.

When he finally did see her, his heart sank with

dread. She stood just inside the vestibule with her bridesmaids gathered around her like a gaggle of geese. She wore a mock veil and carried a frilly bouquet made up of a hundred or more ribbons in a variety of colors and sizes. They came from her five wedding showers, if he remembered correctly. Oh, no. All those gifts would need to be returned.

"I have to talk to Elaine," he announced tightly.

"Now?" Steve asked incredulously.

"Yes." He wasn't putting this off any longer. He walked over to where Father Ecker stood. "I need a few minutes alone with Elaine." He didn't ask if the moment was convenient. He didn't care if he did hold up the entire rehearsal. This was by far more important.

Marching down the center aisle, he sought her out. "Elaine."

Giggling with her friends, she didn't notice him at first.

"Elaine." He tried again.

She glanced away from her maid of honor. "Jason, you're supposed to be in the front of the church," she teased.

"We need to talk," he announced starkly.

"Now?" Her eyes grew round and large.

"Right now."

Elaine cast a speculative glance toward her women friends before following him into the back of the church in the dim light of the vestibule. "What's going on? You haven't been yourself all day."

"I have something to tell you." The best way he could think to do this was to simply say it without offering her any excuses or explanations. He had no justifications to offer for sleeping with Katie.

"You need to talk to me again? Really, Jason, you're carrying this thing a bit far."

"What thing?" Maybe she knew more than she was telling.

"Nerves. Darling, everyone has them."

She didn't appear to be affected. "It's a lot more than nerves."

"You sound so serious." She laughed, making light of his distress.

"I *am* serious." He held her gaze for a long moment before he spoke again. "This afternoon I told you about Katie and me."

"Yes," she said, sounding bored. "We've already been through all that, Jason. Really, you don't have anything to worry about—I understand."

"I saw her last night."

"Katie? Here in San Francisco? I thought you said you met her in high school."

He nodded. "I did. I haven't seen her in ten years . . . the last time I did she was my wife."

Elaine's mouth thinned slightly. "But she isn't now, right?"

"No," he agreed readily enough. He paused because what he had to say next was so damned difficult.

She glared at him with agitation. "Jason, really, can't you see we're holding up the entire rehearsal? I'm beginning to lose patience with you and this woman from your past. So you saw your high school sweetheart after ten years. Big deal."

"That isn't all." His voice sank so low he wondered if she heard him.

Elaine crossed her arms and tapped her foot. "You mean to tell me there's more?"

He nodded, and swallowed hard. Lots more. "Katie and I had dinner together."

She laughed nervously. "So you had dinner with an old girlfriend. You should know by now that I'm not the jealous type. Frankly, Jason, you're making much more of this than necessary. I trust you, darling."

She might as well have kicked him in the balls. It was what he deserved.

"Katie came up to my room afterwards." It demanded

every ounce of fortitude he possessed to face her, but he owed her that much.

"You don't need to tell me anything more," Elaine insisted tightly. "I already said I trust you."

She glared at him as if to will him to keep from telling her what she'd already guessed.

"Your trust isn't as well placed as you think." He ran a hand down his face and found he was shaking with nerves and regret.

"Jason," she insisted in a voice wrapped in steel. "Would you kindly listen to me? This isn't necessary."

"It is," he insisted. This was by far the most difficult thing he'd had to do in his entire life. "Elaine," he said, holding her with his eyes. "I wouldn't hurt you for anything in the world."

"Fine, then let's get back to the rehearsal. Everyone's waiting."

He didn't know why she was making this nearly impossible. "I need to tell you what happened between Katie and me."

"Must you really? Jason, please, this has gone far enough."

"Katie spent the . . ."

"Jason, stop," she snapped. "I don't want to hear it."

". . . Night with me."

It felt as if all the oxygen had been sucked from the room. The silence between them throbbed like a living, breathing animal. Jason waited for her to respond. To shout, to scream, to slap him. Something. Anything.

"I can't tell you how sorry I am," he murmured, his voice so hoarse with regret that he barely recognized it.

"Well," Elaine murmured tightly, "do you feel better now that you've bared your soul?"

"Yes . . ."

Her face tightened with a mild look of displeasure. "Do you have any other confessions you care to make?"

"Ah . . . no."

Her shoulders swelled and sank with a sigh. "Well, that's one thing to be grateful for." She started back toward the sanctuary.

"Elaine, where are you going?"

She tossed him a look over her shoulder that suggested he should know the answer to that. "The rehearsal, where else?"

"But doesn't this change things? I mean . . ." He hesitated and lowered his voice. "I made love to another woman."

"Okay, so you had a momentary lapse. Your timing was incredibly bad, but other than that I'm willing to look past this indiscretion. Just don't let it happen again."

Look past this indiscretion. She made it sound as if his night with Katie meant nothing, as if he'd used the wrong fork at a formal dinner. A minor faux pas.

She turned back to face him. "You aren't thinking of doing something really stupid, are you?"

"I thought . . . I assumed . . ."

"You thought I'd want to cancel the wedding?" She made the very idea sound ludicrous.

"Yes." That was exactly what he'd assumed would happen. He wouldn't blame her if she did decide she wanted out of the marriage. Forgiving him was one thing, but the ramifications of what he'd done went far beyond the obvious. He'd betrayed her faith in him, destroyed her ability to trust him ever again. Surely she understood that. His sleeping with Katie should have told them both something important. He wasn't ready for marriage.

"We're not calling off this wedding just because you couldn't keep your zipper closed."

"But . . ."

"Don't think I'm pleased about this, because I'm not. I'm furious and I have every right to be."

"I know . . ."

"What you did was despicable."

"I couldn't agree with you more."

"And it won't happen again."

"I still think we should . . ."

"Then I don't see what the big deal is," she said, cutting him off. "I'm willing to overlook this one incident. I have to say I'm disappointed; I never thought I'd have this sort of problem with you."

He gave her credit—she handled the news far better than if the tables had been turned. "Then you want to go ahead with the wedding?"

"Of course." She laughed, the sound grating and unnatural. "Of course, we'll still be married. After all the trouble and expense? You're joking, aren't you? I wouldn't dream of calling it off."

"Elaine . . ."

"But I want it understood that I won't tolerate this kind of behavior again."

"I wouldn't think . . ."

"Good. Now let's get back to the others before someone thinks there's something wrong." Without another word, she marched back into the sanctuary.

Rarely had Katie spent a more miserable evening. She enjoyed Wanda and Larry. Liked them. Envied them. Their love for each other was evident, even after fifteen years of togetherness, three children, a mortgage, and all the rest. Being with the couple, listening to them laugh with one another, made it all the more difficult to return to her own home, alone.

That was the crux of it, Katie realized. She was alone when she so desperately wanted the deeply committed relationship the Andersons shared. She longed for a husband, a family. It shouldn't be so much to ask. Nor should it be so difficult. Every man she'd met in the last ten years had fallen short of what she wanted in a husband. After seeing Jase again she understood why. She'd never stopped loving him. He was her heart. Her soul.

Mentally saying his name was like peeling back a fresh

scab. The pain rippled down her spine. Within a matter of hours he would be forever lost to her.

"You're still not feeling well, are you?" Roger whispered. He'd been attentive all evening, and she knew why. When it came time to drop her off, he was going to bring out a dazzling diamond ring and ask her to marry him.

As tempting as the offer was, she couldn't. Roger was her friend. He'd never hurt her, never desert her or leave her emotionally bankrupt the way Jase had. Roger was kind and generous. But to marry him would be cheating this wonderful man out of the kind of wife he deserved.

Katie didn't love him. She was fond of him, cared about him, but she didn't love him. Not the way a wife should love her husband.

"I'm feeling much better," she assured him.

"More champagne?" He replenished her glass without waiting for her answer. He seemed to think a couple of drinks would fix whatever troubled her.

"You know that we met in this very restaurant, don't you?" Larry's gaze slid away from his wife's long enough to glance in Katie's direction.

"That's what Roger said."

Larry waved a breadstick in Roger's direction. "He was here, too."

"So I heard. In fact," Katie said, smiling, "he accepts full credit for getting the two of you together."

"No way." Larry chuckled.

"As I recall," Roger muttered, setting aside the goblet, "I had first dibs on Wanda."

"You make me sound like a piece of meat." Wanda pretended to be outraged, but she didn't fool anyone.

"You were such a cute little thing," Larry teased, and added pointedly, "then."

The other woman glared at her husband and then

laughed. "You try keeping your hourglass figure after three children, fellow."

Larry stood and undulated his hips a couple of times. "I managed just fine, thank you."

Katie couldn't keep from laughing. Roger's gaze captured hers and he reached for her hand, squeezing it gently. He was a handsome man, not the old fart Jase claimed. At forty-three Roger's hair was just beginning to show streaks of silver, giving him a distinguished air. While he did tend to maintain a businesslike attitude, she wouldn't call him pompous.

"Here's to another fifteen equally happy years," Roger said, toasting his friends.

"Here, here," Larry agreed.

Their dinners arrived and soon after they'd eaten, Roger made their excuses, surprising Katie.

After hugs and congratulations, Roger and Katie left the restaurant. She'd worked all day to keep the memories of Jase and the woman who would soon be his bride at bay. Her efforts had worked fairly well until that evening with Larry and Wanda.

For ten long years, Jase had been lost to her. Then life had played a cruel joke and sent him back for one all-too-brief interlude just so she'd know what she'd missed. One night of memories was all she would have to hold onto through the years.

"Thank you for a wonderful evening," she said, as she looped her arm in Roger's. He led the way outside and paid the valet who delivered his BMW.

"I was hoping you'd invite me up for coffee," he said, as they neared her condominium.

"Not tonight."

Although she knew he was disappointed, he didn't let it show. He pulled into the crescent-shaped driveway outside her building and kissed her on the forehead. A touching, sweet gesture of affection. "Sleep well, my love."

"Thanks for everything," she whispered and slid out

of the car. She waved when he pulled away and then greeted the friendly doorman as she entered the lobby.

By the time Katie stepped into the elevator, unexpected tears had filled her eyes. Silly, unexplainable tears. She wasn't sure who she wept for. Jase. Roger. Or herself.

Wiping the moisture from her cheek, she decided she was a mature woman, long past the days of crying over might-have-beens.

She'd fallen in love with Jase far too early in her life, and found him again far too late. Her parents had taught her years ago that life was rarely fair.

She let herself inside her condo and walked over to the large picture window that revealed the bright lights of the city. Her gaze wandered to the thirtieth-floor tower of the St. Regis Hotel.

Hugging one arm around her stomach, she pressed her fingertips to her lips. Fresh tears filled her eyes as she stood and looked at the bright, glittering lights of the city. Once more her gaze returned to the St. Regis and Jase. Closing her eyes, she smiled and blew him a kiss, sending him her love.

Seven

"You're going to go through with the wedding then?" Steve asked Jason in the hallway outside his suite. It was well past midnight and he was scheduled to pick up his tuxedo first thing in the morning.

Elaine's brothers seemed disappointed that he'd cut his bachelor party short, but he wasn't in the mood to celebrate. He'd let the others have their fun, but hadn't participated much himself.

"That's what Elaine wants," Jason said, and slipped the plastic key into the hotel door.

"I can't believe you told her. You're a braver man than I am."

"I didn't have any choice."

"Sure you did. There are some things in life that are best left unsaid."

After the shock of Elaine's reaction, he was almost willing to agree. Frankly, he was sick of the entire matter. "I'll see you in the morning."

"You want me to pick you up?"

"Sure." He didn't show much enthusiasm for a man who was about to be married.

"'Night," Steve said, hesitated, then added, "Jason, don't do anything stupid, okay?"

"Like what?" He resented the question.

"Contact Katie."

"No way," he said emphatically. "She was the one who ran out on me, remember?" As far as he was concerned, she'd done that one too many times. She had some gall, racing across the hotel lobby accusing him of abandoning her. No, he was finished with Katie Kern. He'd learned his lesson. Besides, she'd let him know the entire episode was a mistake and that she wanted him out of her life.

Elaine was right. They'd both put this unfortunate episode behind them and build a meaningful marriage the way they'd planned all these months. Katie had her life and he had his. It was too late for them, far too late.

Walking over to the picture window, Jason stared out over the lights of the city. He jerked his tie back and forth to loosen the knot. By this time tomorrow, he'd be on his honeymoon.

Sitting down in the large, comfortable chair, his feet on the ottoman, he reached for the television remote. No sooner had he found a sports station when the phone rang. He glanced at his wrist and saw that it was almost one. Not the time most folks would make a phone call.

"Hello."

Nothing. A wrong number or a crank call, he wasn't sure which.

"Hello," he said again impatiently. He was in no mood to deal with a jokester.

Then he knew. He wasn't sure how or why he recognized that it was Katie, but he knew beyond a doubt that the person on the other end of the line was his one-time wife.

His hand tightened around the receiver. "Katie?" He breathed her name into the mouthpiece. If he were smart he'd sever the connection now, but he couldn't make himself do it. His heart beat with happy excitement. He'd wanted to talk to her all day, needed her to help him make sense of everything—and she'd walked away.

"I shouldn't have phoned." Her voice was as fragile as

mist on a moor. He heard the regret, the pain, the worry, knew her voice was an echo, a reflection of his own.

Jason clicked off the television, closed his eyes, and leaned back in the chair. "I'm glad you did."

Neither spoke. Jason suspected it was because they were afraid of what the other would say. Or wouldn't say.

Try as he might he couldn't push the memory of their night together from his mind. It had haunted him all day. Would stay with him the rest of his life.

"I . . . I wanted you to know how sorry I am," she whispered.

"Yeah, well, that makes two of us."

"I don't know how I could have let that happen." Her voice was so low, Jason had to strain to hear her.

"I'm not in the habit of that sort of behavior myself." He felt obliged to reassure her of that.

"Nor me."

That much he knew. "Why'd you run away from me this morning?" His day had been hell from the moment she'd raced out of the hotel.

He could hear her soft intake of breath against the mouthpiece.

"What made you say I'd abandoned you?" Jason asked. Her parting shot had burned against his mind all day.

She ignored the questions. "Does she know?"

He hesitated, then murmured, "Yeah, I told her."

"Oh, Jase, she must be so hurt. Hurting Elaine is what I regret the most. My heart aches for her. How . . . how'd she take it?"

He wasn't sure how to answer. Elaine had acted as if infidelity were no big deal. Certainly it wasn't a problem as far as their wedding was concerned. She knew what had happened between him and Katie, but she didn't want him to tell her.

Because he had no answer to give Katie, he asked a question of his own. "Did you tell Daddy Warbucks?"

"No." A bit of defiance echoed in her husky voice. "I'm not sleeping with Roger if that's what you're asking."

It wasn't. Then maybe it was.

"I should go." She was eager to end the conversation.

"No." There were matters that needed settling first. He wouldn't let her break the connection when so many questions remained unanswered.

"The only reason I called was to tell you how very sorry I was. And . . ."

"And?" he coaxed.

"To wish you and . . ."

"Elaine."

"To wish you and Elaine every happiness."

Happiness was the last thing Jason felt. He was bone tired, weary to the very bottom of his soul. "Thanks."

He waited for her to disconnect the line. She didn't. He couldn't make himself do it. The telephone was the only contact he had with her. Would probably ever have.

"Katie?"

She didn't answer right away. "I'm here."

He already knew that. Knew she wanted to maintain the contact with him as long as she could, the same way he wanted to keep hold of her.

"She's all right?"

"She?"

"Elaine." Katie said the name quickly as though voicing it caused her pain. "If I learned you'd slept with another woman two days before our wedding, it would have killed me."

"She's fine." She'd been more upset with the caterers over the asparagus tips than she had been with what he'd done.

"Good . . . I worried about it all day."

So had he, but for naught. Elaine simply hadn't given a damn.

"Why'd you run out on me?" He wasn't going to let her

off the hook so easily. His day had been hell and it had all started when she left him in a huff.

"I . . . don't know that I can tell you."

"Try." He rubbed his hand down his face. "I need to know."

She took her own sweet time answering. "You called her *Sweetheart.*" He heard the hesitation and the pain. "You'd spent the night making love to me and . . . and then you called Elaine your sweetheart."

"I was taken off guard by her phone call. You have to admit, the situation was a bit awkward."

"I know all that. Really, Jase, it doesn't make any difference now, does it? I suppose I was jealous, which is ridiculous in light of the circumstances." She tried to laugh and failed, her voice trembling as she continued. "All at once I was eighteen all over again and I felt," she said as she struggled to regain control of her emotions, "I felt so alone, facing an impossible situation, loving you, wanting you. Only this time it wasn't my family that stood between us, it was life."

"You ran away from me ten years ago, too."

"I didn't," she cried. "I explained what happened."

"This morning," he said, "I was that eighteen-year-old kid again, the same as you. I needed you to help make sense of what happened. Instead you walked out on me."

"All we seem to do is hurt each other."

He didn't disagree with her.

"Good-bye, Jase."

"Good-bye." He was ready to end it now. He'd gotten the answer to his question.

In the morning he'd be marrying Elaine.

Katie slept fitfully all night and was up midmorning. Saturdays she generally did her shopping for the week and took care of any errands. This day would be no different, she decided. It wasn't the end of the world just because Jase was marrying Elaine. No matter how much it felt like it.

She dressed in jeans and a sleeveless blouse and headed for the local grocer's, but soon found herself wandering aimlessly down the aisles, her cart empty. Her mind refused to focus on the matters at hand. Instead it seemed focused on her short conversation with Jase the night before.

There'd been so much she'd wanted to tell him. Even now she didn't know where she'd found the courage to actually contact him. She'd gone to sleep, awakened, her heart heavy and sad. As she lay in bed, she knew she couldn't let it end abruptly with Jase like that. With her running out of the hotel never to see him again. And so she'd phoned, calling herself every kind of fool when he actually answered. She'd expected to wake him from a sound sleep. To her surprise he'd answered on the first ring as if he, too, were having trouble sleeping.

Instead of helping her bring some sort of closure to their relationship, their conversation created longing and wonder. To have found each other after all these years and still have it be too late.

She walked down the aisle and paused in front of the baby food section and was immediately assaulted with a sudden, unexpected flash of pain. Drawing in a deep breath, she forced herself to look straight ahead.

It wasn't until she was at the checkout stand that she realized her entire week's menu consisted of frozen entrees.

Back at the apartment, she noted the flashing light on her answering machine. It was probably Roger and she wasn't in the mood to talk to him. Not today. She was going to be completely indulgent, cater to her own whims and nurture herself. A long walk in Golden Gate Park sounded perfect.

The afternoon was cool and overcast as was often the case in San Francisco in June. Katie wore a light sweater and her tennis shoes as she briskly followed the footpath close to the water. Runners jogged past, daredevils on Rollerblades, kids on skates. The breeze off the bay carried with it the scent of the ocean, pungent and invigorating.

When she'd completed her two-mile trek, she felt better. Her heart was less heavy. She checked her watch and noted that Jase and Elaine had been married all of two hours.

Because she was a glutton for pain, she went out of her way to stroll past the church where Jase had mentioned he and Elaine would be married. The guests would have left long ago. Katie wasn't entirely sure why she was doing this. It wasn't wise, she knew, but she was indulging herself and she wanted to see the church where Jase had married his "sweetheart."

The church was situated on a steep hill overlooking the bay. By the time Katie had walked up the hill, she was breathing hard. She paused, leaned forward, and braced her hands on her knees.

Her gaze studied the sidewalk where she saw bits of birdseed left over from the wedding. A few small seeds had fallen between the cracks. The analogy between her life and those lost seeds didn't escape her. She felt as though her own life had fallen between the cracks. Mentally she gave herself a hard shake. She refused to give in to self-pity.

Slipping inside the darkened church, Katie's gaze went immediately to the huge stained glass window above the pulpit. A couple of older women were busy in the front, setting huge bouquets of arranged flowers around the altar.

Katie recognized that they were probably the very ones used for Jase and Elaine's wedding.

Walking up the side aisle, she heard the murmur of voices as the two women chatted, unaware she was there.

"Never in all my years as an organist have I witnessed what I did this day," the first woman said in hushed tones.

"From what I heard the bride threw a temper tantrum."

Katie's head perked up in order to better listen in on the conversation.

"While the mother dealt with the daughter, the father dealt with the groom. I don't mind telling you I felt sorry for that young man. Not that I blame him. Good grief, if he was going to change his mind, he might have done it a bit sooner than when he was standing in front of the altar."

"Excuse me," Katie said, making her way toward the two. "I couldn't help overhearing. You wouldn't by chance happen to be talking about the Ingram wedding, would you?"

The two women glanced at each other. "No," answered the first.

"Just a minute, Dorothy, I thought that might have been the name."

Dorothy shook her head. "Nope. It was Hopkins. I'm positive it was Hopkins. I played for the Ingram wedding earlier. Don't know when I've seen a more beautiful bride, either. Those two were so in love, why, it did my heart good just being here. Now that's a marriage that'll last."

"Thank you," Katie whispered as she turned away. For a moment she'd dared to hope for a miracle.

Katie speed-walked back to her condominium and took a long, hot shower. She hadn't eaten lunch and wasn't in the mood to cook so she slapped a frozen entree into her microwave. She wasn't sure when she got into the habit of eating her meals in front of the television, but it was well ingrained now. A voice, a friend, someone to share her dinner with so she wouldn't be alone.

Her favorite show was the evening news. The newscaster stood in front of a homeless shelter, a congenial soul who gave the weekend reports. "This evening the men and women dining at Mission House are enjoying

Beef Wellington and succulent baked salmon fit for a king, or, more appropriate, a groom."

Groom. Great, she was going to be assaulted once again. Everywhere she turned people were talking about weddings.

"This groom experienced a sudden change of heart. Unfortunately, it was too late to warn the caterers. Rather than discard the dinner, the groom opted to serve the meal to San Francisco's homeless."

The scene changed to a group of ragged-looking men and women enjoying their elegant dinner. The camera zeroed in on a table of hors d'oeuvres, and petite canapés topped with asparagus spears.

"When asked about the wedding, groom Jason Ingram . . ."

"Jase." A flash of sheer joy raced through Katie as she roared to her feet.

Jase had called off the wedding.

Eight

Jason sat in the cocktail lounge at the St. Regis Hotel, wishing he was the type who found solace in a bottle of good whiskey. He never had been one to drown his sorrows in liquor, but if ever there was a time a man should drink, it would be after a day like this one.

He'd stood before the priest, Elaine at his side and the organ music surrounding them, and realized he couldn't do it. That very morning, he'd had every intention of going ahead with the wedding. Frankly, he couldn't see any other option. It was what Elaine wanted. What his brother, his own flesh and blood, advised. Everyone he knew seemed to think Elaine was perfect for him.

Everyone except him.

Then when he stood before Father Ecker and looked at Elaine, he knew otherwise. He remembered Katie's words on the phone from the night before. She'd claimed that if she'd learned that he'd cheated on her two nights before their wedding, she would have died. The pain of his betrayal would have killed her.

Elaine had barely been troubled by what she referred to as his indiscretion. Not that he'd ever wanted to hurt her. He would have given anything to spare her this embarrassment, save his soul. But that was what marriage would have demanded. In that moment, he realized that no matter how painful this was to them both, he couldn't go through with it.

All this came down on him as the music swirled around them at the foot of the altar. Before the priest could start the wedding, Jason leaned over to Elaine and suggested they speak privately before the ceremony proceeded any further.

Elaine pretended not to hear him.

Fortunately, the priest did hear and paused. Jason tried to tell Elaine how sorry he was, but he couldn't marry her. Then her father had gotten into the act and her mother. Soon the entire wedding party had gathered around them. Everyone seemed to have an opinion, but could reach no consensus.

When Elaine realized that he'd actually called off the wedding, she'd thrown down her bouquet, stomped all over the flowers, and then gone at him with both fists. It'd taken the priest and two ushers to pull her off him.

Jason worked his jaw back and forth to test the discomfort. He'd say one thing for his former fiancee—she packed quite a punch. But the beating Elaine had given him didn't compare with what her father had in store. Jason would almost have preferred a pounding to the financial burden facing him. Elaine's father had left Jason to foot the bill for the dinner and reception. As best as he could figure, Jason would work for the next ten years to pay for the wedding that never was.

He took another swallow of beer and looked up to find his brother and sister-in-law. They looked pleased with themselves, as well they should. Jase had gifted them with his honeymoon. The two were scheduled to fly to Hawaii first thing in the morning. The honeymoon suite awaited them on Waikiki.

"We're checked out of the hotel," Steve said, pulling out the chair across from Jase and plopping himself down.

"I feel a little guilty having Steve and me go on your honeymoon," Lisa told him, sitting next to her husband.

"You're turning down two weeks in Hawaii, all expenses paid?" Jason joked. His brother was no fool.

"No way," Lisa laughed.

"I had vacation time due me anyway. It's a little short notice, is all." Steve gave him a worried look, as if he wasn't square with this even now.

"But you swung it."

"We swung it."

"Enjoy yourselves," Jason said, meaning it. "I sure as hell won't be needing it." He wasn't sure what the future held for him.

"What about you and Katie?"

Jason mowed five fingers through his hair. "I don't know. We're different people now. I'd like to believe that we could make it, but she lives here and I work on the East Coast."

"You can move, can't you? Or she can," Lisa advised. "Don't sweat the small stuff."

"Have you talked to her yet?"

"No." He'd tried phoning her twice, and each time reached her answering machine.

"What are you waiting for, little brother?"

It'd be nice for the swelling to go down on his eye, but he didn't say so. He raised his hand and tentatively tested the tenderness and winced at the pain.

Steve's gaze drifted toward the door. "Time to go, Lisa," he announced unexpectedly. "Jason's got company."

"Who?" He tossed a look over his shoulder and found Katie standing in the doorway. Her eyes lit up with warm excitement when she found him.

"Good luck," Lisa said, kissing him on the cheek as she followed Steve.

Jason had the feeling his luck was about to change. He'd found his pot of gold in his high school sweetheart.

"Jase?" Katie took one look at his face and bit into her lower lip. "What happened?" She gently cupped one side of his jaw and the pain he'd experienced moments earlier vanished.

"You don't want to know," he muttered.

"Elaine's father?"

"Nope," he said with a half-laugh. "Elaine."

"You look . . ."

"Terrible," he finished for her. He'd seen his reflection and knew that his face resembled a punching bag. He had a bruise alongside his chin and one eye was swollen completely shut.

"Not terrible, but so incredibly handsome I can't believe you called off the wedding," she said all in one breath as she slid in the chair recently vacated by his sister-in-law.

"So you finally listened to your messages?"

"My messages. That was you? I thought . . . no, I didn't play them back. I heard about it on the six o'clock news."

There seemed to be no end to his humiliation. First Elaine punching him and now this. "They reported that I'd called off the wedding on the San Francisco news?"

"No, that you had the caterer serve the dinner at the homeless shelter."

"Oh." That salved his ego only a little. "I couldn't see any reason for all that expensive food to go to waste."

"It was a generous, thoughtful thing for you to do."

He smiled, despite the pain it caused. "I never did much care for asparagus canapés."

"Me, either." Now that Katie was here, Jason wasn't sure what to say or where to start.

"I can't believe I'm here with you. You actually stopped the wedding."

He shrugged, making light of it when it was the most difficult thing he'd ever done. "I had to," he said, taking Katie's hand in both of his. "I was in love with another woman. The same woman I've loved since I was a teenager. I've always loved you, Katie."

Her beautiful eyes welled with tears. "Oh, Jase."

"I don't know how many times I told myself it was too late for us, but I couldn't make myself believe it. We live on different coasts . . ."

"I'll move."

"I'm in debt up to my eyebrows for a wedding that never took place."

"I'm really good at managing money. In fact, I know a great place to get a loan. I've got an 'in' with the manager." She knocked down every objection he offered.

"Your 'in' doesn't happen to be Roger, does it?" he asked with a frown. He didn't want any help from Daddy Warbucks.

"No, me."

"You?" He knew she'd done well, just not that well. He felt a fierce pride for her accomplishment and at the same time was a bit intimidated. "You mean to say you'd be willing to give all that up for me?"

"Is this a formal marriage proposal, Jason Ingram?"

The question gave him pause—not that he had any qualms about marrying Katie. He'd already married her once, but his head continued to ring from his last go-around at the altar. The least he should do before considering it a second time was look at his options.

It took him all of two seconds. He was crazy about Katie and had been for more years than he cared to remember.

"Yes," he admitted, "that's exactly what I'm asking."

Her smile was probably one of the most beautiful sights known to man. Her eyes were bright with unshed tears and a happiness that infected him with a joy so profound it was all he could do not to haul her into his arms right then and there.

"I love you so damned much, Jase Ingram."

Her words were a balm to all that had befallen him that day. "I hope you're not interested in long engagements."

"How about three hours?"

"Three hours?"

"We can drive to Reno in that time."

"Are you suggesting we elope, Katie Kern? Again?" It didn't take him long to realize it was a fitting end to their adventure.

"I can be ready in say . . . five minutes."

He chuckled, loving her so much it felt as if his heart couldn't hold it all inside. "Are we going to have a honeymoon this time?"

"You can bet the house on that, Jase Ingram. My guess is it'll last fifty years or longer."

"I only hope that's long enough."

Jason paid for his beer and with their arms wrapped around each other, he brought her up to his room to collect his suitcase.

Eight hours later, they exchanged their vows. The very ones they'd promised each other ten years earlier.

Only this time it was forever.

Satisfy Me

Lori Foster

One

"Do you believe the audacity?" Asia Michaels asked, staring through the dirty window of the company lounge to the newly painted building across the street. Soft pink neon lights flashed Wild Honey with bold provocation, competing with the twinkle of Christmas lights around the door and windows. A porn shop, she thought with awe, right in the middle of their small town. Cuther, Indiana, wasn't known for porn. Nope, it was known for pigs and toiletries, which meant most everyone either farmed or worked in one of the three factories.

Asia worked in a factory as an executive secretary in the marketing department. She liked it, the routine, the security. She'd found independence in Cuther, and peace of mind. Not in a million years had she thought to see a sex shop called Wild Honey erected among the main businesses.

Seated next to Asia at the round table, Becky Harte gaped. She blinked big blue innocent eyes and asked in a scandalized whisper, "You're sure they sell porn?"

Erica Lee, the third in their long-established group and a faithful friend, laughed out loud as she set her coffee and a candy bar on the table. "Well they're sure not raising bees."

Asia shook her head. Erica was probably the most sophisticated of the three, and the least inhibited. Every guy in the factory had asked Erica out at one time or another. Occasionally, Erica said yes.

Now, Becky, she didn't even look at men, even when the men were staring as hard as they could. Becky's fresh-faced appearance and dark blonde curls were beyond cute. Not that Becky seemed to care. If anything, she did her best not to draw male attention. Her best pretty much worked. If Asia had to guess, she'd swear Becky was still a virgin.

Asia took a bite of her doughnut. "We should go check it out," she teased, hoping to get a rise out of her friends.

"Get out of here," Becky rasped, horrified by the mere prospect. "I could *never* go in that place!"

"Why not?" Erica asked. "You refuse to date, so maybe you'd find something that would make your time alone more . . . interesting." She bobbed her eyebrows, making Becky turn three shades of red and sputter.

Laughing, Asia pointed out, "None of us dates, at least not much."

"I date." Erica shook back her shoulder-length black hair. It hung bone-straight, looked like silk, and made every woman who saw it envious. Because her own hair was plain brown and too curly, Asia counted herself among the envious group.

"I just don't meet many guys worth dating twice," Erica explained. "That's all. And it's not like Cuther is a hotbed of eligible males, anyway."

Asia accepted that excuse with silence. Her own reasons for not dating weren't something she cared to discuss. Cuther was a new life, and her old life was well behind her.

Try as they might, none of them could stop looking at the sex shop. "It's rather tastefully decorated, isn't it?"

Becky and Erica stared at her.

"Well, it is." Asia shrugged. "I would have thought the curtains would be red velvet and there'd be lewd signs in the windows. But there aren't." The curtains were actually gauzy, sheer and delicate, in a snowy white, with beige shutters against the red brick. Other than the bright neon sign with the name of the shop, the place looked as subdued as a nail salon or a boardinghouse. And being that it was close to the holidays, there was even a large festive wreath on the door to go with the holiday lights, lending the building a domestic affectation.

Becky leaned forward, motioning for the others to do the same. "When I parked today," she whispered, "I could see inside, and you'll never guess who was in there!"

Erica and Asia looked at each other. "Who?"

"Ian Conrad."

Erica dropped back in her seat. "The new electrician the company hired?"

Becky nodded, making her curls bounce. "He was speaking to the man at the counter."

Erica snorted. "Well, I'll be. And here he acts so quiet."

"Still waters run deep?" Asia speculated aloud.

"I'd like to know what he bought," Erica admitted in a faraway voice.

"Nothing," Becky told her. "That is, he came out empty-handed. Maybe he was just greeting a new proprietor?"

"More like he went window shopping." Erica made a face, her voice rising. "Men are all alike. One woman isn't enough for them. They need outside stimulation, like a vitamin supplement or something."

"We should be more like them," Asia said, without really thinking. "Can you imagine how a guy would act if a woman started buying up porn?"

Erica looked dumbstruck, then leaned forward in excitement. "Let's do it!"

Becky tried to pull away but Erica caught her arm and held on, keeping her within the conspiratorial circle. "I'm serious! None of us is getting any younger. I'm probably the oldest at twenty-eight, but Becky, aren't you twenty-five now?"

Looking distinctly miserable, Becky nodded.

"I'm twenty-six," Asia volunteered, proud because each year took her one more step away from her past and her insecurities, her lack of confidence in all things.

"You see," Erica said, "we're mature women with mature needs, not silly little girls." She rubbed her hands together and her slanted green eyes lit up with anticipation. "Oh, I'd just love to witness Ian Conrad's expression if he went out on a date with a woman, and afterward, when they were alone, she pulled out the props. Ha! Let him deal with not being enough on his own."

Asia sat back and blinked at Erica. "Whatever are you talking about?" And then with insight, "You've got a thing for Ian, don't you?"

"Absolutely not," Erica sniffed. "I'm just talking about guys in general who think they need all that other"—she waved her hand—"*stuff* to be satisfied. As if a woman and her body and her imagination aren't enough."

Becky looked embarrassed, but concerned. "Did a guy, you know, pull out the props on you?"

"Nah, at least not in the middle of things. But I came home once to find him rather occupied."

Becky's eyes widened in titillated fascination. "Ohmigosh."

"You didn't," Asia said, enthralled despite herself.

"Yep. I'd been gone all of four hours and we'd had sex that morning." She muttered under her breath, "The pig."

Asia frowned. "You know, I don't really think there's anything wrong with a mature, consenting couple making use of toys."

Becky looked ready to faint—or die of curiosity—but Erica just shrugged. "Well, me, either, but he sure wasn't a couple. He was there all by his lonesome, just him and a video and some strange . . . hand contraption thing."

Becky puckered up like she'd swallowed a lemon. *"Hand contraption thing?"*

Asia tried to hold it in, but Erica looked so indignant and Becky looked so dazed, she couldn't. She burst out laughing to the point where half the people in the lounge were staring. When she could finally catch a breath, she managed to say, "I wish I could have seen his face!"

"His face?" Erica raised one brow mockingly. "It wasn't his face that drew my attention. No, ladies. It was the place where that contraption connected."

Becky choked, and they all fell into gales of laughter again.

"So what," Asia finally asked, wiping her eyes, "do you think the three of us should do? Buy our own . . ."

She started giggling again and Becky finished for her, "hand contraptions!"

"Honey, please." Erica affected an exaggerated haughtiness. "That gizmo wouldn't do us any good at all."

Becky had tears rolling down her cheeks, she laughed so hard. "You're so bad, Erica."

"Which is why you love me."

"Yep, I guess that's part of it."

"Okay, so what do we do?" Asia really wanted to know. Not that she intended to go into that porn shop and buy anything. Just the idea made her hot with embarrassment.

Then she realized her own thoughts and frowned. Part of her liberation, her new life, was doing as *she* pleased, without concern for what others thought. Why should she be embarrassed? The men from the factory had been moseying over there all day! They could appease their curiosity, so why couldn't she?

"First, we'll share our fantasies."

Fantasies! Good grief, maybe *that* was why she couldn't. Asia wasn't sure she had any fantasies.

Not anymore.

Erica had leaned forward to whisper her comment, but still Asia looked around nervously. By necessity, the lounge was large, able to accommodate shifts for the two hundred plus people who worked there. Employees tended to sit in clusters. The managers with the managers, maintenance with maintenance, and so forth.

Asia and her friends always chose the same table in the corner by the window, separated by a half-wall planter filled with artificial plants. Since Wild Honey had gone in, they often found their favorite table unavailable because everyone wanted to look out that row of windows. Erica had taken to leaving her desk early so she could lay claim to it.

Asia didn't see anyone paying them any mind, although there was someone on the other side of the planter, alone at a table. He wore jeans and a flannel, so she assumed he was one of the workmen, not part of management. But whoever he was, he wasn't listening. He sat alone, a newspaper open in front of his face, his booted foot swinging to music that played only in his head. A half-empty cup of steaming coffee was at his elbow. Even as Asia watched, he rustled the paper, turned the page, and sipped at his drink.

Satisfied, Asia turned back to Erica. "We share fantasies and then what?"

"Then we wait until some guy buys a prop—a movie, a book, a toy, whatever—that relates to our particular fantasy."

"And?" Becky asked, both breathless and bright red.

Erica shrugged. "We approach him. See if he's interested."

Snatching up her foam cup, Asia gulped down a fortifying drink.

Since her first relationship had turned so sour, so . . . *bad,* she'd never gotten to find out what the fireworks were about. She wasn't stupid; she believed awesome sex existed, it just hadn't existed for her. Not in her marriage.

How would it be to have phenomenal sex with a guy who wanted the same things she did? A man who wanted to please her, not the other way around?

She realized both Becky and Erica were staring at her and she asked warily, "What?"

Becky cleared her throat. "Erica asked if you'd want to go first?"

"Me! Why me?"

Becky lifted one narrow shoulder. "I'm too chicken, though I promise to try to work up my nerve."

"You will work up the nerve," Erica promised, and squeezed Becky's hand.

Becky looked skeptical, but nodded. "And Erica says if she goes first, she knows neither of us will."

Asia nearly crumbled her cup, she got so tense. But she wanted to do this. It would be one more step toward total freedom. Not that she believed anything would come of it. And thinking that, she said, "We have to set a time limit. I don't intend to visit that stupid place more than . . . say, three times."

"It's Tuesday," Erica pointed out. "You can start tomorrow right after work, and stop on Friday. If no one turns up, it'll be Becky's turn. But we all have to keep rotating turns until we find someone, agreed?"

Asia thought about it, then nodded. "Agreed. But if in those first three times I don't see a guy buying what he'd need to buy to interest me, then it moves on to Becky's turn."

Becky closed her eyes. "Oh, dear."

"Promise me, Becky."

Becky bit her lip, but finally agreed. "Okay," she whispered, and then with more force, as if a streak of determination existed beneath her innocence, *"Okay."*

Erica laughed. "There you go, hon. So, Asia, what's a fella have to buy to get your motor running?"

This was the embarrassing part. But she'd explain, and they'd understand her reasoning. Asia looked at each woman in turn, then stiffened her backbone. "Something to do with . . ."

Erica and Becky leaned forward, saying in unison, "Yes?"

Asia squeezed her eyes shut, took a deep breath, and blurted, "Spanking."

Cameron O'Reilly choked, then nearly swallowed his tongue. He sputtered, spewing coffee across the front of the flannel he wore today before finally gasping in enough air. A good portion of his steaming coffee went into his lap, but it wasn't nearly as hot as he was.

Spanking! Asia Michaels was into spanking!

As the coffee soaked into his jeans, he leaped from his seat, but at the last second remembered himself and turned his back. He could feel all three of the ladies looking at him, especially *her.* Luckily, he wasn't dressed in his usual suit today. The casual clothes, necessary for the job he did that morning, would help disguise him.

The voice he recognized as Erica Lee muttered, "Klutz."

"Who is he?" he heard Asia whisper and there was a lot of nervousness in her tone.

"Who cares?" Erica said. "Ignore him."

Becky said, "I hope he didn't burn himself." Then they went back to chatting.

Cameron didn't give them a chance to recognize him. He quickly stalked from the lounge. Still poleaxed, he damn near barreled into a wall in his hurry to leave undetected. Asia and spanking! He'd never have guessed it. He groaned, just thinking of Asia with her soft brown curls and big, sexy brown eyes. He'd wanted her for two long months.

But she'd refused to move beyond the platonic acquaintance stage, no matter how many times he tried. She was friendly to him, and ignored any hints for more.

One of the other employees had warned him that Asia was a cold fish, totally uninterested in men. Ha!

He ducked into the men's room and hurried to the sink. In his mind, he pictured Asia stretched out over his lap, her beautiful naked bottom turned up, his large hand on her . . .

And the image ended there.

He just couldn't see himself striking a woman. Not for any reason. But, oh, the other things he'd like to do to that sweet behind.

He grabbed several paper towels and mopped at his soaked jeans. She hadn't known he was listening, of course, or he still wouldn't know her secret. The problem now was how to use it.

He wasn't a kinky man.

He enjoyed sex just like any other guy, but he'd never been a hound dog, never been a womanizer. He'd never done much experimenting beyond what he and his partner found enjoyable, which had stayed pretty much in the bounds of routine stuff, like different positions, different places, different times of the day.

He liked relationships, and he liked Asia.

He wanted her. Soon, and for a long while. He did not want to . . . spank her.

Cameron stared down at his jeans, tautly tented by a raging erection, and knew himself for a liar. He snorted. The idea was exciting as hell, no doubt about that. But mostly because it was sexual in nature. If Asia had said she wanted to roll naked in the snow, *that* would have turned him on too, and he absolutely detested the damn snow. Give him Florida, with hot sandy beaches and bright sunshine over frigid Indiana weather any day.

Of course, if he'd stayed in Florida instead of taking the new supervisor's job, he'd never have met Asia, and he most definitely wouldn't have overheard such an intriguing confession.

He shook his head. What to do?

First, he had to change into his regular clothes. At least the dousing had helped to bring him back under control, otherwise he might have blown it by rushing things. He'd been sitting there listening to her, daydreaming, imagining all types of lewd things while staring blankly at the newspaper, and he'd nearly worked himself into a lather. Her confession had all but pushed him over the edge. At thirty-two, he was too damn old for unexpected boners.

Yet he'd had one. For Asia.

Which meant the next thing he had to do was be in that shop tomorrow when Asia visited. She wouldn't need three days to find him. Hell, he'd never live that long, not with the way he wanted her.

And no way would he let her go off with some other guy. He'd been fantasizing about her since moving to Indiana two months ago, and here was his chance.

The spanking part . . . well, he'd do what he had to do. And if she enjoyed it, great.

After he warmed her bottom, it'd be his turn.

Two

Becky looked faint. "Spanking," she said in a strangled, barely there whisper, clutching her throat.

"I have a theory," Asia hurried to explain. "If a guy gets his kinkier jollies taken care of with props, then he won't expect to fulfill them with a woman."

Erica dropped back in her seat with a guffaw. "You big faker! You really had me going there."

Becky asked, still a bit confused, "So you figure if he buys movies about spanking, he'll have it out of his system and won't try anything like that with you?"

"Bingo."

Erica shook her head. "And here I thought you had a wild side."

"Not even close." Asia thought about it for a moment, then decided it was time for some truths. She could trust Erica and Becky, she knew that. They'd understand. "Actually, I had a wild first husband."

"Get out! You were married?"

"Yes. To a complete and total jerk."

Erica's smile faded. "And he hit you?"

"Not exactly. But he liked to . . . experiment. Everything was geared toward what *he'd* like, whether I liked it or not. And I never did. But he'd claim it was my duty as his wife to try to please him, and I was confused enough then to feel some guilt, because I couldn't please him on my own."

Becky surprised them both by growling, "That bastard."

After giving Becky a long approving look, Erica asked, "How long were you with him?"

"We married right out of college when I was twenty-two. The divorce became final just before my twenty-fifth birthday."

"He did a number on you, didn't he? That's why you don't date."

"Let's just say I like being independent now, thinking my own thoughts and doing my own things. I'm not looking for a relationship, and I don't want—*didn't want*—any part of a quick affair." She tapped her fingers on the tabletop. "But you're right, Erica. I might be missing out on a lot, and to my mind, I've missed enough already. I deserve some satisfaction."

Erica thrust a small fist into the air and said, "Here's to satisfaction," making Becky chuckle.

"So," Asia said, feeling equal parts triumphant for being decisive, anticipation for what might be, and hesitant about the unknown. "That's settled. I'll head over there tomorrow."

"We'll watch from here," Becky told her, and Erica nodded.

Knowing they'd be close would make it easier, Asia decided. "Your turn, Becky."

Becky blanched. "My turn for what?"

"To share a fantasy."

She winced. "I need time to think about it."

As the unofficial moderator, Erica sighed. "All right. You can have until Friday."

Slumping in relief, Becky said, "Friday." She smiled. "I'll be ready."

Cameron stood in the aisle of tapes, surreptitiously watching the door. Unwilling to take a chance on missing Asia, he'd been there for half an hour. Already he'd studied every cover and description of all the more erotic discipline tapes. Some of them were downright disgusting. Pain and pleasure . . . he wasn't at all sure they really mixed. Not that he intended to judge others.

Not that he'd judge Asia.

He had his eye on one in particular, but he waited, wanting Asia to see him buy the damn thing so there'd be no misunderstandings. The cover sported an older English-looking fellow in a straight-backed chair. He had a schoolgirl, of all dumb things, draped over his knees with her pleated skirt flipped up and her frilly panties showing.

Cameron had chosen it because even though the guy appeared stern, the girl wore a vacuous, anxious smile. She seemed to be enjoying herself and that's what he hoped Asia would do. No way in hell could he make her cry—even if she preferred it—which some of the tapes indicated by their covers.

He was engrossed in fantasies too vivid to bear when the tinkling of the front door sounded like a gun blast in his ears. He looked up—and made eye contact with Asia.

Even from the distance separating them, he felt her shock and consternation at seeing him there. She immediately averted her face, her cheeks scalded with color.

The blood surged in his veins. Every muscle in his body tensed, including the one most interested in this little escapade. His cock was suddenly hard enough to break granite.

Cameron couldn't look away as she ducked to the back aisle. He'd already discovered they kept a variety of velvet whips and handcuffs there.

She ducked right back out, her face now pale. Damn. He started toward her, not certain what he'd say but knowing he had to say something. He had the wretched tape in his hand.

"Asia?"

She froze, her back to him, her body strangely still.

Several seconds ticked by, the silence strained, and then she turned. A false, too-bright smile was pinned to her face. "Yes?" And as if she hadn't seen him the second she walked in, she said, "Cameron! What are you doing here?"

As usual, she reached out for a business handshake, keeping their relationship confined.

With no other option coming to mind, he started to accept her hand, realized he held the damn tape, and switched hands. "I'm just . . . ah, looking around."

In horrified fascination, she stared at the movie now held at his side before finally giving him a brisk, quick shake. "It's an interesting place, isn't it?"

"Yes." They stood in the center aisle with display tables loaded down with paperback books of the lustful variety on either side of them. He propped his hip against a table, trying to relax while his testosterone level shot through the roof. "I'm surprised at the diversity. And how upscale it all is." He glanced around, feeling too self-conscious. "I'm not sure what I expected."

"I know what you mean." She relaxed the tiniest bit. "I admit, I never expected a shop like this in conservative Cuther."

The tape in his hand felt like a burning brand. He wanted to set the idiotic thing aside, but that would be defeating the whole purpose of being in the shop in the first place. "Cuther is different," he admitted. "More rural than I'm used to."

"And colder?" she teased, because she knew he'd come from Florida.

Idle conversation in a porn shop, Cameron thought. It was a first for him. "I guess my blood has thinned. I'm almost always cold."

"With the wind chill, it's fifteen below. Everyone is cold."

"True enough."

She tilted her head and her long brown hair flowed

over her coat sleeve. It looked like dark honey and burnished gold, natural shades for a natural woman.

"What about your family?" she asked, taking him by surprise with the somewhat more personal question.

"What about them?"

She smiled, a real smile this time. "You've never said much about them."

"No." Any time he'd talked to her, he'd been trying to get past her walls. Discussing his family had been the farthest thing from his mind.

"It's almost Christmas. Will you be heading home for the holidays?"

"Uh, no." He wouldn't go anywhere until he'd had her. "My family is . . . scattered. We keep in touch by phone, but we don't do the big family get-togethers. We never have."

Her brown eyes warmed, looked a little sad. Thick lashes lowered, hiding her gaze from him. "I thought everyone wanted to be with family this time of year."

He shrugged, wishing she'd change the damn subject, wishing she'd look at him again.

Wishing he had her naked and in his bed.

"I guess not." Then he thought to ask, "What about you?"

She turned partially away, giving him her profile. Even beneath the thick coat, he could see the swells of her breasts, the plumpness of her bottom.

A bottom she wanted him to swat.

Cameron swallowed hard, willing himself to stay in control. "Asia?"

"I'm not sure what I'm doing yet. Mother is . . . well, she remarried and she gets together with her husband's family. I have one sister, but I think she's making it an intimate occasion. Just her husband and two children."

"So you're an aunt?" He liked learning more about her, but she'd picked a hell of a place to open up.

"Yes. I have two adorable nephews, four and six."

He took a step closer. "If you find out you're not doing anything, maybe we could get together?"

"I . . ." Her smile faded. "I don't know."

He could feel her shutting down, closing herself off from him. He hated it. "I'm free," he said, watching for her reaction, "whatever you decide."

She nodded, but didn't say a thing.

Having all but killed that conversational gambit, Cameron looked around for inspiration. "This your first time in here?"

"Yes." Her face colored once again.

Drawn to her, Cameron rubbed the back of his neck and tried to keep his wits. "You looking for anything in particular?"

She gave him such an appalled look, he wanted to kick his own ass. Any idiot would know you didn't ask a lady something like that.

But she surprised him. She cleared her throat, lifted her chin, and pointed down at the video in his hand. "I see you made a selection."

It was stupid, but he felt heat crawling up the back of his neck and prayed she wouldn't notice.

Determined on his course, he held the tape in front of him so she'd get a good look at it and see exactly what it was. "That's right. I suppose I should be paying." He took a small step away.

Asia looked after him.

He edged into another step, willing her to say something, anything. He waited.

Nothing.

"It was, ah, nice speaking with you."

Eyes wide and watchful, she nodded. "You, too."

Damn, damn, damn. Had the tape not been risqué enough? "All right, then." He forced a smile, but it felt more like a grimace. "Take care."

He started to turn away, teeth clenched in disappointment, body on fire.

"Cameron?"

He whipped around. "Yes?"

She didn't look at him, but that was okay, because she asked, "Would you like to . . . maybe do something Friday after work? If you're not busy, that is."

His knees went weak with relief. He didn't know if he'd last till Friday, but he said, "Yeah. Sure. That'd be great."

A tremulous smile brightened her expression. "I could cook you dinner."

"No." He shook his head and walked back to her. "I'll take you out to dinner. Someplace nice. All right?" He didn't want their first date to be only about sex.

She teased, "What? You don't trust my cooking?"

"I imagine you're a terrific cook." It was difficult not to touch her, not to grin like a lecherous moron. But, damn, he was hard and there wasn't a thing he could do about it. He wanted her too much. "This week is my treat, though, okay?"

She studied him closely, then nodded. "All right."

"Do you want to go straight from work?" *Do you want to go now, to my place,* he thought, *where I can get you naked and sate myself on your . . .*

"I'd like to go home and change first. If that's okay."

This smile came easier. At least he had a confirmed date, even if he had a two-day wait. "I'll pick you up at six? Will that give you enough time?"

"Perfect." She wrote her address down for him, then accompanied him to the checkout. Time and again, her gaze went to his movie. Was she excited? He wished like hell she didn't have the thick coat on. He wanted to see her breasts, to see if maybe her nipples were peaked with anticipation.

God, many more thoughts like that and he'd be in real trouble. Luckily, he'd worn his long coat today, which concealed his lower body and straining erection. His jacket wouldn't have hidden a thing.

They stepped outside together, his purchase safely concealed in a plain brown paper bag. He felt like a pervert, even though his logical adult mind told him a grown man could purchase whatever he pleased. But he knew what was in that bag, even if no one else did.

The wind kicked up, blowing Asia's hair. It licked against his chin, scented with female warmth and sweet shampoo. He caught a lock and brought it to his nose, wondering if she'd smell so sweet all over, or would her natural fragrance be spicy, like hot musk? He couldn't wait to find out, to nuzzle her throat and her breasts and her belly . . . between her thighs.

His muscles pulled tight with that thought. "You have beautiful hair," he all but growled.

Her lips parted at his husky tone, and her big eyes stared up at him. "I do?"

He wrapped that silky tendril around his finger and rubbed it with his thumb. "Hmmm. It's almost the exact same shade as your eyes."

Her laugh got carried off on the wind. "You mean plain old brown?"

"There's nothing plain about you, Asia, especially your coloring." They had reached her car, and he opened her door for her. He saw her surprise at the gentlemanly gesture, and it pleased him. "I'll see you at work tomorrow?"

"I'll be there."

Pretending to be much struck, Cameron said, "I just realized. You didn't buy anything. I hope my presence didn't inhibit you?"

Her small nose went into the air. "Not at all. I only wanted to see what they had."

He couldn't resist teasing her. "You didn't find anything you liked, huh?"

Those dark mysterious eyes of hers stared at him, and she said, "I found you, now didn't I?"

Cameron stepped back, stunned and so horny his stomach cramped.

She smiled with triumph. "Tomorrow, Cameron."

He watched her drive away. The next two days would be torture, waiting to get her in his bed, open to him, willing. He shook with need, then glanced down at the bag in his hand.

He'd use the time until then to study up on this kinky preference of hers, just to make sure he got it right.

That thought had him grinning. Were there rules to spanking? A time frame to follow? Did you jump right into it, or ease the way? Did the spanking follow the sex, or was it a form of foreplay?

He didn't know, but he'd sure as hell find out.

He shivered from a particularly harsh blast of icy wind, and realized he'd barely noticed the cold while Asia was close to him. Now that she'd left, he felt frozen. He hurried to his own car.

He had some studying to do.

Asia crawled into bed that night and pulled the thick covers to her chin. The sheets were icy cold, making her shiver, and she curled into a tight ball. It had been so very long since she'd felt a large male body in bed beside her, sharing warmth and comfort.

Sharing pleasure.

During her marriage, she'd learned to dread the nights her husband reached for her. Lovemaking had been tedious at best, uncomfortable and embarrassing at worst. His preferences at trying anything and everything—including discipline—whether she enjoyed it or not, had worn her down. He'd told her it was necessary, that she wasn't exciting enough, her body not sexy enough, to get him aroused without the added elements. After a while she'd begun to believe him, and it had taken a lot for her to finally realize he was the one with the problems, not her.

In the process, she'd gotten completely turned off sex. But she wasn't an idiot. She knew it wasn't always like that.

She didn't think it'd be like that with Cameron.

Thinking his name brought an image of him to mind. She rolled to her back and closed her eyes. Cameron, with his straight black hair. Not as straight or as black as Erica's, but in many ways more appealing, at least to her.

His hair had a chestnut cast to it in the light. And though she knew he was only in his early thirties, a bit of silver showed in his sideburns. His hair was a little too long at the nape, as if regular haircuts weren't high on his list of priorities. And judging by how often it was tousled, he didn't bother much with combs, either. She imagined him showering, shaving, combing his hair—and ending his personal grooming right there. She smiled.

The mental picture of him in the shower lingered, but his suits were so concealing, she could only guess at his physique. He was tall, lean in the middle, and his feet and hands were large. Beyond that, she didn't know.

She liked his eyes best. The many times when they'd spoken, his vivid blue eyes had been very direct. He tended to focus on her with a lot of intensity.

She shivered, but it wasn't from cold.

So many times her mind had wandered while chatting with him. Her heart would race, her skin would flush. She'd thought him dangerous to her, a threat to her independence, and she'd deliberately kept their association as casual, as businesslike, as possible.

But now she'd sought him out.

Would his eyes look that intense, hot from within, when he made love with her? That alone would be nice, she decided, remembering how her husband had always looked . . . distant from her. He'd treated her like nothing more than a convenient body, using her to gain his own pleasure.

Cameron would be aware of her, she was sure.

Was he at home right now, watching that risqué movie? Was he excited? Hard?

Her own soft groan sounded in the silence of her empty bedroom. Rolling to her side, she looked out the window. Snowflakes fell steadily, making patterns on the dark window. She could just make out the faint glow of colored Christmas lights on the house across the street.

Cameron would be alone for Christmas, just like her.

Her heart gave a funny little thump, sort of a poignant pain. The holidays were so lonely, so sad. If she and Cameron were together . . .

No! She wanted this one night of sex, but that was all. She didn't want or need another relationship, and sharing a holiday, especially one as emotional as Christmas, would definitely be a commitment of sorts. Wouldn't it?

She shook her head. Her independence was important to her, and she did just fine on her own. A steady relationship would intrude on that.

Was Cameron watching the movie? Was he thinking of her?

Disturbed by her own conflicting, changing thoughts, she sat up abruptly and turned on the light. Curiosity swamped her, made her body hot and tingly. She reached for the phone and dialed the operator. Cameron was too new to the area to be in the phone book, but the operator had a listing for him.

Asia clutched the phone, daring herself to call him, to ask him . . . what? If he was pleasuring himself? She imagined what that would entail and sensation exploded, like a tide of moist warmth, making her breath catch. She could easily visualize his large strong hand wrapped around his erection. She could see his beautiful blue eyes vague with lust, his hard jaw clenched, thighs and abdomen tensed as he stroked faster and faster . . .

She gasped with the image, feeling her own measure

of burning excitement. Shaking, breathing too hard and fast, she bit her lip and dialed the number.

Cameron's sleep-rough voice answered on the third ring. "Hello?"

Asia froze. Oh, God, he'd been *sleeping*, not indulging in erotic daydreams or self-pleasure! Talk about missing the mark.

Her mouth opened but nothing came out. She'd awakened him when she didn't have a legitimate reason for calling.

"Hello?" he said again, this time with some impatience.

Asia slammed down the phone. Her heart galloped hard enough to hurt her ribs, and her stomach felt funny, kind of tight and sweet. In a rush she turned the light back off and slid under the covers, even pulling them over her head.

Cameron O'Reilly.

He turned her on, no doubt about it. Now if she could just not make a fool of herself, everything might go smoothly.

Cameron stared at the phone. Moving to one elbow he switched on the lamp at his bedside and checked the Caller I.D. *Asia Michaels.* A small curious smile tipped his mouth. There surely weren't two women in all of Cuther with that particular, unique name.

She'd called him—then chickened out.

What had she wanted?

Naked, he eased back against the pillows, plenty warm now, thank you very much.

Very slowly, the smile turned into a toothy grin. Oh, he knew what she wanted, he reminded himself. She wanted sex. She wanted kink.

She wanted him.

Arms crossed behind his head, Cameron glanced at

the tape sitting on his dresser across the room. He hadn't watched it yet. Because of what he'd overheard in the lounge, he hadn't gotten much work done the rest of the day. He'd been too distracted with thoughts of Asia and how he'd make love to her.

His preoccupation on the job meant he'd had to bring several files home to finish on his personal computer. By the time he was done, his eyes were gritty and he'd wanted only a few hours' sleep.

Now he only wanted Asia.

He wasn't at all sure he'd be able to wait until Friday. He needed to taste her before that, just to tide him over.

Soon, he promised himself. Very soon.

Three

"Cameron O'Reilly?" Erica repeated in disbelief, and fanned her face dramatically. "What a hunk!"

"You think?" Asia chewed her bottom lip. *She* thought him sexy as sin, especially now, but did other women think it too? "I mean, I admit I was surprised. He's just such a . . . suit."

Erica snorted. "Honey, all men are the same, white collar and blue collar alike. They're all sex addicts."

"I agree," Becky said. "O'Reilly is hot."

"You been checking him out?" Erica asked in some surprise.

"I'm not blind"—Becky sniffed with mock indignation—"if that's what you mean."

They all chuckled. "I wouldn't mind getting to know him better myself," Erica teased. "But he's never really noticed me. When I talk to him, he's polite, but always businesslike."

Asia fiddled with her coffee stirrer, then admitted, "We've spoken several times." She glanced up, then away. "At length."

"Ah." Erica grinned. "Do tell."

She shrugged. "He sort of . . . sought me out. He comes to my office, hangs around a bit, or catches me in the halls, or right after meetings. I . . . I like him, but I got the feeling he wanted to get more personal, so I . . . brushed him off."

"Are you nuts?"

Asia was sort of wondering that same thing herself, but for different reasons. "I just couldn't see starting something that likely wouldn't go anywhere."

Becky touched her hand. "You were afraid he wouldn't follow up?"

That nettled her new independent streak. "Ha! I wouldn't want him to. It's more likely that *I* wouldn't follow up."

Erica grinned. "That right?"

"Yes." And then, "Why is it always the woman who's supposed to sit around and wait for a damn phone call?"

Erica said, "Amen, sister. You'll get no argument from me. That's why even on dates, I buy my own meals, and I refuse flowers or gifts. If I want something, I can get it for myself. I don't *need* a guy. But sometimes I want one. So I go on *my* schedule, not his."

"Sounds to me," Becky said, "that you both like playing hard to get."

"No playing to it," Erica corrected. "I *am* hard to get."

Asia chuckled. She wasn't playing, either, though her motivation differed from Erica's. "Most of the guys here understand that I'm not interested, that it's a waste of time to want more from me than casual conversation."

Erica nodded knowingly. "But Cameron was new, so he didn't know, and he's been after you?"

"I figured he'd find out soon enough and leave me alone."

"But he didn't?"

She shook her head. "Whenever we're in the same room together, he watches me, and he smiles if our gazes meet." *And what a smile,* she thought privately, *enough to melt a woman's bones,* so, of course it was hell on her reserve.

"And now you know he has kinky sexual preferences," Erica pointed out with a sinner's grin.

"Now I know," Asia corrected, "that he has a healthy outlet. Honest, all the documentation I read said that what one fantasizes isn't generally what one wants in a real-life situation, which is why it's strictly a fantasy. Fantasies are safe. They are not, however, something we'd ever really try or even want to try."

"I used to think about getting stranded on a desert island with three hunks," Erica mused aloud. "None of us had clothes."

Asia and Becky snickered.

"But granted, I like modern luxuries too much to want to rough it just for male attention. Besides, I imagine one day on an island is all it'd take for me to start looking pretty haggard. No lotion, no scented shampoo, no blow dryer . . ."

"No birth control," Becky pointed out.

"And three men fighting for my body? That could get ugly."

"Maybe they'd just share," Asia suggested.

Erica shivered. "To tell you the truth, it's fine as a fantasy, but the idea of three naked sweaty guys bumping up against one another with me in the middle just sort of ruins the fantasy of them being there for *me*."

They were all still chuckling when suddenly Cameron approached. He had his hands in his pants pockets, a crooked smile on his handsome face.

He looked at each woman in turn. "Afternoon, ladies."

Agog, Becky wiggled her fingertips in a halfhearted wave.

Erica lounged back in her seat and grinned. "Mr. O'Reilly."

"Cameron, please." Then to Asia, "I'm sorry to interrupt your break, but could I speak to you for just a moment?"

Asia felt dumbstruck. She glanced at her friends, who made very differing faces at her, then nodded. "Uh, sure."

"In private." He gently took her arm and headed to the back of the lounge, to the large storage closet. Asia almost stalled. *A closet?* She felt workers looking up in casual interest; she felt Erica and Becky staring hard enough to burn a hole into her back.

She felt excitement roil inside her.

As if inviting her into a formal parlor instead of a closet, Cameron gallantly opened the door and gestured her inside.

She only hesitated a moment. He closed the door, leaving them in near darkness. One narrow window over the door let in the lounge's faded fluorescent light. Shadows were everywhere, from boxes and brooms and supplies. Asia backed up to a wall, a little apprehensive, a lot eager, and waited.

He tipped his head at her, frowning slightly. "I wanted to ask you something."

Oh no. No, no, no! He knew she'd called last night! He'd ask her about it, want to know why, and what the heck could she possibly tell him—

"Would you mind too much if I jumped the gun a little here and . . . kissed you?"

Asia froze, her thoughts suspended, her panic redirected, her heart skipping a beat.

"I know, I know." He rubbed the back of his neck, agitated. "The thing is, I can't stop thinking about it—or you—and I doubt I'll get any work done today if I don't." He looked at her, and his voice lowered. "You see, I'm going nuts wanting to taste you."

Taste her? It was like a dream, Asia thought, far removed from reality. Never had she expected any guy to say such a thing to her.

Asia collected her wayward thoughts and replied stupidly, "You are?"

He gave a slow, considering nod, took a step closer. "Would you mind?"

"Uh . . ." She looked around. They had privacy here in the dim closet, never mind that a crowd of people was right outside the door, oblivious to his request.

Even in the shadows, she could see his beautiful blue eyes watching her, hot and expectant. So very aware of her.

Her pulse tripped. She sucked in an unsteady breath and caught his scent—subtle aftershave and heated male flesh. Delicious scents that made her head swim.

He stepped closer still until he nearly touched her, his gaze now on her mouth, hungry and waiting. She licked her lips and started to whisper, "All right—"

And with a soft groan, his mouth was there, covering hers, gentle and warm and firm. His hands flattened on the wall on either side of her head and his chest almost touched hers. Not quite, but she felt the body heat radiating off him in waves, carrying more of that delicious scent for her to breathe in, letting her fill herself up with it until she shook.

"Open your mouth," he murmured against her lips, and like a zombie—a very aroused zombie—she did.

He didn't thrust his tongue into her mouth. No, he licked her lips with a warm, velvet tongue, gentle, easy. Then just inside her mouth, slowly, over the edges of her teeth, her own tongue.

Asia moaned and opened more in blatant invitation, wanting his tongue. Wanting all of him.

He slid in, deep and slow, then out again.

"Jesus." He dropped his head forward and she felt his uneven breaths pelting her cheek. He gave a short, low laugh, roughened by his arousal. "You make me feel like a schoolboy again."

Her heart in her throat, panting and trembling, Asia managed to say, "Made out in a lot of closets, did you?"

"Hmm?" His head lifted, his eyes burning on her face, still eager, still intent.

She swallowed back a groan. "In school."

"Oh." He smiled, looked at her mouth and kissed her again, a brief, teasing kiss to her bottom lip. "No. No, I didn't. But I did walk around with a perpetual hard-on, and damn if that isn't what you do to me."

Was there a proper reply a lady made to such a comment? If so, Asia had no idea what it might be.

His big rough hands settled on her face, cupping her cheeks, his thumbs smoothing over her temples. He looked concerned. Horny and concerned. "I'm sorry if I'm rushing you."

She almost laughed at that. The way he made her feel, she wanted to be rushed. "Do you hear me complaining?"

"No," he said slowly. "No, you're not." His expression turned thoughtful. "Can I take that to mean you want me too?"

He was so blunt! She hadn't expected it of him. In her experience—admittedly limited—well-dressed corporate types were more reserved. She heard lewd jests from the factory workers all the time. And she heard the maintenance guys make ribald jokes throughout the day. But the suits . . . they generally feared sexual harassment charges and any kidding they did remained very private.

Erica claimed all men were the same when it came to sex, but Asia knew that wasn't true. Some men approached sex as a free-for-all. Her ex-husband had been that way. He wanted it whenever he could get it, whoever he could get it from.

Some saw sex as a commitment, others as a challenge.

And some, she hoped, saw it as a mutual exchange of pleasure, best experienced with respect and consideration.

So far, Cameron struck her as that type of man. Finally, she answered, "Yes."

He let out a breath. "You took so long to answer, I wasn't sure." He rubbed her bottom lip with the edge of his thumb, smiling. "You've got a masochistic streak in you, don't you?"

"No, I just wasn't . . . sure how to answer."

This time he laughed. "That'll teach my ego to get excited."

She covered her face with her hands. "I'm making a mess of this aren't I?"

"Not at all. You gave me my kiss, and that was more than I had a right to ask for." Stepping back, he said, "I should let you get back to your friends."

But she didn't want him going through the day thinking she *didn't* want him. Because she did. More so with every blasted second.

Forcing herself to be bold, Asia lifted her chin and looked him right in his sexy blue eyes. "Will you give me another kiss first?"

He stared down at her, that charming crooked smile in place. He leaned back against the wall and said, "Why don't you kiss me this time? Just to be fair?"

He kept taking her by surprise! She'd been under the impression all men liked to be in control, at all times. She realized this proved her theory about the sexually explicit movie he'd purchased. Even though he bought a tape that showed a man dominating in the most elemental way, he'd just offered to let her take the lead. She braced herself.

In for a penny . . . Asia put her hands on his shoulders, then stalled. He was so hard.

His suit coat hid some broad shoulders and a lot of solid muscle. She hadn't realized before, but now the proof was in her hands and it was unbearably enticing. *Would he be that hard all over?*

She shivered. What a thought.

Trailing her fingers downward, she found his biceps and inhaled in triumph. Solid, strong. No underexercised executive here! Cameron O'Reilly was all rugged male.

Eyes closed, Asia flexed her fingers, relishing the feel of hard muscle, strong bones and obvious strength. Her stomach did a little flip of excitement and she stepped into him while going on tiptoe. When he'd kissed her, only their mouths had touched.

But Asia wanted more and she saw no reason to deny herself. She fitted her body to his, soft breasts to broad chest, curving belly to hard abdomen . . . pelvis to pelvis. He groaned low and rough, and then his hands were on the small of her back, pressing her closer, and she felt his solid erection, long and hot, pulsing through the layers of clothes.

"Oh my," she whispered, going well beyond impressed to the realm of awed.

"Give me your mouth, Asia."

No sooner did she comply, kissing him with all the pent-up desire she suffered, than he turned them both so she was the one pressed to the wall. One of his hands slid down her back to her behind, and he gripped her, lifting, bringing her into startling contact with his erection.

He pressed into her rhythmically, rubbing himself against her, setting her on fire, all the while kissing her, soft, eating kisses, deep-driving kisses, wet and hot and consuming.

A rap at the door made them both jump.

Erica called in, "Sorry kiddies, but playtime is over. Time to come in from recess."

Asia slumped against the wall and groaned. She'd totally forgotten her surroundings!

Watching her closely, Cameron cleared his throat. "We'll be right there."

With laughter in her voice, Erica said, "If you wait just two little minutes, the room will be clear and you can escape without notice." They both heard the sound of her retreating footsteps.

"I'm sorry."

Asia looked up. "For what?"

Stroking her cheek gently, he said, "I meant only a simple kiss—well okay, not so simple—but I didn't mean to embarrass you."

She sighed even as her heart softened. What an incredible man. "Cameron, you called a halt," she felt compelled to point out, "and I insisted on one more kiss. I'm the one who should be apologizing."

"Are you sorry?" he asked, and he wore that absorbed expression again, which now looked endearing.

"The truth? Nope." He grinned at her and she added, "I've never done anything like this before. It feels good to be a bit naughty."

"Yeah?" He tilted his head, studying her. "Any time you wanna get naughty, lady, you just let me know."

He was full of surprises. "You're not worried about how it might look to others?"

"You're worth the risk."

The things he said played havoc with her restraint. "I'll keep your offer in mind," she whispered as she opened the door, and they were both relieved to see the room was, indeed, empty.

Tomorrow, she decided, couldn't get here soon enough.

Cameron threw his suit coat over the arm of a chair, kicked his dress shoes into the closet and loosened his tie. All day long, his thoughts had centered on Asia. Damn, but she tasted better, felt better, than he'd imagined. He'd wanted to make love to her there in the closet with the two of them standing, a crowd in the outer room.

He closed his eyes a moment and imagined lifting her long skirt, feeling her grip his shoulders and hook her long slender legs around his waist. He pictured her head back, her eyes closed, her lips parted on a raw cry as he pushed into her.

She would be open, unable to meter the depth of his strokes, and he'd take her so long, so deeply, she'd scream with the pleasure of it. His stomach cramped with lust.

Better *not* to use the closet, he decided with a rueful

grin. He didn't want her stifled in any way, not after the two months he'd spent fantasizing about her. At first, it had been simple lust—she looked exactly as he thought a woman should look. Soft, sexy, capable, and her brown eyes were always bright with intelligence. She was friendly, but not flirtatious. Subtly sensual, with only her natural femininity on display. She didn't flaunt, didn't go out of her way to enhance her looks.

The more he'd gotten to know her, the more he'd wanted her. But she gave him only casual conversation, allowing him to view her generous spirit, her quick smiles and easy nature from an emotional distance. In the two months he'd known her, he'd absorbed all the small glimpses of her character, which had acted as more enticement. He not only wanted her sexually, he just plain wanted her.

Tomorrow night he'd have her.

He didn't know if he'd survive that long.

He tossed his tie onto the chair with his coat and reached into his pants pocket for the gift he'd bought her. He hadn't meant to go shopping, but on the drive home he'd stopped for a red light, and his eye had caught the festive Christmas display in a jewelry store window. Once he saw the bracelet, he wanted it for her.

For a first date, it was a bit extravagant, he thought, but what the hell. He'd known her two months now, necked with her in a closet, fantasized about her endlessly, and besides, he liked to think positive; he had a gut feeling that this would be the first date of many.

He could call it a Christmas gift. After all, he still had hopes of convincing her to spend the day with him.

The exotic burnished gold and topaz-studded bracelet reminded him of Asia's coloring. As he'd told her, she was far from plain. He put the bracelet back in the velvet-lined box and set it on his dresser, then put the spanking tape into the VCR. He picked up the remote and stretched out in his bed on top of the covers, two fat pillows behind his back, one arm folded behind his head.

He hit PLAY, and settled in to be educated.

As the story—*ha! what story?*—started, he thought of Asia and knew there wasn't much he wouldn't do to win her over. Including indulging in a little kinky sex.

Four

Cameron sat behind his desk, a spreadsheet on his computer screen, early the next morning. Steaming coffee filled the cold morning with delicious scents. The windows overlooking the parking lot were decorated with lacy frost, while more snowflakes, fat as cotton balls, drifted down to the sill. The quiet strains of Christmas music from the outer office drifted in.

The knock on the door jarred him and he looked up. "Come in."

Asia peered around the door, smiled at him and asked, "Are you busy?"

Without a single hesitation, he closed out the computer screen. "Not at all."

She inched in, looking furtive and so sexy, his abdomen clenched. Both hands behind her still holding the doorknob, she rested against the closed door. "I hoped you were in."

A glance at the clock showed him she'd come to work almost a half hour early. He'd been there for an hour himself. After watching the tape, he'd found it impossible to relax. He kept seeing Asia in every position depicted by the actors, and when he'd finally drifted off to sleep, he'd dreamed of her. Not since his teens had he awoken in a sweat, but last night he had.

Heart thumping and cock at full attention, Cameron eased out from behind his desk. "Is anything wrong?"

He searched her face, looking for clues to her thoughts.

If she planned to break their date for that night, he'd need to find a way to change her mind.

Her cheeks flushed and her beautiful eyes, locked on his, darkened to mahogany. "Do you mind if I lock this?" she asked, indicating the door.

Cameron stepped closer. "Please do."

The lock clicked like a thunderclap, echoing the sounds of his heartbeat. When she turned to face him again, Cameron murmured, "I'm glad to see you, Asia."

She folded her hands together at her waist. Her long brown hair hung loose, like a rich velvet curtain. The ends curled the tiniest bit, barely reaching the tips of her breasts, which were enticingly molded beneath a beige cashmere sweater. Her neutral-toned patterned skirt ended a mere inch below her knees and was trim enough to outline the shape of her thighs. Wearing flats, she just reached his chin, and she looked up at him.

"I thought maybe we could . . ." She stalled, shifted uncertainly.

His testicles drew tight and his cock flexed at the thought of touching and kissing her again. "Yes?"

She lifted one shoulder in a self-conscious shrug. "I liked kissing you yesterday."

"Liked? I'm surprised I didn't catch on fire." He smiled, trying to take some of the heavy desire from his words. He didn't want to scare her off. There were few people in the building yet. Most wouldn't show up for another twenty-five minutes. He had her all to himself. "I dreamed about you last night."

Her lips parted. "You did?"

Cameron couldn't stop himself from touching her. Using the backs of his knuckles, he smoothed a long tendril of hair—right over her breast. Her nipple puckered, and deliberately he rasped it, teasing her, teasing himself more. He heard the catch of her breath. Her eyes were closed, her chest rising and falling.

"Are you wearing a bra, Asia?" he asked, unable to detect one with his easy touch.

She shook her head. "A . . . a demi bra."

"Meaning your nipples," he murmured, lifting both hands to her, "are uncovered?"

Ah, yes, he could tell now as he caught each tip between his fingers and thumbs and pinched lightly. The cashmere sweater was incredibly soft and did nothing to conceal his touch. Her nipples were tight, pushed up by the bra, but not covered. He gently plucked and rolled and she suddenly grasped his wrists.

"I don't believe this," she moaned.

Cameron didn't remove his hands. She wasn't restraining him so much as holding onto him. He leaned close and nuzzled her temple. "This?" he asked, unsure of her meaning.

"I don't . . . I'm not usually . . ."

He had no idea what she wanted to tell him. "You like this?" He tugged at her nipples, making her sway toward him. Her breasts were very sensitive, he discovered, as heat throbbed beneath his skin.

"I do," she rasped, then dropped her head forward to his shoulder, panting. "I'm not usually so . . . so easy."

Cameron pressed his mouth to the delicate skin of her temple, then her cheekbone. "Easy? I've wanted you for two months." He drew the tender skin of her throat against his teeth, careful not to mark her. "I don't call that easy."

"No, but . . ." She sucked in a breath, then cried out. Her fingers clenched on his wrists and her hips pressed inward, trying to find him. "Cameron, I feel like I'm going to—"

Realization dawned, and he stared at her in wonder. "You want to climax, Asia?"

She didn't answer for the longest time while he continued to toy with her breasts, and she continued to writhe against him. "Oh, please," she finally gasped, nearly beside herself.

Cameron released her, ignoring her soft moan of disappointment, and put an arm around her waist. "C'mere," he said, almost blind with lust.

He led her to his desk. She looked at him with darkened eyes, a little unfocused, a lot hungry. "Just a second," he said and reached for her narrow skirt.

She made a slight sound of surprise when he worked the snug material up to her hips, then lifted her to sit on the edge of the desk. She looked up, a question in her eyes, but he stepped between her thighs and took her mouth, devouring her, his tongue licking, his teeth nipping.

She wrapped both arms around his neck and held on.

He hated panty hose, he thought, as he trailed his fingers up her nylon-clad thighs. Stockings that left her vulnerable to him would have been better, but he'd make do.

He teased her, kissing her while stroking the insides of her thighs until she was nearly frantic. Then he pressed his palm against her mound and they both went still.

"Mmmm," he whispered, his fingers pressing gently, exploring. "You're wet."

She ducked her face into his throat.

Blood roared in his ears, but he made himself move slow and easy. "I can even feel you through your panties and your hose."

"Oh, God." She lurched a little when he stroked over her with his middle finger. "This is awful."

He smiled. "You want me to quit?" he teased.

"Please don't!"

With her legs parted, the panties and panty hose couldn't hide her state of desire. He could feel every sweet inch of her, the curly pubic hair, the swollen lips. Her distended clitoris.

He groaned. With one arm around her holding her

tight, he used the other hand to pet and finger and tease. Her hips shifted, rolled against him. "Is this good, Asia?" he asked, wanting, needing to know if it was enough.

Her head tipped back, lips parted on her panting breaths, her body arched—and then she broke.

Her eyes squeezed shut, her teeth sank into her bottom lip to hold back the moans coming from deep in her throat.

Cameron felt like a world conqueror, watching her beautiful, carnal expressions, feeling the harsh trembling in her body.

"Yes," he murmured, keeping his touch steady, even, despite her frantic movements and the mad dashing of his heart. "That's it, sweetheart. That's it."

By slow degrees, she stilled, her body going boneless. Cameron gathered her close into his arms and held her. His own desire was keen, but at the same time, he felt a heady satisfaction. She smelled warm, a little sweaty despite the frigid winter storm outside and the nip of the air in his office. And she smelled female, the scent guaranteed to fire his blood.

He rocked her gently and smoothed his big hands up and down her narrow back.

Against his throat, she whispered, "I think I'm embarrassed."

"You think?" He couldn't help but chuckle, he felt so damn good. Sexually frustrated, but emotionally sated. "Please don't be. I'm not."

"This was . . . unfair of me."

"This was very generous of you."

That left her speechless. Cameron tangled one hand in her silky hair and tipped her head up to him so he could see her face. "Thank you."

She laughed, groaned and dropped her forehead to his sternum. "I can't wait until tonight, Cameron. I didn't believe it at first, but I know it's going to be so good."

What did she mean, she hadn't believed it at first? Then the rest of what she said hit him and he stilled. "You intend to make love with me tonight?" He had hoped and planned, but he hadn't expected a confirmation.

She looked up in surprise. "You want to, don't you?"

Bemused, he said, "More than I want my next breath."

Her smile was a beautiful thing. "I'm sorry about doing this now. I'd only meant a few more kisses—more of that naughtiness we'd joked about. But then you . . . you touched me and I lost it."

"I'm not sorry, so don't you be, either. I'm glad you're so sensitive, so hot."

She looked down at his tie. "I didn't know I was." Then, "I never was before." She met his gaze with a look of confusion. "I think it's just you."

Cameron didn't bother denying that. He couldn't think of a woman hotter than Asia Michaels. But he'd be damned if he'd explain it wasn't him, taking a chance that she'd find another guy. No way.

"Tonight will be even better," she said, then peeked up at him as if waiting for his reply.

Was this his cue that tonight he was supposed to do something different? Something more . . . forceful? He said, his tone filled with caution, "I want you to be satisfied with me, Asia."

Her eyes brightened, and she threw her arms around his throat again, nearly strangling him. "Thank you." Leaning back, she added with sincerity, "I really am sorry to do this, to leave you . . . unsatisfied. But I never suspected it'd go this far."

He kissed the end of her nose and said, "I'll think of it as extended foreplay."

His phone rang just as she pulled away and began straightening her skirt. Her cheeks were rosy, her eyes slumberous and sated. Watching her, regretting the necessity that kept her beautiful legs hidden from him, Cameron hit a button and said absently, "Yes?"

"You asked that I remind you about the meeting first thing this morning, Mr. Cameron."

"Thank you, Marsha."

He disconnected the line. Marsha was a secretary for the entire floor, which included four supervisors. She kept everyone punctual and was observant as hell.

He looked at Asia. "Do you mind if Marsha knows we're seeing each other?"

She shook her head. "Do you?"

His grin turned wolfish as he stepped past her to unlock and open the door. No one was in the hallway to notice, and for that he was grateful. He wouldn't tolerate gossip about Asia.

"I want everyone to know," he told her, and turned to face her again with a smile. "Maybe it'll keep the rest of the men from pursuing you."

"The guys here?" she asked, and scoffed. "They all know I'm not interested."

"But you are," he reminded her, looking at her breasts, her belly and thighs. "You're interested in *me*."

He waited for her to deny it, but all she did was shrug. "It's strange. You affect me differently."

He sauntered toward her, filled with confidence. "I make you hot."

She looked perplexed as hell when she said, "Yeah."

Cameron shook his head. It had taken her two months to notice the sexual chemistry he'd picked up on within two minutes of meeting her. If it hadn't been for the damned porn shop just opening, she still wouldn't have given him the time of day. He couldn't forget that. Asia with her big bedroom eyes and standoffish ways had a sexual predilection, and last night he'd watched the tape and learned how to appease her.

Her preferences were still foreign to him, but less unappealing. Some of the scenes, in fact, had really turned him on. He'd imagined Asia in place of the overblown actress. He pictured her firm, lush bottom turned up to the warm smacks of a large male hand—*his hand.* The smacking part didn't interest him much, even though the swats had done little more than redden her bottom, and ultimately prepare her for a hard ride.

But the touching afterward, the utter vulnerability and accessibility of the woman's sex to probing fingers and tongue had made him hot as hell. The actress had remained in the submissive position, bent over a foot-stool, hands flat on the floor, knees spread wide, and in Cameron's mind it had been Asia, waiting for him, ready for him.

He sucked in a deep breath, drawing Asia's notice.

Her eyes were again apologetic when she asked, "Are you okay?"

"Other than being hard as a spike, yes."

She smiled. "That might make your meeting difficult."

Cameron took her arm and led her toward the door. "Once you're gone I'll get myself in order. That is, if I can stop thinking about tonight."

The hallway was still clear, not a soul in sight. Memory of the movie still played in his mind, and when Asia turned away, he gave her rump a sound smack. She jumped, whirled to face him with both hands holding her behind and her eyes enormous.

Cameron forced himself to a neutral smile, though the look on her face was priceless, a mixture of surprise and awareness. "I'll see you tonight," he said.

Frowning, rubbing her backside, she gave an absent nod and hurried away.

His palm stung a little, and his cock throbbed. He could do this, he told himself as he went to his desk to gather the necessary files. And if he did it well enough, he'd be able to reel her in.

He wanted Asia Michaels, and one way or another, he'd have her.

***

Asia thought about that rather stinging smack throughout the day. It meant nothing, she told herself, just teasing gone a little overboard. Cameron had been so gentle, so concerned for her and her pleasure, that she trusted him.

But she'd left his office and gone straight to the restroom. After their little rendezvous, she needed to tidy up. And she couldn't stop herself from peeking once she had her panty hose down in the private stall.

Sure enough, Cameron's large handprint, faintly pink and still warm, showed on her white bottom. The sight of that handprint made her heart race with misgivings . . . and something more.

Long after she'd returned to her desk, she'd been aware of the warmth on her cheek, the tingling of that print. It kept Cameron and what they'd done in his office in the forefront of her mind throughout the entire day. She could not stop thinking about him, about the pleasure he'd given her so easily when that type of pleasure had always eluded her. She couldn't put his thoughtfulness or tenderness from her mind.

And she couldn't forget that swat.

As she dressed for the date that night, she again surveyed her bottom. But the mark was long gone, with only the memory remaining. It meant nothing, she told herself yet again, but still her heartbeat sped up whenever she thought of it.

Cameron was right on time. The second she opened her door, he leaned in and kissed her. Snowflakes hung in his dark hair and dusted the shoulders of his black coat. He'd dressed in casual slacks, a dress shirt and sweater.

Asia waited for the verdict as he looked her over from head to toe. Her dress was new, a dark burgundy with gold flecks around the low-scooped neckline and shin-length hem. She wore dark brown leather boots with two-inch heels. Her long hair was in a French braid, hanging down the middle of her back, and gold hoop earrings decorated her ears.

"You look incredible," Cameron murmured, then pulled her close and kissed her again, this time with purpose.

Asia quivered with need. When her mouth was again free, she said, "Maybe . . . maybe we should skip dinner?" She didn't want to eat. She wanted to be alone with Cameron, to find out the extent of these amazing sexual feelings he inspired.

She'd told Erica at a break that she owed her big-time, because if it hadn't been for her, she'd never have discovered the truth. As she'd always suspected, fireworks did exist. You only needed the right man to set them off.

Cameron was evidently the right man.

He took her hand and kissed her palm. She felt the brief touch of his warm, damp tongue and nearly moaned. "Do you need to be up early tomorrow?" he asked.

"No, my weekends are always free."

He took her cloak from her and helped her slip it on. "I hope they won't be free anymore."

Asia had nothing to say to that. She couldn't deny that she wanted to see him again.

"I'll feed you," Cameron continued, "and then we'll go to my place."

She sniffed and turned away, a little put out that he seemed less anxious than she.

Cameron hugged her from behind, chuckling softly. In her ear, he whispered, "The tension will build and build, sweetheart. Just be patient with me, okay?"

She didn't want to be patient, but she figured he had to know more about this than she did. Her experience with sex was that it wasn't much fun most of the time, and other times it was just plain awful.

"All right."

An hour later, Asia was ready to kill him. The restaurant where they had dinner was elegant, expensive and crowded. Festive Christmas music played softly through the speaker system, and fat gold candles, decorated with holly, lit each table.

People talked and smiled and laughed, and Asia felt conspicuous, as if everyone there knew she was aroused, but was too polite to point at her.

Cameron kept her on that keen edge, touching her constantly, her cheek, her chin, her shoulders—touches that seemed innocent but still made her burn because she knew exactly what he could do with those touches, how he could make her body scream in incredible pleasure.

What would it be like when he pushed deep inside her, when he rode her and the friction was within as well as without? She bit her lip hard to keep from gasping aloud with her thoughts.

And still she couldn't stop thinking them.

Feeling his touch through the barrier of clothes had been indescribable, but when he touched naked flesh, would she be able to stand it? When it was his mouth on her nipples, not just his fingers, how much more would she experience? She shuddered at the thought and felt her body turning liquid.

They danced twice, and the way he moved against her should have been illegal. He *knew* what he did to her, and he enjoyed it.

She was on fire, her breath coming too fast and too deep, and still he lingered at the table, watching her closely, talking idly about inconsequential things. Her heart threatened to burst, and though the wind howled outside, she felt feverish and taut.

"Asia?"

She jumped, nearly panicked by the unfamiliar lust and anticipation. She stared at him blankly.

Cameron just smiled. "I asked you where you got your name."

She squeezed her hands together, trying to concentrate

on things other than the way his dark hair fell over his brow, or how his strong jaw moved as he spoke, or the warm male scent of him that made her stomach curl deliciously. His large hands rested on the tabletop, his wrists thick, his fingers long and rough-tipped—fingers that had touched and teased her. Fingers that would be inside her body tonight.

She closed her eyes, remembering.

Cameron smoothed a curl behind her ear, and his voice was rough and low. "Tell me how you got that name, honey."

She swallowed down her growing excitement. "My grandmother's name was Anastasia. My father wanted to name me after her, but my mother thought the name too long."

"So they shortened it to Asia?"

"Yes." Talking required too much concentration.

"It's a beautiful name." His fingertips drifted over her cheek, down her throat, trailed along the neckline of her dress.

She gasped. "Cameron . . ."

"Are you ready to go?" he asked, even as he stood and pulled out her chair.

"More than ready," she muttered. While he tended to the bill, Asia pulled on her wrap and turned to leave. Cameron caught her arm before she'd taken three steps.

They walked in silence to his car. The parking garage was freezing cold and her accelerated breath frosted in the air. Cameron saw her seated, then went around to his side of the car.

They were on the road, only minutes from his apartment, before he asked, "You're not nervous, are you?"

Asia stared at him. She was so beyond nervous, it was all she could do to keep from jumping him. "I'm so excited I can barely stand it."

He kept his profile to her, but that didn't diminish the

beauty of his masculine satisfaction. "Good. I want you excited."

Asia thrust her chin into the air. "I want you excited, too."

Without looking her way, he reached across the seat and caught her arm. His hand trailed down to her wrist, then lifted her fingers into his lap. She inhaled sharply at the well-defined, pulsing erection.

"Believe me, I'm excited," he said simply.

Rather than release him when he replaced his hand on the steering wheel, Asia scooted closer. He was a large man, his sex strong and long. She traced him through his trousers, glancing at his face occasionally to see his jaw locking hard, his nostrils flaring. His blue eyes looked very dark, frighteningly intense.

His penis flexed in her grasp, and she tightened her hold. She stroked him with her thumb, forcing the material of his slacks to rub against him. Her thumb moved up and over the head of his penis—and just that quickly, he grabbed her hand and forced it away.

"No," he said harshly, but without anger. "I won't be able to keep us on the road if you do that."

"When we get to your place," she murmured, understanding now why he enjoyed teasing, because she enjoyed it too, "I'll do that to you again. Only you'll be naked."

Cameron gripped the wheel hard, his mouth open as he sucked in air. "I'll hold you to that, sweetheart." And then he turned in toward his apartment complex.

Five

Cameron kissed her as he opened her car door, kissed her in the parking lot and on the stairs up to his apartment. He couldn't seem to stop kissing her and she didn't try to make him.

Getting his door unlocked was no easy feat with Asia smoothing her soft little hands all over his body, her mouth open on his throat, her fingertips gliding down his abdomen.

He tugged her inside, slammed the door, and fell with her onto the couch. He felt like a caveman, but his control was shot to hell; he'd teased too long.

She shifted around until she laid atop him. "Cameron," she muttered, and then kissed his face, his ear, his jaw.

He caught her, holding her steady so he could devour her sweet mouth. They moved together, hampered by coats and too many clothes and an urgent desire that obliterated reason.

"Damn," he growled, startled as he felt himself sliding off the couch to the floor.

They landed with a thump. He was dumbstruck for a moment, then heard Asia giggle.

"Witch," he groused low, and sat up beside her. He yanked at the fastenings of her cloak and spread it wide. Her breasts heaved, her legs moved restlessly. Cameron lowered himself again, this time with both hands cupping her breasts.

The air filled with their moans and sighs, but again, it

became too frustrating. He didn't want to stop kissing her, but he stood up and jerked his coat off, tossing it aside, then pulled his sweater over his head.

Asia stayed on the floor, sprawled wantonly, watching him. When his chest was bare and her eyes were soft and wide, looking at him, he knelt and began removing her boots. "These are sexy," he said low, tugging them off and eyeing her bare legs beneath. His gaze sought hers and he raised one brow. "No panty hose this time?"

She shook her head. Silky fine tendrils of hair had escaped her braid and framed her face. Her lashes hung heavy, her eyes nearly black with lust. "I wanted to make it easier for you to touch me."

Her words were powerfully arousing. In a rush, he plunged his hands up under her skirt and caught the waistband of her minuscule panties. He started to drag them off her, but seeing her face, the anticipation there, he forced himself to slow down.

He had to remember that Asia had special requirements, a refined inclination toward erotic discipline, and if he wanted to keep her for more than a night or two, he had to adjust. Her pleasure meant everything to him, was half of his own pleasure, so he slowed himself. Instead of pulling her panties off, he cupped her through the thin silk.

"Hot, swollen," he said, watching her back arch. "You want me, don't you sweetheart?"

"Yes," she moaned, her eyes now closing.

He petted her, letting one long finger press between her lips, rub gently over her clitoris.

"Oh, God," she whispered brokenly.

Watching her was almost as good as sex, Cameron decided. She was so beautiful to him, so perfect. So open and honest and giving.

He removed his hand and flipped her onto her stomach.

She froze for a heartbeat, her hands flat on the carpet at either side of her breasts. "Cameron?"

"Let me get this dress off you," he explained, and worked the zipper down her back. The bodice opened and he caught the shoulders, pulling them down to her elbows. She freed her right arm, then her left.

Kneeling between her widespread thighs, Cameron eyed her slender back, the graceful line of her spine. In a rush, he pulled the dress the rest of the way off.

Asia half raised herself, but he pressed a hand to the small of her back and took his time looking at her. Her bottom was plump, her cheeks rounded and firm. He stroked her with both hands, feeling the slide of silken panties over her skin.

"Cameron . . ."

"Shhh." He unfastened her bra and let it fall, freeing her breasts. Leaning over her, his cock nestled securely against that delectable ass, he balanced on one arm. With his free hand he reached beneath her and stroked her breasts, paying special attention to her pointed, sensitized nipples. She gave a ragged moan.

Cameron languidly rubbed himself against her, almost blind with need. It would be so easy to enter her this way. She was wet, hot and slippery and he could sink right in.

He groaned and pushed himself away. He had to do this right.

Before he changed his mind, he kicked off his shoes, sat on the edge of the couch, and pulled off his socks.

Asia was near his feet and she turned her head to look at him curiously. Their eyes met and she started to rise.

Cameron caught her under her arms. Her bra fell completely off, and it stunned him, this first glimpse at her bared body. She wore only transparent, insubstantial panties; they offered her no protection at all.

"You are so beautiful," he said with complete inadequacy.

She smiled shyly, reached for him—and he pulled her across his knees.

For a brief moment, she froze. "Cameron?"

When he didn't answer, determined on his course, Asia twisted to look at him. He controlled her easily, his gaze focused solely on that gorgeous behind. He could see the deep cleft, and the dark triangle of feminine curls covering her mound. He traced her with a fingertip, down the line of her buttocks, in between. She stilled, her breathing suspended.

Her panties were damp with her excitement and he pressed into her, feeling her heat, her swollen lips. His eyes closed. He wanted to taste her, wanted to tongue her and hear her soft cries. Her hands, braced on his thigh, tightened, her nails digging into his muscles even through his slacks.

He had to do this right.

Teeth clenched, Cameron opened his eyes, looked at his big dark hand on her very soft feminine bottom, and forced himself to give her a stinging slap.

She yelped.

"How does that feel?" he rasped, lifting his hand for another.

Asia was frozen on his thighs, not moving, not speaking.

He brought his hand down again, doing his best to meter his strength, to let her feel the warmth of the smack without actually hurting her in any way.

His heart thundered and his pulse roared in his ears. He thought he might split his pants he was so turned on, despite the distaste he felt in striking her. After all, they were minutes away from making love and she was a warm, womanly scented weight over his lap, all but naked and so beautiful—

"You bastard!"

Like a wild woman, she launched herself away from him. Stupefied, Cameron looked at her sprawled on the carpet some feet away, her naked breasts heaving, her eyes wet with tears.

Tears!

Her bottom lip trembled and she said with stark accusation, "I thought you were different!"

Very unsure of himself and the situation, Cameron said, "Uh . . ." And then, "I'm . . . trying to be."

"You hit me!"

He had. Cameron looked at his hand, stinging a little from contact with that beautiful behind, and said again, "Uh . . ."

Asia pushed to her feet. Her breasts swayed, full and still flushed from arousal, the nipples tight points. Feet planted apart in a stance guaranteed to make his blood race, she glared at him.

Slowly, very slowly so he didn't spook her or make this bizarre situation worse, Cameron came to his feet. "You wanted me to," he reminded her.

Her eyes widened even more. "What are you talking about?"

He shrugged, gestured toward his bedroom where the damning tape was still in the VCR. He rubbed the back of his neck and felt a sick foreboding close around him. "You, ah, wanted a guy who was into spanking."

She gasped so hard her breasts jiggled, further exacerbating his desire. "You *listened*!" she accused.

"Not on purpose."

It was as if she hadn't heard him. "You were the guy with the newspaper in the lounge. The guy wearing jeans!"

"Yeah. I, ah, had to work outside that day, to oversee work on the compressors, so my clothes were different." He nearly winced as he admitted that, then thought to add, a bit righteous, "The lounge is a public place and I heard you say plain as day that you were into spanking."

"I said no such thing!"

"Yes, you did." Didn't she? Her face was red, but he

barely noticed with her standing there, the body he'd been dreaming about for two full months more bare than not. "You said you would hook up with the guy who bought a spanking tape. Well, I bought the stupid thing."

"Stupid thing?" she growled, and advanced toward him. "You mean you don't watch them?"

"I never had before." He was mightily distracted from the argument by the way she moved, and how her body moved, and how much he wanted her. "But I'd have bought a tape of monkeys mating if that's what it took to get your attention."

She drew up short, a mere foot away from him. "That's sick!"

Cameron leaned forward, his own temper igniting. "No, sweetheart. That's desperation. I wanted you. You barely acknowledged me, except in that too cool, distantly polite voice that kept miles between us. I heard you in the lounge and took advantage. So what?"

She looked slightly confused for a moment, then pugnacious. "You struck me."

"Because I thought you wanted me to. Hell, do you think *I* wanted to?"

"Didn't you?" She gave a pointed stare to his straining erection.

Cameron grunted. "You're almost naked. You're excited and wet and hot, and I've been hard since the day I first saw you."

She blinked uncertainly. "You're saying you didn't want to swat me?"

Hands on his hips, he leaned down, nose to nose with her. "There are a lot of things I'd rather do to your beautiful naked ass than spank it."

She half turned away, then back. Watching him with suspicion, and what appeared to be sensual curiosity, she asked, "Like what?"

Cameron took a small step forward, further closing

the gap between them. In a lower, more controlled but gravelly voice, he said, "Like pet you, and kiss you—"

"My behind?"

"Hell, yes." Moving slowly, he reached out and caught her shoulders. "I can't imagine any man alive not wanting to kiss your behind."

She giggled at the wording, but flushed at the meaning. "My husband would have never considered . . ."

He released her so fast, he almost tripped. "Husband?"

"Ex-husband."

Clutching his heart, Cameron said, "Thank God." It took him a second to recover from that panic. He hadn't heard anything about her being married. "So you're divorced?"

"Yes."

"You still care about him?"

She laughed, which was a better answer than a straight out "no," but she gave him that too.

"I stopped caring about him almost as soon as I said, 'I do.' Unfortunately, it took longer than that for me to admit it to everyone else and to get the divorce."

He didn't want to talk about any idiot ex-husband. Holding her shoulders again, he said, "Know what I want to do?"

Her hand lifted to his crotch, cuddled his cock warmly. Her smile was sweet and enticing. "I can maybe guess."

He drew a deep breath. "You're willing?"

"No more hitting?"

Cameron kissed her. "It took all my concentration to get it done the first time. Believe me, it was for you, for what I thought you wanted. Not for me."

She looked touched by his gesture. "Then, yes, I'm willing."

Disinclined to take the chance that she might change her mind, Cameron lifted her in his arms and started for his bedroom. "I promise to make it up to you," he said.

And he meant it. Now that he could think clearly, he'd know to concentrate on her responses, not on the dumb conversation he'd overheard. But that made him think of something else.

"Can I ask you a question?"

"That is a question," Asia replied, but she didn't sound put out. She was too engrossed in his chest, caressing his chest hair, finding his nipples and flicking them with her thumbnail until his knees nearly buckled.

Cameron quickly sat on the edge of the bed, Asia braced in his arms. He kissed her, then against her mouth asked, "Why did you require I buy that stupid tape?"

She tucked her face into his throat while she explained her theories—dumb ones, Cameron thought privately—and when she'd finished, she looked up at him.

"My ex-husband was forever trying to force me to do . . . kinky things that turned him on. He said it was the only way I could satisfy him. I didn't like it, and then he'd be angry about it and call me a prude and a cold fish. I used to wish he'd get his jollies that way with a movie or a book." She shrugged. "I wanted us to just make love, like two people who . . ."

Cameron squeezed her, wishing he had her damned ex close at hand so he could offer her retribution. But all he could do was say, "Like two people who loved each other?"

She gave a tiny nod. "Yes." Then she shocked the hell out of him by adding, "I haven't been with anyone since him. I needed to prove to myself first that I was independent, that I didn't believe all his garbage about me not being woman enough. He made me feel so low, and in my head, I knew he was a jerk. I knew he was wrong, too. But no man tempted me."

"Not even me," Cameron admitted, more for himself than her. He'd gained a lot of insight tonight, and most of it broke his heart. He'd handled things all wrong. Asia hadn't wanted him. She hadn't wanted any man.

She'd only needed validation, and instead he'd shot down her beliefs by spanking her. Damn, he was a real idiot.

Asia touched his jaw. "That's not true." She bit her lip, then let out a breath. "I think if it had been anyone other than you in that store, I wouldn't have had the guts to go through with it. But it was you, and I liked you already, and respected you a lot."

"You hid it well," he teased, shaken with relief.

"That's because I wanted you, too, though I was afraid to admit it. It scared me to want someone again."

With a trembling hand, Cameron stroked her throat, her shoulder, her breasts. "Let me show you that there's nothing to be afraid of, sweetheart. Let me show you how it should be." *How it'll always be between us.*

"Yes." Asia closed her eyes on a soft moan. "I think I'd like that."

Like a lick of fire, Cameron's kisses burned her everywhere. With incredible gentleness, he tilted her back on the bed and half covered her. She loved the tingling abrasion of his chest hair over her sensitive nipples. She loved the exciting, not-so-gentle stroke of his hand on her body. He seemed to know exactly how and where to touch her. And he found sensitive places she hadn't known about—the delicate skin beneath her ears, her underarms, below her breasts, the insides of her thighs and backs of her knees.

He kissed her, but not where she wanted his mouth most. Her breasts ached for him, her nipples so tight they throbbed with need, but he kissed around them, his tongue flicking out, leaving damp patches on her heated skin. He kissed her belly, tongued her navel until she squirmed, then put tiny pecks all around her sex, not touching her, but she heard him breathing deeply, inhaling her musky scent with appreciation.

She moaned, then caught her breath as he turned her onto her stomach.

"Easy," he whispered, his mouth brushing over her shoulders, down the length of her spine. He caught her panties and stripped them off. Through dazed eyes, Asia looked over her shoulder and saw him lift them to his face and inhale deeply. He gave a rough, growling groan of appreciation, and when his gaze met hers, his blue eyes burned like the hottest fire.

As promised, he kissed her bottom, especially the pink handprint on her left cheek. He murmured words of apology but she barely heard them because his hand slipped between her thighs. His long fingers just barely touched her, teasing and taunting while his mouth continued, so very gentle, so careful.

She couldn't hold still. She pressed her face into the bedclothes and squirmed. *"Cameron."*

He turned her over again, and this time when his fingers went between her thighs he parted her and pressed his middle finger deep.

Her hips lifted sharply off the mattress and she cried out.

"Asia," he whispered huskily. "Baby, I want to watch you come again."

Oh, God, she thought, almost frantic with need. How was she supposed to answer that demand?

He didn't give her a chance to worry about it. He lowered his head and sucked her nipple into the moist heat of his mouth. His tongue curled around her and he drew on her, even as his finger began sliding in and out.

She moaned and gasped and clutched at the sheets on his bed. Cameron switched to her other breast, licking, plucking with his lips. She braced herself, but he took her by surprise with his teeth, catching her tender nipple and tugging insistently.

"Oh, God."

"Open up for me, Asia," he whispered, and worked another finger into her. "Damn, you're snug."

He had large hands, she thought wildly, feeling herself stretched taut, but with his tongue licking her nipple she didn't have time to worry about it. He kept moving his hand, deep, harder, and the rough pad of his thumb pressed to her clitoris, giving a friction so sweet she screamed. Her muscles clamped down on the invading, sliding fingers and she shook with an orgasm so powerful she went nearly insensate.

When she was able to breathe again, she realized Cameron had moved and now had his head resting low on her belly, his arm around her upper thighs. With a lot of concentration, she lifted a hand and threaded her fingers through the cool silk of his dark hair. "That was . . ." Words were beyond her. How could she describe such a remarkable thing?

"Very nice," he answered, and she felt his breath on her still-hot vulva. Her legs were obscenely sprawled, she realized, but when she started to close them, he shushed her and petted her back into the position he wanted.

He turned his face inward and kissed her belly, then pressed his cheek to her pubic hair. "I love your scent," he growled, and Asia knew his arousal was razor sharp, that once again he'd skipped his own pleasure for her.

"Cameron," she chided gently, and some insidious emotion too much like love, squeezed at her heart. He kept saying her name, giving to her, pleasing her. He didn't take her for granted. She wasn't just an available woman. He wanted *her.*

"Bend your knees for me, love," he said.

Asia blushed at just the thought, and the pleasure of being called "love." She shifted her legs slightly farther apart.

He pulled them wider, bent her knees for her. He stroked his fingers through her curls, tweaked one, smoothed another. "You're beautiful," he said, looking at her too closely. "All pink and wet and swollen. For me."

She tipped her head back, staring at the ceiling and trying not to groan. But she was fully exposed to him, overly sensitive from her recent release, and it was unbearably erotic even while mortification washed over her.

Cameron repositioned himself directly between her thighs, urging them wider still so that they accommodated his broad shoulders. Using his thumbs, he opened her even more and just when she thought she couldn't bear it another second, he lowered his head and his rough velvet tongue lapped the length of her, up to but not quite touching her clitoris.

Her hips rose sharply off the bed as her back bowed and the breath in her lungs escaped in a rush. *"Cameron."*

He licked again, and again. His mouth was scalding, his tongue rasping against already aroused tissues. Asia gripped the sheets, trying to anchor herself, trying to keep still, but she strained against him, wanting and needing more.

He teased and tasted her everywhere except where she most wanted to feel the tantalizing flick of his tongue. "Please," she barely whispered.

And with a soft groan, he drew her in, suckling at her clitoris, nipping with his teeth. Asia moaned with the unbelievable pleasure of it, her entire body drawing tight and then melting on wave after wave of sensation.

She didn't know she'd cried until she felt Cameron kissing the tears from her cheeks, murmuring softly, reassuringly—and sinking deep into her body with a low, long groan.

"Oh," she said, and got her eyes to open.

"Hi," he whispered, withdrawing inch by inch, and then pressing in again. He filled her up, stretched her already sensitive vulva unbearably, and the friction was incredible.

Dark color slashed his cheekbones and his blue eyes burned with an inner fire, intense and wild and tender.

"You're making love to me," she said, awed and a little overwhelmed because she'd thought her body was spent, as boneless as oatmeal. Yet she couldn't stop herself from countering his every move.

"I'm making love *with* you," he corrected.

"But I'm not doing anything," she said, thinking of all the ways she should have kissed him and touched him in turn.

His beautiful smile made her heart do flip-flops. "You're you— that's all you need to do."

"Cameron." She lifted limp arms to wrap around his neck and squeeze him tight. He kissed her lax mouth, and she felt his smile and kissed him back.

After a minute or two of that, she felt the need to shift and did, only to find the one position that really gratified was wrapping her legs around his waist.

He groaned, then drove a tiny bit harder, farther into her, until it was both an awesome pleasure and a small pain, a joining so complete that she was a part of him, and he of her.

She answered his groan with a gasp, her hips lifting into his, urging him on.

"That's it," he said, and cupped her buttocks in his hands, working her against him, his face a fierce study of concentration.

Incredibly, the feelings began to well again, taking her by surprise with the suddenness of it. "It can't be," she said.

And he said, "Hell, yes," and started driving fast and deep and faster still.

Asia tightened her hold on him, overwhelmed with it all as she experienced yet one more orgasm, this one deeper, slower, longer, not as cataclysmic, but still so sweetly satisfying she wanted to shout aloud with the pleasure of it.

No sooner did she relax than Cameron rubbed his face into her throat and began his own orgasm. She heard his rumbling growl start low in his chest, felt the fierce pounding of his heart, the light sweat on his back and the heat that poured off his naked body.

"Asia," he groaned, and his body shuddered heavily, then collapsed on hers.

Too lethargic to move, Asia managed a pucker to kiss his ear, then dozed off.

Ten minutes later, Cameron levered himself up to look at her. She snored softly, making him grin like the village idiot, and she looked beautiful, melting his heart. *Mine,* he thought with a surge of possessiveness that took him by surprise. Asia Michaels was his, in every sense of the word.

As gently as possible, he disengaged their bodies and removed the condom. He doubted she'd even noticed when he'd rolled it on, she'd been so spent. Smiling, he located the sheet at the foot of the bed. Asia stirred, rolling to her side and curling up tight from the chill of the air.

The lights were still on and he could see the fading imprint of his hand on her soft bottom. He closed his eyes, wanting to groan but not wanting to awaken her. What an ass he'd been.

Tomorrow they'd talk more, he'd tell her how he felt and give her the bracelet, and with any luck at all, she'd understand.

He reached over and flipped off the lights. She turned toward him, snuggled close, and resumed snoring.

Oh, yeah, she was his all right. Now he just had to let her know that.

Six

Asia stirred, smiling even before her eyes were open, and feeling good—achy but good—all the way down to her toes. Cameron O'Reilly. Wow. The man really knew how to make love.

She rolled to her side and reached for him, but found only cold sheets. Jerking up in an instant, she looked around, but he was gone. Her discarded clothes from the night before were now neatly folded over a chair, waiting, it seemed, for her to get dressed.

The blankets, which had been irreparably tossed during their lovemaking, were now straightened and smoothed over her, keeping her warm.

She looked out the wide window and saw snow and more snow, and a sun so bright it hurt her eyes.

She groaned. It was two days till Christmas Eve. Of course, the man had things to do, yet she'd slept in. In his bed. Inconveniencing him.

Humiliation rolled over her. Some independent broad she turned out to be. She'd spent the night when she hadn't even been invited. What must he think? Was he wondering how to get rid of her?

She'd just shoved the covers aside and slipped one naked leg off of the bed, shivering at the touch of cool air on her bare skin, when Cameron opened the door. He paused, standing there in nothing more than unsnapped jeans and a healthy beard shadow. His blue eyes were sharp and watchful.

As if shaking himself, he continued into the room and said, "Good morning."

Asia didn't want to meet his gaze, but she refused to be a coward. Attempting a smile, she said, "Give me a minute to get dressed and I'll get out of your way."

Strange after the night of incredible, uninhibited sex, but she suddenly felt naked. Cameron didn't help, staring at her with blatant sexual interest. She could use the sheet from the bed, but again, that seemed cowardly. She had no modesty left, not with this man.

"I'm cooking breakfast," he said. "I was hoping you'd stay and eat with me."

She held her dress in her hands. It was tangled, the sleeves inside out, and wrinkled almost beyond repair. She stared at it stupidly, not even sure where to start.

Cameron pushed away from the dresser and took the dress, tossing it aside. He retrieved a flannel robe from his closet and held it out to her.

Not seeing too many options, especially since her brain refused to function in any normal capacity, Asia slipped her arms into the robe. Cameron wrapped it around her, tied the belt and rolled up the sleeves.

"It makes me hot," he said, "to see you in my things."

Asia stared at him. Her mouth opened, but nothing came out.

"Almost as hot," he continued when she stayed mute, "as it made me to wake up this morning with you in my bed, warm and soft." He touched her cheek. "I could wake up like this a lot, Asia."

Thrown for an emotional loop, she started to turn away, but Cameron caught her arm and led her out of the room. "I'm fixing bacon and I don't want it to burn."

His apartment was slightly smaller than hers, with a kitchen-dinette combination. Asia sat at the thick pine table and watched Cameron complete the meal. Barefoot and bare-chested, he moved around the small kitchen with domestic ease. Her ex-husband had never cooked. He didn't even know how to boil water.

Cameron's hair was still disheveled, hanging over his brow with a rakish appeal. Muscles flexed in his shoulders and arms and down his back as he bent this way and that, turning bacon, pouring juice, as he turned to wink at her occasionally, or smile, or just gaze.

He asked her if fried eggs were okay, and how she liked her toast.

Asia answered more by rote than anything else. With the memories of the night, and Cameron in the kitchen looking sexy as the original sin, food was the farthest thing from her mind. But when he set her plate in front of her, she dug in.

And he watched her eat, smiling like a contented fool, his big bare feet were on either side of hers.

Finally, she laid her fork aside. Nothing had happened quite as she'd expected and she felt lost. "What," she grouched, "are you staring at?"

His smile widened. "You." He reached out and smoothed her hair, his fingers lingering. "I've never seen a woman with smudged makeup and tangled hair look quite so sexy."

His compliment put her over the edge. She shoved her chair back and stood up.

Cameron came to his feet, too. They stared at each other over the table, facing off.

Asia drew a deep breath. "This is ridiculous."

"I know. There's so much I want to say to you, but I'm not sure where to start."

She blinked, then covered her ears. "Stop it! Just stop . . . taking me by surprise."

Holding her gaze, Cameron rounded the table until he could clasp her wrists and pull her hands down. "I want to see you again, Asia."

"You mean you want to have sex with me again."

"Hell, yes. I want you right now. I wanted you the second I woke up. I'll want you tonight and tomorrow too."

She laughed, a near hysterical sound. "Will you stop?"

"No." Shaking his head, he said, "Not until you tell me how you feel."

"I feel . . ." She wasn't at all sure how she felt, and gestured helplessly. "Frustrated."

Cameron stroked her arms, bending to look her in the eyes. "I didn't satisfy you last night?"

Her laugh this time was genuine. "You did! Ohmigod, did you satisfy me."

"Well, then . . . ?"

"Cameron." She pulled away. She couldn't think, and she sure as hell couldn't talk, when he touched her. "This was all a . . . lark. You overheard my ridiculous pact with Erica and Becky, and because of that, you reacted and we had . . . better sex than I knew existed."

Cameron's jaw locked, but he kept quiet, letting her talk.

She drew another breath to fortify herself. "But that's all it is, all it was meant to be. You didn't intend for me to spend the night and intrude on your life."

"Are you done?"

He sounded angry, confusing her more. "Yes."

He went to the kitchen windowsill and lifted a small package wrapped in silver foil paper and tied with a bright red ribbon. "Everything you just said is bullshit and you know it. I've wanted you since the day I met you. And yes, it started out purely sexual, and it'll always be partly sexual. You turn me on, Asia, no way to deny that when I get a boner just hearing your name. But I like you a lot, too. Hell," he said, rubbing his neck the way he always did when he was annoyed, "I'm damn near obsessed with you."

Asia bit her lip, doing her best to keep her eyes off that gaily wrapped gift.

"I want you. It makes me nuts to think about any other

guy with you." He paced away, then back again. "I want you to spend the weekend with me."

"But . . . it's Christmas."

"That's right. And if you stay with me, it'll be the nicest Christmas I've ever had."

"You don't have any other plans?"

"If I did, I'd change them." He handed her the gift. "I bought you this. Before we slept together, because even if things hadn't gotten intimate so soon, I still wanted you to have it."

She held the gift with fascination. "Why?"

"Because you're special to me. The way you affect me is special, and the way I feel around you is special. I wanted you to know it."

"Oh."

"Well," he said, once again smiling, although now his smile looked a bit strained. "Open it."

Sitting back down in the chair, Asia pulled aside the crisp paper. She felt like a child again, filled with anticipation. When she opened the velvet box and saw the bracelet, tears welled in her eyes. "Oh, Cameron."

"You like it?" he asked anxiously.

"I love it." She looked up at him, seeing him through a sheen of tears. "It's absolutely perfect."

Cameron knelt down in front of her, lifted the bracelet from the box and clasped it around her slender wrist. "You're perfect. The bracelet is just decoration."

"Cameron?"

He lifted his gaze to hers, still holding her hand.

"May I spend Christmas with you?"

He sucked in a breath, then let it out with an enormous grin. "You may. You may even spend the entire week with me."

Giggling with pure happiness, Asia threw her arms around him. "You're so wonderful."

He squeezed her tight. "I know you want to take things slow and easy, honey. So I'm not rushing you." As he spoke, he lifted her in his arms and started back down the hall. "Your ex pulled a number on you, and I'd like to demolish the bastard. But I want you to know I'll be patient. We can do whatever you want, however you want. You just tell me."

Asia felt ready to burst. "I really do care about you, Cameron."

He froze, shuddered, then squeezed her tight and hurried the rest of the way to the bed. "That's a start," he said, lowering them both to the mattress. "Do you think by New Year's you might be telling me you love me? Because Asia, I . . ." He stopped and frowned. "I'm rushing you, aren't I?"

"You think you love me?" she asked in lieu of giving him an answer. "Is that what you were going to say?"

"I know how I feel." He untied the belt of the robe and parted it, looking down at her body. "And yes, I love you." He bent and lazily kissed her breasts. "Hell, I'm crazy nuts about you." He started kissing his way down her belly, and Asia wasn't able to say another thing. All she could do was gasp.

Epilogue

"A Valentine's Day engagement." Becky sighed. "How romantic."

Asia smiled in contentment. "I'm so happy. I didn't know a man like Cameron existed, and now I've not only discovered him, I have him for my own."

Erica gave her a smug grin. "You see how well my plans turn out."

"What I see," Asia said, leaning over the lounge table to wag a finger at her two friends, "is that neither of you have fulfilled your end of the bargain."

Erica laughed. "We were too amused watching things unfold for you. You and Cameron have stolen the show."

"Uh-huh. I think you both just chickened out."

Erica said, "No way," but Becky just looked around, as if seeking escape.

Erica and Asia both caught her hands. "C'mon, Becky," Asia teased, "you know it's well past your turn!"

Looking tortured, Becky said, "I don't know if I can."

"Trust me." Erica patted her shoulder. "You can."

"And you should," Asia added. "I mean, look how it turned out for me."

Becky folded her arms on the table and dropped her head. She gave a small groan.

Asia and Erica shared a look. "'Fess up, Becky," Asia urged. "You've had two months instead of two days to think about it. So let's hear the big fantasy."

"I know I'm going to regret this," came her muffled voice. "But if you both insist . . ."

"We do!"

She lifted her head, looked around the lounge and leaned forward to whisper into two ears.

"Wow," Asia said when she'd finished.

"All right!" Erica exclaimed, and lifted a fist in the air.

Cameron showed up just then, forcing the women to stifle their humor. He bent down and planted a kiss on Asia's mouth. "You want to leave right after work to pick out the ring?"

Erica shook her head. "In a hurry, big boy?"

"Damn right."

To everyone's relief, Cameron got along fabulously with both Becky's timid personality, and Erica's outrageous boldness.

Asia couldn't imagine being any happier. Now, if only her two friends could find the same happiness. She eyed Becky, who still blushed with her confessed fantasy. Maybe, she thought, doing some silent plotting, she could give Becky a helping hand. She tugged Cameron to his feet and said good-bye to her friends.

Once they were in the hallway, she said, "How well do you know George Westin?"

"Well enough to know he's got a reputation with the ladies. Why?"

"I think he may just be perfect."

Cameron narrowed his eyes. "For what?"

"No, for who."

"Erica?"

"Ha! They're both too cocky. They'd kill each other within a minute." She smoothed her hand over his shoulder, then patted him. "No, I was thinking of Becky."

Cameron shook his head. "I don't know, sweetheart. She's so shy, he'd probably have her for lunch."

Asia just grinned. There was no one else in the hall, so she put her arms around him, loving him so much it hurt, and said, "You, Cameron O'Reilly, haven't heard Becky's fantasy. I'm thinking George might get a big surprise."

Cameron kissed her. "If it's half as nice as the surprise I got, then he's one lucky cuss."

"I love you, Cameron."

He patted her bottom in fond memory. "I love you, too, Asia. Now and forever."

Please turn the page for an exciting sneak peek at Lori Foster's new novel JAMIE, coming in June 2005!

One

The relentless rain came down, accompanied by ground-rattling thunder and great flashes of lightning. Jamie liked storms . . . but not this one. This time he felt more than the turbulence of the weather. The air crackled with electricity—and good intentions. Determination. Resolve.

They hunted him. Well meaning, but destructive all the same. He had only himself to blame. He'd allowed them to become friendly. He hadn't been aloof enough, had interfered too many times. But God, what other choices did he have? Watch them suffer? Feel their pain?

No, he couldn't. He had enough of his own pain to deal with.

Sitting on the plank floor, his back to a wall, his knees drawn up, he stared out at the darkness. Not a single lamp glowed in his home. The fireplace remained cool and empty. A chill skated up his spine, and he laid his forehead to his knees, trying to block them out, wanting to pray that they wouldn't find him, but unable to summon the right words in the midst of so many feelings bombarding him.

Then it dawned on him. His head shot up, his black eyes unseeing. *Not just the townsfolk.* No, someone else crept up his mountain. Someone else wanted him.

Without conscious decision, he came to his feet and padded barefoot across the cold floor. No locks protected his doors; he didn't need them. He shoved the heavy wood open and moved out to the covered porch. Rain immediately blew in against him, soaking his shirt and jeans, collecting in his beard and long hair until he looked, felt, like a drowned rat.

Something vaguely close to excitement stirred in his chest, accelerating his heartbeat, making his blood sing. He lifted his nose to the wind, let his heavy eyelids drift shut . . . and he knew. He saw the first visitor, alone, a stranger. A woman. Seeking him out. *Needing* him.

This he could do.

Half-furious and half-thrilled for the distraction, he stepped inside the house and shoved his feet into rubber boots. Forgoing a jacket, sensing the limitations of his time-frame, Jamie stepped off the porch and into the pouring rain.

Storms were different in the woods, with leaves acting as a canopy, muffling the patter of the rain, absorbing the moisture. Once, long ago, he had hoped they might absorb some of the emotions that assaulted him. But they hadn't. Even from such a distance, high up the mountain in the thick of the trees where no one ever ventured, he'd still gotten to know the townsfolk, first the children, then the others.

And they'd gotten to know him.

Despite his efforts to the contrary, they were starting to care. They didn't know that their caring could destroy him, could strip away the last piece of self-respect he had. And he couldn't tell them.

Twice as dark as it'd be in the open, Jamie made his way cautiously away from his home, down an invisible trail known only to him. He walked and walked, mud caked up to his knees, his clothes so wet they were useless. Pausing beside a large tree that disappeared into the sky, he looked down the hillside.

Clint Evans, the new sheriff who'd listened to Jamie's dire warnings without much disbelief, picked his way tirelessly up the hillside. Jamie narrowed his eyes, knowing this was Julie's doing, that she wanted him at her wedding.

He would have gone. To make sure everything stayed safe. To keep watch. She didn't need to send her hulking new lover after him. He should be pleased it wasn't Joe, because Joe wouldn't give up, no matter what. Worse, it could have been Alyx, Joe's sister, who surprised him once when she'd gotten too close for Jamie to send her away. She'd actually been in his home, and damn her, she wanted in his heart. She wanted his friendship. They all did.

Jamie closed his eyes and concentrated on breathing, concentrated on feeling the other intruder. His eyes snapped open and he lifted a hand to shield his vision from the downpour. There, farther up the hill from Clint, she shivered and shook, miserable clear to her bones, tears mixing with the rain and mud on her face.

Jamie felt . . . something. He didn't know what. Odd, because it was only people he cared about that he couldn't read clearly. When he cared, emotional reactions mixed with his truer senses, muddling his readings.

Maybe *she* didn't know what she felt, so how could *he* know?

Dismissing Clint from his mind, already knowing what Clint would see and what he'd do, Jamie pushed away from the tree. The woman wore no hat and her hair was plastered to her skull. A redhead, Jamie thought, although with her hair soaked it looked dark enough to be brown. He didn't have to survey her to know of her pale skin sprinkled with a few freckles, or her blue eyes, now bloodshot. Her face, more plain than otherwise, served as a nice deception to her body.

She had incredible breasts and a small waist. Her legs were long and shapely, and she had an ass that would excite many men—if they noticed. But her quiet demeanor and ordinary appearance put them off. As she wanted. She hid—just as Jamie did.

They had that in common.

Holding tight to a skinny tree, she tried and failed to take a few more steps up the mountain. Her feet gained no purchase in the slick mud, and she fell forward with a gasp that got her a mouthful of mud. Moaning, she rolled to her back and just laid there, more tears coming as she labored for breath.

Jamie picked his way toward her, and with each step he took a sense of alarm that expanded until her fear and worry and pain became his own. She hurt. Fever robbed her of strength. Her lungs labored and her eyes burned.

Before Jamie could get to her, before he could warn her not to move, she tried to stand again. She got upright, then one foot slipped out from under her and her arms floundered in the air—and she fell back. Hard.

She didn't roll down the hill.

The rock kept her from doing so.

In seconds, Jamie reached her. He touched her cheek and knew the fever wasn't that bad. Sick, yes, but not so sick that he had to worry. The bump on her head . . . that worried him. He patted her cheeks, unwilling to speak, knowing that Clint drew nearer, and he simply couldn't deal with them both right now.

Tipping a leaf to gather the moisture off it, Jamie wiped some of the mud from her face. Her hair spiked up in front when he pushed it away from her eyes. He tapped her cheeks again, smoothed his thumb along her cheekbone, and her eyes opened. As he already knew, they were blue—deep, dark blue, like a sky at midnight. At first vague, her gaze sharpened the moment her eyes met his.

Jamie half-expected hysterics, which was absurd given he should have known exactly what she'd do. But still, her reaction surprised him. Her eyes widened, then her lashes sank down and she said, "Jamie Creed. Thank God."

The Brass Ring

Lisa Jackson

One

The old merry-go-round picked up speed, ancient gears grinding as black smoke spewed from the diesel engine and clouded the summer-blue Oregon sky.

Shawna McGuire clung to the neck of her wooden mount and glanced over her shoulder. Her heart swelled at the sight of Parker Harrison. Tall, with the broad shoulders of a natural athlete and brown hair streaked gold by the sun, he sat astride a glossy striped tiger. His blue eyes were gazing possessively at her and a camera swung from his neck.

Shawna grinned shamelessly. Tomorrow morning she and Parker would be married!

The carousel spun faster. Colors of pink, blue, and yellow blurred together.

"Reach, Shawna! Come on, you can do it!" Parker yelled, his deep voice difficult to hear above the piped music of the calliope and the sputtering engine.

Grinning, her honey-gold hair billowing away from her face, she saw him wink at her, then focus his camera and aim.

"Go for it, *Doctor!*" he called.

The challenge was on and Shawna glanced forward again, her green eyes fixed on the brass ring with fluttering pastel ribbons, the prize that hung precariously near the speeding carousel. She stretched her fingers, grabbed as she passed the ring and swiped into the air, coming up with nothing and nearly falling off her painted white stallion in the bargain. She heard Parker's laughter and looked back just in time to see him snatch the prize. A big, gloating smile spread easily across his square jaw and the look he sent her made her heart pound wildly.

She thought about her plans for the wedding the following morning. It was almost too good to be true. In less than twenty-four hours, under the rose arbor at Pioneer Church, she'd become Mrs. Parker Harrison and they would be bound for a weeklong honeymoon in the Caribbean! No busy hospital schedules, no double shifts, no phones or patients—just Parker.

She glimpsed Parker stuffing the ring and ribbons into the front pocket of his jeans as the merry-go-round slowed.

"That's how it's done," he said, cupping his hands over his mouth so that she could hear him.

"Insufferable, arrogant—" she muttered, but a dimple creased her cheek and she laughed gaily, clasping her fingers around the post supporting her mount and tossing back her head. Her long hair brushed against her shoulders and she could hear the warm sound of Parker's laughter. She was young and in love—nothing could be more perfect.

When the ride ended she climbed off her glazed white horse and felt Parker's strong arms surround her. "That was a feeble attempt if I ever saw one," he whispered into her ear as he lifted her to the ground.

"We all can't be professional athletes," she teased, looking up at him through gold-tipped lashes. "Some of us have to set goals, you know, to achieve higher intellectual and humanistic rewards."

"Bull!"

"Bull?" she repeated, arching a golden brow.

"Save that for someone who'll believe it, Doctor. I won and you're burned."

"Well, maybe just a little," she admitted, her eyes

shining. "But it is comforting to know that should I ever quit my practice, and if you gave up completely on tennis, we could depend on your income as a professional ring-grabber."

"I'll get you for that one, Dr. McGuire," he promised, squeezing her small waist, his hand catching in the cotton folds of her sundress. "And my vengeance will be swift and powerful and drop you to your knees!"

"Promises, promises!" she quipped, dashing away from him and winding quickly through the crowd. Dry grass brushed against her ankles and several times her sandals caught on an exposed pebble, but she finally reached a refreshment booth with Parker right on her heels. "A bag of buttered popcorn and a sack of peanuts," she said to the vendor standing under the striped awnings. She felt out of breath and flushed, and her eyes glimmered mischievously. "And this guy," she motioned to Parker as he approached, "will foot the bill."

"Henpecked already," Parker muttered, delving into his wallet and handing a five-dollar bill to the vendor. Someday—" he said, blue eyes dancing as he shucked open a peanut and tossed the nut into his mouth.

"Someday what?" she challenged, her pulse leaping when his eyes fixed on her lips. For a minute she thought he was going to kiss her right there in the middle of the crowd. If he did, she wouldn't stop him. She couldn't. She loved him too much.

"Just you wait, lady—" he warned, his voice low and throaty, the vein in the side of his neck pulsing.

Shawna's heart began to thud crazily.

"For what?"

A couple of giggling teenage girls approached, breaking the magical spell. "Mr. Harrison?" the taller, red-haired girl asked, while her friend in braces blushed.

Parker looked over his shoulder and twisted around. "Yes?"

"I told you it was him!" the girl in braces said, nearly

jumping up and down in her excitement. Her brown eyes gleamed in anticipation.

"Could we, uh, would you mind—" the redhead fumbled in her purse "—could we get your autograph?"

"Sure," Parker said, taking the scraps of paper and pen that had been shoved into his hand and scribbling out his name.

"I'm Sara and this is Kelly. Uh—Sara without an 'h.'"

"Got it!" Parker finished writing.

"Is, um, Brad here?"

"'Fraid not," Parker admitted, the corner of his mouth lifting as he snapped the cap back onto the pen.

"Too bad," Sara murmured, obviously disappointed as she tucked her pen and paper into her purse.

But Kelly smiled widely, displaying the wires covering her teeth. "Gee, thanks!"

The two girls waved and took off, giggling to themselves.

"The price of fame," Parker said teasingly.

"Not too bad for a has-been," Shawna commented dryly, unable to hide the pride in her voice. "But it didn't hurt that you're Brad Lomax's coach. He's the star now, you know."

Parker grinned crookedly. "Admit it, McGuire, you're still sore 'cause you didn't get the ring." Draping his arm possessively around her shoulders, he hugged her close.

"Maybe just a little," she said with a happy sigh. The day had been perfect despite the humidity. High overhead, the boughs of tall firs swayed in the sultry summer breeze and dark clouds drifted in from the west.

Shawna's feet barely hit the ground as they walked through the "Fair from Yesteryear." Sprawled over several acres of farmland in the foothills of the Cascade Mountains, the dun-colored tents, flashy rides, and booths were backdropped by spectacular mountains. Muted calliope music filled the summer air, and barkers, hawking their wares and games, shouted over the noise of the crowd. The smells of horses, sawdust, popcorn, and caramel wafted through the crowded, tent-lined fields that served as fairgrounds.

"Want to test your strength?" Shawna asked, glancing up at Parker and pointing to a lumberjack who was hoisting a heavy mallet over his head. Swinging the hammer with all of his might, the brawny man grunted loudly. The mallet crashed against a springboard and hurled a hearty weight halfway up a tall pole.

Parker's lips curved cynically. "I'll pass. Don't want to ruin my tennis arm, you know."

"Sure."

Parker ran his fingers through his sun-streaked hair. "There is another reason," he admitted.

She arched an eyebrow quizzically. "Which is?"

"I think I'll save my strength for tomorrow night." His voice lowered and his eyes darkened mysteriously. "There's this certain lady who's expecting all of my attention and physical prowess."

"Is that right?" She popped a piece of popcorn into his mouth and grinned. "Then you'd better not disappoint her."

"I won't," he promised, his gaze shifting to her mouth.

Shawna swallowed with difficulty. Whenever he looked at her that way, so sensual and determined, her heart always started beating a rapid double-time. She had to glance away, over his shoulder to a short, plump woman who was standing in front of a tent.

Catching Shawna's eye, the woman called, "How about I read your fortune?" With bright scarves wrapped around her head, painted fingernails, and dangling hooped earrings, she waved Shawna and Parker inside.

"I don't know—"

"Why not?" Parker argued, propelling her into the darkened tent. Smelling of sawdust and cloying perfume, the tent was dark and close. Shawna sat on a dusty pillow near a small table and wondered what had possessed her to enter. The floor was covered with sawdust and straw, the only illumination coming from a slit in the top of the canvas. The place gave her the creeps.

Placing a five-dollar bill on the corner of the table, Parker sat next to Shawna, one arm still draped casually over her shoulders, his long legs crossed Indian style.

The money quickly disappeared into the voluminous folds of the Gypsy woman's skirt as she settled onto a mound of pillows on the other side of the table. "You first?" she asked, flashing Shawna a friendly, gold-capped smile.

Shrugging, Shawna glanced at Parker before meeting the Gypsy woman's gaze. "Sure. Why not?"

"Good!" Lady Fate clapped her wrinkled palms together. "Now, let me read your palm." Taking Shawna's hand in hers, she gently stroked the smooth skin, tracing the lines of Shawna's palm with her long fingers.

"I see you have worked long and hard in your job."

That much was true, Shawna thought wryly. She'd spent more hours than she wanted to count as a bartender while going to college and medical school. It had been years of grueling work, late shifts, and early morning classes, but finally, just this past year, she'd become a full-fledged internist. Even now, juggling time between her clinic and the hospital, she was working harder than she'd ever expected.

"And you have a happy family."

"Yes," Shawna admitted proudly. "A brother and my parents."

The woman nodded, as if she saw their faces in Shawna's palm. "You will live a long and fruitful life," she said thickly and then her fingers moved and she traced another line on Shawna's hand, only to stop short. Her face clouded, her old lips pursed and she dropped Shawna's wrist as quickly as she had taken it earlier. "Your time is over," she said gently, kindness sparking in her old brown eyes.

"What?"

"Next," Lady Fate said, calling toward the flap used as a door.

"That's all?" Shawna repeated, surprised. She didn't know much about fortune-telling, but she'd just begun to enjoy the game and some of her five-dollar future was missing.

"Yes. I've told you everything. Now, if you'll excuse me—"

"Wait a minute. What about my love life?" Glancing at Parker in the shadowed room, Shawna winked.

Lady Fate hesitated.

"I thought you could see everything," Shawna said. "That's what your sign says."

"There are some things better left unknown," the woman whispered softly as she started to stand.

"I can handle it," Shawna said, but felt a little uneasy.

"Really, you don't want to know," Lady Fate declared, pursing her red lips and starting to stand.

"Of course I do," Shawna insisted. Though she didn't really believe in any of this mumbo jumbo, she wanted to get her money's worth. "I want to know everything." Shawna thrust her open palm back to the woman.

"She's very stubborn," Parker interjected.

"So I see." The fortune-teller slowly sat down on her pillows as she closed Shawna's fingers, staring straight into her eyes. "I see there is a very important man in your life—you love him dearly, too much, perhaps."

"And?" Shawna asked, disgusted with herself when she felt the hairs on the back of her neck prickle with dread.

"And you will lose him," the woman said sadly, glancing at Parker and then standing to brush some of the straw from her skirt. "Now go."

"Come on," Parker said, his eyes glinting mischievously. "It's time you got rid of that love of your life and started concentrating on me." He took Shawna by the hand and pulled her from the dark tent.

Outside, the air was hot and muggy but a refreshing change from the sticky interior of the tiny canvas booth. "You set her up to that, didn't you?" Shawna accused, still uneasy as she glanced back at the fortune-teller's tent.

"No way! Don't tell me you believed all of that baloney she tried to peddle you!"

"Of course not, but it was kind of creepy." Shuddering, she rubbed her bare arms despite the heat.

"And way off base." Laughing, he tugged on her hand and led her through a thicket of fir trees, away from the crowd and the circus atmosphere of the fair.

The heavy boughs offered a little shade and privacy and cooled the sweat beading on the back of Shawna's neck.

"You didn't believe her, did you?" he asked, his eyes delving deep into hers.

"No, but—"

"Just wait 'til the medical board gets wind of this!"

She couldn't help but smile as she twisted her hair into a loose rope and held it over her head, and off her neck. "You're laughing at me."

"Maybe a little." Stepping closer, he pinned her back against the rough bark of a Douglas fir, his arms resting lightly on her shoulders. "You deserve it, too, after all that guff you gave me about that damned brass ring."

"Guilty as charged," she admitted. She let her hair fall free and wrapped her hands around his lean, hard waist. Even beneath his light shirt, she could feel the ripple of his muscles as he shifted.

"Good." Taking the brass ring from his pocket, he slipped the oversized band onto her finger. "With this ring, I thee wed," he said quietly, watching the ribbons flutter over her arm.

Shawna had to blink back some stupid tears of happiness that wet her lashes. "I can't wait," she murmured, "for the real thing."

"Neither can I." Placing his forehead agai[illegible] stared at the dimpled smile playing on her lips.

Shawna's pulse leaped. His warm breath fanned [illegible] face, his fingers twined lazily in a long strand of her honey-gold hair and his mouth curved upward in a sardonic smile. "And now, Dr. McGuire, prepare yourself. I intend to have my way with you!" he said menacingly.

"Right here?" she asked innocently.

"For starters." He brushed his lips slowly over hers and Shawna sighed into his mouth.

She felt warm all over and weak in the knees. He kissed her eyelids and throat and she moaned, parting her lips expectantly. His hands felt strong and powerful and she knew that Parker would always take care of her and protect her. Deep inside, fires of desire that only he could spark ignited.

"I love you," she whispered, the wind carrying her words away as it lifted her hair away from her face.

"And I love you." Raising his head, he stared into her passion-glazed eyes. "And tomorrow night, I'm going to show you just how much."

"Do we really have to wait?" she whispered, disappointment pouting her lips.

"Not much longer—but we had a deal, remember?"

"It was stupid."

"Probably," he agreed. "And it's been hell." His angular features grew taut. "But weren't you the one who said, 'Everything meaningful is worth the wait'?"

"That's a butchered version of it, but yes," she said.

"And we've made it this far."

"It's been agony," she admitted. "The next time I have such lofty, idealistic and stupid ideas, go ahead and shoot me."

Grinning, he placed a kiss on her forehead. "I suppose this means that I'll have to give up my mistress."

"Your *what!*" she sputtered, knowing that he was teasing. *His mistress!* This mystery woman—a pure ıantasy—had always been a joke between them, a joke that hurt more than it should have. "Oooh, you're absolutely the most arrogant, self-centered, egotistical—"

Capturing her wrists, he held them high over her head with one hand. "Go on," he urged, eyes slowly inching down her body, past her flashing green eyes and pursed lips, to the hollow of her throat where her pulse was fluttering rapidly, then lower still, to the soft mounds of her breasts, pushed proudly forward against apricot-colored cotton, rising and falling with each of her shallow breaths.

"—self-important, presumptuous, insolent bastard I've ever met!"

Lowering his head, he kissed the sensitive circle of bones at the base of her throat and she felt liquid inside. "Leave anything out?" he asked, his breath warm against her already overheated skin.

"A million things!"

"Such as?"

"Mistress," she repeated and then sucked in a sharp breath when she felt his moist tongue touch her throat. "Stop it," she said weakly, wanting to protest but unable.

"Aren't you the woman who was just begging for more a few minutes ago?"

"Parker—"

Then he cut off her protest with his mouth slanting swiftly over hers, his body pressed urgently against her. He kissed her with the passion that she'd seen burning in him ever since the first time they'd met. Her back was pinned to the trunk of the tree, her hands twined anxiously around his neck, wanton desire flowing from his lips to hers.

His hips were thrust against hers and she could feel the intensity of his passion, his heat radiating against her. "Please—" she whispered and he groaned.

His tongue rimmed her lips and then tasted of the sweetness within her open mouth.

"Parker—" She closed her eyes and moaned softly.

Suddenly every muscle in his body tensed and he released her as quickly as he'd captured her. Swearing, he stepped away from her. "You're dangerous, you know that, don't you?" His hands were shaking when he pushed the hair from his eyes. "I—I think we'd better go," he said thickly, clearly trying to quell the desire pounding in his brain.

Swallowing hard, she nodded. She could feel a hot flush staining her cheeks, knew her heart was racing out of control, and had trouble catching her breath. "But tomorrow, Mr. Harrison—you're not going to get away so easily."

"Don't tease me," he warned, his mouth a thin line of self-control.

"Never," she promised, forest-green eyes serious.

Linking his fingers with hers, he pulled her toward the parking lot. "I think we'd better get out of here. If I remember correctly, we have a wedding rehearsal and a dinner to get through tonight."

"That's right," she groaned, combing her tangled hair with her fingers, as they threaded their way through the cars parked in uneven rows. "You know, I should have listened to you when you wanted to elope."

"Next time, you'll know."

"There won't be a next time," she vowed as he opened the door of his Jeep and she slid into the sweltering interior. "You're going to be stuck with me for life!"

"I wouldn't have it any other way." Once behind the wheel, he cranked open the windows and turned on the ignition.

"Even if you have to give up your mistress?"

Coughing, he glanced at her. One corner of his mouth lifted cynically as he maneuvered the car out of the bumpy, cracked field that served as a parking lot. "The things I do for love," he muttered and then switched on the radio and shifted gears.

Shawna stared out the window at the passing countryside. In the distance, dark clouds had begun to gather around the rugged slopes of Mount Hood. Shadows lengthened across the hilly, dry farmland. Dry, golden pastures turned dark as the wind picked up. Grazing cattle lifted their heads at the scent of the approaching storm and weeds and wildflowers along the fencerows bent double in the muggy breeze.

"Looks like a storm brewing." Parker glanced at the hard, dry ground and frowned. "I guess we could use a little rain."

"But not tonight or tomorrow," Shawna said. "Not on our wedding day." *Tomorrow,* she thought with a smile. She tried to ignore the Gypsy woman's grim prediction and the promise of rain. "Tomorrow will be perfect!"

". . . and may you have all the happiness you deserve. To the bride and groom!" Jake said, casting a smile at his sister and holding his wineglass high in the air.

Hoisting her glass, Shawna beamed, watching her dark-haired brother through adoring eyes.

"Here, here," the rest of the guests chimed in, glasses clinking, laughter and cheery conversation filling the large banquet room of the Edwardian Hotel in downtown Portland. The room was crowded with family and friends, all members of the wedding party. After a rehearsal marred by only a few hitches, and a lovely veal dinner, the wine, toasts and fellowship were flowing freely in the elegant room.

"How was that?" Jake asked, taking his chair.

"Eloquent," Shawna admitted, smiling at her brother. "I didn't know you had it in you."

"That's because you never listened to me," he quipped, and then, setting his elbows on the table, winked at Parker. "I hope you have better luck keeping her in line."

"I will," Parker predicted, loosening his tie.

"Hey, wait a minute," Shawna protested, but laughed and sipped from a glass of cold Chablis.

"I can't wait until tomorrow," Gerri, Shawna's best friend, said with a smile. "I never thought I'd see this day, when someone actually convinced the good doctor to walk down the aisle." Shaking her auburn hair, Gerri leaned back and lit a cigarette, clicking her lighter shut to add emphasis to her words.

"I'm not married to my work," Shawna protested.

"Not anymore. But you were. Back in those days when you were in med school, you were no fun. I repeat: *No fun!*"

Parker hugged his bride-to-be. "I intend to change all that, starting tomorrow!"

"Oh, you do, do you?" Shawna said, her gaze narrowing on him. "I'll have you know, Mr. Harrison, that *you'll* be the one toeing the line."

"This should be good," Jake decided. "Parker Harrison under a woman's thumb."

"I'll drink to that!" Brad Lomax, Parker's most famous student, leaned over Shawna's shoulder, spilling some of his drink on the linen tablecloth. His black hair was mussed, his tie already lost, and the smell of bourbon was heavy on his breath. He'd been in a bad mood all evening and had chosen to drown whatever problems he had in a bottle.

"Maybe you should slow down a little," Parker suggested, as the boy swayed over the table.

"What? In the middle of this celebration? No way, man!" To add emphasis to his words, he downed his drink and signaled to the waiter for another.

Parker's eyes grew serious. "Really, Brad, you've had enough."

"Never enough!" He grabbed a glass of champagne from a passing waiter. "Put it on his tab!" Brad said, cocking his thumb at Parker. "This is his las' night of freedom! Helluva waste if ya ask me!"

Jake glanced from Parker to Brad and back again. "Maybe I should take him home," he suggested.

But Brad reached into his pocket, fumbled around and finally withdrew his keys. "I can do it myself," he said testily.

"Brad—"

"I'll go when I'm damned good and ready." Leaning forward, he placed one arm around Parker, the other around Shawna. "You know, I jus' might end up married myself," he decided, grinning sloppily.

"I'd like to be there on the day some girl gets her hooks into you," Parker said. "It'll never happen."

Brad laughed, splashing his drink again. "Guess again," he said, slumping against Shawna.

"Why don't you tell me about it on the way home?" Parker suggested. He helped Brad back to his feet.

"But the party's not over—"

"It is for us. We've got a pretty full schedule tomorrow. I don't want you so hung over that you miss the ceremony."

"I won't be!"

"Right. 'Cause I'm taking you home right now." He set Brad's drink on the table and took the keys from his hand. Then, leaning close to Shawna, he kissed her forehead. "I'll see you in the morning, okay?"

"Eleven o'clock, sharp," she replied, looking up at him, her eyes shining.

"Wouldn't miss it for the world."

"Me, neither," Brad agreed, his arm still slung over Parker's broad shoulders as they headed for the door. "'Sides, I need to talk to you, need some advice," he added confidentially to Parker.

"So what else is new?"

"Be careful," Jake suggested. "It's raining cats and dogs out there—the first time in a couple months. The roads are bound to be slick."

"Will do," Parker agreed.

Jake watched them leave, his eyes narrowing on Parker's broad shoulders. "I don't see why Parker puts up with Brad," he said, frowning into his drink.

Shawna lifted a shoulder. "You know Brad is Parker's star student, supposedly seeded ninth in the country. Parker expects him to follow in his footsteps, make it to the top—win the grand slam. The whole nine yards, so to speak."

"That's football, sis. Not tennis."

"You know what I mean."

"He's that good?" Obviously, Jake didn't believe it, and Shawna understood why. As a psychiatrist, he'd seen more than his share of kids who'd gotten too much too fast and couldn't handle the fame or money.

Leaning back in her chair, Shawna quoted, "The best natural athlete that Parker's ever seen."

Jake shook his head, glancing again at the door through which Parker and Brad had disappeared. "Maybe so, but the kid's got a temper and a chip on his shoulder the size of the Rock of Gibraltar."

"Thank you for your professional opinion, Dr. McGuire."

"Is that a nice way of saying 'butt out'?" Jake asked.

Shawna shook her head. "No, it's a nice way of saying, let's keep the conversation light—no heavy stuff, okay? I'm getting married tomorrow."

"How could I forget?" Clicking the rim of his glass to hers, he whispered, "And I wish you all the luck in the world." He took a sip of his wine. "You know what the best part of this marriage is, don't you?"

"Living with Parker?"

"Nope. The fact that this is the last day there will be two Dr. McGuires working at Columbia Memorial. No more mixed-up messages or calls."

"That's right. From now on, I'll be Dr. Harrison." She wrinkled her nose a bit. "Doesn't have the same ring to it, does it?"

"Sounds great to me."

"Me, too," she admitted, looking into her wineglass and smiling at the clear liquid within. "Me, too."

She felt a light tap on her shoulder and looked up. Her father was standing behind her chair. A tall, rotund man, he was dressed in his best suit, and a sad smile curved his lips. "How about a dance with my favorite girl?" he asked.

"You've got it," she said, pushing back her chair and taking his hand. "But after that, I'm going home."

"Tired?"

"Uh-huh, and I want to look my best tomorrow."

"Don't worry. You'll be the prettiest bride ever to walk down that aisle."

"The wedding's going to be in the rose garden, remember?" She laughed, and her father's face pulled together.

"I don't suppose I can talk you into saying your vows in front of the altar?"

"Nope. Outside," she said, glancing out the window into the dark night. Rain shimmered on the window panes. "I don't care if this blasted rain keeps falling, we're going to be married under the arbor in the rose garden of the church."

"You always were stubborn," he muttered, twirling her around the floor. "Just like your mother."

"Some people say I'm a chip off the old block, and they aren't talking about Mom."

Malcolm McGuire laughed as he waltzed his daughter around the room. "I know this is the eleventh hour, but sometimes I wonder if you're rushing things a bit. You haven't known Parker all that long."

"Too late, Dad. If you wanted to talk me out of this, you shouldn't have waited this long," she pointed out.

"Don't get me wrong; I like Parker."

"Good, because you're stuck with him as a son-in-law."

"I just hope you're not taking on too much," he said

thoughtfully. "You're barely out of med school and you have a new practice. Now you're taking on the responsibilities of becoming a wife—"

"And a mother?" she teased.

Malcolm's eyebrows quirked. "I know you want children, but that can come later."

"I'm already twenty-eight!"

"That's not ancient, Shawna. You and Parker, you're both young."

"And in love. So quit worrying," she admonished with a fond grin. "I'm a big girl now. I can take care of myself. And if I can't, Parker will."

"He'd better," her father said, winking broadly. "Or he'll have to answer to me!"

When the strains of the waltz drifted away, he patted Shawna's arm and escorted her back to her chair. He glanced around the room as she slipped her arms through the sleeves of her coat. "So where is that husband-to-be of yours? Don't tell me he already skipped out."

"Very funny." She lifted her hair out of the collar of her raincoat and said, "He took Brad Lomax home a little earlier. But don't worry, Dad, he'll be there tomorrow. I'll see you then."

Tucking her purse under her arm, she hurried down the stairs, unwilling to wait for the elevator. On the first floor, she dashed through the lobby of the old Victorian hotel, and shouldered open the heavy wood door.

The rain was coming down in sheets and thunder rumbled through the sky. Just a summer storm, she told herself, nothing to worry about. Everything will be clean and fresh tomorrow and the roses in the garden will still have dewy drops of moisture on their petals. It will be perfect! Nothing will ruin the wedding. Nothing can.

Two

Shawna stared at her reflection as her mother adjusted the cream-colored lace of her veil. "How's that?" Doris McGuire asked as she met her daughter's gaze in the mirror.

"Fine, Mom. Really—" But Shawna's forehead was drawn into creases and her green eyes were dark with worry. *Where was Parker?*

Doris stepped back to take a better look and Shawna saw herself as her mother did. Ivory lace stood high on her throat, and creamy silk billowed softly from a tucked-in waist to a long train that was now slung over her arm. Wisps of honey-colored hair peeked from beneath her veil. The vision was complete, except for her clouded gaze. "Parker isn't here yet?" Shawna asked.

"Relax. Jake said he'd let us know the minute he arrived." She smoothed a crease from her dress and forced a smile.

"But he was supposed to meet with Reverend Smith half an hour ago."

Doris waved aside Shawna's worries. "Maybe he got caught in traffic. You know how bad it's been ever since the storm last night. Parker will be here. Just you wait. Before you know it, you'll be Mrs. Parker Harrison and Caribbean-bound."

"I hope so," Shawna said, telling herself not to worry. So Parker was a few minutes late; certainly that wasn't something to be alarmed about. Or was it? Parker had never been late once in the six weeks she'd known him.

Glancing through the window to the gray day beyond, Shawna watched the yellow ribbons woven into the white slats of the arbor in the church garden. They danced wildly over the roses of the outdoor altar as heavy purple clouds stole silently across the sky.

Doris checked her watch and sighed. "We still have time to move the ceremony inside," she said quietly. "I'm sure none of the guests would mind."

"No!" Shawna shook her head and her veil threatened to come loose. She heard the harsh sound of her voice and saw her mother stiffen. "Look, Mom, I'm sorry, I didn't mean to snap."

"It's okay—just the wedding-day jitters. But try to calm down," her mother suggested, touching her arm. "Parker will be here soon." But Doris's voice faltered and Shawna saw the concern etched in the corner of her mother's mouth.

"I hope you're right," she whispered, unconvinced. The first drops of rain fell from the sky and ran down the windowpanes. Glancing again out the window to the parking lot, Shawna hoped to see Parker's red Jeep wheel into the lot. Instead, she saw Jake drive up, water splashing from under the wheels of his car as he ground to a stop.

"Where did Jake go?" she asked. "I thought he was in the rose garden . . ." Her voice drifted off as she watched her brother dash through the guests who were moving into the church.

"Shawna!" Jake's voice boomed through the door and he pounded on the wood panels. "Shawna!"

The ghost of fear swept over her.

"For God's sake, come in," Doris said, opening the door.

Jake burst into the room. His hair was wet, plastered to

his head, his tuxedo was rumpled, and his face was colorless. "I just heard—there was an accident last night."

"An accident?" Shawna repeated, seeing the horror in his gaze. "No—"

"Parker and Brad were in a terrible crash. They weren't found until a few hours ago. Right now they're at Mercy Hospital—"

"There must be some mistake!" Shawna cried, her entire world falling apart. Parker couldn't be hurt! Just yesterday they were at the fair, laughing, kissing, touching . . .

"No mistake."

"Jake—" Doris reproached, but Jake was at Shawna's side, taking hold of her arm, as if he were afraid she would swoon.

"It's serious, sis."

Disbelieving, Shawna pinned him with wide eyes. "If this is true—"

"Damn it, Shawna, do you think I'd run in here with this kind of a story if I hadn't checked it out?" he asked, his voice cracking.

The last of her hopes fled and she clung to him, curling her fingers over his arm as fear grew in her heart. "Why didn't anyone tell me? I'm a doctor, for God's sake—"

"But not at Mercy Hospital. No one there knew who he was."

"But he's famous—"

"It didn't matter," Jake said soberly. His eyes told it all and for the first time Shawna realized that Parker, her beloved Parker, might die.

"Oh, my God," she whispered, wanting to fall to pieces, but not giving in to the horror that was coldly starting to grip her, wrenching at her insides. "I've got to go to him!"

"But you can't," her mother protested weakly. "Not now—"

"Of course I can!" Flinging off her veil, she gathered her skirts and ran to the side door of the church.

"Wait, Shawna!" Jake called after her, running to catch up. "I'll drive you—"

But she didn't listen. She found her purse with the car keys, jumped into her little hatchback, and plunged the keys into the ignition. The car roared to life. Shawna rammed it into gear and tore out of the parking lot, the car wheels screeching around the curves as she entered the highway. She drove wildly, her every thought centered on Parker as she prayed that he was still alive.

Jake hadn't said it, but it had been written in his eyes. *Parker might die!* "Please God, no," she whispered, her voice faltering, her chin thrust forward in determination. "You can't let him die! You can't!"

She shifted down, rounding a curve and nearly swerving out of her lane as the car climbed a steep street. Fir trees and church spires, skyscrapers and sharp ravines, a view of the Willamette River and the hazy mountains beyond were lost to her in a blur of rainwashed streets and fear.

Twice her car slid on the slick pavement but she finally drove into the parking lot of the hospital and ignored a sign reserving the first spot she saw for staff members. Her heart hammering with dread, she cut the engine, yanked on the brake and ran toward the glass doors, oblivious to the fact that her dress was dragging through mud puddles and grime.

As she ran to the desk in the emergency room, she wiped the water from her face. "I need to see Parker Harrison," she said breathlessly to a calm-looking young woman at the desk. "I'm Dr. McGuire, Columbia Memorial Hospital." Flashing credentials in the surprised woman's face, she didn't wait for a response. "I'm also Mr. Harrison's personal physician. He was brought in here early this morning and I have to see him!"

"He's in surgery now—"

"Surgery!" Shawna said, incredulous. "Who's the doctor in charge?"

"Dr. Lowery."

"Then let me see Lowery." Shawna's eyes glittered with authority and determination, though inside she was dying. She knew her requests were unreasonable, against all hospital procedures, but she didn't care. Parker was in this hospital, somewhere, possibly fighting for his life, and come hell or high water, she was going to see him!

"You'll have to wait," the nurse said, glancing at Shawna's wet hair, her bedraggled wedding dress, the fire in her gaze.

"I want to see him. Now."

"I'm sorry, Dr. McGuire. If you'd like, you could wait in the doctors' lounge and I'll tell Dr. Lowery you're here."

Seeing no other option, Shawna clamped her teeth together. "Then, please, tell me how serious he is. Exactly what are his injuries? How serious?"

"I can't give out that information."

Shawna didn't move. Her gaze was fixed on the smaller woman's face. "Then have someone who can give it out find me."

"If you'll wait."

Swallowing back the urge to shake information out of the young woman, Shawna exhaled a deep breath and tried to get a grip on her self-control. "Okay—but, please, send someone up to the lounge. I need to know about him, as his physician and as his fiancée."

The young nurse's face softened. "You were waiting for him, weren't you?" she asked quietly, as she glanced again at Shawna's soiled silk gown.

"Yes," Shawna admitted, her throat suddenly tight and tears springing to her eyes. She reached across the counter, took the nurse's hand in her own. "You understand—I have to see him."

"I'll send someone up as soon as I can," the girl promised.

"Thank you." Releasing her grip, Shawna suddenly felt the eyes of everyone in the waiting room boring into her back. For the first time she noticed the group of people assembled on the molded-plastic couches as they waited to be examined. Small children whined and cuddled against their mothers and older people, faces set and white, sat stiffly in the chairs, their eyes taking in Shawna's disheveled appearance.

Turning back to the young nurse, she forced her voice to remain steady. "Please, I want to know if there's any change in his condition." *Whatever that is,* she added silently.

"Will do, Dr. McGuire. The doctors' lounge is just to the left of the elevator on the second floor."

"Thank you," Shawna said, scooping up her skirts and squaring her shoulders as she started down the hall. The heels of her soaked satin pumps clicked on the tile floor.

"Shawna! Wait!" Jake's voice echoed through the corridor. In a few swift strides he was next to her, oblivious to the eyes of all the people in the waiting room. Still dressed in his tuxedo, his wet hair curling around his face, he looked as frantic as she felt. "What did you find out?" he asked softly.

"Not much. I'm on my way to the lounge on the second floor. Supposedly they'll send someone up to give me the news."

"If not, I'll check around—I've got connections here," Jake reminded her, glancing at all the pairs of interested eyes.

"You what?"

"Sometimes I consult here, at Mercy, in the psychiatric wing. I know quite a few of the staff. Come on," he urged, taking her elbow and propelling her toward the elevators. "You can change in the women's washroom on the second floor."

"Change?" she asked, realizing for the first time that he was carrying her smallest nylon suitcase, one of the suitcases she'd packed for her honeymoon. Numb inside, she took the suitcase from his outstretched hand. "Thanks," she murmured. "I owe you one."

"One of many. I'll add it to your list," he said, but the joke fell flat. "Look, Mom went through that," he gestured at the bag, "and thought you could find something more suitable than what you're wearing." Frowning, he touched her dirty gown.

The sympathy in Jake's eyes reached out to her and she felt suddenly weak. Her throat was hot, burning with tears she couldn't shed. "Oh, Jake. Why is this happening?" she asked, just as the elevator doors whispered open and they stepped inside.

"I wish I knew."

"I just want to know that Parker will be all right."

"I'll find out," he promised as the elevator groaned to a stop and Shawna stepped onto the second floor. Pushing a button on the control panel, Jake held the doors open and pointed down the hallway. "The lounge is right there, around the corner, and the washroom—I don't know where *that* is, but it must be nearby. I'll meet you back in the lounge as soon as I find Tom Handleman—he's usually in charge of ER—and then I'll be back to fill you in."

"Thanks," she whispered. The brackets around Jake's mouth deepened as he grimaced. "Let's just hope Parker and Brad are okay."

"They will be! They have to be!"

"I hope so. For your sake."

Then he was gone and Shawna, despite the fact that she was shaking from head to foot, found the washroom. Trying to calm herself, she sluiced cold water over her face and hardly recognized her reflection in the mirror over the sink. Two hours before she'd been a beaming bride, primping in front of a full-length mirror. Now, she looked as if she'd aged ten years. Eyes red, mouth surrounded by lines of strain, skin pale, she stripped off her wedding dress, unable to wear it another minute. Then she changed into a pair of white slacks, a cotton sweater, and a pair of running shoes, the clothes she had thought she would wear while holding hands with Parker and running along the gleaming white beach at Martinique.

Parker. Her heart wrenched painfully.

Quickly folding her dress as best she could and stuffing it into the little bag, she told herself to be strong and professional. Parker would be all right. He had to be.

Quickly, she found the lounge. With trembling hands, she poured herself a cup of coffee. Groups of doctors and nurses were clustered at round tables chattering, laughing, not seeming to care that Parker, her Parker, was somewhere in this labyrinthine building clinging to his very life. Forcing herself to remain calm, she took a chair in a corner near a planter filled with spiky leafed greenery. From there she could watch the door.

Doctors came and went, some with two days' growth of beard and red-rimmed eyes, others in crisply pressed lab coats and bright smiles. Each time the door opened, Shawna's gaze froze expectantly on the doorway, hoping that Jake would come barging into the room to tell her the entire nightmare was a hellish mistake; that Parker was fine; that nothing had changed; that later this afternoon they would step on a plane bound for white sand, hot sun, and aquamarine water . . .

"Come on, Jake," she whispered to herself, watching the clock as the second hand swept around the face, the minutes ticking by so slowly the waiting had become excruciating. She eavesdropped, listening to the conversations buzzing around her, dreading to overhear that Parker was dead, hoping to hear that his injuries were only superficial. But nothing was said.

Please, let him be all right! Please.

Somehow she finished her coffee and was shredding

her cup when Jake pushed open the door and headed straight for her. Another young man was with him—tall and lean, with bushy salt and pepper hair, wire-rimmed glasses, and a sober expression. "Dr. McGuire?" he asked.

Bracing herself for the worst, Shawna met the young man's eyes.

"This is Tom Handleman, Shawna. He was just in ER with Parker," Jake explained.

"And?" she asked softly, her hands balling into fists.

"And he'll live," Tom said. "He was pinned in the car a long time, but his injuries weren't as bad as we'd expected."

"Thank God," she breathed, her voice breaking as relief drove aside her fears.

"He has several cracked ribs, a ruptured spleen, a concussion and a fractured patella, including torn cartilage and ripped ligaments. Besides which, there are facial lacerations and contusions—"

"And you don't think that's serious!" she cut in, the blood draining from her face.

Jake met her worried eyes. "Shawna, please, listen to him."

"I didn't say his condition wasn't serious," Tom replied. "But Mr. Harrison's injuries are no longer life-threatening."

"Concussion," she repeated, "ruptured spleen—"

"Right, but we've controlled the hemorrhaging and his condition has stabilized. As I said, his concussion wasn't as bad as Lowery and I had originally thought."

"No brain damage?" she asked.

"Not that we can tell. But he'll have to have knee surgery as soon as his body's well enough for the additional trauma."

She ran a shaking hand over her forehead. *Parker was going to be all right!* She felt weak with relief. "Can I see him?"

"Not yet. He's still in recovery," Tom said quietly. "But

in a few hours, once he's conscious again—then you can see him."

"Was he conscious when he was brought in?"

"No." Dr. Handleman shook his head. "But we expect him to wake up as soon as the anesthetic wears off."

Jake placed his hand on Shawna's shoulder. "There's something else," he said quietly.

His grim expression and the fingers gripping her shoulder warned her. For the first time, she thought about the other man in Parker's car. "Brad?" she whispered, knowing for certain that Parker's star pupil and friend was dead.

"Brad Lomax was DOA," Tom said softly.

"Dead on arrival?" she repeated, the joy she'd felt so fleetingly stripped away.

"He was thrown from the car and his neck was broken."

"No!" she cried.

Jake's fingers tightened over her shoulders as she tried to stand and deny everything Tom was saying. She could see heads swing in her direction, eyes widen in interest as doctors at nearby tables heard her protest.

"I'm sorry," Tom said. "There was nothing we could do."

"But he was only twenty-two!"

"Shawna—" Jake's fingers relaxed.

Tears flooded her eyes. "I don't believe it!"

"You're a doctor, Miss McGuire," Tom pointed out, his eyes softening with sympathy. "You know as well as I do that these things happen. Not fair, I know, but just the way it is."

Sniffing back her tears, Shawna pushed Jake's restraining hands from her shoulders. Still grieving deep in her heart, she forced her professionalism to surface. "Thank you, Doctor," she murmured, extending her hand though part of her wanted to crumple into a miserable heap. As a doctor, she was used to dealing with death, but it was never easy, especially at a time like this, when the person who had lost his life was someone she'd known, someone Parker had loved.

Tom shook her hand. "I'll let you know when Mr. Harrison is awake and in his room. Why don't you go and rest for a couple of hours?"

"No—I, uh, I couldn't," she said.

"Your choice. Whatever I can do to help," he replied before turning and leaving the room.

"Oh, Jake," she said, feeling the security of her brother's arm wrap around her as he led her from the lounge. "I just can't believe that Brad's gone—"

"It's hard, I know, but you've got to listen to me," he urged, handing her the nylon suitcase he'd picked up and helping her to the elevator. "What you'll have to do now is be strong, for Parker. When he wakes up and finds out that Brad is dead, he's going to feel guilty as hell—"

"But it wasn't his fault. It couldn't have been."

"I know," he whispered. "But Parker won't see the accident that way—not at first. The trauma of the accident combined with an overwhelming sense of guilt over Brad's death might be devastating for Parker. It would be for anyone." He squeezed her and offered a tight smile. "You'll have to be his rock, someone he can hold on to, and it won't be easy."

She met his gaze and determination shone in her eyes. "I'll do everything I can for him," she promised.

One side of Jake's mouth lifted upward. "I know it, sis."

"The only thing that matters is that Parker gets well."

"And the two of you get married."

Her fingers clenched around the handle of her suitcase and she shook a wayward strand of hair from her eyes. "That's not even important right now," she said, steadfastly pushing all thoughts of her future with Parker aside. "I just have to see that he gets through this. And I will. No matter what!"

***

The next four hours were torture. She walked the halls of the hospital, trying to get rid of the nervous tension that twisted her stomach and made her glance at the clock every five minutes.

Jake had gone back to the church to explain what had happened to the guests and her parents, but she'd refused to give up her vigil.

"Dr. McGuire?"

Turning, she saw Dr. Handleman walking briskly to her.

"What's happened?" she asked. "I thought Parker was supposed to be put in a private room two hours ago."

"I know," he agreed, his face drawn, "but things changed. Unfortunately, Mr. Harrison hasn't regained consciousness. We've done tests, the anesthesia has worn off, but he's still asleep."

Dread climbed up her spine. "Meaning?"

"Probably that he'll come to in the next twenty-four hours."

"And if he doesn't?" she asked, already knowing the answer, panic sending her heart slamming against her rib cage.

"Then we'll just have to wait."

"You're saying he's in a coma."

Tom pushed his glasses up his nose and frowned. "It looks that way."

"How long?"

"We can't guess."

"How long?" she repeated, jaw clenched, fear taking hold of her.

"Come on, *Dr.* McGuire, you understand what I'm talking about," he reminded her as gently as possible. "There's no way of knowing. Maybe just a few hours—"

"But maybe indefinitely," she finished, biting back the urge to scream.

"That's unlikely."

"But not out of the question."

He forced a tired smile. "Prolonged coma, especially after a particularly traumatic experience, is always a possibility."

"What about his knee?"

"It'll wait, but not too long. We can't let the bones start to knit improperly, otherwise we might have more problems than we already do."

"He's a tennis pro," she whispered.

"We'll take care of him," he said. "Now, if you want, you can see him. He's in room four-twelve."

"Thank you." Without a backward glance, she hurried to the elevator, hoping to stamp down the panic that tore at her. On the fourth floor, she strode briskly down the corridor, past rattling gurneys, clattering food trays, and the soft conversation of the nurses at their station as she made her way to Parker's room.

"Excuse me, miss," one nurse said as Shawna reached the door to room four-twelve. "But Mr. Harrison isn't allowed any visitors."

Shawna faced the younger woman and squared her shoulders, hoping to sound more authoritative than she felt. "I'm Dr. McGuire. I work at Columbia Memorial Hospital. Dr. Harrison is my patient and Dr. Handleman said I could wait for the patient to regain consciousness."

"It's all right," another nurse said. "I took the call from Dr. Handleman. Dr. McGuire has all privileges of a visiting physician."

"Thank you," Shawna said, entering the darkened room and seeing Parker's inert form on the bed. Draped in crisp, white sheets, lying flat on his back, with an IV tube running from his arm and a swath of bandages over his head, he was barely recognizable. "Oh, Parker," she whispered, throat clogged, eyes suddenly burning.

She watched the slow rise and fall of his chest, saw the washed-out color of his skin, the small cuts over his face, noticed the bandages surrounding his chest and kneecap, and she wondered if he'd ever be the same, wonderful man she'd known. "I love you," she vowed, twining her fingers in his.

Thinking of the day before, the hot sultry air, the brass ring, and the Gypsy woman's grim fortune, she closed her eyes.

You love him too much—you will lose him, the fortune-teller had predicted.

"Never," Shawna declared. Shivering, she took a chair near the bed, whispering words of endearment and telling herself that she would do everything in her power as a doctor and a woman to make him well.

Three

A breakfast cart rattled past the doorway and Shawna started, her eyelids flying open. She'd spent all day and night at Parker's bedside, watching, waiting, and praying.

Now, as she rubbed the kinks from her neck and stretched her aching shoulder muscles, she looked down at Parker's motionless form, hardly believing that their life together had changed so drastically.

"Come on, Parker," she whispered, running gentle fingers across his forehead, silently hoping that his eyelids would flutter open. "You can do it."

A quiet cough caught her attention and she looked up to the doorway, where her brother lounged against the door frame. "How's it going?" Jake asked.

She lifted a shoulder. "About the same."

He raked his fingers through his hair and sighed. "How about if I buy you a cup of coffee?"

Shaking her head, Shawna glanced back at Parker. "I don't think I could—"

"Have you eaten anything since you've been here?"

"No, but—"

"That's right, no buts about it. I'm buying you breakfast. You're not doing Parker any good by starving yourself, are you, Doctor?"

"All right." Climbing reluctantly to her feet, she stretched again as she twisted open the blinds. The morning rays of late summer sun glimmered on the puddles outside. Deep in her heart, Shawna hoped the sunlight would wake Parker. She glanced back at him, her teeth sinking into her lower lip as she watched the steady rise and fall of his chest, noticed the bandage partially covering his head. But he didn't move.

"Come on," Jake said softly.

Without protest, she left the room. As she walked with Jake to the cafeteria, she was oblivious to the hospital routine: the nurses and orderlies carrying medication, the incessant pages from the intercom echoing down the corridors, the charts and files, and the ringing phones that normally sounded so familiar.

Jake pushed open the double doors to the dining room. Trays and silverware were clattering, and the smell of frying bacon, sizzling sausages, maple syrup, and coffee filled the air. Despite her despondency, Shawna's stomach grumbled and she let Jake buy her a platter of eggs, bacon, and toast.

Taking a seat at a scarred Formica table, she sat across from her brother and tried to eat. But she couldn't help overhearing the gossip filtering her way. Two nurses at a nearby table were speaking in a loud whisper and Shawna could barely concentrate on her breakfast.

"It's a shame, really," a heavyset nurse was saying, clucking her tongue. "Parker Harrison of all people! You know, I used to watch his matches on TV."

"You and the rest of the country," her companion agreed.

Shawna's hands began to shake.

"And on his wedding day!" the first woman said. "And think about that boy and his family!"

"The boy?"

"Brad Lomax. DOA. There was nothing Lowery could do."

Shawna felt every muscle in her body tense. She was chewing a piece of toast, but it stuck in her throat.

"That explains the reporters crowded around the front door," the smaller woman replied.

"For sure. And that's not all of it. His fiancée is here, too. From what I hear she's a doctor over at Columbia Memorial. Been with him ever since the accident. She came charging over here in her wedding dress, demanding to see him."

"Poor thing."

Shawna dropped her fork and her fists curled in anger. *How dare they gossip about Parker!*

"Right. And now he's comatose. No telling when he'll wake up."

"Or if."

Shawna's shoulders stiffened and she was about to say something, but Jake held up his hand and shook his head. "Don't bother," he suggested. "It's just small talk."

"About Parker and me!"

"He's a famous guy. So was Brad Lomax. Loosen up, Shawna, you've heard hospital gossip before."

"Not about Parker," she muttered, her appetite waning again as she managed to control her temper. The two nurses carried their trays back to the counter and Shawna tried to relax. Of course Parker's accident had created a stir and people were only people. Jake was right. She had to expect curiosity and rumors.

"I know this is hard. But it's not going to get much better, at least for a while." He finished his stack of pancakes and pushed his plate to one side. "You may as well know that the reporters have already started calling. There were several recordings on your phone machine this morning."

"You were at my apartment?"

"I took back your bag and I gave the wedding dress to Mom. She's going to have it cleaned, but isn't sure that it will look the same."

"It doesn't matter," Shawna said. She wondered if

she'd ever wear the gown again. "How're Mom and Dad?"

"They're worried about you and Parker."

"I'll bet," she whispered, grateful for her parents and their strength. Whereas Parker was strong because he'd grown up alone, never knowing his parents, Shawna had gotten her strength from the support and security of her family.

"Mom's decided to keep a low profile."

"And Dad?"

"He wants to tear down the walls of this hospital."

"It figures."

"But Mom has convinced him that if you need them, you'll call."

"Or you'll tell them, if I don't," Shawna guessed.

Smiling slightly, he said. "They're just trying to give you some space—but you might want to call them."

"I will. Later. After Parker wakes up."

Jake raised one brow skeptically, but if he had any doubts, he kept them to himself. "Okay, I'll give them the message."

She quit pretending interest in her food and picked up her tray. She'd been away from Parker for nearly half an hour and she had to get back.

"There's something you should remember," Jake said as they made their way through the tightly packed Formica tables, setting their trays on the counter.

"And what's that?"

"When you leave the hospital, you might want to go out a back entrance, unless you're up to answering a lot of personal questions from reporters."

"I understand. Thanks for the warning."

She turned toward the elevator, but Jake caught her elbow.

"There is one other thing. Brad Lomax's funeral is the day after tomorrow. Mom already arranged to send a spray of flowers from you and Parker."

Shawna winced at the mention of Brad's name. His death was still difficult to accept. And then there was the matter of Parker and how he would feel when he found out what had happened to his protegé. "Mom's an angel," Shawna decided, "but I think I'd better put in an appearance."

"The funeral's for family only," Jake told her. "Don't think about it."

Relieved, Shawna said, "I'll try not to. I'll see you later." Waving, she dashed to the stairwell, unable to wait for the elevator. She had to get back to Parker and make sure she was the one who broke the news.

Parker felt as if his head would explode. Slowly he opened an eye, ignoring the pain that shot through his brain. He tried to lift a hand to his head, but his cramped muscles wouldn't move and his struggling fingers felt nothing save cold metal bars.

Where am I? he wondered, trying to focus. There was a bad taste in his mouth and pain ripped up one side of his body and down the other. His throat worked, but no sound escaped.

"He's waking up!" a woman whispered, her voice heavy with relief. The voice was vaguely familiar, but he couldn't place it. "Call Dr. Handleman or Dr. Lowery! Tell them Parker Harrison is waking up!"

What the hell for? And who are Lowery and Handleman? Doctors? Is that what she said?

"Parker? Can you hear me? Parker, love?"

He blinked rapidly, focusing on the face pressed close to his. It was a beautiful face, with even features, pink-tinged cheeks, and worried green eyes. Long, slightly wavy honey-colored hair fell over her shoulders to brush against his neck.

"Oh, God, I'm so glad you're awake," she said, her voice thick with emotion. Tears starred her lashes and for the first time he noticed the small lines of strain near her mouth and the hollows of her cheeks.

She's crying! This beautiful young woman was actually shedding tears. He was amazed as he watched her tears drizzle down her cheeks and one by one drop onto the bedsheets. She was crying for him! But why?

Her hands were on his shoulders and she buried her face into the crook of his neck. Her tenderness seemed right, somehow, but for the life of him, he couldn't understand why. "I've been so worried! It's been three days! Thank God, you're back!"

His gaze darted around the small room, to the television, the rails on the bed, the dripping IV hanging over his head, and the baskets and baskets of flowers sitting on every available space in the room. It slowly dawned on him that he was in a hospital. The pain in his head wasn't imagined, this wasn't all a bad dream. Somehow he'd landed in a hospital bed, completely immobilized!

"Good morning, Mr. Harrison!" a gruff male voice called.

The woman straightened and quickly brushed aside her tears.

Shifting his gaze, Parker saw a man he didn't recognize walk up to the bed and smile down at him. A doctor. Dressed in a white lab coat, with an identification tag that Parker couldn't make out, the man stared down at Parker from behind thick, wire-framed glasses. Taking Parker's wrist in one hand, he glanced at his watch. "I'm Dr. Handleman. You're a patient here in Mercy Hospital and have been for the past three days."

Three days? What in God's name was this man talking about? Partial images, horrible and vague, teased his mind, though he couldn't remember what they meant.

Drawing his brows together in concentration, Parker tried to think, strained to remember, but his entire life was a blur of disjointed pieces that were colorless and dreamlike. He had absolutely no idea who these people were or why he was here.

"You're a very lucky man," the doctor continued, releasing his wrist. "Not many people could have survived that accident."

Parker blinked, trying to find his voice. "Accident?" he rasped, the sound of his own voice unfamiliar and raw.

"You don't remember?" The doctor's expression clouded.

"Wh-what am I doing here?" Parker whispered hoarsely. His eyes traveled past the doctor to the woman. She was leaning against the wall, as if for support. Wearing a white lab coat and a stethoscope, she had to be a member of the staff. *So why the tears?* "Who are you?" he asked, his bruised face clouding as he tried to concentrate. He heard her muted protest and saw the slump of her shoulders. "Do I know you?"

Four

Shawna's heart nearly stopped. "Parker?" she whispered, struggling to keep her voice steady as she took his bandaged hand in hers. "Don't you remember me?"

His gaze skated over her face and he squinted, as if trying to remember something hazy, but no flash of recognition flickered in his eyes.

"I'm Shawna," she said slowly, hoping to hide the tremble of her lips. "Shawna McGuire."

"A doctor?" he guessed, and Shawna wanted to die.

"Yes—but more than that."

Tom Handleman caught her eye, warning her not to push Parker too hard, but Shawna ignored him. This was important. Parker had to remember! He couldn't forget—not about the love they'd shared, the way they had felt and cared about each other.

"We were supposed to be married," she said quietly, watching his thick brows pull together in consternation. "The day after your accident, at Pioneer Church, in the rose arbor . . . I waited for you."

He didn't say a word, just stared at her as if she were a complete stranger.

"That's enough for now," Tom Handleman said, stepping closer to the bed, snapping on his penlight, trying to end the emotional scene. "Let's take a look at you, Mr. Harrison."

But before Tom could shine his penlight into Parker's eyes, Parker grabbed the doctor's wrist. The crisp sheets slid from one side of the bed, exposing his bare leg and the bandages, still streaked with dried blood. "What the hell's going on?" he demanded, his voice gruff and nearly unrecognizable. "What happened to me? What's she talking about?" He glanced back to Shawna. "What marriage? I've never even been engaged—" Then his eyes dropped to Shawna's left hand and the winking diamond on her ring finger.

"Mr. Harrison, please—"

"Just what the hell happened to me?" Parker repeated, trying to sit up, only to blanch in pain.

"Parker, please," Shawna whispered, restraining him with her hands. She could feel his shoulder muscles, hard and coiled, flexing as he attempted to sit upright. "Just calm down. We'll straighten this all out. You'll remember, I promise." But she had to fight the catch in her throat and her professionalism drained away from her. She couldn't be cool or detached with Parker. "Dr. Handleman's your physician."

"I don't *know* any Handleman. Where's Jack Pederson?"

"Who?" Handleman asked, writing quickly on Parker's chart.

Shawna glanced nervously to the doctor. "Jack was Parker's trainer."

"Was?" Parker repeated, his features taut from pain and the effort of trying to remember those tiny pieces of his past that teased him, rising just to the surface of his mind only to sink deeper into murky oblivion. "Was?"

"That was a couple of years ago," Shawna said quickly.

"What're you talking about? Just last Saturday, Jack and I—" But he didn't finish and his features slackened suddenly as he turned bewildered blue eyes on Handleman. "No, it wasn't Saturday," he whispered, running one hand through his hair and feeling, for the first time, the bandages surrounding his head. Involuntarily his jaw tightened. "Maybe you'd better fill me in," he said, dropping his hand and pinning Tom Handleman with his gaze. "What the hell happened to me?"

"You were in an accident. Several days ago."

Parker closed his eyes, trying vainly to remember.

"From what the police tell me, a truck swerved into your lane, your Jeep crashed through the guardrail, and you were pinned inside the vehicle for several hours. They brought you in here, we performed surgery, and you've been unconscious ever since."

Parker seemed about to protest, but didn't. Instead he listened in stony silence as Tom described his injuries and prognosis.

"So, now that you're awake and the swelling in your leg has gone down, we'll do surgery on that knee. It will all take a little time. You'll be in physical therapy for a while, then you'll be good as new—or almost."

"How long is 'a while?'"

"That depends upon you and how everything heals."

"Just give me an educated guess."

Handleman crossed his arms over his chest, folding Parker's chart against his lab coat. "I'll be straight with you, Mr. Harrison."

"I'd appreciate that—and call me Parker."

"Fair enough, Parker. It could take anywhere from three months to a year of physical therapy before you can play tennis again. But, if you set your mind to it, work hard, I'll bet you'll be walking without crutches in six months."

Parker's jaw was rock hard and his eyes, clouded, moved from Tom's face to Shawna's. "Okay. That answers one question. Now, tell me about the driver of the truck—is he okay?"

"Not a scratch," Tom replied. "You missed him completely, even though he was all over the road. He was too drunk to report the accident."

A muscle jerked in Parker's jaw as he tried to remember. Horrifying images taunted him, but he couldn't quite make them out. Nonetheless his heart began to beat unsteadily and his hands, beneath bandages, had started to sweat. "There's something else, though," he said, rubbing his eyes. "Something—I can't remember. Something . . . important." *God, what is it?*

Shawna cleared her throat. Though she tried to appear calm, Parker read the hint of panic in the way she glanced at Handleman and toyed with the strand of pearls at her neck. "Maybe that's enough for you right now," she said.

"You know something, both of you. Something you're keeping from me."

Shawna, feeling the urge to protect him, to lie if she had to, to do anything to keep him from the horrid truth, touched his arm. "Just rest now."

"Is that your professional advice?" Parker asked. "Or are you trying to put me off?"

"Professional," Tom said quickly, rescuing Shawna. "A nurse will be in to take your temperature and order you some lunch—"

"Wait a minute." Parker's voice was stern. "Something's wrong here, I can feel it. There's something you're not telling me about the accident." *What the hell is it?* Then he knew. "Someone else was involved," he said flatly. "Who?"

Shawna's shoulders stiffened a bit and her fingers found his on the cold metal railing.

Handleman offered a professional smile. "Right now all you have to worry about is—"

Parker sat bolt upright, tearing the IV tubing from the rail of the bed and ignoring the jab of pain in his knee. He kicked off the sheets and tried to climb out of bed. "What I have to worry about is who was with me. Where is he—or she?" Fire flared in his eyes as Handleman tried to restrain him. "I have the right to know!"

"Whoa—Parker, settle down," Handleman said.

"Who, dammit!"

"Brad Lomax," Shawna whispered, unable to meet the confused torture in his eyes.

"Lomax?"

"He was in the car with you. He drank too much at our wedding rehearsal dinner and you were taking him home."

"But I don't remember—" He swallowed then, his eyes clouding. Somewhere deep in his mind he remembered the squeal of tires, the shatter of glass, felt his muscles wrench as he jerked hard on the steering wheel, heard a terrifying scream. "Oh, God," he rasped. "Who is he?"

"A tennis pro. Your student." Shawna felt her eyes grow moist as she watched the skin over his cheekbones turn white and taut.

"I was driving," he said slowly, as if measuring each agonizing word. "Lomax. How is he?"

"I'm afraid he didn't make it," Tom replied, exchanging glances with Shawna.

"He was killed in the wreck?" Parker's voice was sharp and fierce with self-loathing. "I killed him?"

"It was an accident," Shawna said quickly. "An unfortunate one—his seat belt malfunctioned and he was pinned under the Jeep."

Parker blinked several times, then lay back on the pillows as he struggled with his past. This couldn't be happening—he didn't even know these people! Maybe if he just went back to sleep he'd wake up and this hellish dream with the beautiful woman and clouded jags of memory would go away. "Does Lomax have any family?"

Just you, Shawna thought, but shook her head. "Only an uncle and a couple of cousins, I think."

"I think you'd better get some rest now," Tom advised, motioning to a nurse standing by the door. "I want Mr. Harrison sedated—"

"No!" Parker's eyes flew open.

"This has all been such a shock—"

"I can handle it," Parker said tightly, his face grim and stern. "No sedative, no painkillers. Got it?"

"But—"

"Got it?" he repeated, some of his old fire returning. "And don't try slipping anything into this!" He lifted his fist with the IV tubes attached.

Handleman's mouth became a thin white line. "Lie back down, Mr. Harrison," he said sternly, waiting until Parker reluctantly obeyed. "Now, it's my job to see that you're taken care of—that you rest. But I'll need your help. Either you contain yourself or I'll have the nurse sedate you."

Muscles rigid, eyes bright with repressed fury, Parker stared at the ceiling.

"Good. Just let me know if you change your mind about the sedatives or the painkillers. Now, Shawna, I think Mr. Harrison needs his rest."

"Wait a minute," Parker insisted, reaching for Shawna's hand again. "I want to talk to you. Alone." His gaze drilled past Handleman's thick glasses, and fortunately, the doctor got the message. With a nod of his head, he tucked his clipboard under his arm, left the room, and closed the door.

"Tell me," he said, forcing himself to be calm, though his fingers clenched tightly over hers.

"About what?"

"Everything."

Shawna sighed and sagged against the bed. How could she begin to explain the whirlwind fantasy that had been their relationship? How could she recount how Parker had seen the potential in a streetwise juvenile delinquent and had turned him into one of the finest young tennis players in the nation—a boy who had become a younger brother to him?

"Tell me," he insisted, hungry for knowledge of himself.

"First things first. What do you remember?"

"Not enough!" he said sharply, then took a deep breath. "Not nearly enough."

"I'll tell you what I can," she said, "but you've got to promise to stay calm."

"I don't know if that's possible," he admitted.

"Then we haven't got a deal, have we?"

Swearing under his breath, he forced a grin he obviously didn't feel. "Okay," he said. "Deal."

"Good."

"Something tells me I should remember you."

"Most definitely," she agreed, feeling better than she had since the accident and grinning as she blinked back tears. Then, as all her bravado crumbled, she touched him gently on his forehead. "Oh, Parker, I've missed you—God, how I've missed you." Without thinking, she leaned forward and kissed him, brushing her lips suggestively over his and tasting the salt from her own tears.

But Parker didn't respond, just stared at her with perplexed blue eyes.

Shawna cleared her throat. "Fortunately, that part—the loneliness—is over now," she said, quickly sniffing back her tears. "And once you're out of here, we'll get married, and go to the Bahamas, have a ton of children, and live happily ever after!"

"Hey, whoa. Slow down," he whispered. Rubbing one hand over his jaw, he said, "Tell me about Brad Lomax."

Shawna realized he wouldn't give up. Though she felt the urge to protect him, she decided he had to face the truth sooner or later. She wanted to soften the blow, but she had to be honest with him. "Brad Lomax," she said uneasily, "was a hellion, and he was a terror on the tennis courts, and you saw something in him. You recognized his raw talent and took him under your wing. You and he were very close," she admitted, seeing the pain in his eyes. "You knew him a lot longer than you've known me."

"How close?" Parker asked, his voice low.

"You were his mentor—kind of a big brother. He looked up to you. That night, the night of the accident, he'd had too much to drink and wanted to talk to you. You offered to take him home."

A muscle worked in his jaw. "Why did he want to talk to me?"

Shawna lifted a shoulder. "I don't know. No one does. I suppose now that no one ever will."

"I killed him," Parker said quietly.

"No, Parker. It was an accident!" she said vehemently.

"How old was he?"

"Don't do this to yourself."

"How old was he?" His eyes drilled into hers.

"Twenty-two," she whispered.

"Oh, God." With a shudder, he closed his eyes. "I should have been the one who died, you know."

Shawna resisted the overpowering urge to cradle his head to her breast and comfort him. The torture twisting his features cut her to the bone. "Don't do this, Parker. It's not fair."

Parker stared up at her with simmering blue eyes. His expression was a mixture of anguish and awe, and his hand reached upward, his fingers slipping beneath her hair to caress her nape.

She trembled at his touch, saw the torment in his gaze.

"I don't remember where I met you. Or how. Or even who you are," he admitted, his voice husky, the lines near his mouth softening as he stared up at her. "But I do know that I'm one lucky son of a bitch if you were planning to marry me."

"Am—as in present tense," she corrected, her throat hot with unshed tears. "I still intend to march down the aisle with you, Parker Harrison, whether you're in a cast, on crutches, or in a wheelchair."

She felt his fingers flex as he drew her head to his, and he hesitated only slightly before touching his lips to hers.

"I will remember you," he promised, eyes dusky blue. "No matter what it takes!"

Her heart soared. All they needed was a little time!

Tom Handleman, his expression stern behind his wire-rimmed glasses, poked his head into the room. "Doctor?"

"That's my cue," Shawna whispered, brushing her lips against Parker's hair. "I'll be back."

"I'm counting on it."

She forced herself out of the room, feeling more lighthearted than she had in days. So what if Parker didn't remember her? What did it matter that he had a slight case of amnesia? The important consideration was his health, and physically he seemed to be gaining strength. Although mentally he still faced some tough hurdles, she was confident that with her help, Parker would surmount any obstacle fate cast his way. It was only a matter of time before he was back on his feet again and they could take up where they'd left off.

Jake was waiting for her in the hallway. Slouched into one of the waiting-room chairs, his tie askew, his shirtsleeves rolled over his forearms, he groaned as he stretched to his feet and fell into step with her. "Good news," he guessed, a wide grin spreading across his beard-stubbled jaw.

"The best!" Shawna couldn't contain herself. "He's awake!"

"About time!" Jake winked at her. "So, when's the wedding?"

Shawna chuckled. "I think Parker and I have a few bridges to cross first."

"Meaning Brad's death?"

"For one," she said, linking her arm through her brother's and pushing the elevator button. "You can buy me lunch and I'll explain about the rest of them."

"There's more?"

"A lot more," she said as they squeezed into the

crowded elevator and she lowered her voice. "He doesn't remember me—or much else for that matter."

Jake let out a long, low whistle.

"You're used to dealing with this, aren't you, in your practice?" she asked eagerly.

"I've seen a couple of cases."

"Then maybe you can work with him."

"Maybe," he said, his gray eyes growing thoughtful.

As the elevator opened at the hallway near the cafeteria, Shawna sent him a teasing glance, "Well, don't trip all over yourself to help."

"I'll do what I can," he said, massaging his neck muscles. "Unfortunately, you'll have to be patient, and that's not your strong suit."

"Patient?"

"You know as well as I do that amnesia can be tricky. He may remember everything tomorrow, or . . ."

"Or it may take weeks," she said with a sigh. "I can't even think about that. Not now. I'm just thanking my lucky stars that he's alive and he'll be all right."

Maybe, Jake thought, steering Shawna down the stainless steel counter and past cream pies, pudding, and fruit salad. Only time would tell.

Parker tried to roll off the bed, but a sharp pain in his knee and the IV tube stuck into his hand kept him flat on his back. He had a restless urge to get up, walk out of the hospital, and catch hold of the rest of his life—wherever it was.

He knew who he was. He could remember some things very clearly—the death of his parents in a boating accident, the brilliance of a trophy glinting gold in the sun. But try as he might, he couldn't conjure up Brad Lomax's face to save his soul.

And this Shawna woman with her honey-gold hair, soft lips, and intense green eyes. She was a doctor and they'd planned to be married? That didn't seem to fit. Nor did her description of his being some heroic do-gooder who had saved a boy from self-destruction while molding him into a tennis star.

No, her idealistic views of his life didn't make a helluva lot of sense. He remembered winning, playing to the crowd, enjoying being the best; he'd been ruthless and unerring on the court—the "ice man," incapable of emotion.

And yet she seemed to think him some sort of modern-day Good Samaritan. No way!

Struggling for the memories locked just under the surface of his consciousness, he closed his eyes and clenched his fists in frustration. Why couldn't he remember? Why?

"Mr. Harrison?"

He opened one eye, then the other. A small nurse was standing just inside the door.

"Glad you're back with us," she said, rolling in a clattering tray of food—if that's what you'd call the unappetizing gray potatoes-and-gravy dish she set in front of him. "Can I get you anything else?"

"Nothing," he replied testily, his thoughts returning to the beautiful doctor and the boy whose face he couldn't remember. *I don't want anything but my past.* Sighing, the nurse left.

Parker shoved the tray angrily aside and closed his eyes, willing himself to remember, concentrating on that dark void that was his past. Shawna. Had he known her? How? Had he really planned to marry her?

Sleep overcame him in warm waves and bits of memory played with his mind. Dreaming, he saw himself dancing with a gorgeous woman in a mist-cloaked rose garden. Her face was veiled and she was dressed in ivory silk and lace, he in a stiff tuxedo. Her scent and laughter engulfed him as they stopped dancing to sip from crystal glasses of champagne. Sweeping her into his arms again, he spilled champagne on the front of her gown and she tossed back her head but her veil stayed in place, blocking his view of her eyes as he licked the frothy bubbles from the beaded lace covering her throat.

"I love you," she vowed, sighing. "Forever."

"And I love you."

Light-headed from the drink and the nearness of her, he captured her lips with his, tasting cool, effervescent wine on her warm lips. Her fingers toyed his bow tie, loosening it from his neck, teasing him, and he caught a glimpse of her dimpled smile before she slipped away from him. He tried to call out to her, but he didn't know her name and his voice was muted. Desperate not to lose her, he grasped at her dress but clutched only air. She was floating away from him, her face still a guarded mystery. . . .

Parker's eyes flew open and he took in a swift breath. His hand was clenched, but empty. The dream had been so real, so lifelike, as if he'd been in that garden with that beautiful woman. But now, in his darkened hospital room, he wondered if the dream had been part of his memory or only something he wanted so fervently he'd created the image.

Had the woman been Shawna McGuire?

Dear God, he hoped so. She was, without a doubt, the most intriguing woman he'd ever met.

The next evening, in her office at Columbia Memorial Hospital on the east side of the Willamette River, Shawna leaned back in her chair until it creaked in protest. Unpinning her hair, letting it fall past her shoulders in a shimmering gold curtain, she closed her eyes and imagined that Parker's memory was restored and they were getting married, just as they planned.

"Soon," she told herself as she stretched and flipped through the pages of her appointment book.

Because she couldn't stand the idea of spending hour upon hour with nothing to do, she had rescheduled her vacation—the time she had meant to use on her honeymoon—and today had been her first full day of work since the accident. She was dead tired. The digital clock on her desk blinked the time. It was eight-fifteen, and she hadn't eaten since breakfast.

She'd finished her rounds early, dictated patient diagnoses into the tiny black machine at her desk, answered some correspondence and phone calls, and somehow managed to talk to the amnesia specialist on staff at Columbia Memorial. Her ears still rang with his advice.

"Amnesia's not easy to predict," Pat Barrington had replied to her questions about Parker. A kindly neurosurgeon with a flushed red face and horn-rimmed glasses, he'd told Shawna nothing she hadn't really already known. "Parker's obviously reacting to the trauma, remembering nothing of the accident or the events leading up to it," Barrington had said, punching the call button for the elevator.

"So why doesn't he remember Brad Lomax or me?"

"Because you're both part of it, really. The accident occurred right after the rehearsal dinner. Subconsciously, he's denying everything leading up to the accident—even your engagement. Give him time, Shawna. He's not likely to forget you," Barrington had advised, clapping Shawna on her back.

Now, as Shawna leaned back in her chair, she sighed and stared out the window into the dark September night. "Time," she whispered. Was it her friend or enemy?

Five

Two weeks later, Shawna sipped from her teacup and stared through the kitchen window of her apartment at the late afternoon sky. Parker's condition hadn't changed, except that the surgery on his knee had been a success. He was already working in physical therapy to regain use of his leg, but his mind, as far as Shawna and the wedding were concerned, was a complete blank. Though Shawna visited him each day, hoping to help him break through the foggy wall surrounding him, he stared at her without a flicker of the warmth she'd always felt in his gaze.

Now, as she dashed the dregs of her tea into the sink, she decided she couldn't wait any longer. Somehow, she had to jog his memory. She ached to touch him again, feel his arms around her, have him talk to her as if she weren't a total stranger.

"You're losing it, McGuire," she told herself as she glanced around her kitchen. Usually bright and neat, the room was suffering badly from neglect. Dishes were stacked in the sink, the floor was dull, and there were half-filled boxes scattered on the counters and floor.

Before the wedding she'd packed most of her things, but now she'd lost all interest in moving from the cozy little one-bedroom apartment she'd called home for several years. Nonetheless, she had given her notice and would have to move at the end of the month.

Rather than consider the chore of moving, she stuffed

two packets of snapshots into her purse and found her coat. Then, knowing she was gambling with her future, she grabbed her umbrella and dashed through the front door of her apartment.

Outside, the weather was gray and gloomy. Rain drizzled from the sky, ran in the gutters of the old turn-of-the-century building, and caught on the broad leaves of the rhododendron and azaleas flanking the cement paths.

"Dr. McGuire!" a crackly voice accosted her. "Wait up!"

Shawna glanced over her shoulder. Mrs. Swenson, her landlady, clad in a bright yellow raincoat, was walking briskly in her direction. Knowing what was to come, Shawna managed a smile she didn't feel. "Hi, Mrs. Swenson."

"I know you're on your way out," Mrs. Swenson announced, peering into the bushes near Shawna's front door and spying the lurking shadow of Maestro, Shawna's yellow tabby near the steps. Adjusting her plastic rain bonnet, Mrs. Swenson pursed her lips and peered up at Shawna with faded gold eyes. "But I thought we'd better talk about your apartment. I know about your troubles with Mr. Harrison and it's a darned shame, that's what it is—but I've got tenants who've planned to lease your place in about two weeks."

"I know, I know," Shawna said. If her life hadn't been shattered by the accident, she would already have moved into Parker's house on the Willamette River. But, of course, the accident had taken care of that. "Things just haven't exactly fallen into place."

"I know, I know," Mrs. Swenson said kindly, still glancing at the cat. "But, be that as it may, the Levertons plan to start moving in the weekend after next and your lease is up. Then there's the matter of having the place painted, the drapes cleaned, and whatnot. I hate to be pushy . . . but I really don't have much choice."

"I understand," Shawna admitted, thinking over her

options for the dozenth time. "And I'll be out by Friday night. I promise."

"That's only four days away," Mrs. Swenson pointed out, her wrinkled face puckering pensively.

"I've already started packing." Well, not really, but she did have some things in boxes, things she'd stored when she and Parker had started making wedding plans. "I can store my things with my folks and live either with them or with Jake," she said. The truth of the matter was, deep down, she still intended to move into Parker's place, with or without a wedding ring. In the past few weeks since the accident, she'd discovered just how much she loved him, and that a certificate of marriage wasn't as important as being with him.

"And what're you planning to do about that?" the old woman asked, shaking a gnarled finger at Maestro as he nimbly jumped onto the window ledge. With his tail flicking anxiously, he glared in through the window to the cage where Mrs. Swenson's yellow parakeet ruffled his feathers and chirped loudly enough to be heard through the glass.

"He's not really mine—"

"You've been feeding him, haven't you?"

"Well, yes. But he just strayed—"

"Two years ago," Mrs. Swenson interjected. "And if he had his way my little Pickles would have been his dinner time and time again."

"I'll take him with me."

"Good. Saves me a trip to the animal shelter," Mrs. Swenson said. Shawna seriously doubted the old woman had the heart to do anything more dastardly than give Maestro a saucer of milk—probably warmed in the microwave. Though outwardly a curmudgeon, Myrna Swenson had a heart of gold buried beneath a crusty layer of complaining.

"I'll tell Eva Leverton she can start packing."

"Good!" Shawna climbed into her car and watched as

Mrs. Swenson cooed to the bird in the window. She flicked on the engine, smothered a smile, and muttered, "Pickles is a dumb name for a bird!" Then slamming the car into gear, she drove away from the apartment complex.

More determined than ever to help Parker regain his memory, Shawna wheeled across the Ross Island bridge and up the steep grade of the west hills to Mercy Hospital.

Today Parker would remember her, she decided with a determined smile as she pulled on the emergency brake and threw open the car door. Sidestepping puddles of rainwater, she hurried inside the old concrete and glass of Mercy Hospital.

She heard Parker before she saw him. Just as the elevator doors parted on the fourth floor, Parker's voice rang down the gray-carpeted hallway.

"Hey, watch out, you're killing me!" he barked and Shawna smothered a grin. One of the first signs of patient improvement was general irritability, and Parker sounded as if he was irritable in spades.

"Good morning," Shawna said, cautiously poking her head into the room.

"What's good about it?" Parker grumbled.

"I see our patient is improving," she commented to the orderly trying to adjust the bed.

"Not his temperament," the orderly confided.

"I heard that," Parker said, but couldn't help flashing Shawna a boyish grin—the same crooked grin she'd grown to love. Her heart did a stupid little leap, the way it always did when he rained his famous smile on her.

"Be kind, Parker," she warned, lifting some wilting roses from a ceramic vase and dropping the wet flowers into a nearby trash basket. "Otherwise he might tell the people in physical therapy to give you the 'torture treatment,' and I've heard it can be murder."

"Humph." He laughed despite his ill humor and the orderly ducked gratefully out the door.

"You're not making any friends here, you know," she said, sitting on the end of his bed and leaning back to study him. Her honey-colored hair fell loose behind her shoulders, and a small smile played on her lips.

"Am I supposed to be?"

"If you don't want your breakfast served cold, your temperature to be taken at four A.M., or your TV cable to be mysteriously tampered with."

"I'd pay someone to do it," Parker muttered. "Then maybe I wouldn't have to watch any more of that." He nodded in the direction of the overhead television. On the small screen, a wavy-haired reporter with a bright smile was sitting behind a huge desk while discussing the worldwide ranking of America's tennis professionals.

"*—and the tennis world is still reeling from the unfortunate death of Brad Lomax, perhaps the brightest star in professional tennis since his mentor, Parker Harrison's, meteoric burst onto the circuit in the midseventies.*"

A picture of Brad, one arm draped affectionately over Parker's broad shoulders, the other hand holding a winking brass trophy triumphantly overhead, was flashed onto the screen. Brad's dark hair was plastered to his head, sweat dripped down his face, and a fluffy white towel was slung around his neck. Parker, his chestnut hair glinting in the sun, his face tanned and unlined, his eyes shining with pride, stood beside his protégé.

Now, as she watched, Shawna's stomach tightened. Parker lay still, his face taut and white as the newscaster continued. "*Lomax, whose off-court escapades were as famous as his blistering serves, was killed just over two weeks ago when the vehicle Parker Harrison was driving swerved off the road and crashed down a hundred-foot embankment.*

"*Harrison is still reported in stable condition, though there're rumors that he has no memory of the near-collision with a moving van which resulted in the—*"

Ashen-faced, Shawna snapped the television off. "I don't know why you watch that stuff!"

Parker didn't answer, just glanced out the window to the rain-soaked day and the gloomy fir boughs visible through his fourth-floor window. "I'm just trying to figure out who I am."

"And I've told you—"

"But I don't want the romanticized version—just the facts," he said, his gaze swinging back to hers. "I want to remember—for myself. I want to remember *you.*"

"You will. I promise," she whispered.

He sighed in frustration, but touched her hand, his fingers covering hers. "For the past week people have been streaming in here—people I should know and don't. There have been friends, reporters, doctors, and even the mayor, for heaven's sake! They ask questions, wish me well, tell me to take it easy, and all the time I'm thinking, 'who the hell are you?'"

"Parker—" Leaning forward, she touched his cheek, hoping to break through the damming wall blocking his memory.

"Don't tell me to be patient," he said sharply, but his eyes were still warm as they searched her face. "Just take one look around this room, for crying out loud!" Everywhere there were piles of cards and letters, huge baskets of fruit, tins of cookies and vases of heavy-blossomed, fragrant flowers. "Who *are* these people?" he asked, utterly perplexed.

Shawna wanted to cry. "People who care, Parker," she said, her voice rough as her hands covered his, feeling the warmth of his palms against her skin. She treasured the comfort she felt as his fingers grazed her cheekbones. "People who care about us."

He swore under his breath. "And I can't remember half of them. Here I am with enough flowers to cover all the floats in the Rose Parade and enough damned fruit and banana bread to feed all the starving people in the world—"

"You're exaggerating," she charged.

"Well, maybe just a little," he admitted, his lips twisting into a wry grin.

"A lot!"

"Okay, a lot."

She stroked his brow, hoping to ease the furrows in his forehead. "Unfortunately, neither of us can undo what's happened. Don't you think that I would change things if I could? That I would push back the hands of the clock so that I could have you back—all of you?" She swallowed against a huge lump forming in her throat.

He rested his forehead against hers. His gaze took in every soft angle of her face, the way her lashes swept over her eyes, the tiny lines of concern etching the ivory-colored skin of her forehead, the feel of her breath, warm and enticing against his face. Old emotions, cloaked in that black recess of the past, stirred, but refused to emerge. "Oh, why can't I remember you?" His voice was so filled with torment and longing, she buried her face in his shoulder and twisted her fingers in the folds of his sheets.

"Try," she pleaded.

"I have—over and over again." His eyes were glazed as he stroked her chin. "If you believe anything, believe that I want to remember you . . . everything about you."

The ache within her burned, but before she could respond, his palms, still pressed against her cheeks, tilted her face upward. Slowly, he touched her lips with his. Warm and pliant, they promised a future together—she could feel it!

Shawna's heart began to race.

His lips moved slowly and cautiously at first, as if he were exploring and discovering her for the first time.

Tears welled unbidden to her eyes and she moaned, leaning closer to him, feeling her breath hot and constricted in her lungs.

Love me, she cried mutely. *Love me as you did.*

The kiss was so innocent, so full of wondering, she felt

as flustered and confused as a schoolgirl. "I love you," she whispered, her fingers gripping his shoulders as she clung to him and felt hot tears slide down her cheeks. "Oh, Parker, I love you!"

His arms surrounded her, drawing her downward until she was half lying across him, listening to the beat of his heart and feeling the hard muscles of his chest.

The sheets wrinkled between them as Parker's lips sought hers, anxious and moist, pressing first against her mouth and then lower, to the length of her throat as his hands twined in the golden sun-bleached strands of her hair. "I have the feeling I don't deserve you," he murmured into her ear, desire flaring in his brilliant blue eyes.

From the hallway, Jake cleared his throat. Shawna glanced up to see her brother, shifting restlessly from one foot to the other as he stood just outside the door.

"I, uh, hope I'm not disturbing anything," he said, grinning from one ear to the other, his hands stuffed into the pockets of his cords as he sauntered into the small room.

Shawna hurriedly wiped her cheeks. "Your timing leaves a lot to be desired."

"So I've been told," he replied, before glancing at Parker. "So, how's the patient?"

"Grumpy," Shawna pronounced.

"He didn't look too grumpy to me." Jake snatched a shiny red apple from a fruit basket and polished it against his tweed sports jacket.

"You didn't see him barking at the orderly."

One side of Jake's mouth curved cynically as he glanced at Parker. "Not you, not the 'ice man.'" Still grinning, he bit into the apple.

"This place doesn't exactly bring out the best in me," Parker said, eyeing the man who had almost become his brother-in-law.

"Obviously," Shawna replied. "But if everything goes

well in physical therapy today and tomorrow, and you don't get on Dr. Handleman's bad side again, you'll be out of here by the end of the week, only doing physical therapy on an outpatient basis."

"No wonder he's in a bad mood," Jake said, taking another huge bite from the apple. "Outpatient physical therapy sounds as bad as the seventh level of hell, if you ask me."

"No one did," Shawna reminded him, but smiled at her brother anyway. Jake had a way of helping her find humor in even the most trying times. Even as children, she could count on him and his cockeyed sense of humor to lift her spirits even on her worst days.

Jake tossed his apple core deftly into a trash can. "Two points—or was that three?" he asked. When neither Parker nor Shawna answered, he shoved his fingers through his hair. "Boy, you guys are sure a cheery group."

"Sorry," Shawna said. "As I told you, Grumpy isn't in a great mood."

Jake glanced from Shawna to Parker. "So, what can we do to get you back on your feet?"

"You're the psychiatrist," Parker replied stonily. "You tell me."

Shawna reached into her purse. "Maybe I can help." Ignoring her brother's questioning gaze, she reached into her purse and withdrew a thick packet of photographs. "I thought these might do the trick."

Her hands were shaking as one by one, she handed him the snapshots of the fair. Her heart stuck in her throat as she saw the pictures of herself, her long blond hair caught in the breeze, her green eyes filled with mischief as she clung to the neck of that white wooden stallion on the carousel and stretched forward, reaching and missing the brass ring with the fluttering ribbons.

Other photos, of Parker trying to catch a peanut in his mouth, of Parker flaunting his prized brass ring, and of the dark-eyed fortune-teller, beckoning them inside her ragtag tent, brought back her memories of the fair. Now, in the hospital room, only a little over two weeks later, the old-time fair seemed ages past, and the fortune-teller's prediction loomed over Shawna like a black cloak.

Parker studied each picture, his eyes narrowed on the images in the still shots. His brow furrowed in concentration.

Shawna held her breath. Couldn't he see the adoration shining in her eyes as she gazed into the camera? Or the loving way he had captured her on film? And what about the pictures of him, grinning and carefree? Wasn't it obvious that they had been two people hopelessly head over heels in love?

For a minute, she thought he reacted, that there was a flicker of recognition in his gaze, but as suddenly as it had appeared, it was gone.

"Nothing?" she asked, bracing herself.

He closed his eyes. "No—not nothing," he said, his voice dry and distant. "But what we shared—what was there at the fair—it's . . . gone."

"Just misplaced," Jake said quickly as if feeling the searing wound deep in Shawna's soul. "You'll find it again."

"I'd like to think so," Parker admitted but he still seemed vexed, his thick brows knitted, his chin set to one side, as if he were searching for a black hole in the tapestry her pictures had woven.

"Look, I've got to run," Jake said quickly, looking at his sister meaningfully. "Mom and Dad are expecting you for dinner tonight."

"But I can't," she said, unable to leave Parker. She felt that if she were given just a few more minutes, she could cause the breakthrough in Parker's memory.

"Don't stay on my account," Parker cut in, glaring angrily at the pictures spread across his bed.

Shawna saw them then as he did, pictures of a young couple in love, their future bright and untarnished, and she cringed inside, knowing instinctively what he felt—the anger and the resentment, the pain and the blackness of a time he couldn't remember.

"Maybe I shouldn't have brought these," she said hurriedly, scooping the photographs into the purse.

He snatched one out of her hands, the photo of her with her face flushed, her long hair billowing over the neck of the glossy white carousel horse. "I'll keep this one," he said, his features softening a little, "if you don't mind."

"You're sure?"

"Positive."

"Let's go." Jake suggested. "You can come back later. But right now, Mom and Dad are waiting."

Shawna felt her brother's hand over her arm, but she twisted her neck, craning to stare at Parker who didn't move, just studied the photograph in his hands. Impatiently, Jake half dragged her through the building.

"That was a stupid move!" Jake nearly shouted, once they were outside the hospital. "He's not ready for pictures of the past, can't you see that?" Jake's expression turned dark as he opened the car door for her, then slid behind the wheel and shoved the Porsche into gear.

"You can't just skip into his room and hand him pictures of a rose-colored future that could have been, you know. It takes time! Think about him, not just yourself! Where's your professionalism, *Doctor?*"

"Back in my medical bag, I guess," Shawna said, staring blindly out the windows. "I'm sorry."

"It's not me you have to apologize to." He let out a long, disgusted breath, then patted her shoulder. "Just hang in there. Try to think of Parker as another patient—not your fiancé, okay?"

"I will, but it's hard."

"I know," he said, "but he needs all your strength

now—and your patience." Jake turned off the main highway and veered down the elm-lined driveway of his parents' house. "Okay, sis. Show's on. Stiff upper lip for Mom and Dad," he teased, reaching across her and pushing open the car door.

As Shawna walked up the flagstone path, she steadfastly shoved all her doubts aside. Tomorrow she'd see Parker again and when she did, she wouldn't push too hard. She'd be patient and wait until the walls blocking his memory eroded—even if it killed her.

Long after Shawna left his room, Parker stared at the small photograph in his hand. Without a doubt, Dr. Shawna McGuire was the most fascinating, beautiful, and stubborn woman he'd ever met.

He knew now why he'd fallen in love with her. Though he was loath to admit it and despite all the problems he now faced, he was falling in love with her again. The depth of his feelings was a surprise. She aroused him sensually as well as intellectually. Doctor McGuire, though she professed her love, was a challenge. Just being near her, smelling her perfume, seeing the glimmer of mystique in her intelligent green eyes, was enough to drive him to distraction and cause an uncomfortable heat to rise in his loins.

Unfortunately, he had to be careful. No longer was he a recent tennis star with a future bright as the sun, acting in commercials and coaching younger, upcoming athletes. Now his future was unsure.

He glanced down and the woman in the photograph smiled up at him. She swore she loved him and he believed her. And, if he let himself, he could easily get caught in her infectious enthusiasm. Several times, when he'd kissed her, he'd seen images in his mind—smelled the salty air of the beach, or fresh raindrops in her hair, heard the tinkle of her laughter, felt the driving beat of her heart. Reality mixed with sights and smells that were as elusive as a winking star—bright one minute, dim and clouded the next.

And now, lying in the hospital bed, with months, perhaps years of physical therapy staring him in the face, what could he offer her?

A big, fat nothing. Because no matter how she deluded herself, Shawna was wrong about one thing: Parker would never be the man he was before the accident. His perception, with his memory, had changed.

Brad Lomax was gone, as was Parker's ability to coach and play tennis. The man Shawna McGuire had fallen in love with no longer existed and this new man—the one who couldn't even remember her—was a pale substitute. How long could she love a faded memory, he wondered. When would that love, so freely given, turn to duty?

Glancing again at the woman in the picture, Parker ached inside. Yes, he wanted her, maybe even loved her. But he wouldn't let her live a lie, sacrifice herself because she believed in a dream that didn't exist.

Gritting his teeth, Parker took the snapshot of Shawna and crushed it in his fist—then feeling immediately contrite, he tried to press the wrinkles from the photo and laid it, facedown, in a book someone had left by his bed.

"Help me," he prayed, his voice echoing in the empty room. "Help me be whole again."

Six

Shawna snatched a patient's chart from the rack next to the door of the examination room. She was running late and had to force herself into gear. "Get a move on, Doctor," she muttered under her breath as she glanced quickly over the patient information file. The patient, Melinda James, was new to the clinic, had an excellent health record, and was eighteen years old.

"Good afternoon," Shawna said, shoving open the door to find a beautiful black-haired girl with round eyes perched on the edge of the examination table. She looked scared as her fingers clamped nervously over a sheet she'd pulled over her shoulders, and Shawna felt as if the girl wanted to bolt. "I'm Dr. McGuire," she said calmly. "And you're Melinda?"

Melinda nodded and chewed nervously on her lip.

"So what can I do for you?"

"I, uh, saw your name in the paper," Melinda said quickly, glancing away. "You're the doctor who's engaged to Parker Harrison, right?"

Shawna's stomach tightened at the mention of Parker. Was Melinda a reporter, pretending to be a patient just to get an inside story on Parker, or was there something else?

"That's right, but I really don't see what that has to do with anything." She clamped the chart to her chest. "Do you know Parker?"

"He's got amnesia, doesn't he?"

Shawna tried to keep her tongue in check. Obviously the girl was nervous—maybe she was just making conversation. "I can't discuss Parker's condition. Now—" she glanced down at her chart. "Is there a reason you came to see me? A health reason?"

The girl sighed. "Yes I, uh, I've only been in Portland a few months so I don't have a doctor here. I went to a pediatrician in Cleveland," Melinda continued, "but I'm too old for a pediatrician now and I've got this problem, so I made an appointment with you."

"Fair enough." Shawna relaxed a little and took a pen from the pocket of her lab coat. "What was the pediatrician's name?"

Melinda seemed hesitant.

"I'll need this information in case we need to contact him for his files," Shawna explained, offering the girl an encouraging smile.

"Rankin, Harold Rankin," Melinda said quickly and Shawna scrawled the physician's name in the appropriate spot on the form. "Thanks." Pushing her suspicions aside, Shawna set the chart on a cabinet. "You said you had a problem. What kind of problem?"

Melinda twisted the sheet between her fingers. "I'm sick." Avoiding Shawna's eyes, she said in a rush, "I can't keep anything down and I'm not anoretic or whatever it's called. I don't understand what's wrong. I've had the flu for over a month and it just won't go away. I've never been sick for this long."

"The flu?" Shawna said, eyeing the girl's healthy skin color and clear eyes. "You're feverish? Your muscles ache?"

"No, not really. It's just that one minute I'm feeling great; the next I think I might throw up."

"And do you?"

"Sometimes—especially in the afternoon." Melinda wrung her hands anxiously together and sweat beaded her forehead. "And sometimes I get horrible cramps."

"Anything else? Sore throat?"

Shaking her short glossy hair, Melinda sighed. "I kept hoping I would get better, but—" She shrugged and the sheet almost slipped from her fingers.

"Well, let me take a look at you. Lie down." Shawna spent the next fifteen minutes examining Melinda carefully, as the girl nearly jumped off the examination table each time she was touched.

"When was the date of your last menstrual period?" Shawna finally asked, once the examination was over and Melinda was sitting, sheet draped over her on the table.

"I don't know. A couple of months ago, I guess."

"You *guess?*" Shawna repeated.

"I don't keep track—I'm real irregular."

"How irregular?"

"Well, not every month. I skip around a little."

"Could you be pregnant?"

Melinda's eyes widened and she licked her lips. "I—I don't get sick in the morning. Never in the morning."

Shawna smiled, trying to put the girl at ease. "It's different with everyone. I had a patient who only was sick at night."

Melinda chewed on her lower lip. "I—uh, it's possible, I guess," she whispered.

"Why don't we run a quick test and see?" Shawna asked.

"When will I know?"

"In a little while. I have a friend in the lab. The pregnancy test is relatively easy; but if there's something else, we won't know about it for a couple of days. Now, why don't you try to remember the date of your last period."

Melinda closed her eyes as Shawna drew a small vial of blood from her arm and had a nurse take the filled vial to the lab.

"I don't know. I think it was around the Fourth of July."

Shawna wasn't surprised. All of Melinda's symptoms pointed toward pregnancy. "This is nearly October," she pointed out.

Melinda's lower lip protruded defiantly. "I said I was irregular."

"Okay. No need to worry about it, until we know for sure." She checked her watch. "It's still early—the hospital lab can rush the results if I ask."

"Would you?"

"Sure. You can get dressed and meet me in my office in a few hours—say four o'clock?"

"Fine." Melinda grudgingly reached for her clothes and Shawna, feeling uneasy, left the room.

By the time Shawna returned to her office after seeing the rest of her patients and finished some paperwork, she was ready to call it a day. It was four o'clock and she was anxious to drive to Mercy Hospital to spend some time with Parker.

But first she had to deal with Melinda James.

"Well?" Melinda asked as she plopped into the chair opposite Shawna's desk.

Shawna scanned the report from the lab, then glanced at the anxious girl.

"Your test was positive, Melinda. You're going to have a baby."

Melinda let out a long sigh and ran her fingers through her hair. "I can't believe it," she whispered, but her voice lacked conviction and for the first time Shawna wondered if Melinda had been suspicious of her condition all along. "There's no chance that"—she pointed to the pink report—"is wrong."

"Afraid not."

"Great," Melinda mumbled, blinking back tears.

"I take it this isn't good news."

"The worst! My dad'll kill me!"

"Maybe you're underestimating your dad," Shawna suggested.

"No way!"

"What about the father of your child?" Shawna asked.

Tears flooded the girl's eyes. "The father?" she repeated, swallowing with difficulty and shaking her head.

"He has the right to know."

"He can't," Melinda said, her voice low and final, as if she had no choice in the matter.

"Give him a chance."

Melinda's eyes were bright with tears. "I can't tell him," she said. "He thinks this is all my responsibility. The last thing he wants is a baby."

"You don't know—"

"Oh, yes I do. He said so over and over again."

Shawna handed her a couple of tissues and Melinda dabbed her eyes but was unable to stem the flow of her tears.

"I—I was careful," she said, blinking rapidly. "But he'll blame me, I know he will!"

"Sometimes a man changes his mind when he's actually faced with the news that he's going to be a father."

"But he can't!" Melinda said harshly, obviously hurting deep inside.

Shawna walked around the desk and placed her arm around the young woman's shaking shoulders. "I don't want to pry," she said evenly. "What's going on between you and the father isn't any of my business—"

"If you only knew," Melinda whispered, glancing at Shawna with red-rimmed eyes, then shifting her gaze. Standing, she pushed away Shawna's arm. "This is my problem," she said succinctly. "I—I'll handle it."

"Try not to think of the baby as a problem, okay?" Shawna advised, reaching for a card from a small holder on her desk. "Take this card—it has Dr. Chambers's number. He's one of the best obstetricians in the city."

"What I need now is a shrink," Melinda said, still sniffing.

"My brother's a psychiatrist," Shawna said quietly, locating one of Jake's business cards. "Maybe you should talk with him—"

Melinda snatched the cards from Shawna's outstretched hand. "I—I'll think about it. After I talk with the father."

Shawna offered the girl an encouraging smile. "That's the first step."

"Just remember—this was *your* idea!"

"I'll take full responsibility," Shawna replied, but read the message in the young woman's eyes. More clearly than words, Melinda had told her Shawna didn't know what she was saying. Anger and defiance bright in her eyes, Melinda James walked briskly out the door.

Shawna watched her leave and felt the same nagging doubts she had when she'd first talked to the girl. "You can't win 'em all," she told herself thoughtfully as she hung her lab coat in the closet and quickly ran a brush through her hair. But she couldn't shake the feeling that Melinda, despite her vocal doubts, had known she was pregnant all along.

She reached for her purse and slung it over her shoulder, but stopped before slipping her arms through her jacket. Feeling a little guilty, she called directory assistance in Cleveland and asked for the number of Harold Rankin, Melinda's pediatrician.

"There are several H. Rankins listed," the operator told her.

"I'm looking for the pediatrician. He must have an office number." The operator paused. "I'm sorry. There is no Doctor Rankin listed in Cleveland."

"Unlisted? Look, I'm a doctor myself. I need to consult with him about a patient and I don't have his number," Shawna said, new suspicions gnawing at her.

The operator muttered something under her breath. "I really can't—"

"It's important!"

"Well, I guess I can tell you this much, there's no Dr.

Harold Rankin listed or unlisted in Cleveland. Just a minute." For a few seconds all Shawna could hear was clicking noises. "I'm sorry—I checked the suburbs. No Dr. Harold Rankin."

"Thank you," Shawna whispered, replacing the receiver. So Melinda had lied—or the doctor had moved. But that was unlikely. Shawna remembered Melinda's first words. *"I saw your name in the paper. . . . You're the doctor who's engaged to Parker Harrison, aren't you? . . . He's got amnesia, right?"*

Without thinking about what she was doing, Shawna buttoned her jacket and half ran out the door of her office. She waved good-bye to the receptionist, but her mind was filled with Melinda's conversation and the girl's dark grudging glances. No, Melinda James wasn't a reporter, but she was hiding something. Shawna just couldn't figure out what it was. As she took the elevator down to the underground parking garage, she was alone, her keys gripped in one hand. What did a pregnant eighteen-year-old girl have to do with Parker? she asked herself, suddenly certain she wouldn't like the answer.

Parker's leg throbbed, rebelling against his weight as he attempted to walk the length of the physical therapy room. His hands slipped on the cold metal bars, but he kept himself upright, moving forward by sheer will. Every rigid, sweat-covered muscle in his body screamed with the strain of dragging his damned leg, but he kept working.

"That's it, just two more steps," a pert therapist with a cheery smile and upturned nose persuaded, trying to encourage him forward.

Gritting his teeth he tried again, the foot slowly lifting from the floor. Pain ripped through his knee and he bit his lower lip, tasting the salt of his sweat. *Come on, Harrison,* he said to himself, squeezing his eyes shut, *do it for*

Shawna, that beautiful lady doctor who's crazy enough to love you.

In the past few weeks, he'd experienced flashes of memory, little teasing bits that had burned in his mind. He could remember being with her on a sailboat—her tanned body, taut and sleek. She'd been leaning against the boom as the boat skimmed across clear green water. Her blond hair had billowed around her head, shimmering gold in the late afternoon sun, and she'd laughed, a clear sound that rippled across the river.

Even now, as he struggled to the end of the parallel bars, he could remember the smell of fresh water and perfume, the taste of her skin and the feel of her body, warm and damp, as she'd lain with him on the sand of some secluded island.

Had they made love? That one delicious recollection escaped him, rising to the surface only to sink below the murky depths of his memory, as did so much of his life. Though he knew—he could sense—that he'd loved her, there was something else stopping him from believing everything she told him of their life together—something ugly and unnamed and a part of the Brad Lomax tragedy.

"Hey! You've done it!" the therapist cried as Parker took a final agonizing step.

While thinking of the enigma that was his relationship with Shawna, he hadn't realized that he'd finished his assigned task. "I'll be damned," he muttered.

"You know what this means, don't you?" the therapist asked, positioning a wheelchair near one of the contraptions that Parker decided were designed for the sole purpose of human torture.

"What?"

"You're a free man. This is the final test. Now, if your doctor agrees, you can go home and just come back here for our workouts."

Parker wiped the sweat from his eyes and grinned. He'd be glad to leave this place! Maybe once he was home he'd start to remember and he could pick up the pieces of his life with Shawna. Maybe then the dreams of a mystery woman that woke him each night would disappear, and the unknown past would become crystal clear again.

The therapist tossed him a white terry towel and a nurse appeared.

Parker wiped his face, then slung the towel around his neck.

Placing her hands on the handles of the wheelchair, the nurse said, "I'll just push you back to your room—"

"I'll handle that," Shawna said. She'd been standing in the doorway, one shoulder propped against the jamb as she watched Parker will himself through the therapy. She'd witnessed the rigid strength of his sweat-dampened shoulders and arms, seen the flinch of pain as he tried to walk, and recognized the glint of determination in his eyes as he inched those final steps to the end of the bars.

"If you're sure, Doctor—" the nurse responded, noting Shawna's identification tag.

"Very sure." Then she leaned over Parker's shoulder and whispered, "Your place or mine?"

He laughed then. Despite the throb of pain in his knee and his anguish of not being able to remember anything of his past, he laughed. "Get me out of here."

"Your wish is my command." Without further prompting, she rolled him across the polished floors of the basement hallway and into the waiting elevator, where the doors whispered closed. "Alone at last," she murmured.

"What did I do to deserve you?" he asked, glancing up at her, his eyes warm and vibrant.

Her heart constricted and impulsively she jabbed the stop button before leaning over and pressing her lips to his. "You have been, without a doubt, the best thing that ever happened to me," she said, swallowing back a thick lump in her throat. "You showed me there was more to life than medical files, patient charts, and trying to solve everyone else's problems."

"I can't believe—"

"Of course not," she said, laughing and guessing that he was going to argue with her again, tell her he didn't deserve her love. "You've been right all along, Parker," she confided. "Everything I've been telling you is a lie. You don't deserve me at all. It's just that I'm a weak, simple female and you're so strong and sexy and macho!"

"Is that so?" he asked, strong arms dragging her into his lap.

She kissed him again, lightly this time. "Well, isn't that what you wanted to hear?"

"Sounded good," he admitted.

Cocking her head to one side, her blond hair falling across his shoulder, she grinned slowly. "Well, the strong and sexy part is true."

"But somehow I don't quite see you as a 'weak, simple female.'"

"Thank heaven. So just believe that you're the best thing in my life, okay? And no matter what happens, I'm never going to take the chance of losing you again!"

"You won't," he murmured, pulling her closer, claiming her lips with a kiss so intense her head began to spin. She forgot the past and the future. She could only concentrate on the here and now, knowing in her heart the one glorious fact that Parker, her beloved Parker, was holding her and kissing her as hungrily as he had before the accident—as if he did indeed love her all over again.

Her breath caught deep in her lungs and inside, she was warming, feeling liquid emotion rush through her veins. She felt his hands move over her, rustling the lining of her skirt to splay against her back, hold her in that special, possessive manner that bound them so intimately together. Delicious, wanton sensations whispered through her body and she tangled her hands in his hair.

"Oh, what you do to me," he whispered in a voice raw and raspy as his fingers found the hem of her sweater and moved upward to caress one swollen breast. Hot and demanding, his fingers touched the soft flesh and Shawna moaned softly as ripples of pleasure ran like wildfire through her blood.

"Parker, please—" She cradled his head against her, feeling the warmth of his breath touch her skin. His lips teased one throbbing peak, his tongue moist as it caressed the hard little button.

Shawna was melting inside. Rational thought ceased and she was only aware of him and the need he created.

"Oh, Shawna," he groaned, slowly releasing her, his eyes still glazed with passion as a painful memory sizzled through his desire. "You're doing it again," he whispered, rubbing his temple as if it throbbed. "Shawna—stop!"

She had trouble finding her breath. Her senses were still spinning out of control and she stung from his rejection. Why was he pulling away from her? "What are you talking about?"

Passion-drugged eyes drilled into hers. "I remember, Shawna."

Relieved, she smiled. Everything was going to be fine. She tried to stroke his cheek but he jerked away. "Then you know how much we loved each—"

"I remember that you teased me, pushed me to the limit in public places. Like this."

"Parker, what are you talking about?" she cried, devastated. What was he saying? If he remembered, then surely he'd know how much she cared.

"It's not all clear," he admitted, helping her to her feet. "But there were times, just like this, when you drove me out of my mind!" He reached up and slapped the control panel. The elevator started with a lurch and Shawna nearly lost her footing.

"I don't understand—" she whispered.

The muscles of his face tautened. "Remember the fair?" he said flatly. "At the fir tree?"

She gasped, recalling rough bark against her bare back, his hands holding her wrists, their conversation about his "mistress."

"It was only a game we played," she said weakly.

"Some game." His eyes, still smoldering with the embers of recent passion, avoided hers. "You know, somehow I had the impression that you and I loved each other before—that we were lovers. You let me think that." His eyes were as cold as the sea.

"We were," she said, then recognized the censure in the set of his jaw. "Well, almost. We'd decided to wait to get married before going to bed."

Arching a brow disdainfully, he said through clenched teeth, "*We* decided? You're a doctor. I'm a tennis pro. Neither one of us is a kid and you expect me to believe that we were playing the cat-and-mouse game of waiting 'til the wedding."

"You said you remembered," she whispered, but then realized his memory was fuzzy. Certain aspects of their relationship were still blurred.

"I said I remembered part of it." But the anger in his words sounded hollow and unsure, as if he were trying to find an excuse to deny the passion between them only moments before.

The elevator car jerked to a stop and the doors opened on the fourth floor. Shawna, her breasts still aching, reached for the handles of the wheelchair, but Parker didn't wait for her. He was already pushing himself down the corridor.

In the room, she watched him shove the wheelchair angrily aside and flop onto the bed, his face white from the effort.

"You're memory is selective," she said, leaning over the bed, pushing her face so close to his that she could read the seductive glint in his blue eyes.

"Maybe," he admitted and stared at her lips, swallowing with difficulty.

"Then why won't you just try to give us a chance? We were good together, sex or no sex. Believe me." She heard him groan.

"Don't do this to me," he asked, the fire in his eyes rekindling.

"I'll do whatever I have to," she whispered, leaning closer, kissing him, brushing the tips of her breasts across his chest until he couldn't resist.

"You're making a big mistake." He pressed her close to him.

"Let me."

"I'm not the same man—"

"I don't care, damn it," she said, then sighed. "Just love me."

"That would be too easy," he admitted gruffly, then buried his face in her hair, drinking in the sweet feminine smell that teased at his mind every night. He held her so fiercely she could feel the heat of his body through her clothes. Clinging to him, she barely heard the shuffle of feet in the doorway until Parker dragged his lips from hers and stared over her shoulder.

Twisting, half expecting to find Jake with his lousy sense of timing, she saw a young black-haired girl standing nervously on one foot, then the other.

"Melinda?" Shawna asked, her throat dry. "Are you looking for me?"

"No," Melinda James said quietly, her large, brown eyes lifting until they clashed with Parker's. "I came to see him, on your advice."

"My advice—what—?" But a dark doubt steadily grew in her heart and she gripped Parker's shoulders more tightly, as if by clinging to him, she could stop what was to come. "No—there must be some mistake," she heard herself saying, her voice distant, as if in a dream.

"You told me to talk to him and that's . . . that's why

I'm here," Melinda said, her eyes round with fear, large tears collecting on her lashes. "You see, Parker Harrison is the father of my child."

Seven

"He's what?" Shawna whispered, disbelieving.

"It's true."

"Wait a minute—" Parker stared at the girl, not one flicker of recognition in his eyes. "Who are you?"

Shawna wanted to tell him not to believe a word of Melinda's story, but she didn't. Instead she forced herself to watch his reaction as Melinda, hesitantly at first, then with more conviction, claimed she and Parker had been seeing each other for several months, long before he'd started dating Shawna, and that she'd become pregnant with his child.

Parker blanched, his mouth drawing into a tight line.

"This is absurd," Shawna finally said, praying that Parker would back her up.

"How old are you?" he asked, eyes studying the dark-haired girl.

"Eighteen."

"Eighteen?" he repeated, stunned. His eyes narrowed and he forced himself to stand. "And you're saying that you and I—"

"—were lovers," Melinda clarified.

Shawna couldn't stand it a minute more. "This is all a lie. Parker, this girl came into my office, asked all sorts of questions about you and your amnesia, and then had me examine her."

"And?"

"And she *is* pregnant. That much is true. But . . . but

. . . she's lying . . . you couldn't have been with her. *I* would have known." But even though her words rang with faith, she couldn't help remembering all the times Parker had taunted her by pretending to have a mistress. *I suppose I'll have to give up my mistress,* he'd said at the fair, teasing her, but wounding her just the same. Her old doubts twisted her heart. Was it possible that he'd actually been seeing someone and that the person he'd been with had been this girl?

"You don't remember me?" Melinda asked.

Parker closed his eyes, flinching a bit.

"I saw you the night of the accident," she prodded. "You . . . you were with Brad and he was drunk."

Parker's eyes flew open and pain, deep and tragic, showed in their vibrant blue depths.

"You stopped by my apartment and Brad became violent, so you hauled him back to the car."

"She's making this up," Shawna said. "She must have read about it in the papers or heard it on the news." But her voice faltered as she saw Parker wrestling with a memory.

"I've met her before," he said slowly. "I was at her apartment."

"No!" Shawna cried. She wouldn't believe a word of Melinda's lies—she couldn't! Parker would never betray her! She'd almost lost Parker once and she wasn't about to lose him again, not to this girl, not to anyone. "Parker, you don't honestly believe—"

"I don't know *what* to believe!" he snapped.

"But we've been through so much together . . ." Then she turned her eyes on Melinda and all of her professionalism and medical training flew out the window. No longer was Melinda her patient, but just a brash young woman trying to tarnish the one man Shawna loved. "Look," she said, her voice as ragged as her emotions. "I don't really know who you are or why you're here torturing him or even how you got into this room, but I want you out, now!"

"Stop it, Shawna," Parker said.

But Shawna ignored him. "I'll call the guards if I have to, but you have no right to come in here and upset any of the patients—"

"I'm *your* patient," Melinda said, satisfaction briefly gleaming in her eyes.

"I referred you to—"

"He's the father of my child, dammit!" Melinda cried, wilting against the wall and sobbing like the girl she was.

"She can stay," Parker pronounced as Tom Handleman, his lab coat flapping behind him, marched into the room. "What the devil's going on here?" he demanded, eyeing Shawna. "Who's she?" He pointed an accusing finger at the huddled figure of Melinda.

"A friend of mine," Parker said, his voice ringing with quiet authority.

"Parker, no!" Shawna whispered, ignoring Tom. "She lied to me this morning—told me the name of her previous physician in Cleveland. I tried to call him—there is no Dr. Harold Rankin in the area."

"Then he moved," Melinda said, stronger because of Parker's defense. "It's—it's been years."

"She has to leave," Shawna decided, turning to Tom, desperation contorting her face.

"Maybe she can help," Tom suggested.

"Help?" Shawna murmured. "She's in here accusing him, lying to him, lying to me—"

Melinda stood, squaring her shoulders and meeting Parker's clouded gaze. "I—I understand why you feel betrayed, Dr. McGuire. First Parker lied to you and then I had to lie this morning. But I just wanted to find out that he was all right. No one would let me in here. Then *you* convinced me that I had to tell him about the baby—"

"Baby?" Handleman asked, his face ashen.

"—and I decided you were right. Every father has the

right to know about his child whether he wants to claim him or not."

"For cryin' out loud!" Tom whispered. "Look, Miss—"

"James," Melinda supplied.

"Let her stay," Parker said.

"You remember me," she said.

Shawna wanted to die as they stared at each other.

"I've met you," Parker admitted, his face muscles taut. "And I don't mean to insult you, Miss James—"

"Melinda. You called me Linnie. Don't you remember?" Her chin trembled and she fought against tears that slid from her eyes.

"I'm sorry—"

"You have to remember!" she cried. "All those nights by the river—all those promises—"

Good Lord, what was she saying? Shawna's throat closed up. "Parker and I were—are—going to be married, and neither one of us believes that he's the father of your child. This is obviously just some way for you and your boyfriend to take advantage—"

"No!" Melinda whispered. "I don't care what *you* believe, but Parker loves me! He—he—" her eyes darted quickly around the room and she blinked. "Oh, please, Parker. Remember," she begged.

Parker gripped the arms of his wheelchair. "Melinda," he said softly. Was it Shawna's imagination or did his voice caress the younger woman's name? "I don't remember ever sleeping with you."

"You deny the baby?"

He glanced at Shawna, his eyes seeming haunted. She could only stare back at him. "Not the baby. I'm just not sure it's mine."

Shawna shook her head. "No—"

"Then maybe you'd want a simple paternity test," Melinda suggested.

"Hey—hold the phone," Tom Handleman cut in. "Let's all just calm down. Right now, Miss James, I'm asking you to leave." Then he glanced at Shawna. "You, too, Dr. McGuire. This has been a strain on Parker. Let's all just give it a rest."

"I'm afraid I can't do that," Melinda said staunchly, seeming to draw from an inner reserve of strength. "Don't get me wrong, Parker. I'm not interested in ruining your reputation or trying to damage your professional image, but my baby needs his father."

"So you want money," Parker said cynically.

"Money isn't what I'm after," Melinda said, and Shawna felt a chill as cold as a December wind cut through her. "I want to give my baby a name and I want him to know who his father is. If it takes a paternity test to convince you or a lawsuit, I don't care." Swallowing back a fresh onslaught of tears, she walked unsteadily out of the room.

Shawna turned a tortured gaze to Parker. "You remember her?"

He nodded and let his forehead drop to his hand. "A little."

Dying inside, Shawna leaned against the bed. After all these weeks, Parker still barely admitted to remembering her—only disjointed pieces of their relationship. And yet within fifteen minutes of meeting Melinda James he conceded that he recognized her. Dread settled over her.

Sick inside, she wondered if Melinda's ridiculous accusations could possibly be true. Did Parker remember Melinda because they had slept together? Was her face so indelibly etched in his mind because of their intimacy? But that was ridiculous—she knew it and deep down, so did he!

She felt that everything she'd believed in was slowly being shredded into tiny pieces.

"You—you and Brad. You saw her that night?" she asked, her voice barely audible over the sounds of the hospital.

He nodded, his jaw extending. "Yes."

"And you remember?"

"Not everything."

"Maybe she was Brad's girl. Maybe the baby is his."

Parker's eyes narrowed. "Maybe. I don't know."

Tom placed his hand over Shawna's arm and guided her to the door. "Don't torture yourself," he said in a concerned whisper. "Go home, think things through. I guarantee you Parker will do the same. Then tomorrow, come back and take him home."

"Home?" she repeated dully.

"Yes, I'm releasing him tomorrow." He glanced over his shoulder to Parker. "That is, unless Miss James's visit sets him back."

"I hope not," Shawna said, staring at Parker with new eyes, trying to smile and failing miserably. "Look, I really need to talk to him. Just a few minutes, okay?"

"I guess it won't hurt," Tom decided, "but keep it short. He's had one helluva shock today."

"Haven't we all?" Shawna said as Tom closed the door behind him.

Parker didn't look at her. He scowled through the window to the gray day beyond.

Had he betrayed her? Shawna couldn't believe it. Melinda had to be lying. But why? And why had Parker gone to visit the young girl before taking Brad home? Was it to call off their affair? Or had he needed to see her just one more time before the wedding? Shawna's stomach churned at the thought of them lying together, kissing—

"So much for the knight in shining armor, huh?" he mocked.

"I don't believe a word of her lies. And I really don't think you do, either."

"That's the tricky part," he admitted, staring up at the ceiling. "I know I've seen her—been with her, but—"

"—But you don't remember." Tossing her hair over her shoulder, she leaned against the bed.

"She has no reason to lie."

"Neither do I, Parker. I don't know anything about that girl, but I know what we shared and we didn't cheat or lie or betray one another."

"You're sure of that?"

"Positive," she whispered, wishing that awful shadow of doubt would disappear from her mind. "I only wish I could prove it."

Parker watched her blink back tears, saw her fine jaw jut in determination, and loved her for all of her pride and faith in him. Her blond hair draped across her shoulder to curl at her breast, and her eyes, fierce with indignation and bright with unshed tears, were as green as a night-darkened forest. How he loved her. Even lying here, charged with fathering another woman's child, he loved Shawna McGuire. But not because of any memories that had surfaced in his mind. No, this love was new, borne from just being near her. Never had he met any woman so proud and free-spirited, so filled with giving and fighting for what she believed in. And what she believed in was him.

"Do you think you're the father of Melinda's baby?" she finally asked, so close he could touch her.

"I don't know."

She blanched, as if in severe pain. Without thinking he took her hand in his and pulled her gently forward, so that she was leaning over him.

"But I do know that if I ever did anything that would hurt you this much, I have to be the worst bastard that ever walked the earth."

She swallowed. "You . . . you wouldn't."

"I hope to God you're right." His throat felt dry, and though the last thing he intended to do was kiss her again, he couldn't stop himself. He held her close, tilting her chin up with one finger and molding his mouth possessively over hers. "I don't want to ever hurt you, Shawna," he rasped hoarsely. "Don't let me."

"You won't." She felt the promise of his tongue as it gently parted her lips, then heard the sound of voices in the hall. She couldn't think when he held her, and she needed time alone to recover from the shock of Melinda James's announcement. Besides, she'd promised Dr. Handleman she wouldn't upset Parker. "Look, I don't want to, but I've got to go. Doctor's orders."

"To hell with doctor's orders," he muttered, his arms flexing around her, thwarting her attempts at escape.

"Don't mess with the medical profession," she warned, but the lilt she tried for didn't materialize in her voice.

"Not the whole profession," he said slowly, "just one very beautiful lady doctor."

Oh, Parker! Her throat thickened. "Later," she promised, kissing him lightly on the tip of the nose and hearing him moan in response.

"You're doing it again," he whispered.

"What?"

"Driving me crazy." His gaze slid down her body and stupidly, like a schoolgirl, she blushed and ran for the door.

As she drove home, her thoughts were tangled in a web of doubt and despair. Was it possible? Could Melinda's story be true?

"Don't be absurd," she told herself as she maneuvered her little car through the twisted streets of Sellwood. Maple and alder trees had begun to drop their leaves, splashing the wet streets with clumps of gold, brown, and orange.

As Shawna climbed out of the car, a cold autumn breeze lifted her hair from her face, cooled the heat in her cheeks.

"Hey, about time you showed up!" Jake accosted her as he climbed out of a battered old Chevy pickup. "I thought you'd be home half an hour ago."

She'd forgotten all about him, and the fact that he'd offered to help her move. "I—I'm sorry. Uh, something came up," she said, trying to concentrate.

"Oh, yeah?" Jake's brows raised expectantly. "Don't tell me the coach is gonna be released."

"Tomorrow," Shawna said, her voice catching before her brother saw the pain in her eyes.

"Hey—whoa. What happened?" Jake grabbed both her shoulders, then forced her chin upward with one finger and stared down at her.

"You wouldn't believe it."

"Try me." One arm over her shoulders, Jake walked her to the front door and unlocked the dead bolt. The apartment was a mess. Boxes and bags were scattered all over the living-room floor, piled together with pictures, furniture, and clothes.

Shawna flopped in the nearest corner and told Jake everything, from the moment Melinda James had walked into her office until the time when she'd dropped the bomb about Parker being the father of her unborn child.

"And you bought that cockamamy story?" Jake asked, flabbergasted.

"Of course not." Shawna felt close to tears again.

"I hope not! It's ridiculous."

"But Parker did."

"What?"

"He claims to remember her, and admits that he visited her the night Brad was killed!"

Stricken, Jake sat on a rolled carpet. His eyes narrowed thoughtfully. "I don't believe it."

"Neither did I, but you should have been there." Outside, Maestro meowed loudly. "I'm coming," Shawna called, every muscle in her body suddenly slack as she tried to stand and couldn't.

"I'll let him in." Jake opened the door and the bedraggled yellow tabby, wet from the rain, dashed into the house and made a beeline for Shawna. He cried until she petted him. "At least I can trust you," she said, her spirits lifting a little as the tabby washed his face and started to purr noisily.

"You can trust Parker, too," Jake said. "You and I both know it. That guy's crazy about you."

"Tell him," she said.

Jake frowned at his sister. "Okay, so this lunatic girl has made some crazy claims and Parker can't remember enough to know that she's lying. It's not the end of the world." He caught her glance and sighed. "Well, almost the end," he admitted, and even Shawna had to smile. "Now, come on. What's your next step?"

"You're not going to like it," Shawna said, opening a can of cat food for the cat.

"Try me."

"When the movers come tomorrow, I'm going to have them take my things to Parker's."

"His house?" Jake asked, his brows shooting up. "Does he know about this?"

"Nope." She straightened and her gaze narrowed on her brother. "And don't you tell him about it."

"I wouldn't dare," Jake said with obvious respect for Parker's volatile temper. "What about Mom and Dad?"

"I'll explain."

"Good luck. That's one dogfight I don't want any part of."

"I don't blame you." Why was this happening, and why now? She couldn't help thinking back to the Gypsy fortune-teller and her grim prediction.

"Shawna?" Jake asked, concern creasing his brow. "Are you okay?"

She nodded, her chin inching upward proudly. "I'm fine," she said. "I just have to stick by Parker 'til all of this is resolved one way or the other."

"Can I help?"

"Would you mind taking care of Maestro, just for a few days?"

Jake eyed the tabby dubiously. As if understanding he was the center of attention, Maestro leaped to the counter and arched his back as he rubbed up against the windowsill.

"I'm allergic to cats."

"He's outside most of the time."

"Bruno will eat him alive."

Shawna couldn't help but laugh. Bruno was a large mutt who was afraid of his own shadow. "Bruno will stick his big tail between his legs and run in the other direction."

"Okay."

"By the way," she said, feeling better. "You should work on that dog's obvious case of paranoia!"

"Maybe I should work on yours," Jake said, clapping her on the back. "You and I both know that Parker wasn't unfaithful to you."

"But he doesn't know it," Shawna replied, her convictions crumbling a little.

"You'll just have to convince him."

"I'm trying. Believe me." She pushed her hair from her eyes and rested the back of her head against the wall. "But that's not the only problem. What about Melinda and her baby? Why is she lying? How does Parker know her? As much as this mess angers me, I can't forget that Melinda is only eighteen, unmarried, and pregnant."

"Does she have any family?"

"I don't know." Shawna blew a strand of hair from her eyes. "All she said was that her dad would kill her when he found out. I think she was just using a turn of phrase. At least I hope so."

"But you're not sure."

"That's one of the most frustrating things about all of this. I don't know a thing about her. I've never even heard her name before and now she claims to be carrying my fiancé's child."

"Maybe there's something I could do."

"Such as?"

"I don't know, but *something.*"

"Not this time," she decided, grateful for his offer. "But thanks. This one I've got to handle by myself."

"I don't believe it!" Doris McGuire exclaimed. Sitting on her antique sofa, she stared across the room at her daughter. "Parker, and some, some girl?"

"That's what she claims," Shawna said.

"She's lying!"

"Who is?" Malcolm McGuire opened the front door and shook the rain from his hat, then tossed the worn fedora over the arm of an oak hall tree in the foyer. "Who's lying?" he repeated as he strode into the den and kissed Shawna's cheek. "You're not talking about Parker, are you?"

"Indirectly," Shawna admitted.

"Some young girl claims she's pregnant with Parker's child!" Doris said, her mouth pursed, her eyes bright with indignation. "Can you believe it?"

"Hey, slow down a minute," Malcolm said. "Let's start at the beginning."

As Shawna explained everything that had happened since she'd first met Melinda, Malcolm splashed a stiff shot of Scotch into a glass, thought twice about it, and poured two more drinks, which he handed to his daughter and wife.

"You don't believe it, do you?" he finally asked, searching Shawna's face.

"Of course not."

"But you've got doubts."

"Wouldn't you?"

"Never!" Doris declared. Malcolm's face whitened a bit.

"Sometimes a man can make a mistake, you know," he said.

"He was *engaged* to Shawna, for goodness sake!"

"But not married to her," Malcolm said slowly.

"Dad?" Did he know something? She studied the lines of her father's face as he finished his drink and sat heavily on the edge of the couch.

"I have no idea what Parker was up to," Malcolm said. "But I warned you that we didn't know all that much about him, didn't I? Maybe he had another girlfriend, I don't know. I would never have believed it before, but now? Why would she lie?"

Why indeed?

"But let's not judge him too harshly," Malcolm said. "Not until all the facts are in."

"I don't think you understand the gravity of the situation," Doris replied.

"Of course I do. Now, tell me about Parker. What does he have to say?"

"Not much." Shawna told her parents about the scene in the hospital room.

Malcolm cradled his empty glass in both hands and frowned into it. Doris shook her head and sighed loudly, though her back was ramrod stiff. "He'll just have to submit to a paternity test—prove the child isn't his and then get on with his life."

"Maybe it's not that simple," Malcolm said quietly. "He has a career to think of. All this adverse publicity might affect it."

"We're talking about the man Shawna plans to marry," Doris cut in, simmering with fury, "and here you are defending his actions—if, indeed, he was involved with that . . . that *woman!*"

"She's barely more than a girl," Shawna said.

"Eighteen is old enough to know better!"

Malcolm held up his hand to calm his wife. "I'm just saying we should all keep a level head."

Now that she'd said what she had to say, Shawna snatched her jacket from the back of a wing chair. "I think Dad's right—we should just low-key this for now."

"The girl is pregnant!"

"I know, I know. But I've decided that what I'm going to do is try and help Parker through this. It's got to be as hard on him as it is on me. That's one of the reasons I've decided to move in with him."

"Do what?" Doris was horrified. She nearly dropped her drink and her pretty face fell.

"He's being released from the hospital tomorrow. And I'm taking him home—to his house—with me."

"But you can't—you're not married. And now, with that girl's ridiculous accusations—"

"All the more reason to try and help jog his memory." Shawna saw the protests forming on her mother's lips and waved them off.

"Look, I've already made up my mind. If things had turned out differently, I'd already be married to him and living in that house. He and I would still have to deal with Melinda—unless this is all a convenient story of hers just because he's lost his memory. So, I'm going to stand by him. I just wanted you to know how to get in touch with me."

"But—"

"Mom, I love him." Shawna touched her mother's shoulder. It felt stiff and rigid under Doris's cotton sweater. "I'll call you in a couple of days."

Then, before her mother or father could try to change her mind, she walked out of the room, swept her purse off an end table, and opened the front door. She was glad to drive away from her parents' house because she needed time alone, time to think and clear her head. Tomorrow she'd have the battle of her life with Parker. He'd already told her he didn't want her tied to him as a cripple, that they couldn't marry until he was strong enough to support them both. Now, after Melinda's allegations, he'd be more adamant than ever.

Well, that was just too damned bad. Shawna intended to stand by him no matter what, and if he never walked again, she still intended to marry him. All she had to do was convince him that she was right. Involuntarily, she crossed her fingers.

Parker shoved the dinner tray aside. He wasn't hungry and didn't feel like trying to force food down his throat. With a groan, he reached for the crutches near his bed.

Dr. Handleman and the idiot down in physical therapy didn't think he was ready for crutches, but he'd begged them off a candy striper. Tomorrow he was going home and he wasn't about to be wheeled down the hall like a helpless invalid.

Gritting his teeth against a stab of pain in his knee, he slid off the bed and shoved the crutches under his arms. Then, slowly, he moved across the room, ignoring the throbbing in his knee and the erratic pounding of his heart. Finally he fell against the far wall, sweating but proud that he'd accomplished the small feat of walking across the room.

Breathing hard, he glanced out the window to the parking lot below. Security lamps glowed blue, reflecting on the puddles from a recent shower. Parker had a vague recollection of another storm. . . .

Rain had been drizzling down a windshield, wipers slapping the sheeting water aside as he had driven up a twisting mountain road. Someone—was it Brad?—had been slumped in the passenger seat. The passenger had fallen against Parker just as the Jeep had rounded a corner and there, right in the middle of the road, a huge truck with bright glaring headlights was barreling toward them, out of control. The truck driver blasted his horn, brakes squealed and locked, and Parker, reacting by instinct alone, had wrenched hard on the wheel, steering the Jeep out of the path of the oncoming truck and through the guardrail into the black void beyond.

Now, as he stood with his head pressed to the glass, Parker squeezed his eyes shut tight, trying to dredge up the memories, put the ill-fitting pieces of his past into some order.

He remembered Melinda—he'd seen her that night. But she was just a girl. Surely he wouldn't have slept with her!

Impatient with his blank mind, he swore and knocked over one of his crutches. It fell against the table, knocking over a water glass and a book. From the pages of the book fluttered a picture—the single snapshot of Shawna on the carousel.

In the photograph, her cheeks were rosy and flushed, her eyes bright, her hair tossed wildly around her face. He'd been in love with her then. He could feel it, see it in her expression. And now, he'd fallen in love with her again and this time, he suspected, his feelings ran much deeper.

Despite the searing pain in his knee, he bent down, but the picture was just out of reach, in the thin layer of dust under the bed, and he couldn't coax the snapshot back to him, not even with the aid of his crutch.

He frowned at the irony. He couldn't reach the picture just as he couldn't have her, wouldn't chain her to a future so clouded and unsure. She deserved better than a man who might never walk without a cane—a man who couldn't even remember if he'd betrayed her.

Eight

Bracing herself, knowing full well that she was in for the fight of her life, Shawna walked into Parker's hospital room. "Ready?" she asked brightly.

"For what?" Parker was standing near his bed, fully dressed in gray cords and a cream-colored sweater, and balancing precariously on crutches.

"To go home." She picked up his duffel bag and tossed it over her shoulder, overlooking the storm gathering in his eyes. "Hurry up, I'm double-parked."

"I'll call a cab," he said quietly.

"No reason. Your house is on my way."

"To where?"

"The rest of my life."

Taking in a swift breath, he shoved one hand through his hair and shook his head. "You're unbelievable," he muttered.

"So you've said. Come on."

"Mr. Harrison?" A nurse pushed a wheelchair into his room and Parker swore under his breath.

"I don't need *that.*"

"Hospital regulations."

"Change them," he said, jaw tight.

"Come on, Parker, don't buck the system now," Shawna said, grabbing the handles of the wheelchair from the nurse. "Everyone has to use these chairs in order to get out."

Muttering to himself he slid into the chair and grumbled all the way along the corridor.

"I see we're in good spirits today," Shawna commented drily.

"Don't start in with that hospital 'we' talk, okay? I'm sick to death of it."

"My mistake. But don't worry. I'll probably make a few more before the day is over." She wheeled him into the elevator and didn't say a word until they were through the emergency room doors—the same door she'd run through weeks ago in her soggy wedding dress. That day felt like a lifetime ago.

Once they were in the car and through the parking lot, Shawna drove south, down the steep fir-cloaked hills of west Portland toward Lake Oswego and Parker's rambling Tudor house on the cliffs.

He stared out the window in silence, his eyes traveling over the familiar landscape. Leaves of the maple and oak trees had turned vibrant orange and brown, swirling in the wind and hanging tenaciously to black branches as Shawna drove toward the river. She glanced at Parker and noticed the tight pinch at the corners of his mouth and the lines of strain on his forehead as his stone house loomed into view.

Rising a full three stories, with a sharply gabled roof and dormers, the Tudor stood high on the cliffs overlooking the green waters of the Willamette. Trees and shrubbery flanked a broad, pillared porch and leaded glass windows winked in the pink rays from a setting sun.

Shawna cut the engine in front of the garage. She was reaching for the handle of her door when his voice stopped her.

"Aren't you going to ask me about Melinda?"

She froze and her stomach twisted painfully. Inadvertently she'd been avoiding the subject. "Is there something you want to tell me?"

Swallowing, he glanced away, then stared straight into

her eyes. "I—I'm starting to remember," he admitted, weighing his words. "Part of the past is getting a little more clear."

She knew what was coming and died a bit inside, her fingers wrapping around the steering wheel as she leaned back in her seat. "The part with Melinda," she guessed, fingers clenched tight over the wheel.

"Yes."

"You . . . remember being with her?"

"Partly."

"Sleeping with her?"

She saw him hesitate, then shake his head. "No, but there's something . . . something about her. If only I could figure it out."

Licking her lips nervously, she forced her gaze to meet his. "I don't believe you betrayed me, Parker," she admitted, her voice rough. "I just can't."

"Maybe it would be easier if you did," he whispered.

"Why?"

"Because I feel—this tremendous responsibility."

She touched him then, her fingers light on his sweater, beneath which she could feel the coiled tension in his shoulders. "Give it time."

"I think we're running out." Then, as quickly as he'd brought up the subject, he jerked on the door handle and shoved the car door open. Cool wind invaded the interior as he gripped the frame and tried to struggle to his feet.

"Hey—wait!" She threw open her door and ran around the car just as he extracted himself from his seat and balanced on one leg, his face white with strain. "What do you think you're doing?" she demanded.

"Standing on my own," he said succinctly.

She caught his meaning, but refused to acknowledge it. "Sure, but you were almost flat on your face," she chastised. "How do you think Dr. Handleman would like it if you twisted that knee again and undid all his work?"

"I don't really give a damn what he does or doesn't like."

"Back to your charming sweet self, I see," she said, though her heart was pounding a rapid double-time. "Personally I'd hate to see you back in that hospital bed—in traction or worse—all because of your stupid, bullheaded male pride." She opened the hatchback of her car and wrestled with the collapsible wheelchair, noting that he'd paled slightly at the mention of the hospital. Good! He needed to think that one over. "So, quit being a child and enjoy being pampered."

"Pampered by whom?"

"Me." She locked the wheelchair and rolled it toward his side of the car.

"I don't want to be pampered."

"Oh, I think you will. Think of it as a reward for all those grueling hours you'll be spending with the physical therapist. I already hired him—he starts tomorrow."

"You did *what?*" Parker was livid, the fire in his eyes bright with rage. "I'm not going to—"

"Sure you are. And you're going to get off this self-reliant-male ego kick right now!"

She pushed the wheelchair next to him, but he held up a hand, spreading his fingers in her face. "Hold on, just one minute. I may not remember a lot about my past, but I know one thing, I never let any woman—even a lady doctor—push me around."

"Not even Melinda James?" Shawna snapped, instantly regretting her words when she saw his face slacken and guilt converge over his honed features.

"I'll deal with Melinda," he said, his voice ringing with authority, "in my own way." Then, ignoring the wheelchair, he reached down and tugged on the crutches she'd wedged into the car.

"You can't—"

"I can damned well do as I please, Dr. McGuire," he said cuttingly. "I'm not in a hospital any longer. You're not the boss." He slammed the crutches under his arms and swung forward, landing on his good leg with a jarring thud as he started up the flagstone path leading to the back door.

"You'll be back in the hospital before you know it if you don't watch out," she warned. Walking rapidly, she caught up with him.

"You can go home now, Shawna," he advised.

"I am."

Cocking his head to one side, he asked testily, "You're what?"

"Home."

"What?" he roared, twisting to look at her, his crutch wedging in the chipped mortar to wrench out from under him. He pitched forward, grabbing frantically at the lowest branches of a nearby willow tree and landing with a thud on the wet grass.

"Parker!" Shawna knelt beside him. "I'm sorry—"

"Wasn't your fault." But he winced in pain, skin tight over his cheeks. "Now, tell me I heard wrong."

"I moved in this morning," she said, but her eyes were on his leg and without asking she pushed up his pant leg, to make sure that the stitches in his knee hadn't ruptured.

"I'm all right." He caught her wrist. "You are *not* my doctor. And you're not moving in here."

"Too late," she said, reaching into her pocket with her free hand and extracting a key ring from which dangled the keys to his house, car, and garage. "You gave these to me—for better or for worse, remember."

"We didn't get married."

"Doesn't matter. I'm committed to you, so you'd better get used to it!" She met his gaze steadily, her green eyes bright with defiance and pride. His fingers were still circling her wrist, warm against her skin, and her breathing, already labored, caught in her throat as his eyes moved from hers to the base of her neck and lower still.

"Whether the ceremony happened or not, I consider myself your wife, and it will take an act of God for you to get rid of me."

"What about another woman's child?"

Her heart constricted. "We'll just have to deal with that together, won't we?" Nervously, she licked her lips, her self-confidence slowly drifting away.

He studied her mouth. "Maybe I need to stand alone before I can stand with someone," he said, sun glinting off the burnished strands of his hair.

"Are you telling me you won't let me live here?" She could barely concentrate. Her thoughts centered on her wrist and the provocative movement of his fingers against her skin. And his eyes, blue as the sea, stared into hers, smoldering with desire, yet bewildered.

"I just don't think we—you and I—can act like this accident didn't happen, pretending that Melinda James doesn't exist, that our lives will mesh in some sort of fairy-tale happy ending, when there are so many things pulling us apart." He glanced down at her lips and then to her hair, shining a radiant gold in the afternoon sunlight.

"Please, Parker, just give me a chance. I—I don't mean to come on like gangbusters, but we need time alone together, to work things out."

He pulled her close, kissing her as passionately as she'd ever been kissed, his lips possessive and strong with a fire she knew burned bright in his soul.

Responding, she cradled his head to hers, feeling the texture of his hair, and the warmth of his breath.

He shifted, more of his weight falling across her, his arms strong as they circled her waist.

"Parker, please—just love me," she whispered against his ear. He groaned a response. "Let me help you—help us." She placed both of her hands on his cheeks and held his head between her palms. "I can't let go, Melinda or no Melinda. Baby or no baby."

Before he could respond, Shawna heard the back door swing open and there, standing on the porch, her eyes dark with unspoken accusation, was Melinda James.

"What the devil?" Parker whispered. "How'd you—? Don't even answer! It doesn't matter."

Shawna realized that he'd probably given her a set of keys, too, long before he'd met Shawna, and the wound she'd tried so hard to bind opened again, fresh and raw.

"Remind me to have my locks changed," Parker muttered.

Shawna dusted off her skirt and tried to help him to his feet, but he pushed her hands aside, determined to stand by himself.

"I—I didn't know she would be here," Melinda said quietly, but her dark eyes darted quickly from Shawna to Parker and back again.

"I live here," Shawna said.

Melinda nearly dropped her purse. "You what?"

Parker's brows shot up. "Hold on a minute. I live here. Me. Alone."

"Not anymore," Shawna said, cringing at how brash she sounded. Two months ago she would never have been so bold, but now, with her back against the wall and Parker's physical and mental health at stake, she'd fight tooth and nail to help him.

"You invited her?" Melinda asked, surveying Parker with huge, wounded eyes.

"She invited herself." He forced himself upright and started propelling himself forward.

"Are—are you all right?" Melinda asked.

"Just dandy," he snapped, unable to keep the cynicism from his voice. "I think we'd all better go into the house, and straighten out a few things." He glanced over his shoulder to Shawna, who was attempting to comb the tangles from her hair with her fingers. "Coming, Doctor?"

"Wouldn't miss it for the world," she quipped back, managing a smile though her insides were shredding.

What would she do if he threw her out, insisted that he cared about Melinda, that the child was his?

"One step at a time," she reminded herself, following him inside.

Melinda was already halfway down the hall to the den. "I don't like this," Shawna confided in Parker as she caught up with him.

"Neither do I." His gaze wandered to her face and she could feel his eyes taking in the determined slant of her mouth. "But then there's a lot of things I don't like—things I'm not sure about."

"Such as?"

Before she could walk down the two steps to the den, he leaned forward, balanced on his crutches, and touched her shoulder. "Such as you," he admitted, eyes dark and tormented. "It would be easy to fall in love with you, Shawna—too easy. I must have been one helluva lucky guy—"

"You still are."

"—but now, things have changed. Look at me! I still can't walk. I may never walk without these infernal things!" He shook one crutch angrily, his expression changing to violent anger and frustration. "And then there's Melinda. I can't say her story isn't true. I don't know! I can't remember."

"I'll help you."

He let out a weary sigh and rested his forehead against hers. Involuntarily her fingers caught in the thick threads of his sweater. So desperately, she wanted him to understand, remember, recapture that fleeting love they'd shared.

One of his hands stroked her cheek, as if he couldn't quite believe she was real. "You—you've got a medical practice—a future, and you're a gorgeous, intelligent woman. Any man would count himself lucky if you just looked sideways at him."

"I'm not interested in 'any man,'" she pointed out. "Just one."

"Oh, Shawna," he moaned, his voice as low as the wind rustling through the rafters of the old house. Against her cheek, his fingers trembled.

A hot lump filled her throat. "How come I feel like you're trying to push me away?"

"Because I am. I have to. I can't tie you down to this!" He gestured to his legs, furious that they wouldn't obey his commands.

"Let me make that decision." Tears filled her eyes, but she smiled bravely just the same. "I'll decide if you're so horrible that any sane woman wouldn't be interested in you."

From the doorway to the den, Melinda coughed. She glanced guiltily away, as if she didn't mean to eavesdrop, but hadn't been able to stop herself from witnessing the tender scene between Parker and Shawna. "If you want me to, I'll leave," she said, chin quivering.

"Not yet." Straightening, Parker rubbed one hand around his shoulders, as if to relieve a coiled tension in his muscles. "Not yet." He swung his crutches forward and hobbled down the two steps into the den.

Steeling herself, Shawna followed, only to find that Melinda had already lit a fire in the grate and had placed a carafe of coffee on the table. "You've been here a while."

Melinda shrugged but resentment smoldered in her large brown eyes. "I, um, didn't expect you."

Parker met the questions in Melinda's gaze. "I think we'd better set a few ground rules. First of all, I don't remember you, not in the way you think I should," he said to Melinda. "But, if that child is really mine, I'll do right by you."

"That's all I'd expect," Melinda replied quickly. "I'm just concerned for my baby."

Shawna's hands shook. Just thinking that Parker

might have a child with someone else, even a child conceived before they had met, tore at her soul. I can handle this, she told herself over and over again, trying to convince herself.

"Okay, so how did we meet?" Parker said, leaning forward and cringing a little when a jab of pain shot through him.

"I—I was a friend of Brad's. I, uh, used to watch him play and you coached him. Brad—he introduced us."

"How did you know Brad?"

Melinda looked down at her hands. "We went to school together in Cleveland, before he dropped out," she explained. "We, uh, used to date."

"But then you met Parker," Shawna prodded.

"Yes, and, well, Brad was seeing someone else, Parker and I hit it off, and then," she licked her lips. "We fell in love. Until you came along."

Shawna exhaled slowly. How much of Melinda's story was fact and how much fantasy? If only Parker could remember! She wanted to hate the girl but couldn't. Melinda was afraid of something, or someone; it was written all over her downcast face.

"Do you have any family?" Parker asked.

"Not around here. My dad's a widower."

"Does he know that you're pregnant?"

"I didn't know until I saw *her* yesterday," Melinda said, then her shoulders slumped. "Though I guess I kinda expected it. But Dad, even if he did know, he wouldn't care. I haven't lived at home for a couple of years."

"I thought you said he'd kill you," Shawna whispered.

"I guess I was wrong. Melinda swallowed hard and Shawna almost felt sorry for her. "Look, I made a mistake. It's no big deal," she said, her temper flaring. "The thing is I'm in trouble, okay? And it's *his* fault. You know I'm not lying, you're the one who did the test."

Shawna slowly counted to ten. She couldn't lose her self-control. Not now. "Fine. Let's start over."

"I didn't come here to talk to you."

"This involves all of us," Parker said.

Shawna asked, "Did you finish high school?"

"Yep." Melinda flopped onto one of the cushions of the leather couch and stared at the ceiling. "I was going to be a model. Until I met Parker."

"After Brad."

"Right."

Shawna wondered how much, if any, of the girl's story were true. "And then you were swept off your feet?"

"That's about it," Melinda said, her smile faltering.

Parker's expression was unreadable. He stared at Melinda, his lips pressed together, as if he, too, were trying to find flaws in her words, some key to what had really happened. "Then you won't mind if I have a friend of mine look up your father, just to verify a few things," Parker said slowly.

Beneath her tan, Melinda blanched, but said, "Do what you have to do. It won't change anything, and at least then maybe she'll believe me." Disturbed, she slung her purse over her shoulder and left, the heels of her boots echoing loudly on the tiles of the foyer. A few seconds later Shawna heard the front door slam.

"Does anything she said sound true?" she asked.

"I don't know." Parker sighed heavily and, groaning, pushed himself to his feet. "I just don't know." Leaning one shoulder against the stones of the fireplace, he stared into the glowing red embers of the fire. "But she seemed pretty sure of herself. That seems to be a trait of the women I knew."

The firelight flickered on his face, causing uneven red shadows to highlight the hard angle of his jaw. He added, "You know you can't stay here."

"I have to."

"You don't owe me any debts, if that's what you think."

"You need someone to look after you."

"Like hell!" he muttered, his eyes blazing with the

reflection of the coals. "What I don't need is anyone who thinks they owe me."

"You just don't understand, do you?" she whispered, so furious she was beginning to shake again. "You just don't understand how much I love you."

"Loved. Past tense."

Standing, she tossed her hair away from her face and met his fierce, uncompromising stare. "One accident doesn't change the depth of my feelings, Parker. Nor does it, in any way, shape or form, alter the fact that I love you for life, no matter what. Legally, I suppose, you can force me out of here. Or, you could make my life here so intolerable that I'd eventually throw in the towel and move. But you can't, *can't* destroy the simple fact that I love you and always will." Into the silence that followed, she said, "I've made up the guest room for you so you won't have to hassle with the stairs. I've moved all of your clothes and things down here."

"And you—where do you intend to sleep?"

"Upstairs—for now. Just until this Melinda thing is straightened out."

"And then?"

"Then, I hope, you'll want me to sleep with you."

"As man and wife?"

"Yes. If I can ever get it through that thick skull of yours that we belong together! So," she added fiercely, "if we're finished arguing, I'll make dinner." Leaving him speechless, she marched out of the room, fingers crossed, hoping that somehow, some way, she could help him remember everything.

Parker stared after her in amazement. Nothing was going as he'd planned. Ever since she'd bulldozed her way back into his life, he seemed to have lost control—not only of his past, but of his future.

Unfortunately, he admired her grit and determination, and even smiled to himself when he remembered how emphatic she'd become when she'd told him she intended to sleep with him. Any other man would jump at the chance of making love to her—but then any other man could jump and make love. So far he hadn't done either since the accident. He was sure he couldn't do one. As for the other, he hoped that he was experiencing only a temporary setback. He smiled a little. Earlier, when he'd fallen on the ground and he'd kissed Shawna, he'd felt the faintest of stirrings deep within.

Now, he found his crutches and pushed himself down the hallway toward the kitchen. Shawna was so passionate, so full of life. Why would he betray her with a woman who was barely out of childhood?

He leaned one shoulder against the wall and watched Shawna working in the kitchen. She'd tied a towel over her wool skirt, clipped her hair loosely away from her face, and kicked her shoes into a corner. In stocking feet and reading glasses, she sliced vegetables near the sink. She was humming—actually humming—as she worked, and she seemed completely at home and comfortable in his house, as though their argument and Melinda's baby didn't exist.

Watching her furtively, listening to the soft sound of her voice, seeing the smile playing upon her lips, he couldn't help feeling as lighthearted as she. She was a beautiful, intriguing woman—a woman with determination and courage—and she gave her love to him so completely.

So how could he have betrayed her? Deep inside, he knew he wouldn't have cheated on her. Yet he couldn't dismiss the fact that he vaguely remembered Melinda James.

She glanced up sharply, as if sensing him for the first time, and she blushed. "I didn't hear you."

"It's okay, I was just watching."

"Well, come in and take a center seat. No reason to hide in the hall," she teased.

Parker grinned and hobbled into the kitchen where

he half fell into one of the caned chairs. "Don't let me disturb you," he said.

"Wouldn't dream of it!" She pushed her glasses onto the bridge of her nose and continued reading a recipe card. "You're in for the thrill of your life," she declared. "*Coq au vin* à la Shawna. This is going to be great."

"I know," he admitted, folding his arms over his chest, propping his bad leg on a nearby chair, and grinning to himself. Great it would be, but he wasn't thinking about the chicken in wine.

Nine

Shawna eyed the dining room table critically. It gleamed with a fresh coat of wax and reflected the tiny flames of two creamy white candles. She'd polished the brass candlesticks and placed a fresh bouquet of roses and baby's breath between the flickering candles.

Tonight, whether Parker was agreeable or not, they were going to celebrate. She'd been living with him for over three weeks in a tentative truce. Fortunately, Melinda hadn't intruded, though Parker had spoken with her on the phone several times.

"Buck up," she told herself, as she thought about the girl. Melinda was pregnant and they couldn't ignore her. Even though neither she nor Parker had brought up the subject of Melinda's baby, it was always in the air, an invisible barrier between them.

In the past weeks, Parker had spent his days in physical therapy, either at Mercy Hospital or here, at the house.

Shawna rearranged one drooping flower and frowned. As a doctor, she knew that Parker was pushing himself to the limit, forcing muscles and ligaments to work, as if regaining full use of his leg would somehow trip his memory. Though Shawna had begged him to slow down, he'd refused to listen, mule-headedly driving himself into a state of utter exhaustion.

Finally, at the end of the third week, he'd improved to the point that he was walking with only the aid of a cane.

To celebrate, she'd taken the afternoon off and had been waiting for him, cooking and cleaning and feeling nearly as if she belonged in his house—almost as if she were his wife.

She heard his car in the drive. Smiling, she hurried into the kitchen to add the last touches to the beef stroganoff simmering on the stove.

Parker opened the back door and collapsed into one of the kitchen chairs. His hair was dark with sweat and his face was gaunt and strained as he hung his cane over the back of his chair. He winced as he lifted his bad leg and propped it on a stool. Glancing up, he forced a tired smile. "Hi."

Shawna leaned over the counter separating kitchen from nook. "Hi, yourself."

"I thought you had the late shift."

"I traded so that we could have dinner together," she said.

"Sounds good." But he really wasn't listening. He was massaging his knee, his lips tightening as his fingers touched a particularly sensitive spot.

"You've been pushing yourself too hard again," she said softly, worried that he would do himself more damage than good.

"I don't think so."

"I'm a doctor."

He rolled his eyes. "Don't I know it?"

"Parker, please," she said, kneeling in front of him and placing a kiss on his sweat-dampened forehead. "Take it easy."

"I can't."

"There's plenty of time—"

"Do you really believe that?" He was staring at her suspiciously, as if he thought she was lying to him.

"You've got the rest of your—"

"Easy for you to say, *Doctor,*" he snapped. "You're not facing the rest of your life with this!" He lifted his cane, then, furious with the damned thing, hurled it angrily across the room. It skidded on the blue tiles and smashed into a far wall.

Shawna wanted to lecture him, but didn't. Instead she straightened and pretended interest in the simmering sauce. "I, uh, take it the session wasn't the best."

"You take it right, Doctor. But then you know everything, don't you?" He gestured toward the stove. "What I should eat, where I should sleep, how fast I should improve—all on your neat little schedule!"

His words stung and she gasped, before stiffening her back and pretending he hadn't wounded her. The tension between them had been mounting for weeks. He was disappointed, she told herself.

But he must have recognized her pain. He made a feeble gesture of apology with his hand, then, bracing his palms on the table, forced himself upright.

"I wish things were different," he finally said, gripping the counter with both hands, "but they're not. You're a good woman, Shawna—better than I deserve. Do yourself a favor and forget about me. Find yourself a whole man."

"I have," she whispered, her throat swollen tight. "He's just too pigheaded to know it."

"I mean it—"

"And so do I," she whispered. "I love you, Parker. I always will. That's just the way it is."

He stared at her in amazement, then leaned back, propping his head against the wall. "Oh, God," he groaned, covering his face with his hands. "You live in such a romantic dream world." When he dropped his hands, his expression had changed to a mask of indifference.

"If I live in a dream world," she said quietly, "it's a world that you created."

"Then it's over," he decided, straightening. "It's just . . . gone. It vanished that night."

Shawna ignored the stab of pain in her heart. "I don't believe you and I won't. Until you're completely well and have regained all of your memory, I won't give up."

"Shawna—"

"Remember that 'for better or worse' line?"

"We didn't get married."

Yet, she thought wildly. "Doesn't matter. In my heart I'm committed to you, and only when you tell me that you remember everything we shared and it means nothing to you—then I'll give up!"

"I just don't want to hurt you," he admitted, "ever again."

"You won't." The lie almost caught on her tongue.

"I wish I was as sure as you."

Her heart squeezed as she studied him, his body drenched in sweat, his shoulder balanced precariously against the wall.

As if reading the pity in her eyes, he swore, anger darkening his face. Casting her a disbelieving glance, he limped down the hall to his room and slammed the door so hard that the sound echoed through the old house.

Shawna stared after him. Why couldn't he remember how strong their love had been? *Why?* Feeling the need to break down and cry like a baby, she steeled herself. In frustration, she reached for the phone, hoping to call her brother or her friend Gerri or anyone to whom she could vent her frustrations. But when she placed the receiver to her ear, she heard Parker on the bedroom extension.

"That's right . . . everything you can find out about her. The name's James—Melinda James. I don't know her middle name. She claims to have been living in Cleveland and that she grew up with Brad Lomax."

Quietly, Shawna replaced the receiver. It seemed that no matter where she turned or how fiercely she clung to the ashes of the love she and Parker had once shared, the winds of fate blew them from her fingers.

Dying a little inside, she wondered if he was right. Maybe the flames of their love couldn't be rekindled.

"Give him time," she told herself, but she knew their time was running out. She glanced around the old Tudor house, the home she'd planned to share with him. She'd moved in, but they were both living a lie. He didn't love her.

Swallowing against the dryness in her throat, she turned toward the sink and ran water over the spinach leaves in a colander. She ignored the tears that threatened to form in the corners of her eyes. *Don't give up!* part of her insisted, while the other, more reasonable side of her nature whispered, *Let him go.*

So intent was she on tearing spinach, cutting egg, and crumbling bacon that she didn't hear the uneven tread of his footsteps in the hall, didn't feel his gaze on her back as she worked, still muttering and arguing with herself.

Her first indication that he was in the room with her was the feel of his hands on her waist. She nearly dropped her knife as he bent his head and rested his chin on her shoulder.

"I'm not much good at apologies," he said softly.

"Neither am I."

"Oh, Shawna." His breath fanned her hair, warm and enticing, and her heart took flight. He'd come back! "I know you're doing what you think is best," he said huskily. "And I appreciate your help."

She dropped the knife and the tears she'd been fighting filled her eyes. "I've done it because I want to."

His fingers spanned her waist. "I just don't understand," he admitted, "why you want to put up with me."

She wanted to explain, but he cut her off, his arms encircling her waist, her body drawn to his. His breath was hot on the back of her head and delicious shivers darted along her spine as he pulled her close, so close that her back was pressed against the taut muscles of his chest. A spreading warmth radiated to her most outer limbs as his lips found her nape.

"I—I love you, Parker."

His muscles flexed and she silently prayed he would return those three simple words.

"That's why I'm working so hard," he conceded, his voice rough with emotion. "I want to be able to remember everything."

"I can wait," she said.

"But I can't! I want my life back—all of it. The way it was before the accident. Before—"

He didn't say it, but she knew. *Before Brad was killed, before Melinda James shattered our lives.*

"Maybe we should eat," she said, hoping to divert him from the guilt that ran rampant every time he thought about Brad.

"You've worked hard, haven't you?"

"It's a—well, it was a celebration."

"Oh?"

"Because you're off crutches and out of the brace," she said.

"I've still got that." He pointed to where the cane still lay on the floor.

"I know, but it's the final step."

"Except for my memory."

"It'll come back," she predicted, sounding more hopeful than she felt. "Come on, now," she urged. "Make yourself useful. Pour the wine before I ruin dinner and the candles burn out."

During dinner Shawna felt more lighthearted than she had in weeks. At the end of the meal, when Parker leaned forward and brushed his lips over hers, she thought fleetingly that together they could face anything.

"Thanks," he whispered, "for putting up with me."

"I wouldn't have it any other way." She could feel her

eyes shining in the candlelight, knew her cheeks were tinged with the blush of happiness.

"Let's finish this—" he said, holding the wine bottle by its neck, "—in the gazebo."

A dimple creased her cheek. "The gazebo?" she repeated, and grinned from ear to ear as she picked up their wineglasses and dashed to the hallway where her down coat hung. Her heart was pounding with excitement. Just two months earlier, Parker had proposed in the gazebo.

Hand in hand, they walked down a flagstone path that led to the river. The sound of water rushing over stones filled the night air and a breeze, fresh with the scent of the Willamette, lifted Shawna's hair.

The sky was clear and black. A ribbon of silver moonlight rippled across the dark water to illuminate the bleached wood and smooth white rocks at the river's edge. On the east bank, lights from neighboring houses glittered and reflected on the water.

Shawna, with Parker's help, stepped into the gazebo. The slatted wood building was built on the edge of Parker's property, on the ridge overlooking the Willamette. The gazebo was flanked by lilac bushes, no longer fragrant, their dry leaves rustling in the wind.

As Shawna stared across the water, she felt Parker's arms slip around her waist, his breath warm against her head, the heat from his body flowing into hers.

"Do—do you remember the last time we were here?" she whispered, her throat swollen with the beautiful memory.

He didn't say anything.

"You proposed," she prodded.

"Did I?"

"Yes." She turned in his arms, facing him. "Late in the summer."

Squinting his eyes, fighting the darkness shrouding his brain, he struggled, but nothing surfaced. "I'm sorry," he whispered, his night-darkened eyes searching hers.

"Don't apologize," she whispered. Moonlight shifted across his face, shadowing the sharp angles as he lowered his head and touched his lips to hers.

Gently, his fingers twined in her hair. "Sometimes I get caught up in your fantasies," he admitted, his lips twisting cynically.

"This isn't a fantasy," she said, seeing her reflection in his eyes. "Just trust me."

He leaned forward again, brushing his lips suggestively over hers. "That's the trouble. I do." He took the wine and glasses and set them on the bench. Placing his palms on her cheeks, he stared into her eyes before kissing her again. Eagerly she responded, her heart pulsing wildly at his touch, her mouth opening willingly to the erotic pressure of his tongue on her lips.

She felt his hands quiver as they slid downward to rest near her neck, gently massaging her nape, before pushing the coat from her shoulders. The night air surrounded her, but she wasn't cold.

Together, they slid slowly to the weathered floorboards and Parker adjusted her down coat, using its softness as a mattress. Then, still kissing her, he found the buttons of her blouse and loosened them, slipping the soft fabric down her shoulders.

Slowly he bent and pressed his moist lips against the base of her throat.

In response, she warmed deep within, stretching her arms around him, holding him tight, drinking in the smell and feel of him.

"Shawna," he whispered.

"Oh, Parker, love," she murmured.

"Tell me to stop."

"Don't ever stop," she cried.

He shuddered, as if trying to restrain himself, then, in one glorious minute, he crushed his lips to hers and kissed her more passionately than ever before. His hands caressed her skin, tearing at her blouse and the clasp of her bra, baring her breasts to the shifting moonlight. Slowly he lowered his head and touched each proud nipple with his lips, teasing the dark peaks to impatient attention.

"Ooh," she whispered, caught up in the warm, rolling sensations of his lips and tongue as he touched her, stoking fires that scorched as they raced through her blood and burned wantonly in her brain.

Reckless desire chased all rational thought away.

Her breath tangled with his and his hands touched her, sweeping off her skirt until she was naked in the night. Her skin was as white as alabaster in the darkness. Despite the cool river-kissed wind, she was warm deep inside, as she throbbed with need for this one special man.

His moist lips moved over her, caressing her, arousing her, stealing over her skin and causing her mind to scream with the want of him.

She found the hem of his sweater and pushed the offending garment over his head. He groaned in response and she unsnapped his jeans, her fingers sliding down the length of his legs as she removed the faded denim until, at last, they lay naked in the tiny gazebo—his body gleaming with a dewy coat of sweat, hers rosy with the blush of desire.

"I will always love you," she promised as he lowered himself over her, twisting his fingers in her hair, his eyes blue, lusting flames.

"And I'll always love you," he vowed into her open mouth as his hands closed over her breasts, gently kneading the soft, proud nipples, still wet from his kiss.

Her fingers moved slowly down his back, touching firm smooth muscles and the gentle cleft of his spine.

Though her eyes wanted to close, she willed them open, staring up at him, watching the bittersweet torment on his face as he delved inside, burying himself in her only to withdraw again and again. Her heart slamming wildly, her blood running molten hot, she arched upward, moved by a primitive force and whispering words of love.

Caught in her own storm of emotion and the powerful force of his love, she lost herself to him, surrendering to the vibrant spinning world that was theirs alone. She felt the splendor of his hands, heard him cry out her name.

In one glorious moment he stiffened, his voice reverberating through the gazebo and out across the river, and Shawna, too, convulsed against his sweat-glistened body.

His breath was rapid and hot in her ear. "This . . . could be dangerous," he whispered hoarsely, running a shaking hand through his hair.

Still wrapped in the wonder and glow of passion, she held him close, pressed her lips to his sweat-soaked chest. "Don't talk. For just tonight, let's pretend that it's only you and me, and our love."

"I'm not much good at pretending." Glancing down at her plump breasts, he sighed, then reached past her to a glass on the bench. Swirling wine in the goblet, he said, "I don't think we should let this happen again."

"I don't think we have a choice."

"Oh, Shawna," he whispered, drinking his wine and setting the empty glass on the floor before he reached behind her, to wrap the coat over her suddenly chilled shoulders before holding her close. "This isn't a question of love," he said.

Crushed, she couldn't answer.

"I just think we both need time."

"Because of Melinda's baby."

"The baby has something to do with it," he admitted, propping himself against the bench. He drew her draped body next to his and whispered against her neck. "But there's more. I don't want to tie you down."

"But you're not—"

"Shh. Just listen. I'm not the man you were in love with before the accident. Too much has changed for us to be so naive to think that everything will be just as we'd planned, which, for the record, I still can't remember."

"You will," she said, though she felt a gaping hole in her heart.

Parker slid from behind her and reached for his clothes. He'd never intended to make love to her, to admit that he loved her, for crying out loud, but there it was—the plain simple truth: He loved her and he couldn't keep his hands off her.

"I think I'll go for a drive," he said, yanking his sweater over his head and sliding with difficulty into his jeans.

"Now?"

"I need time to think, Shawna. We both do," he said abruptly. Seeing the wounded look in her eyes he touched her cheek. "You know I care about you," he admitted, stroking her hair. "But I need a little space, just to work things out. I don't want either of us to make a mistake we'll regret later."

"Maybe we already have," she said, clutching her coat over her full breasts. She lifted her chin bravely, though deep inside, she was wounded to the core. Just minutes before he was loving her, now he was walking away!

"Maybe," he groaned, then straightened and hobbled to the door.

Shawna watched him amble up the path and shuddered when she heard the garage door slam behind him. He was gone. It was that simple. Right after making love to her for the first time, he'd walked away. The pain in her heart throbbed horribly, though she tried to believe that his words of love, sworn in the throes of passion, were the only real truth.

***

Brittle night wind raced through the car as Parker drove, his foot on the throttle, the windows rolled down. He pushed the speed limit, needing the cold night air to cool the passion deep in his soul. He was rocked to his very core by the depth of his feelings for Shawna. Never would he have believed himself capable of such all-consuming physical and mental torture. He wanted her—forever. He'd been on the verge of asking her to marry him back in the gazebo and damning the consequences.

"You're a fool," he chastised, shifting down, the car squealing around a curve in the road. Lights in the opposite lane dazzled and blinded him, bore down on him. "A damned fool."

The car in the oncoming lane passed, and memories crashed through the walls of his blocked mind. One by one they streamed into his consciousness. He remembered Brad, passed out and unconscious, and Melinda crying softly, clinging to Parker's shoulder. And Shawna—Lord, he remembered her, but not as he saw her now. Yes, he'd loved her because she was a beautiful, intelligent woman, but in the past, he hadn't felt this overpowering awe and voracious need that now consumed him.

He strained to remember everything, but couldn't. "Give it time," he said impatiently, but his fingers tightened over the wheel and he felt a desperate desire to know everything.

"Come on, come on," he urged, then realized that he was speeding, as if running from the black hole that was his past.

With difficulty, he eased up on the throttle and drove more cautiously, his hot blood finally cooled. Making love to Shawna had been a mistake, he decided, though a smile of satisfaction still hovered over his lips at the thought of her ivory-white body stretched sensually in the gazebo, her green eyes luminous with desire.

"Forget it," he muttered, palms suddenly damp. Until he remembered everything and knew she loved the man he was today, not the person she'd planned to marry before the accident, he couldn't risk making love to her again.

And that, he thought, his lips twisting wryly, was a crying shame.

Ten

"He's pushing too hard," Bob Killingsworth, Parker's physical therapist, admitted to Shawna one afternoon. She had taken the day off and had intended to spend it with Parker, but he was still in his indoor pool, swimming, using the strength of his arms to pull himself through the water. Though one muscular leg kicked easily, the other, the knee that had been crushed, was stiff and inflexible and dragged noticeably.

"That's it!" Bob called, cupping his hands around his mouth and shouting at Parker.

Parker stood in the shallow end and rubbed the water from his face. "Just a couple more laps."

Glancing at his watch, Bob frowned. "I've got to get to the hospital—"

"I don't need a keeper," Parker reminded him.

"It's all right," Shawna whispered, "I'll stay with him."

"Are you sure?"

"I *am* a doctor."

"I know, but—" Bob shrugged his big shoulders. "Whatever you say."

As Bob left, Shawna kicked off her shoes.

"Joining me?" Parker mocked.

"I just might." The tension between them crackled. Since he'd left her the night they had made love, they had barely spoken. With an impish grin, she slid quickly out of her panty hose and sat on the edge of the pool near the diving board, her legs dangling into the water.

"That looks dangerous, Doctor," Parker predicted from the shallow end.

"I doubt it."

"Oh?" Smothering a devilish grin, Parker swam rapidly toward her, his muscular body knifing through the water. She watched with pride. In two weeks, he'd made incredible strides, physically if not mentally.

He'd always been an athlete and his muscles were strident and powerful. His shoulders were wide, his chest broad and corded. His abdomen was flat as it disappeared inside his swimming trunks to emerge again in the form of lean hips and strong legs—well, at least one strong leg. His right knee was still ablaze with angry red scars.

As he reached the deep end of the pool, he surfaced and his incredible blue eyes danced mischievously. He tossed his hair from his face and water sprayed on her blouse.

"What's on your mind?" she asked, grinning.

"I thought you were coming in."

"And I thought I'd change first."

"Did you?" One side of his mouth lifted into a crafty grin.

"Oh, Parker, no—" she said, just as she felt strong hands wrap over her ankles. "You wouldn't—"

But he did. Over her protests, he gently started swimming backward, pulling her off her bottom and into the pool, wool skirt, silk blouse, and all.

"You're despicable!" she sputtered, surfacing, her hair drenched.

"Probably."

"And cruel and . . . and heartless . . . and—"

"Adorable," he cut in, laughing so loudly the rich sound echoed on the rafters over the pool. His hands had moved upward over her legs, to rest at her hips as she hung by the tips of her fingers at the edge of the pool.

"That, too," she admitted, lost in his eyes as he studied

her. Heart pounding erratically, she could barely breathe as his head lowered and his lips brushed erotically over hers.

"So are you." One strong arm gripped her tighter, so fierce and possessive that her breath was trapped somewhere between her throat and lungs, while he clung to the side of the pool with his free hand. "Oh, so are you."

Knowing she was playing with proverbial fire, she warned herself to leave, but she was too caught up in the wonder of being held by him, the feel of his wet body pressed against hers, to consider why his feelings had changed. She didn't care that her clothes were ruined. She'd waited too long for this glorious moment—to have him hold her and want her again.

His tongue rimmed her mouth before parting her lips insistently. Moaning her surrender she felt his mouth crush against hers, his tongue touch and glide with hers, delving delicately, then flicking away as she ached for more. Her blood raced uncontrollably, and her heart hammered crazily against her ribs.

She didn't know why he had chosen this moment to love her again. She could only hope that he'd somehow experienced a breakthrough with his memory and could remember everything—especially how much they had loved each other.

His warm lips slid lower on her neck to the base of her throat and the white skin exposed between the lapels of her soggy blouse. The wet silk clung to her, and her nipples, proudly erect, were visible beneath the thin layer of silk and lace, sweetly enticing just above the lapping water.

Lazily, as if he had all the time in the world, his tongue touched her breast, hot as it pressed against her skin. She cried out, couldn't help herself, as he slowly placed his mouth against her, nuzzling her, sending white-hot rivulets of desire through her veins.

She could only cling to him, holding his head against

her breast, feeling the warmth within her start to glow and a dull ache begin to throb deep at her center.

She didn't resist as with one hand he undid the buttons of her blouse, baring her shoulders, and letting the sodden piece of silk drift downward into the clear depths of the pool. Her bra, a flimsy scrap of lace, followed.

She was bare from the waist up, her breasts straining and full beneath his gaze as clear water lapped against her white skin.

"You are so beautiful," he groaned, as if her beauty were a curse. He gently reached forward, softly stroking her skin, watching in fascination as her nipple tightened, his eyes devouring every naked inch of her skin. "This is crazy, absolutely crazy," he whispered. Then, almost angrily, he lifted her up and took one bare nipple into his mouth, feasting hungrily on the soft white globe, his hand against her back, causing goose bumps to rise on her skin.

"Love me," she cried, aching to be filled with his spirit and soul. Her hands tangled in the hair of his chest and her eyes glazed as she whispered, "Please, Parker, make love to me."

"Right here?" he asked, lifting his head, short of breath.

"I don't care . . . anywhere."

His lips found hers again and as he kissed her, feeling her warm body in the cool water, a jagged piece of memory pricked his mind. Hadn't there been another time, another place, when Shawna—or had it been another woman—had pleaded with him to make love to her?

The sun had been hot and heat shimmered in vibrant waves over the river. They were lying in a canoe, the boat rocking quietly as he'd kissed her, his heart pounding in his ears, her suntanned body molded against his. She'd whispered his name, her voice rough with longing, then . . .

***

Just as suddenly as the memory had appeared, it slipped away again.

"Parker?"

He blinked, finding himself in the pool with Shawna, her green eyes fixed on his, her white skin turning blue in the suddenly cold water.

"What is it?"

"I don't know," he admitted, frustrated all over again. If only he could remember! If only he could fill the holes in his life! He released her and swam to the edge of the pool. "I think maybe you'd better get dressed," he decided, hoisting his wet body out of the water and reaching for a towel. "I—I'm sorry about your clothes."

"No—"

But he was already limping toward the door.

Dumbfounded, she dived for her blouse and bra, struggled into them, and surfaced at the shallow end. "You've got a lot of nerve," she said, breathing rapidly, her pride shattered as she climbed, dripping out of the pool. "What was *that?*" Gesturing angrily, she encompassed the entire high-ceilinged room to include the intimacy they'd just shared.

"A mistake," he said, wincing a little. Snatching his cane from a towel rack, he turned to the door.

"Mistake?" she yelled. "Mistake?" Boiling, her female ego trampled upon one too many times, she caught up to him and placed herself, with her skirt and blouse still dripping huge puddles on the concrete, squarely in his path. "Just like the other night was a mistake?"

His gaze softened. "I told you—we need time."

But she wasn't listening. "I know what you're doing," she said, pointing an accusing finger at him. "You're trying to shame me into leaving!"

"That's ridiculous!"

"Is it? Then explain what that scene in the pool was all

about! We nearly made love, for crying out loud, and now you're walking out of here as if nothing happened. Just like the other night! That's it, isn't it? You're trying to mortify me!" All her pent-up emotions exploded, and without thinking she slapped him, her palm smacking as it connected with his jaw. The sound reverberated through the room.

"Thank you, Dr. McGuire," he muttered, his temper erupting. "Once again your bedside manner is at its finest!" Without another word he strode past her, limping slightly as he yanked open the door and slammed it shut behind him.

Shawna slumped against the brick wall. She felt as miserable and bedraggled as she looked in her wet clothes. Stung by his bitterness and the cruelty she'd seen in his gaze, she closed her eyes, feeling the cold of the bricks permeate her damp clothes. Had he set her up on purpose? Her head fell to her hands. Had he planned to make love to her only to throw her aside, in order to wound her and get her out of his life? "Bastard!" she cursed, flinging her wet hair over her shoulder.

Maybe she should leave. Maybe there was no chance of ever recovering what they had lost. Maybe, just maybe, their love affair was truly over. Sick at heart, she sank down against the wall and huddled in a puddle of water near the door.

Then her fists clenched tightly and she took a long, steadying breath. She wouldn't give up—not yet, because she believed in their love. She just had to get him to see things her way!

Parker slammed his bedroom door and uttered a quick oath. What had he been thinking about back there in the pool? Why had he let her get to him that way? He yanked off his wet swim trunks and threw them into a corner.

Muttering to himself, he started to struggle into a pair of old jeans when the door to his room swung open and

Shawna, managing to hold her head high though her clothes were wet and dripping and her hair hung lankily around her face, said, "You've got company."

"I don't want—"

"Too late. She's here."

"She?" he repeated, seeing the pain in her eyes.

"Melinda. She's waiting in the den."

Parker zipped up his jeans, aware of her gaze following his movements. He didn't care, he told himself, didn't give one damn what she thought. Grabbing a T-shirt and yanking it over his head, he frowned and made a sound of disgust. "What's she doing here?" he finally asked, holding onto the rails of the bed as he hobbled toward the door.

"Your guess is as good as mine, but I don't think I'll stick around to find out. You know the old saying, three's a crowd."

He watched as she marched stiffly upstairs. He could hear her slamming drawers and he cringed as he made his way to the den.

Melinda was there all right. Standing next to the windows, she straightened as he entered. "So Shawna's still here," she said without any trace of inflection.

"So far."

"And she's staying?" Melinda asked, not meeting his eyes.

"That remains to be seen." He flinched as he heard Shawna stomping overhead. A light fixture rattled in the ceiling. Cocking his head toward an old rocker, he said, "Have a seat."

"No. I'm not staying long. I just came to find out what you intend to do—about the baby, I mean. You do remember, don't you? About the baby?"

Sighing wearily, he stretched his bad leg in front of him and half fell onto the raised hearth of the fireplace. The stones were cold and dusty with ash, but he couldn't have cared less. "What do you want to do?" he asked.

"I don't know." Her chin quivered a little and she

chewed on her lower lip. "I suppose you want me to have an abortion."

His skin paled and he felt as if she'd just kicked him in the stomach. "No way. There are lots of alternatives. Abortion isn't one."

She closed her eyes. "Good," she whispered, obviously relieved as she wrapped her arms around herself. "So what about us?"

"Us?"

"Yes—you and me."

He heard Shawna stomp down the stairs and slam the front door shut behind her. Glancing out the window, he saw her, head bent against the wind as she ran to her car. Suddenly he felt as cold as the foggy day.

"Parker?"

He'd almost forgotten Melinda and he glanced up swiftly. She stared at him with wounded eyes and it was hard for him to believe she was lying—yet he couldn't remember ever loving her.

"We have a baby on the way." Swallowing hard, she fought tears that began to drizzle down her face and lowered her head, her black hair glossy as it fell over her face. "You still don't believe me," she accused, her voice breaking.

"I don't know what to believe," he admitted. Leaning his head back against the stones, he strained for images of that night. His head began to throb with the effort. Dark pieces emerged. He remembered seeing her that rainy night, thought she'd held him and cried into the crook of his neck. Had he stroked her hair, comforted her? God, if he could only remember!

"You're falling in love with her again," she charged, sniffing, lifting her head. When he didn't answer, she wiped at her eyes and crossed the room. "Don't be fooled, Parker. She'll lie to you, try to make you doubt me. But this," she patted her abdomen, "is proof of our love."

"If it's mine," he said slowly, watching for any sign that

she might be lying. A shadow flickered in her gaze—but only for an instant—then her face was set again with rock-solid resolve.

"Just think long and hard about the night before you were supposed to get married, Parker. Where were you before the accident? In whose bed?"

His skin tightened. Surely he hadn't— Eyes narrowing, he stared up at her. "If I was in your bed, where was Brad?" he asked, as memory after painful memory pricked at his conscience only to escape before he could really latch on to anything solid.

"Passed out on the couch," she said bitterly, hiking the strap of her purse over her shoulder. "He'd drunk too much."

He almost believed her. Something about what she was saying was true. He could sense it. "So," he said slowly, "if I'd planned to stay with you that night, why didn't I take Brad home first?"

She paled a bit, then blinked back sudden tears. "Beats me. Look, I'm not trying to hassle you or Shawna. I just took her advice by giving you all the facts."

"And what do you expect to get out of it?" he asked, studying the tilt of her chin.

"Hey, don't get the wrong idea, you don't *have* to marry me—we never had that kind of a deal, but I do want my son to know his father and I would expect you to . . ." She lifted one shoulder. "You know . . . take care of us."

"Financially?"

She nodded, some of her hard edge dissipating. "What happened—the accident and you losing your memory—isn't really fair to the baby, is it?"

"Maybe nothing's fair," he said, then raked his fingers through his hair. He'd never let anyone manipulate him and he had the distinct feeling that Melinda James was doing just that. Scowling, he felt cornered, and he wanted to put her in her place. But he couldn't. No matter what the truth of the matter was, her unborn child hadn't asked to be brought into a world with a teenager for a mother and no father to care for him.

When the phone rang, she stood. "Think about it," she advised, swinging her purse over her shoulder and heading toward the door.

Closing his eyes, he dropped his face into his hands and tried to think, tried to remember sleeping with Melinda, making love to her.

But he couldn't remember anything. Though he strained to concentrate on the dark-haired young woman who claimed to be carrying his child, the image that swam in front of his eyes was the flushed and laughing face of Shawna McGuire as she clung to the neck of a white carousel stallion.

Once again he saw her laughing, her blond hair billowing behind her as she reached, grabbing blindly for a ribboned brass ring. Or was the image caused by looking too long at photographs of that fateful day?

Think, Harrison, think!

A fortune-teller with voluminous skirts sat by a small table in a foul-smelling tent as she held Shawna's palm. Gray clouds gathered overhead, rain began to pepper the ground, the road was dark and wet, and Brad was screaming. . . .

Parker gritted his teeth, concentrating so much his entire head throbbed. He had to remember. He had to!

The phone rang again, for the fourth or fifth time, and he reached to answer it just in time to hear the smooth voice of Lon Saxon, a friend and private detective. "That you, Parker?"

"Right here," Parker replied.

"Good. I've got some of the information you wanted on Melinda James."

Parker's guts wrenched. Here it was. The story. "Okay, tell me all about her."

***

Shawna's fingers were clammy on the wheel as she turned into the drive of Parker's house. After driving aimlessly through the damp streets of Portland, she decided she had to return and confront him. She couldn't run from him and Melinda's baby like some wounded animal.

Silently praying that Melinda had already left, Shawna was relieved to see that the girl's tiny convertible wasn't parked in the drive.

"Remember that he loves you," she told herself as she flicked off the engine and picked up the white bags of hamburgers she'd bought at a local fast-food restaurant. "Just give him time."

Inside, the house was quiet, and for a heart-stopping minute, Shawna thought Parker had left with Melinda. The den was dark and cold, the living room empty. Then she noticed a shaft of light streaming from under the door of his bedroom.

She knocked lightly on the panels, then poked her head inside.

He was still dressed in the old jeans but his shirt was hanging limply from a post on the bed, and his chest was stripped bare. His head was propped by huge pillows and he stared straight at her as if he'd never seen her before.

"Truce?" she asked, holding up two white bags of food.

He didn't move, except to shift his gaze to the bags.

"Was it bad? With Melinda?"

"Did you expect it to be good?"

Hanging on to her emotions, she walked into the room and sat on the bed next to him. The mattress sagged a little, but still he didn't move.

Though her hands were trembling, she opened one bag and held out a paper-wrapped burger. When he ignored the offering she set it, along with the white sacks, on the nightstand. "I didn't expect anything. Every day has a new set of surprises," she admitted, tossing her hair over her shoulders and staring straight at him, refusing to flinch. "Look, let's be completely honest with each other."

"Haven't we been?"

"I don't know," she admitted. "I—I just don't know where I stand with you anymore."

"Then maybe you should move out."

"Maybe," she said slowly, and saw a streak of pain darken his eyes. "Is that what you want?"

"Honesty? Isn't that what you said?"

"Yes." She braced herself for the worst.

His jaw grew rock hard. "Then, *honestly,* I want to do the right thing. If the baby's mine—"

"It isn't," she said.

The look he gave her cut straight through her heart. "Do you know something I don't?"

"No, but—*Yes.* I do know something—something you don't remember—that we loved each other, that we would never have betrayed each other, that Melinda's baby *can't* be yours."

"I remember her," he said softly.

She gave a weak sound of protest.

His throat worked. "And I remember being with her that night—holding her. She was crying and—"

"No! This is all part of her lies!" Shawna screamed, her stomach twisting painfully, her breath constricted and tight. She wanted to lash out and hit anyone or anything that stood in her way. "You're lying to me!"

"Listen to me, damn it!" he said, grabbing her wrist and pulling her forward so that she fell across his chest, her hair spilling over his shoulders. "I remember being with her that night. Everything's not clear, I'll grant you that. But I was in her apartment!"

"Oh, no," she whispered.

"And there's more."

"Parker, please—"

"You were the one who wanted honesty, remember?" His words were harsh, but there wasn't any trace of mockery in his eyes, just blue, searing torment.

"No—"

"Her story checks out, at least part of it. I had a private detective in Cleveland do some digging. Her mother's dead. Her father is an unemployed steelworker who hasn't held a job in ten years! Melinda supported him while she went to high school. He was furious with her when he found out she was pregnant."

Shawna's fingers clenched over the sheets. "That doesn't mean—"

"It means she's not a chronic liar and she obviously has some sense of right and wrong."

"Then we'll just have to wait, won't we?" she asked dully, her entire world black. "Until you regain your memory or the baby's born and paternity tests can be run."

"I don't think so," he said thoughtfully. She didn't move, dread mounting in her heart, knowing the axe was about to fall. "She told me she wants me to recognize the baby as mine and provide support."

"She wants you to marry her, doesn't she? She expects it?"

"No—" he let his voice drop off.

"But you're considering it!" Shawna gasped, all her hopes dashed as the realization struck her. Parker was going to do the noble deed and marry a girl he didn't know! Cold to the bone, she tried to scramble away, but he held her fast. "This is crazy—you *can't* marry her. You don't even remember her!"

"I remember enough," he said, his voice oddly hollow.

For the first time Shawna considered the horrid fact that he might be the baby's father, that he might have betrayed her the week and night before their wedding, had one last fling with a young girl. "I . . . I don't think I want to hear this," she whispered.

"You wanted the truth, Shawna. So here it is: I'm responsible for Melinda's predicament and I can't ignore that responsibility or pretend it doesn't exist, much as I might want to." His eyes searched her face and she recognized his pain—the bare, glaring fact that he still loved her. She could smell the maleness of him, hear the beating of his heart, feel the warmth of his skin, and yet he was pushing her away.

"Please, Parker, don't do this—"

"I have no choice."

"You're claiming the baby," she whispered, eyes moist, insides raw and bleeding.

"Yes." His jaw was tight, every muscle in his body rigid as he took in a long, shaky breath. "So—I think it would be better for everyone involved if you moved out."

She closed her eyes as her world began spinning away from her. All her hopes and dreams were just out of reach. She felt his grip slacken. Without a word, she walked to the door. "I—I'll start packing in the morning," she whispered.

"Good."

Then, numb from head to foot, she closed the door behind her. As she slowly mounted the stairs, she thought she heard him swear and then there was a huge crash against one of the walls, as if a fist or object had collided with plaster. But she didn't pay any attention. All she could think about was the horrid emptiness that was her future—a future barren and bleak without Parker.

Eleven

Tossing off the covers, Shawna rolled over and stared at the clock. Three A.M. and the room was pitch black except for the green digital numbers. Tomorrow she was leaving, giving up on Parker.

Before a single tear slid down her cheek, she searched in the darkness for her robe. Her fingers curled in the soft terry fabric and she fought the urge to scream. How could he do this? Why couldn't he remember?

Angry with herself, Parker, and the world in general, she yanked open the door to her room and padded silently along the hall and down the stairs, her fingers trailing on the banister as she moved quietly in the darkness. She didn't want to wake Parker, though she didn't really know why. The thought that he was sleeping peacefully while she was ripped to ribbons inside was infuriating.

In the kitchen she rattled around for a mug, the powdered chocolate, and a carton of milk. Then, while her cocoa was heating in the microwave, she felt a wild need to escape, to run away from the house that trapped her with its painful memories.

Without really thinking, she unlocked the French doors of the dining room and walked outside to the balcony overlooking the dark Willamette. The air was fresh and bracing, the sound of the river soothing as it flowed steadily toward the Columbia.

Clouds scudded across a full moon, filtering thin

beams of moonlight, which battled to illuminate the night and cast shadows on the river. Leaves, caught in the wind, swirled and drifted to the ground.

Shivering, Shawna tightened her belt and leaned forward over the rail, her fingers curling possessively around the painted wood. This house was to have been hers, but losing the house didn't matter. Losing Parker was what destroyed her. She would gladly have lived in a shack with him, if only he could have found his way back to her. But now it was over. Forever.

She heard the microwave beep. Reluctantly she turned, her breath catching in her throat when she found Parker staring at her, one shoulder propped against the open French door.

"Couldn't sleep, either?" he asked, his night-darkened gaze caressing her face.

"No." She lifted her chin upward, unaware that moonlight shimmered silver in her hair and reflected in her eyes. "Can I get you a cup?" she asked, motioning toward the kitchen. "Hot chocolate's supposed to do the trick."

"Is that your professional opinion?" For once there was no sarcasm in his voice.

"Well, you know me," she said, laughing bitterly at the irony. "At least you did. But maybe you don't remember that I don't put too much stock in prescriptions—sleeping pills and the like. Some of the old-fashioned cures are still the best. So, if you want, I'll fix you a cup."

"I don't think so."

Knowing she should leave, just brush past him, grab her damned cocoa and hightail it upstairs, she stood, mesmerized, realizing that this might be their last moment alone. She couldn't help staring pointedly at his bare chest, at his muscles rigid and strident, his jeans riding low over his hips. Nor could she ignore his brooding and thoughtful expression. His angular features were dark and his eyes, what she could see of them, were focused on her face and neck. As his gaze drifted lower to linger at the cleft of her breasts and the wisp of white lace from her nightgown, she swallowed against her suddenly dry throat.

"I thought you should have this," he said quietly as he walked across the balcony, reached into the pocket of his jeans, and extracted the brass ring he'd won at the fair. Even in the darkness she recognized the circle of metal and the ribbons fluttering in the breeze. "You should have caught this that day."

"You remember?" she asked quickly as her fingers touched the cold metal ring.

"Pieces."

Hope sprang exuberantly in her heart. "Then—"

"It doesn't change anything."

"But—"

His hand closed over hers, warm and comforting, as his fingers forced hers to curl over the ring. "Take it."

"Parker, please, talk to me!" Desperate, she pleaded with him. "If you remember—then you know the baby—"

His jaw grew rock hard. "I don't know for sure, but you have to accept that the baby is mine," he said, his eyes growing distant. He turned then, limping across the balcony and through the kitchen.

For a few minutes Shawna just stared at the damned ring in her hands as memory after painful memory surfaced. Then, unable to stop herself from trying one last time, she practically flew into the house and down the hall, her bare feet slapping against the wooden floors. "Parker, wait!"

She caught up with him in his bedroom. "Leave it, Shawna," he warned.

"But you remember!" Breathless, her heart hammering, she faced him. "You know what we meant to each other!"

"What I remember," he said coldly, though his gaze said differently, "is that you wouldn't sleep with me."

"We had an agreement," she said weakly, clasping the post of his bed for support. "Maybe it was stupid, but—"

"And you teased me—"

"I what?" But she'd heard the words before. Stricken, she could only whisper, "It was a joke between us. You used to laugh!"

"I told you then you'd drive me to a mistress," he said, his brows pulling down sharply over his eyes.

"You're doing this on purpose," she accused him. "You're forcing yourself to be cruel—just to push me away! All that business about having a mistress . . . you were kidding . . . it was just a little game . . . oh, God." She swayed against the post. Had she really been so blind? Had Parker and Melinda—? Numb inside she stumbled backward. Before she could say or do anything to further degrade herself, she scrambled out of the room.

"Shawna—"

She heard him call, but didn't listen.

"I didn't mean to—"

But she was already up the stairs, slamming the door shut, embarrassed to tears as she flipped on the light and jerked her suitcases from the closet to fling them open on the bed.

"Damn it, Shawna! Come down here."

No way! She couldn't trust herself, not around him. She wouldn't. She felt close to tears but wouldn't give in to them. Instead she flung clothes—dresses, sweaters, underwear, slacks—anything she could find into the first suitcase and slammed it shut.

"Listen to me—"

Dear God, his voice was closer! He was actually struggling up the stairs! What if he fell? What if he lost his balance and stumbled backward! "Leave me alone, Parker!" she shouted, snapping the second suitcase shut. She found her purse, slung the strap over her shoulder, slipped into her shoes, and hauled both bags to the landing.

He was there. His face was red from the exertion of the climb, and his eyes were blazing angrily. "Look," he said, reaching for her, but she spun out of his grasp and he nearly fell backward down the steep stairs.

"Stop it!" she cried, worried sick that he would stumble. "Just stop it!"

"I didn't mean to hurt you—"

"Too late! But it doesn't matter. Not anymore. It's over. I'm leaving you alone. That's what you want, isn't it? It's what you've been telling me to do all along. You've got your wish."

"Please—"

Her traitorous heart told her to stay, but this time, damn it, she was going to think with her head. "Good luck, Parker," she choked out. "I mean it, really. I—I wish you the best." Then she ran down the stairs, feeling the tears filling her eyes as she fled through the front door.

The night wind tore at her robe and hair as she raced down the brick path to the garage and the safety of her little hatchback. Gratefully, she slid behind the steering wheel and with trembling fingers flicked on the ignition. The engine roared to life just as Parker opened the kitchen door and snapped on the overhead light in the garage.

Shawna sent up a silent prayer of thanks that he'd made it safely downstairs. Then she shoved the gearshift into reverse and the little car squealed out of the garage.

Driving crazily along the empty highway toward Lake Oswego, she could barely breathe. She had to fight to keep from sobbing hysterically as she sought the only safe refuge she knew. Jake—her brother—she could stay with him.

Slow down, she warned herself, as she guided the car toward the south side of the lake where Jake lived in a small bungalow. *Please be home,* she thought as she parked, grabbed her suitcases, and trudged up the front steps to the porch.

The door opened before she could knock and Jake, his dark hair falling in wild locks over his forehead, his jaw stubbled, his eyes bleary, grabbed the heaviest bag. "Come on in, sis," he said, eyeing her gravely.

"You knew?"

"Parker called. He was worried about you."

She let out a disgusted sound, but when Jake kicked the door shut and wrapped one strong arm around her, she fell apart, letting out the painful sobs that ripped at her soul.

"It's okay," he whispered.

"I wonder if it will ever be," Shawna said, before emitting a long, shuddering sigh and shivering from the cold.

"Come on," Jake suggested, propelling her to the tiny alcove that was his kitchen. "Tell me what happened."

"I don't think I can."

"You don't have much choice. You talk and I'll cook. The best omelet in town."

Shawna's stomach wrenched at the thought of food. "I'm not hungry."

"Well, I am," he said, plopping her down in one of the creaky kitchen chairs and opening the refrigerator, "So, come on, spill it. Just what the hell happened between you and Parker tonight?"

Swallowing hard, Shawna clasped her hands on the table and started at the beginning.

Parker could have kicked himself. Angry with himself, the world, and one lying Melinda James, he ignored the fact that it was the middle of the night and dialed his lawyer.

The phone rang five times before he heard Martin Calloway's groggy voice. "Hello?" he mumbled.

"Hello. This is—"

"I know who it is, Harrison. Do you have any idea what time it is?"

"Vaguely."

"And whatever's on your mind couldn't wait 'til morning?"

"That's about the size of it," Parker said, his gaze roving around the dark, empty kitchen. Damn, but the house felt cold without Shawna. "I want you to draw up some papers."

"Some papers," Martin repeated dryly. "Any particular kind?"

"Adoption," Parker replied flatly, "and postdate them by about six or seven months."

"Wait a minute—what the hell's going on?"

"I've had a breakthrough," Parker said, his entire life crystal clear since his argument with Shawna. "Something happened tonight that brought everything back and now I need to straighten out a few things."

"By adopting a child that isn't born yet?"

"For starters—I don't care how you handle it—I just want to make sure the adoption will be legal and binding."

"I'll need the mother's signature."

"I don't think that will be a problem," Parker said. "Oh—and just one other thing. I want to keep the fact that I'm remembering again a secret."

"Any particular reason?"

"There's someone I have to tell—after we get whatever letters of intent for adoption or whatever it's called signed."

"I'll work on it in the morning."

"Great."

Parker hung up and walked restlessly to his bedroom. He thought about chasing Shawna down at Jake's and admitting that he remembered his past, but decided to wait until everything was settled. This time, he wasn't going to let anything come between them!

***

If Shawna had known the torment she was letting herself in for, she might have thought twice about leaving Parker so abruptly. Nearly a week had dragged by, one day slipping into the next in a simple routine of patients, hospitals, and sleepless nights. Though Shawna fought depression, it clung to her like a heavy black cloak, weighing down her shoulders and stealing her appetite.

"You can't go on like this," Jake said one morning as Shawna, dressed in a skirt and blouse, sipped a cup of coffee and scanned the newspaper without interest.

"Or *you* can't?" Shawna replied.

Jake's dog, Bruno, was lying under the table. With one brown eye and one blue, he stared at Maestro and growled as the precocious tabby hopped onto the window ledge. Crouching behind a broad-leafed plant, his tail twitching, Maestro glared longingly past the glass panes to the hanging bird feeder where several snowbirds pecked at seeds.

Jake refused to be distracted. "If you don't believe that you're moping around here, take a look in the mirror, for Pete's sake."

"No, thank you."

"Shawna, you're killing yourself," Jake accused, sitting angrily in the chair directly across from hers.

"I'm leaving, just as soon as I find a place."

"I don't care about that, for crying out loud."

"I'm not 'moping' or 'killing myself' so don't you dare try to psychoanalyze me," she warned, raising her eyes to stare at him over the rim of her cup. He didn't have to remind her that she looked bad, for heaven's sake. She could feel it.

"Someone's got to," Jake grumbled. "You and Parker are so damned bullheaded."

Her heartbeat quickened at the sound of his name. If only he'd missed her!

"He looks twice as bad as you do."

"That's encouraging," she muttered, but hated the sound of her voice. Deep down, she wanted Parker to be happy and well.

"Talk to him."

"No."

"He's called twice."

Frowning, Shawna set her cup on the table. "It's over, Jake. That's the way he wanted it, and I'm tired of being treated as if my emotions don't mean a damned thing. Whether he meant to or not, he found my heart, threw it to the ground, and then stomped all over it."

"So now you don't care?"

"I didn't say that! And you're doing it again. Don't talk to me like you're my shrink, for Pete's sake."

Jake wouldn't be silenced. "Okay, so I'll talk like your brother. You're making one helluva mistake here."

"Not the first."

"Cut the bull, Shawna. I know you. You're hurting and you still love him even if you think he's a bastard. Isn't it worth just one more chance?"

She thought of the brass ring, still tucked secretly in the pocket of her robe. "Take a chance," Parker had told her at the fair that day. Dear Lord, it seemed ages ago.

"I'm out of chances."

Jake leaned over the table, his gaze fastened on her. "I've never thought you were stupid, Shawna. Don't change my mind, okay?" Glancing at the clock over the stove, he swore, grabbing his suit jacket from the back of a chair. "Do yourself a favor. Call him back." With this last bit of brotherly advice, Jake swung out the door, then returned, his face flushed. "And move your car, okay? Some of us have to work today."

She felt like sticking her tongue out at him, but instead she grabbed her purse and keys and swung her coat over her shoulders. The beginning of a plan had begun to form in her mind—and if Jake was right about Parker . . .

"You don't have to leave," Jake said as they walked down the frost-crusted path to the garage. "Just move that miserable little car of yours."

"I think I'd better get started."

"Doing what?" he asked. "You have the next couple of days off, don't you?"

She grabbed the handle of her car door and flashed him a secretive smile as she climbed inside, "Maybe you're right. Maybe I should do more than mope around here."

"What's that supposed to mean?" he asked suspiciously.

"I'm not sure. But I'll let you know." Waving with one hand, she rammed her car into gear and backed out of his driveway. With only the barest idea of what she was planning, she parked in front of the house and waited until Jake had roared out of sight.

Spurred into action, she hurried back inside Jake's house, called her friend Gerri, and threw some clothes into a bag.

Her heart was in her throat as she climbed back into her car. She could barely believe the plan that had formed in her mind. Ignoring the screaming protests in her mind, she drove through the fog, heading north until she slammed on the brakes at the street leading toward the Willamette River and Parker's house.

Her hands were damp. What if he wasn't home? Or worse yet, what if he had company? Perhaps Melinda? *Well, that would be too damned bad. Because it's now or never!*

Her muscles were so rigid they ached as she drove, her jaw firm with determination as Parker's huge house loomed to the side of the road. Without hesitation, she cranked the wheel, coasted along the long asphalt drive and parked near the brick path leading to the front door.

Then, with all the confidence she could gather, she marched up the path and rang the bell.

Twelve

Shawna held her breath as the door swung inward, and Parker, dressed in cords and a soft sweater, stared at her. Her heart started knocking against her rib cage as she looked into his eyes.

"Well, if this isn't a surprise," he drawled, not moving from the door. His face was unreadable. Not an emotion flickered in his eyes.

"I had a few things to sort out," she said.

"And are they sorted out?"

Nervously, she licked her lips. "Just about. I thought maybe we should talk, and I'm sorry I didn't return your calls."

Still suspicious, he pushed open the door. "Fair enough."

"Not here," she said quickly. "Someplace where we won't be disturbed."

"Such as?"

Shawna forced a friendly smile. "For starters, let's just drive."

He hesitated a minute, then shrugged, as if it didn't matter what she wanted to discuss—nothing would change. Yanking his fleece-lined jacket off the hall tree, he eyed his cane hanging on a hook but left it.

Striding back to the car, Shawna held her breath and felt his eyes bore into her back as he walked unsteadily after her and slid into the passenger side of the hatchback.

Without a word, she climbed behind the wheel and

started out the drive. A surge of self-doubts assailed her. If he had any idea that she planned to kidnap him for the weekend, he'd be furious. She might have ruined any chance they had of ever getting back together again.

But it was a risk she had to take. The longer they were apart, she felt, the more likely stubborn pride would get in their way.

She put the little car through its paces, heading west amidst the fog still clinging to the upper reaches of the west hills. "So talk," Parker suggested, his arms crossed over his chest, his jean jacket stretched tight over his shoulders.

"I've had a lot of time to think," she said, gambling, not really knowing what to say now that he was sitting in the seat next to hers, his legs stretched close, his shoulder nearly touching hers. "And I think I acted rashly."

"We both behaved like children," he said, staring straight ahead as the city gave way to suburbs. Parker looked around, as if noticing for the first time that they'd left Portland far behind. Ahead the blue-gray mountains of the coast range loomed into view. "Where're we going?" he asked, suddenly apprehensive.

"To the beach." She didn't dare glance at him, afraid her emotions were mirrored in her eyes.

"The *beach?*" he repeated, stunned. "Why?"

"I think more clearly when I'm near the ocean." That, at least, wasn't a lie.

"But it's already afternoon. We won't be back until after dark."

"Is that a problem?"

"I guess not."

"Good. I know this great candy store in Cannon Beach—"

He groaned, and Shawna, glimpsing him from the corner of her eye, felt a growing sense of satisfaction. So he did remember—she could see it in his gaze. Earlier in the summer they'd visited Cannon Beach and eaten saltwater taffy until their stomachs ached. So just how much did he recall? Everything? What about Melinda? Shawna felt dread in her heart but steadfastly tamped it down. Tonight she'd face the truth—all of it. And so would Parker!

Once at the tiny coastal town, with its weathered buildings and cottages, they found a quaint restaurant high on the cliffs overlooking the sea. The beach was nearly deserted. Only a few hardy souls braved the sand and wind to stroll near the water's ragged edge. Gray-and-white seagulls swooped from a steely sky, and rolling whitecapped waves crashed against jagged black rocks as Shawna and Parker finished a meal of crab and crusty French bread.

"Want to take a walk?" Shawna asked.

Deep lines grooved around his mouth. "Didn't bring my wheelchair," he drawled, his lips thinning.

She said softly, "You can lean on me."

"I don't think so. I really should get back." His eyes touched hers for a moment and then he glanced away, through the window and toward the sea.

"Melinda's expecting you?"

His jaw worked. "Actually, it's a case of my lawyer wants to meet with her attorney. That sort of thing."

She braced herself for the showdown. "Then we'd better get going," she said as if she had every intention of driving him back to Portland. "I wouldn't want to keep her waiting."

Parker paid the check, then ambled slowly toward the car. Shawna pointed across the street to a mom-and-pop grocery and deli. "I'll just be a minute. I want to pick up a few things," she said, jaywalking across the street.

"Can't you get whatever it is you need in Portland?"

Flashing him a mischievous smile, she shook her head. He noticed the luxuriant honey-blond waves that swept the back of her suede jacket. "Not fresh crab. Just give me a minute."

Rather than protest, he slid into the hatchback and Shawna joined him a few minutes later. She swallowed back her fear. Until this moment, she'd been fairly honest with him. But now, if she had the courage, she was going to lie through her teeth.

"It's almost sunset," she said, easing the car into the empty street.

The sun, a fiery luminous ball, was dropping slowly to the sea. The sky was tinged rosy hues of orange and lavender. "I'd noticed."

"Do you mind if I take the scenic route home, through Astoria?"

Frowning, Parker rubbed the back of his neck and shrugged. "I guess not. I'm late already."

So far, so good. She drove north along the rugged coastline, following the curving road that wound along the crest of the cliffs overlooking the sea. Contorted pines and beach grass, gilded by the sun's final rays, flanked the asphalt. Parker closed his eyes and Shawna crossed her fingers. Maybe, just maybe, her plan would work.

"Here we are," Shawna said, pulling up the hand brake as the little car rolled to a stop.

Parker awakened slowly. He hadn't meant to doze, but he'd been exhausted for days. Ever since Shawna had moved out of his house, he'd spent sleepless nights in restless dreams filled with her, only to wake up drenched with sweat and hot with desire. His days, when he wasn't consulting his lawyer about Melinda's child, had been filled with physical therapy and swimming, and he could finally feel his body starting to respond. The pain in his injured leg had slowly lessened and his torn muscles had grudgingly started working again. For the first time since the accident, he'd felt a glimmer of hope that he would eventually walk unassisted again. That knowledge was his driving force, though it was a small comfort against the fact that he'd given up Shawna.

But only temporarily, he reminded himself, knowing that one way or another he would make her love him, not for what he once was, but for the man he'd become. But first, there was the matter of Melinda's baby, a matter which should have been completed this afternoon. If he'd had any brains at all, he never would have agreed to drive to the beach with Shawna, but he hadn't been able to stop himself.

When he had opened the door and found her, smiling and radiant on his doorstep, he hadn't been able to resist spending a few hours with her.

Now, he blinked a couple of times, though he knew he wasn't dreaming. "Where?" In front of her car was a tiny, weathered, run-down excuse of a cabin, behind which was the vibrantly sun-streaked ocean.

"Gerri's cabin."

"Gerri?"

"My friend. Remember?" She laughed a little nervously. "Come on, I bet you do. You seem to be remembering a lot lately. More than you're letting on."

But Parker still wasn't thinking straight. His gaze was glued to the gray shack with paned windows and a sagging porch. "What're we doing here?" Was he missing something?

She pocketed her keys, then faced him. "We're spending the weekend together. Here. Alone. No phone. No intrusions. Just you and me."

He smiled until he saw that she wasn't kidding. Her emerald eyes sparkled with determination. "Hey—wait a minute—"

But she wasn't listening. She climbed out of the car and grabbed the grocery bag.

"Shawna!" He wrenched open the door, watching in disbelief as she mounted the steps, searched with her fingers along the ledge over the porch, then, glancing back with a cat-who-ate-the-canary smile, held up a rusted key. *She wasn't joking!* "You can't do this—I've got to be back in Portland tonight!" Ignoring the pain in his knee, he followed after her, limping into the dark, musty interior of the cabin.

She was just lighting a kerosene lantern in the kitchen. "Romantic, don't you think?"

"What does romance have to do with the fact that you shanghaied me here?"

"Everything." She breezed past him and he couldn't help but notice the way her jeans fit snugly over her hips, or the scent of her hair, as she passed.

"I have a meeting—"

"It'll wait."

His blood was boiling. Just who the hell did she think she was—kidnapping him and then flirting with him so outrageously? If only she'd waited one more day! "Give me your keys," he demanded.

She laughed, a merry tinkling sound that bounced over the dusty rafters and echoed in the corners as she knelt on the hearth of a river-rock fireplace and opened the damper.

"I'm serious," Parker said.

"So am I. You're not getting the keys." She crumpled up a yellowed piece of newspaper, plunked two thick pieces of oak onto the grate, and lit a fire. Immediately flames crackled and leaped, climbing hungrily over the dry wood.

"Then I'll walk to the road and hitchhike."

"Guess again. It's nearly a mile. You're still recovering, remember?"

"Shawna—"

"Face it, Parker. This time, you're mine." Dusting her hands, she turned to face him and her expression had changed from playful and bright to sober. "And this time, I'm not letting you go. Not until we settle things once and for all."

Damn the woman! She had him and she knew it! And deep in his heart he was glad, even though he worried about his meeting with Melinda James and her attorney. He glanced around the room, past the sheet-draped furniture and rolled carpets to the windows and the view of the sea beyond. The sky was painted with lavender and magenta and the ocean, shimmering and restless, blazed gold. Worried that he might be blowing the delicate negotiations with Melinda, Parker shoved his hands into the pockets of his cords and waited. Protesting was getting him nowhere. "I'll have to make a call."

"Too bad."

He swore under his breath. "Who knows we're here?"

"Just Gerri. She owns this place."

Since Gerri was Shawna's best friend, he didn't doubt that she'd keep her mouth shut. "What about Jake or your folks?"

She shook her head and rolled out the carpet. "As I said, it's just you, me, the ocean, and the wind. And maybe, if you're lucky, white wine and grilled salmon."

"I'm afraid you'll live to regret this," he said, groaning inwardly as he deliberately advanced on her. Firelight caught in her hair and eyes, and a provocative dimple creased her cheek. The very essence of her seemed to fill the empty cracks and darkest corners of the cabin. He hadn't realized just how much he'd missed her until now. "We probably both will."

"I guess that's a chance we'll just have to take." She met his gaze then, her eyes filled with a love so pure, so intense, he felt guilty for not admitting that he remembered everything—that he, at this moment, had he been in Portland, would be planning for their future together. Reaching forward, he captured her wrist in his hand, felt her quivering pulse. "I want you to trust me," he said, his guts twisting when he recognized the pain in her eyes.

"I do," she whispered. "Why do you think I kidnapped you?"

"God only knows," he whispered, but his gaze centered on her softly parted lips and he felt a warm urgency invade his blood. "You know," he said, his voice turning silky, "I might just mete out my revenge for this little stunt."

He was close to her now, so close she could see the flecks of blue fire in his eyes. "Try me."

Would she never give up? He felt an incredible surge of pride that this gorgeous, intelligent woman loved him so tenaciously she would fight impossible odds to save their relationship. A vein throbbed in his temple, his thoughts filled with desire, and he gave in to the overpowering urge to forget about the past, the present, and the future as he gazed hungrily into her eyes. "I do love you. . . ." he whispered, sweeping her into his arms.

Shawna's heart soared, though she didn't have time to catch her breath. The kiss was hard, nearly brutal, and filled with a fierce passion that caused her heart to beat shamelessly.

She moaned in response, twining her arms around his neck, her breasts crushed against his chest, her blood hot with desire. He pulled her closer still, holding her so tight she could barely breathe as his tongue pressed against her teeth. Willingly, her lips parted and she felt him explore the velvety recesses of her mouth.

"God, I've missed you," he whispered, his voice rough as his lips found her throat and moved slowly downward.

She didn't stop him when he pushed her jacket off her shoulders, nor did she protest when he undid the buttons of her blouse. Her eyes were bright when he kissed her lips again.

The fire glowed red and yellow and the sound of the

sea crashing against rocks far below drifted through the open window as she helped him out of his clothes.

"Shawna—are you sure?" he asked, and groaned when she kissed his chest.

"I've always been sure," she whispered. "With you." Tasting the salt on his skin, feeling the ripple of his muscles, she breathed against him, wanton with pleasure when he sucked in his abdomen, his eyes glazing over.

"You're incredible," he murmured, moving suggestively against her, his arousal evident as her fingers played with his waistband, dipping lower and teasing him.

"So are you."

"If you don't stop me now—"

"Never," she replied and was rewarded with his wet lips pressing hard against hers. All control fled, and he pushed her to the carpet, his hands deftly removing her clothes and caressing her all over until she ached for more. Blood thundered in her ears, her heart slammed wildly in her chest, and she could only think of Parker and the desire throbbing hot in her veins. "I love you, Parker," she said, tears filling her eyes at the wonder of him.

Firelight gleamed on his skin as he lowered himself over her, touching the tip of her breasts with his tongue before taking one firm mound possessively with his mouth and suckling hungrily. His hand was on her back, spread wide over her skin, drawing her near as he rubbed against her, anxious and aroused.

"I should tell you—"

"Shh—" Twining her fingers in the hair of his nape, she drew his head down to hers and kissed him, moving her body erotically against his. She pushed his cords over his hips, her fingers inching down his muscular buttocks and thighs, a warm, primal need swirling deep within her. His clothes discarded, she ran her fingers over his skin and turned anxious lips to his.

If he wanted to stop, he couldn't. His muscles, glistening with sweat and reflecting the golden light from the fire, strained for one second before he parted her legs with one knee and thrust deep into her.

"Shawna," he cried, his hand on her breasts, his mouth raining kisses on her face. "Love me."

"I do!" Hot inside, and liquid, she captured him with her legs, arching against him and holding close, as if afraid he would disappear with the coming night.

With each of his long strokes, she felt as if she were on that carousel again, turning faster and faster, spinning wildly, crazily out of control.

Tangled in his passion, she shuddered, and the lights of the merry-go-round crackled and burst into brilliant blue and gold flames. Parker cried out, deeply and lustily, and it echoed with her own shriek of pleasure. Tears filled her eyes with each hot wave of pleasure that spread to her limbs.

Parker kissed the dewy perspiration from her forehead, then took an old blanket from the couch and wrapped it over them.

"My darling, I love you," he murmured, his voice cracking.

"You don't have to say anything," she whispered, but her heart fairly burst with love.

"Why lie?" Levering himself on one elbow, he brushed the honey-streaked strands of hair from her face and stared down at her. "You wouldn't believe me anyway. You've always insisted that I loved you." He kissed her gently on the cheek. "You just have no idea how much." His gaze lowered again, to the fullness of her breasts, the pinch of her waist, the length of her legs. "I love you more than any sane man should love a woman," he admitted, his voice thick with emotion.

"Now, we can forget about everything except each other," she whispered, winding her arms around his neck. "I love you, Parker Harrison. And I want you.

And if all I can have of you is this one weekend—then I'll take it."

"Not good enough, Doctor," he said, his smile white and sensual as it slashed across his jaw. "With you, it has to be forever."

"Forever it is," she whispered, her voice breaking as she tilted her face eagerly to his.

Gathering her into his arms, he made love to her all night long.

Thirteen

Shawna stretched lazily on the bed, smiling to herself as she reached for Parker again. But her fingers rubbed only cold sheets. Her eyes flew open. "Parker?" she called, glancing around the tiny bedroom. Where was he?

Morning light streamed into the room and the old lace curtains fluttered in the breeze.

"Parker?" she called again, rubbing her eyes before scrambling for her robe. The little cabin was cold and she didn't hear any sounds of life from the other room. There was a chance he'd hobbled down to the beach, but she doubted he would climb down the steep stairs of the cliff face. Worried, she crossed the small living room to peer out a side window, and her fears were confirmed. Her hatchback was gone. He'd left. After a night of intense lovemaking, he'd gone.

Maybe he's just gone to the store, or to find a phone booth, she told herself, but she knew better, even before she found a hastily scrawled note on the table. Her hands shook as she picked up a small scrap of paper and read:

Had to run home for a while. I'll be back or send someone for you. Trust me. I do love you.

She crumpled the note in her hand and shoved it into the pocket of her robe. Her fingers grazed the cold metal of the brass ring he'd won at the fair all those weeks ago and she dropped into one of the old, dilapidated chairs. Why had he returned to Portland?

To settle things with Melinda.

And after that?

Who knows?

Her head fell to her hands, but she tried to think positively. He did love her. He had admitted it over and over again the night before while making love, and again in the note. So why leave? Why take off and abandon her now?

"Serves you right," she muttered, thinking how she'd shanghaied him to this cabin.

She had two options: she could walk into town and call her brother, or trust Parker and wait it out. This time, she decided to give Parker the benefit of the doubt.

To pass the time, she cleaned the house, stacked wood, even started lamb stew simmering on the stove before changing into clean clothes. But at five-thirty, when he hadn't shown up again, she couldn't buoy her deflated spirits. The longer he was away, the more uncertain she was of the words of love he had whispered in the night.

"He'll be back," she told herself, knowing he wouldn't leave her stranded, not even to pay her back for tricking him. Nonetheless, she slipped into her shoes and jacket and walked outside.

The air was cool and as the sun set, fog collected over the waves. A salty breeze caught and tangled in her hair as she threaded her way along an overgrown path to the stairs. Brambles and skeletal berry vines clung to her clothes and dry beach grass rubbed against her jeans before she reached the weathered steps that zigzagged back and forth along the cliff face and eventually led to the beach. She hurried down, her shoes catching on the uneven boards and exposed nails, to the deserted crescent-shaped strip of white sand. Seagulls cried over the roar of the surf and foamy waves crashed against barnacle-riddled shoals. Far to the north a solitary lighthouse knifed upward, no light shining from its gleaming white tower.

Shawna stuffed her hands in her pockets and walked along the water's edge, eyeing the lavender sky and a few stars winking through tattered wisps of fog. She walked aimlessly, her thoughts as turbulent as the restless waves.

Why hadn't Parker returned? Why? Why? Why?

She kicked at an agate and turned back toward the stairs, her eyes following the ridge. Then she saw him, standing at the top of the cliff, balanced on the weather-beaten stairs. His hair ruffling in the wind, Parker was staring down at her.

He'd come back!

Her heart took flight and she started running along the water's edge. All her doubts were washed away with the tide. He waved, then started down the stairs.

"Parker, no! Wait!" she called, her breath short. The steps were uneven, and because of his leg, she was afraid he might fall. Fear curled over her heart as she saw him stumble and catch himself. "Parker—don't—"

But her words were caught in the wind and drowned by the roar of the sea. Adrenaline spurred her on, her gaze fastened on the stairs. He was slowly inching his way down, his hands gripping the rail, but she was still worried.

Her legs felt like lead as she raced across the dry sand toward the stairs, her heart hammering, slamming against her ribs, as his eyes locked with hers. He grinned and stepped down, only to miss the final sun-bleached stairs.

"No!" she cried, as he scrambled against the rail, swore, then pitched forward. In an awful instant, she watched as he fell onto the sand, his strong outstretched arms breaking his fall. But his jeans caught on a nail, the fabric ripped, and his bad leg wrenched.

He cried out as he landed on the sand.

"Parker!" Shawna flew to his side, dropping to her knees in the sand, touching his face, her hands tracing the familiar line of his jaw as his eyes blinked open.

"You—you were supposed to catch me," he joked, but the lines near his mouth were white with pain.

"And you weren't supposed to fall! Are you all right?" She cradled his head to her breast, her eyes glancing down to his leg.

"Better now," he admitted, still grimacing a little, but his blue gaze tangled in hers.

"Let me see—"

Ignoring his protests, she ripped his pant leg further and probed gently at his knee.

He inhaled swiftly.

"Well, you didn't do it any good, but you'll live," she thought aloud, relieved that nothing seemed to have torn. "But you'll have to have it looked at when we get back." She tossed her hair over her shoulder and glared at him. "That was a stupid move, Harrison—" she said, noticing for the first time a crisp white envelope in the sand. "What's this?"

"The adoption papers," he replied, stretching his leg and grimacing.

"Adoption—?" Her eyes flew to his.

"Melinda's agreed to let me adopt the baby."

"You—?"

"Yep." Forcing himself to a standing position, he steadied himself on the rail as Shawna scanned the legal forms. "It didn't even take much convincing. I agreed to send her to school and take care of the baby. That's all she really wanted."

Shawna eyed him suspiciously and dusted off her hands to stand next to him. "Are you sure you're okay?"

His eyes darkened with the night. "I'm fine, now that everything's worked out. You know the baby isn't really mine. Melinda was Brad's girlfriend. I just couldn't remember the connection for a while."

She couldn't believe her ears. "What triggered your memory?"

"You did," he said affectionately. "You literally jarred me to my senses when you moved out."

Dumbstruck, she felt her mouth open and close—then her eyes glimmered furiously. "That was days ago!"

"I called."

Trying to hold on to her indignation, she placed her hands on her hips. "You could have said something last night!"

"I was busy last night," he said and her heart began to pound. "So, do you want to know what happened?"

"Of course."

"The night of the wedding rehearsal, I drove Brad to Melinda's apartment and they had a knock-down-drag-out about her pregnancy. He didn't want to be tied down to a wife and kid—thought it would interfere with his career." Parker whitened at the memory. "Melinda was so upset she slapped him and he passed out on the couch. That's why I remembered her, because I held her, told her everything would work out, and tried to talk some sense into her. Later, I intended to give Brad the lecture of his life. But," he sighed, "I didn't get the chance."

"So why did she claim the baby was yours?"

"Because she blamed me for Brad's death. It was a scheme she and her father cooked up when they read in the papers that I had amnesia. But she couldn't go through with it."

"Because you remembered."

"No, because she finally realized she had to do what was best for the baby. Nothing else mattered."

"That's a little hard to believe," Shawna whispered.

He shrugged. "I guess the maternal instinct is stronger than either of us suspected. Anyway, I told her I'd help her through school, but I want full custody of the child." His eyes narrowed on the sea and now, as if to shake off the past, he struggled to stand. "It's the least I can do for Brad."

"Be careful," she instructed as she brushed the sand from her jeans. She, too, was reeling. Parker was going to be a father!

Wincing a little, he tried his leg, then slung his arm over Shawna's shoulders. "I guess I'll just have to lean on you, he whispered, "if you'll let me."

"You think I wouldn't?"

Shrugging, he squeezed her shoulder. "I've been kind of an ass," he admitted.

"That's for sure," she agreed, but she grinned up at him as they walked toward the ocean. "But I can handle you."

"Can you? How about a baby?"

She stopped dead in her tracks. "What are you saying, Parker?" They were at the water's edge, the tide lapping around her feet.

"I'm asking you to marry me, Shawna," he whispered, his gaze delving deep into hers. "I'm asking you to help me raise Brad's baby, as if it were ours, and I'm begging you to love me for who I am, not the man I was," he said, stripping his soul bare, his eyes dark with conviction.

"But I do—"

"I'm not the same man you planned to marry before," he pointed out, giving her one last door to walk through, though his fingers tightened possessively around her shoulders.

"Of course you are. Don't you know that no matter what happens in our lives, what tragedy strikes, I'll never leave you—and not just out of some sense of duty," she explained, "but because I love you."

She saw the tears gather in his eyes, noticed the quivering of his chin. "You're sure about this?"

"I haven't been chasing you down for weeks, bulldozing my way into your life just because I thought it was the right thing to do, Parker."

"I know, but—"

"'I know but' nothing. I love *you*—not some gilded memory!"

"All this time I thought—"

"That's the problem, Parker, you didn't think," she said, poking a finger into his broad chest and grinning.

"Oh, how I love you," he said, his arms pulling her swiftly to him, his lips crashing down on hers, his hands twining in the long silky strands of her hair.

The kiss was filled with the wonder and promise of the future and her heart began to beat a wild cadence. "I'll never let you go now," he vowed.

"I don't want to."

"But if you ever decide to leave me," he warned, his eyes drilling into hers. "I'll hunt you down, Shawna, I swear it. And I'll make you love me again."

"You won't have to." She heard the driving beat of his heart over the thrashing sea, saw pulsating desire in his blue eyes, and melted against him. "I'll never leave." She tasted salt from his tears as she kissed him again.

"Good. Then maybe we can exchange this—" Reaching into his pocket, he withdrew the beribboned brass ring.

"Where did you get that?"

"In the cabin, where you were supposed to be."

"But what're you going to do?"

"We don't need this anymore." Grinning wickedly, he hurled the ring with its fluttering ribbons out to sea.

"Parker, no!" she cried.

But the ring was airborne, flying into the dusk before settling into the purple water.

"As I was saying, we'll exchange the brass ring for two gold bands."

She watched as pastel ribbons drifted beneath the foaming waves. When he tilted her face upward, her eyes were glistening with tears. Finally, Parker had come home. Nothing separated them.

"Will you marry me, Dr. McGuire?"

"Yes," she whispered, her voice catching as she flung her arms around his neck and pressed her eager lips to his. He loved her and he remembered! Finally, they would be together! "Yes, oh, yes!" Her green eyes shimmered in the deepening shadows, her hands urgent as desire and happiness swept through her.

"Slow down, Shawna," he whispered roughly. But even as he spoke, her weight was dragging them both down to the sea-kissed sand. "We've got the rest of our lives."

Dear Reader,

My next new novel for Zebra Books is DEEP FREEZE. If you like mystery/thrillers and romance, then you're sure to love this one. Pick up a copy in March 2005! DEEP FREEZE is the story of Jenna Hughes, a harried single mother of two, who senses that someone is stalking her. It's the coldest winter in fifty years in Oregon and with the first snowfall comes a cold certainty that someone is watching and waiting. Jenna fears for the lives of her two teenage daughters as well as for herself as a serial killer who calls himself as The Ice Man begins to prowl and kill. As the days pass and the nights lengthen Jenna can trust no one, including Sheriff Shane Carter, a handsome but reclusive lawman. The Ice Man has his sights set on Jenna and her family as the frigid winter becomes her enemy.

DEEP FREEZE will certainly make your blood run cold. For an excerpt of the story, just turn the page!

Meanwhile, be certain to visit *www.lisajackson.com* and *www.themysterymansion.com.* I've updated the web sites and they've got cool contests, games and polls that I think you'll have a lot of fun with. Write me and let me know what you think of the books, vote for your favorite character, play games, visit the lairs of the villians or take part in a quest.

Of course, there's an excerpt of DEEP FREEZE on the web site too . . . so check it out!

Keep reading!

Lisa Jackson

HER BIGGEST FAN . . .

When she wakes up, she's very cold. Colder than she's ever been in her life. She can't move or speak. And then she sees him. The one who took her. And before she dies, she wishes she could scream. . . .

IS ABOUT TO BECOME . . .

Former movie star Jenna Hughes left Hollywood for an isolated farm in Oregon to get away from fame. But someone has followed her—an obsessed fan whose letters are personal and deeply disturbing. And while Jenna's already shaken up by what she's seen on paper, she'd be terrified if she knew what Sheriff Shane Carter is investigating. It's a shocking case that started with the discovery of a dead woman in the woods. Now two more women are missing, one of whom bears a striking resemblance to Jenna. . . .

HER WORST NIGHTMARE. . . .

As a winter storm bears down on the Pacific Northwest, a merciless killer's grisly work has only just begun. And Jenna is getting closer to meeting her biggest fan . . . one who wants nothing more than to see her dead. . . .

Please turn the page for an exciting sneak peek at
Lisa Jackson's
newest romantic suspense thriller
DEEP FREEZE,
coming in March 2005!

She was there.

Inside.

Somewhere in the rambling log home.

No doubt Jenna Hughes felt secure. Innocently safe.

But she was wrong.

Dead wrong.

As the first flakes of winter snow drifted from the gray sky and the wind screamed down the gorge, he watched from his hiding spot, a blind he'd built high in the branches of an old-growth Douglas fir that towered from this high ridge. Her ranch stretched out below in frozen acres that abutted the Columbia River.

The rustic old house was the core of what he considered her compound. Graying logs and siding rising two stories to peaked gables and dormers. From lights behind the ice-glazed windows, cozy patches of light glowed against the frozen ground, reminding him of his own past, of how often he'd been on the outside, in the freezing weather, teeth chattering as he stared at the smoke rising from the chimney of his mother's warm, forbidden house.

But that was long ago.

Now, focusing the military glasses on the panes, he caught a glimpse of her moving through her house. But just a teaser, not much, not enough to focus on her. Her image disappeared as she turned down a hallway.

He refocused, caught a bit of movement in the den, but it was only the dog, a broken-down German shepherd who slept most of the day.

Where was she?

Where the hell had she gone?

Be patient, his inner voice advised, trying to soothe him. *Soon you'll be able to do what you want.*

The snowflakes increased, powdering the branches, covering the ground far below and he glanced down at the white frost. In his mind's eye he saw drops of blood in the icy crystals, warm as it hit the ground, giving off a puff of steam, then freezing slowly in splotches of red.

A thrill tingled up his spine just as a stiff breeze, cold as Lucifer's piss, screamed down the gorge, stinging the bit of skin above his ski mask. The branches above and around him danced wildly and beneath the mask, he smiled. He embraced the cold, felt it was a sign. An omen.

The snow was now falling in earnest. Icy crystals falling from the sky.

Now was the time.

He'd waited so long.

Too long.

A light flashed on in the master bedroom and he caught another glimpse of her long hair braided into a rope that hung down her back, baggy sweatshirt covering her curves, no makeup enhancing an already beautiful face. His pulse accelerated as she walked past a bank of windows, then into a closet. His throat went dry. He refocused the glasses, zoomed in closer on the closet door. Maybe he'd catch a glimpse of her naked, her perfectly honed body, an athlete's body with large breasts and a nipped-in waist and muscles that were both feminine and strong. His crotch tightened.

He waited.

Ignored a light being snapped on in another part of the house. Knew it was probably one of her kids.

Come on, come on, he thought impatiently. His mouth turned dry as sand and lust burned through his chilled blood. The master bedroom with its yellowed-pine walls and softly burning fire remained empty. What the hell was taking her so long?

God, he wanted her. He had for a long, long time.

He licked his lips against the cold as she reappeared, wearing a black bra and low-slung black jeans. God, she was beautiful. Nearly perfect in those tight pants. "Strip 'em, Jenna," he muttered under breath that fogged through his insulated mask. Her breasts nearly fell from the sexy black undergarment. But she headed into her bathroom and he readjusted the lens as she leaned over a sink and applied lipstick and mascara. He saw her backside, that sweet, sweet ass straining against the black denim as she leaned closer to the mirror and within that smooth glass surface, he stared at her wide eyes, silvery green and rimmed in thick black lashes. For a second she seemed to catch his eye, to look right at him and she hesitated, mascara wand in hand. Little lines appeared between her arched eyebrows, a hint of worry. As if she knew. Her eyes narrowed and his heart pounded hard against his ribs.

Turning quickly, she stared out the window, to the gathering darkness and the snow now falling steadily. Was it fear he saw in her hazel eyes? Premonition?

"Just you wait," he whispered, his voice lost in the shriek of the wind, the snow becoming thick enough that her image was blurred, his erection suddenly rock-hard as he imagined what he would do to her.

But that instant of fear was gone and her lips pulled into a half smile, as if she'd been foolish. She flipped off the bathroom light, then headed back to her bedroom. She yanked a sweater from her bed and pulled it over her head. For a few seconds he felt ecstasy, watching as her arms uplifted and for a heartbeat she was blindfolded and trapped in the garment, but then her head poked through a wide cowl neck and her arms slid through the sweater's sleeves. She pulled her rope of hair from the neckline and walked quickly out of view, snapping the lights off as she ented the hallway.

Hot desire zinged through his blood at the thought of her.

Beautiful.

Arrogant.

Proud.

And soon, very soon, to be brought to her knees.